Part one

Chapter one

The man studied the papers on his desk forlornly. Until recently he had been proud of his career. In sixty years he had achieved a remarkable amount. Yet there was something that haunted him. He couldn't get these notions out of his head. They pestered him constantly, making the glass of wine he was holding all but compulsory. With a sigh he raised his gaze to the wall. Everything had been painted white. Quite why the decorators had chosen this colour scheme he had yet to fathom. It seemed to be company policy; the design was ubiquitous. Tiredly he pushed his spectacles to the top of his nose. While doing so he took a sip of his red wine. Normally it was an occasional treat at the end of the week. But how could he do without it when his waking life had become a nightmare? For once he wasn't comforted by the plum aftertaste. Slowly he turned to view the window. Outside a storm was raging. The sky was a desolate grey as rain fell from the heavens. The wind blew it sideways, bombarded his window as if a thousand machine guns had been trained upon it. At the moment his heart matched the weather. Whenever he regained his composure he was blasted to pieces again. How could things have changed so quickly? Less than a few months ago he was happy. Six decades didn't prepare him for what he had recently experienced.

When he considered the events a lump formed in his throat. His eyes filled with tears as the emotional dam in his heart burst. If he couldn't control himself he would end up a nervous wreck. No longer did he feel a dynamic person. Until now he had always considered himself young. Every minute of every day he had ever lived pressed upon him. His chest tightened as if an anvil had been placed on it. None of his achievements mattered anymore. Previously he took pride in his fine education. Even that seemed as hollow as everything else. He wrote the brochure for his summer camp. It wasn't a strange event; he had done the same for years before. This booklet brought children through the gates more effectively than the Pied Piper. They had been promised a summer they would never forget. As he looked back on things he was dumbstruck by how correct he was. Tragically this promise came true in the wrong way. When he prepared to take in the youths he had no idea that this year would be so brutal. When facing these experiences he wished he had never had it printed. It would have saved everyone involved a great deal of money and heartbreak. He continuously pined for better times; for years where things were simpler. If he could change time he would tear up the adverts. Never would he forgive himself for what had transpired. He might not have caused it, but by opening for business he had condemned so many. If he had kept the site closed that year he would have saved many from the carnage that took place.

With a grunt he threw the glass at the wall. What good was alcohol? It couldn't absolve himself of the guilt consuming him. It couldn't restore the face he had lost in the sight of his colleagues. It could only drag him deeper into his web of despair. But freeing himself of its grasp didn't make him feel better. As he sat with his head in his hands he sobbed openly. In all his life he had never known such pain. There were so many people to mourn for. The premises that brought so much joy now bore sickening scarlet stains. For ten minutes he cried, lost in the caverns of his own soul. Yet from the surface he noticed a weak light. As the seconds ticked by he felt himself returning to the room. When he raised his head he knew what he had to do. Nothing that happened had been his fault. Personally he had done nothing wrong. Writing his story was the only way he could begin to heal from his torment. With renewed vigour he tore open a drawer. Grabbing as much paper as he could, he took a pen from his desk. All these forms could wait. If he was to continue living he had to sort his own head out. By now everyone around him knew every sordid detail of the affair. Despite nothing happening in his presence he pictured it constantly. Pressing the pen against the paper, he paused momentarily. Was this really a good idea? He had never been one for talking. He found it didn't help anything in the grand scheme of things. What made him think writing his feelings would be any different? Before he could stop himself he began to etch the first few words of his story. Nobody would ever see this. Presumably he would tear it up the moment he finished the final sentence. Even so, he had faith that it would be allow him to heal.

"Inika truly is the best place to be a businessman," he spoke as he wrote, not knowing quite where to start. "There are so many kingdoms- an infinite number. All of them are separated by border portals," his mind drifted back to the explanation his teacher gave him as a child. "Nothing can cross them; that technology is a secret of the government. No two realms are the same. Some don't have inhabitants. Others are just like ours, even if they are technologically advanced. Some you simply wouldn't want to go to. Their inhabitants are all sorts of monsters. We should be grateful we are not living in such a place. All we have to worry about are a few scattered predators."

As he wrote those words he wasn't sure he believed them. Given what had happened he could no longer define what a monster is. As a youngster he believed they were hideous beasts hiding under bridges. However, with age comes wisdom. The events of that summer concluded what he knew deep down. Human beings can be just as vile as any demon lurking in the shadows. Strangely he already felt a little better. Perhaps it was simply the distraction the task was providing. Straight away he began work on the second paragraph. The first sentence of the previous one had hit the nail right on the head. As the citizens of his realm couldn't pass through the portals, all holidays had to be taken internally. Anyone offering retreats could earn a large sum in this place. Summer camps for juveniles are particularly lucrative. There were almost endless streams of parents waiting to send their children off for a month. In return for their payment they got a great deal of time to themselves. As the second paragraph came to an end he reread what he had written. Almost immediately he scolded himself. His intention had been to document the horrific events imposed upon him. So far he appeared to be churning out a letter for potential investors. Yet he had to start somewhere. Unknowingly he had found something that was perfect for him. He began to rise through the desolate layers of his soul beautifully. What he had so far was an ideal beginning. Even so, he had to go deeper. A surgeon has to slice a patient open for their own benefit. If he was to heal properly he had to probe his open wounds. Pressing the pen to the page again, he started right at the beginning. His mind drifted to the start of the horrendous nightmare. Only then could he explore the matter properly.

The consensus was that the children were in for a summer they would never forget. In all ten of the buses the kids were chatting excitedly. Over one hundred individuals had been sent by their parents for the best month of the year. This summer camp had been heralded as one of the greatest treats they could have. Thus, after a little persuasion, they had managed to get their parents to send them there. Those who had been there before knew what to expect. They mainly sat in groups, knowing full well that excitement would get them nowhere. The atmosphere was charged as they anticipated the fun they would have. Already friendships were beginning to form. Children who had never met before were going to bond in ways they could never have imagined. Hopefully these relationships would survive past the end of their holiday. Their guardians had been just as excited as their offspring were when they boarded the vehicles. Of course, they loved their children with all their hearts; this went without saying. However, it is nice to get a small break occasionally. They knew the juvenile members of their families would be well cared for while away. Until the time they returned home there would be plenty of time for adult bonding. Taking a small break from the usual routine does everyone wonders. One large check enabled everyone involved to recuperate from the stresses of life. Certainly the children never considered this. It would be a miracle if they remembered their parents at all as they noisily rode the buses to their temporary haven.

It was a lovely day for travelling. The hot summer sun baked the countryside as they drove past endless fields. Serene cows in glorious green pastures stood beautifully against the mountainous backdrops. There was certainly a magical aspect to the scenery as they went past. Overhead there wasn't a cloud in the sky. This was perfect weather for having fun. Numerous ball games would allow them to become friends quickly. Sunscreen their parents had given them would lie forgotten in their bags as they lost themselves in the moment. If the buses were a little hot they didn't care. Why would they when they knew exactly what was coming? Not a single face lacked a smile as they headed for their destination. For the first time in their lives they had been given a taste of freedom. With their parents far away they could be themselves without having to worry about anything. Muddy clothes that were normally scorned would simply be washed. Petty arguments that would earn bad tempers would be cast aside swiftly. One of the hills they passed was covered completely in forest. It was impossible to see anything other than delicious green while it was in view. Someone could spend the rest of their days hiding there. Nothing had ever seemed as paradisiacal as it did that wonderful day. Naturally the only ones who focused on it were those at the back. They had been to the camp before. There once was a time when they were as hyperactive as the youngest were. As the years rolled on they found it easier to control their emotions. This wasn't to say that they didn't feel a sense of glee. They too were happy to be away from home for a period. It just so happened that restraint comes with age.

Bryan Ackerman couldn't wait to arrive at the camp. At only ten, this was the first time his parents had let him stray from home. Sitting next to him was his best friend. Somehow he had persuaded them to let him go. Even at his young age he knew the boy's parents were tight with money. For them to send him off for such a holiday must have taken a great deal of nagging. For the three hours they were on the bus they did nothing but talk about the summer. Since school was over they saw no need to even discuss it. Certainly there were people they were glad to have a break from. A month away from those individuals would surely do them the world of good. Bryan held the brochure open on his lap. Almost every night he had read it. When he went to bed he fell asleep thinking of the good things that would come his way. Such use had now left it in pieces. Pages hung out at all sorts of strange angles. If it wasn't for a few pieces of tape it would disintegrate completely. Naturally he didn't care about this. All he needed was to catch a glimpse of hysterically happy children. That seemed to get him through all sorts of things lately. Now the day was finally upon him; he was about to begin his break from life. His excitement was almost too much for his skull to contain. If he could he would get out and push the bus to make it go faster. If there was a motorway they would be there by now. Instead his region only had small, winding country roads. This wasn't all bad. At least if Jordan became boring he could look at the scenery. With one hand he brushed part of his black hair aside. Surprisingly his friend was quite reserved. Even though he was just as joyous to be going, he couldn't quite free himself in the same way as everyone else. Perhaps part of him knew that this was his only chance. There was a strong possibility that his parents would make the trip a one-time event. Once they started secondary school the last nail would be hammered into the coffin of their childhoods. He was probably there to ensure he had a good time while he was still a kid. Such a thought was enough to keep him from giving in to his emotions. There was definitely a hint of sadness in his eyes. Was this going to be the only time he would go to camp? How could he enjoy it knowing it might never happen again?

"What do you think we'll do first?!" Bryan asked him, trying to draw the lad out of his shell.

"Dunno," Jordon replied with a shrug, "wouldn't mind a game of football."

That was probably the one thing his friend was known for. When they had PE he was always the first to be chosen. Other primary schools visiting for matches tended to learn very quickly just how good he is. Hopefully he would find someone capable of rising to his level during the holiday. It was terrible that he was never challenged. With a bit of luck someone might even beat him. That would surely wipe away the complacent air he seemed to have acquired of late. Secretly the boy wished he was as good as his friend. That year at school the children had started to form archetypes of cliques. He knew from television that these things happened. He never imagined it might shake his closest friendships. During break-times he had started going off to the sports field rather than play with him. As time goes by he sees less of him by the week. There might come a time when they don't talk at all. Truly it would be a dark day if that was the case. Other people could almost sense they were different. While waiting for the bus, the other children overlooked the black haired boy. Why would they notice him when there was a blonde budding athlete next to him? This was something that bothered the young man slightly. They treated him as somewhat inferior because he wasn't in one of their primordial cliques. Of course, he didn't know that was here to stay. A few years in the future the social structure would leave him immensely unhappy. Yet until then he would find some sort of comfort amongst his peers.

Behind them was another of the buses. It was servicing the county beneath theirs; on the quiet country roads it was easy for even cumbersome vehicles to catch up with each other. Bryan had no idea that there was a similar little boy less than fifty metres away from him. Clement Forney had a personality that closely mirrored his contemporary. This blonde haired male was also smart. He could be so quiet at times that his parents had to check to see if he was even in his bedroom. One day he was going to have to try to slip out. That would surely give his parents a fright. It would be difficult for him to play such a trick. His thirteen year old brother was in the room next to him. Somehow, through the noise of the music he listened to, he was able to tell exactly what he was doing. Merely thinking about the racquet was enough to give the boy a headache. His mother often claims that one day he will enjoy it. That was something he was always ready to dispute. If he ever liked such terrible songs he would need to see a doctor. Recently he had noticed changes in his sibling. When he looked into the street a few weeks ago he had been kissing a girl. Apparently that was something else he would look forwards to later on. If that wasn't bad enough, the smell was sometimes strong enough to kill a horse. Many times his parents had to almost force him into the shower when they couldn't stand it anymore. Most worrying was the fact he wasn't fun anywhere. Until recently they played together all the time. Sometimes they still do when they are on their own. Now he seems so moody Clement almost feels as if he doesn't know him. Evidently his parents hadn't felt up to talking to him about such things. One day they would sit him down to discuss puberty. But that would be after he returned from camp. A single conversation would forever remove his innocence. One part of his childhood would be lost in less than an hour. It seemed cruel to not allow him one last holiday as a child. He had the rest of his life to focus on more mature things. A month of blissful ignorance would not harm him at all.

They were sitting together on the bus. Unlike the other older boys he wasn't chatting at the back. Although he had changed, he still loved his brother more than anything. Ironically he wasn't one to show this bond. For months he had begged his parents not to let him tag along. Couldn't they have sent him to another camp instead? Sadly they hadn't listened to his protests at all. Why would they when they thought they knew better? Everything he tried failed spectacularly. He told them he would be better off someone smaller, where the staff could give him proper attention. They shrugged off his suggestion, as if he was making out the boy was a dangerous misfit. Of course, nothing could be further from the truth. In reality he was only trying to look after the lad. One problem was that the older boys would inevitable target him. If they felt he had somehow wronged them, their first port of call would be to attack his younger brother. Evidently their son might have to live with these consequences for some time. Secretly he was dreading the thought of having to spend a whole month there. It wasn't helped by the presence of his sibling. If only they had listened to him. Now he would pay the price for their actions. In general the boys were very good friends. He felt drawn to protect the smaller child. A small growth spurt had left Adam much taller than others his age. Strangely, Clement had always been shorter than his peers. When he sat next to the ten year old he towered above him. Hopefully their bond would survive the holiday they were about to embark upon.

"Don't let the other kids push you around," he told him helpfully. "I know you get picked on at school. Don't let them ruin this for you too."

Clement turned to look at the scenery when he heard those words. The bullying wasn't that severe, but it did make him burn with rage. Being pushed about on the playground was, relatively speaking, a minor occurrence. Still, having it happen every day for two years was more than he could handle. When it happened he wanted nothing more than to push the aggressors into some sort of black hole. Merely picturing their smug faces was enough to raise his heart rate. It pounded in his chest as his face screwed up in anger. Adam could sense that he was in no mood to talk. When he was in primary school he was there to protect the boy. As soon as he left, the other children knew he was a sitting duck for their juvenile psychopathy. Every day he tried to discover the secret of just how bad things were. Not once was he able to make any sort of ground. In some twisted way they had convinced him that he should lie to protect his abusers. His own parents haven't discovered why their previously nice young man has been irritable at times. More often than not he found himself wanting to beat the yobs that do such things. Couldn't they see he was a decent human being? What could they gain from malice other than a sick sadistic pleasure? Sensing he wasn't going to get any information from the boy, he joined him in gazing out the window. The finest shades of green in nature soothed his eyes. When he saw them he felt some of his anger leaving him. That was probably for the best. He didn't want to spend all day thinking about hurting those that attacked his brother.

The last half an hour dragged on for geological eras. Who could have thought that thirty minutes would go so slowly? During this period everyone grew increasingly excited. In the last five minutes the children were unbearably noisy. Surprisingly there were no signs indicating where the camp was. Someone from the outside world would never be able to find the place. Eventually they came to a large pair of gates. These metal structures looked as if they could withstand a dinosaur charging into them. Even so, if they looked closely they could see signs of age beginning to set in. One hinge had rusted from exposure to the elements. Bryan studied them, waiting for someone to walk over to open them. He watched in awe as the bolt slid backwards electronically. It was quite impressive for a ten year old. Nobody he knew had such things installed on their property. At a reasonable speed the unseen motors pulled the gate aside. Finally the bus was able to move forwards through them. Their dream holiday was less than minutes from beginning. When the vehicle accelerated they could see the camp properly. It was truly a wonderful place to be. From the looks of things it was a square at least four miles in perimeter. That meant they would have plenty of room to play sports. Surrounded on all sides by forest, no-one would see what they were doing. News of any mischief they embarked upon would never reach the outside world. In effect, it was a boy's paradise. The buildings also appeared wonderful. Pretty log cabins looked as if they could house half a town. Nobody could wait for the fun to begin. They wanted to explore more than a starving dog wants to be fed. For many this was the first time in their lives they wouldn't have their parents to answer to. The journey had shown just how wild they would become while unchained. In front of a large cabin were several wooden picnic tables. Eight people were sitting round one, talking as they feasted on some sort of curry. From their demeanours the lad knew he would get on well with them. Not one of their faces lacked a smile. More than one giggled pleasantly at some unknown joke. Surely they were caring people who would deal with any problems he had.

He was so focused on them that he didn't notice the bus had stopped. At the end of the field it came to a halt, the driver switching off the engine. With a startling roar the doors opened. This was it; the boys were being unleashed on the world. This wasn't just a camp for males. Girls were more than welcome to attend. Fortunately the administration had the presence of mind to segregate them into different fields. Less than a mile away they were probably about to have just as much fun as they were. As soon as the doors opened they began to pour through them. Who could possibly resist the urge after months of waiting? Ironically they didn't do much once they were outside. Bryan and Jordon waited for the others to leave before doing so themselves. Those who were already on the soft grass were frolicking peacefully. Since it was by no means late they would naturally have a day in the sun. The older boys were in no hurry to leave. Maybe it was because they had been through this many times in the past. Yes, they were excited, but they didn't feel as if they had won the jackpot. It took the prompting of the bus driver to get them to stand up. Jordon certainly didn't need to be told twice. He almost skipped to the door, leaving his best friend far in the distance. This made him slightly upset. No longer did he urge the lad to run along with him. Instead he barely seemed to notice he was there. Had their relationship really deteriorated that far? For the first time he caught a glimpse of what life would be like once they were no longer on speaking terms. That was something he was in no hurry to actually endure. Once Jordon had been tempted away from him he would be alone. Merely thinking about it made his eyes go scarlet. This boy was his friend. How could he just abandon him in such a way?

"This is magical," he told himself as he finally stepped from the vehicle.

As soon as the last person left the doors shut. With a groan they closed; this was surely the horn announcing the start of their holiday. About a hundred boys were standing around, playfully talking to each other. So many new friendships would form that there had to be someone Bryan liked. Yet he stood around on his own, not knowing what to do. It was as if he had no place amongst them. His own best friend had left him in solitude. Even so, things could only get better. He would find others he could associate himself with. Countless activities would provide opportunities for him to meet everyone. So what if his chum had abandoned him? That only demonstrated how little Jordon truly cared for him. When he looked at the older boys he found them all together. Their faces looked rather strange given the circumstances. This camp catered to teenagers as well. Why weren't they happy about being here? He could go as far as to say they looked troubled. Nevertheless, he didn't dig too deeply into the matter. If they chose not to have fun it wasn't his problem. Thinking about the next month filled him with joy. At that age it seemed as if it would never end. Perhaps if he acted in a certain way he could draw the experience out forever. But logic told him it was impossible. All too soon he would be getting back on the bus to go home. Once he arrived he would be bombarded with questions. This would be his parents' way of trying to pretend they weren't glad to have had a break themselves. He wasn't stupid; this was as much about the pair of them as it was about him. But he wasn't going to moan about their perceived lack of loyalty. He knew that if there was anything wrong they come running. With that sort of love at hand, how could he fault their desire for a few weeks alone?

He turned to view one of the log cabins. From it came three men, all dressed in black outfits. Their short-sleeved shirts allowed horrible sunburns to develop. As they moved he caught a glimpse of the normal flesh hidden by the fabric. The change in tone was almost ridiculous. These were people who had spent a great deal of time outside. Their faces wore smiles as they approached the boys. Despite this, he didn't feel as if there was any warmth in them. They were the same grins he had seen teachers use while dealing with difficult pupils. Still, they were making an effort to be pleasant. He couldn't complain, considering the alternative. Who would want to spend a month with obnoxiously grumpy people? How could you have fun if the leaders were miserable round the clock? Once they were ten feet from the horde they stopped. With great authority one of them spoke, all eyes suddenly fixed on the trio. Some of the older children looked as if they would vomit as they listened to him. Perhaps they had left girlfriends behind. Maybe the thought of being away from them was enough to sicken them. Certainly such a thought would make the ten year olds want to retch themselves. Despite this the boy managed to listen to what the adults were saying. He supposed it was only right he paid attention. He didn't want to make enemies of them on the first day. If they wanted to they could make things very unpleasant for him.

"Make your way into that cabin there," he told them firmly as he pointed to one of the buildings. "There you will be given your uniforms. If you have any questions, ask one of the older boys."

Perhaps if he was a few years older he would have noticed there was a slightly harsh tone to his voice. Sadly as a ten year old he wasn't a master of subtext. When he finished speaking a few of the teenagers rolled their eyes. Were they going to get hundreds of idiotic questions from the prepubescents? Amazingly they didn't get one as they walked along. Slowly at first, the group managed to cross the grass as they were instructed. Only two boys did not do so. One was about the same age as him, the other a little older. He had no idea who they were. Adam held Clement tightly, not wanting him to go with the others. The brothers stood in silence for a moment. How could he say what was on his mind? Someone so young couldn't understand that his older brother wasn't trying to be a killjoy. Ironically he would be protecting him if he begged a bus driver to take him as far from the place as possible. Clement knew something was wrong. On the bus he had spoken about bullying. Just before they drove through the gates, he looked as if he was about to be sick. From his perspective he was worrying about nothing. This wasn't a state school; this was a company. If someone had a bad experience they wouldn't return the following year. It was in their best interests to make sure everyone enjoyed their holiday. Even so, he would probably have problems with some of the children. But his older brother would surely help him out. He was as defensive as a pack of guard dogs at times. There was no way abuse would last for long while he was around.

"I have some money on me. I could probably bribe a driver to take you home," he begged him to leave one last time.

"You two!" One of the adults shouted at them. "I told you what to do, now get on with it!"

His voice was much angrier than it had been the first time. Clement was shocked at such an outburst. What would the month be like if these men were in charge of everything? Just thinking about it made tears form in his eyes. For a long time he had waited for this break. Now it seemed it could be just as bad as at home. Adam noticed the effect the man had had on him. There was no way either of them would get away now. The bus drivers were clueless as to what the place was actually like. No amount of explaining would get them to believe their stories. It was incredibly distressing to consider. These men drove for a living; they could take the children far away from this place. Yet they would never do so. Those who could help them simply would not. With the barking of that statement, he knew both of them would be trapped here for the duration of the holiday. But maybe he was underestimating the kid. Perhaps he would pull through it. At the back of his mind he knew this was wishful thinking. How could someone so soft endure a month of torture? The other children would eat him alive. For them he was an easy target to harass at will. He would inevitably spend quite a lot of time defending the boy. Fortunately this was perfectly fine by him. Of course he would go out of his way to help the lad. If he couldn't do that for a blood relative, who could he do it for?

"Come on," he told his brother, taking hold of his arm. "You don't want to make these men angry," he whispered as he pulled his brother forwards.

"Why?" Clement replied, confused.

He didn't get an answer to his question. This was something he would find out soon enough. What good would come from ensuring he was fearful from the offset? However, the boy was smart enough to read into the statement. At school there were horrible teachers who would shout for no reason. They often appeared to target people just because they existed. Was this what the men would do if he didn't listen to their instructions? If so it wasn't the end of the world. He would simply have to try to stay out of their way. Naturally he had no experience of the camp. The truth was far more horrific than he could ever have imagined. As swiftly as they could they reached the log cabins. Adam turned back for a moment just as they were entering the attractive structure. Smiles adorned the faces of all three men. These weren't the looks of people pleased that the children were following their commands. Instead they were grins of sadistic delight. Once again they had ensnared an innocent soul. As soon as they were inside, Clement stopped dead in his tracks. He couldn't believe what he was seeing. Everyone was changing into white overalls. Four more men were inside, checking names against lists so they could distribute the ugly clothing. Was this seriously what they were going to be wearing for a month? Baggy white trousers and t-shirts weren't exactly what he had expected when he told his parents he wanted to go. Of course, he knew they were going to receive clothes when they arrived. Yet he was clueless as to why these particular garments had been chosen. Even worse was the lack of privacy he felt. Changing in front of others was not a problem, but they were getting undressed wherever they fancied. Once again the older boys stuck together, not speaking to the children as they wondered when the fun would start. A sinking feeling gripped Clement as he was ushered towards the man. Perhaps this wasn't going to be the haven he thought it was.

"Remember," Adam whispered towards his younger sibling. "Don't do anything to upset the adults."

Bryan barely noticed the pair as he hurried to get changed. He had never been to camp before. Unlike Clement, he didn't even have a reference to work with. As this was his first time, anything that happened set the precedent. How could he know if something was bad if he had nothing to compare it with? Still, he wasn't sure if changing in such a fashion was appropriate. Shouldn't they be getting dressed in their private cabins? Whatever his opinions were, he wasn't one to disobey an authority figure. Thus he did as he was told; leaving his clothes in a mess as he sported what he had been given. It was so loose around him that he giggled when he looked down at himself. Once again the excitement of events to come overcame him. Many of the people he saw around him looked rather friendly. If he made an effort to reach out to them he would surely be rewarded with friendship. In his mind he could picture the fun they were going to have. He would try so many things during the summer, some of which he would enjoy. Whole new worlds of entertainment previously unknown to him would appear before his eyes. When he returned to school he would have many stories to tell the others. Apparently not everyone felt such joy to finally commence the break. Most of the older boys looked as if they wished they had never got out of bed. There was quite a lot of tension coming from their group. If they could they would be back on the buses in the blink of an eye. But why would they come if they weren't going to let themselves enjoy the events? Couldn't they have stayed at home if their previous experiences were than bad? Frankly he couldn't understand their attitudes. Regardless of their shared misery, he would not let them ruin this period for him. Surely once they got into the swing of things they would enjoy what the camp had to offer.

"He's over there," he thought to himself as he found Jordon in the crowd.

He could see no point in going over to him. He didn't feel particularly fond of someone who abandoned him when someone else was in the vicinity. A strange sort of rage grew within him when he considered the boy's actions. This was not the behaviour of a person who cared for him at all. Earlier on he considered how their relationship would deteriorate over the next few years. Perhaps, at least from the boy's perspective, it was already over. Shockingly the youngster wasn't that concerned about it. If he wanted to run off with others, he was welcome to. Such a person was obviously not worth his time. Still, even in light of these thoughts he couldn't shake the primordial anger surging in his heart. For the first time in his life he wanted to hit his own friend. At first he watched him with neutral eyes. Now they had narrowed in what could only be described as fury. For two minutes he looked at him, laughing with his new friends. At school he was going to be so alone. But why should he dwell on it? It was something he was just going to have to live with. Perhaps he could share addresses with the new friends he would make. They could write to each other while waiting for camp to come around again. Logically that would help deal with the loneliness he would have to endure. Now he had changed, there was nothing to do except stand around until they were told what their first activity would be. He wondered what they would do. Hopefully they would break off into smaller groups. Bryan felt far more comfortable in such circumstances than if the horde went out as one unit.

"Hello," someone next to him said, attracting his attention.

"Hello," he replied, looking at the boy.

When he turned he saw someone of the same age. His hair was fairly light, although it would never be considered blonde. If it was it was a very dirty shade, as if straw had been peppered with spots of mud. As he responded he did so with a smile. This could be it; he could make friends with this youngster. His new acquaintance returned his grin with one of his own. Perhaps the two were more similar than appearances would suggest. Maybe he didn't have any friends here either. It made sense that one of them would have to make the first move. Why hadn't he thought of that? It was possible that the fact he hadn't reached out to people was why he didn't have any friends to begin with. Such a notion made him rather upset. Could it be true? Was his predicament of his own making? Even if it was, it didn't matter. If social withdrawal was the issue, he would quickly correct it. The children seemed a little edgier than usual after being ordered to change. It was, in a way, perfectly understandable. Couldn't they just do something fun first? When it was time to eat they could sort all these things out. None of the adults appeared to notice how desperate they were to explore their temporary home. Bryan held a different viewpoint. Obviously these people were stern in nature. There was every reason to believe they simply didn't care about the boys' need to expend energy. They were the batteries waiting to release their charges into whatever game set up for them. However, batteries are capable of being stored. The children could wait until the adults had finished dealing with them. For five minutes nothing really happened. Gingerly the two lads tried to talk, comparing interests to see if they had much in common. In all honesty, there weren't that many similarities. Bryan knew that was something he had to work on. If he wanted this person to stick around he was going to have to find something to bind them together. Perhaps a sport would allow them to bond over the course of the month.

"I'm Chad," the kid told him after a while, perhaps as eager to make friends as he was.

"Bryan," he replied, the two sharing a nervous smile.

"I wish we could go back outside," Bryan told him.

"It's horrible being stuck in here."

Neither of them was under the delusion that they looked good in their outfits. Frankly they resembled people of weight loss programs trying on their old clothes. How were they supposed to run around in such things? They were so baggy you could probably fit both of them in a single garment. Both of them turned their heads when the doors opened once more. Could they finally be going out for some fresh air? Having been cooped up all day, nothing would be better than smelling freshly mown grass. Yet there was something wrong with the sound the doors made. It was too aggressive, as if someone had flung them open in anger. Outside the strong sunlight made it difficult to see who was there. Having numerous people in the way didn't help either. Still, they could make out who it was. Those who had been eating outside were now standing in the entrance to the log cabin. At first Bryan was pleased to see them. Now they had their clothes, the only other thing to do was to assign bunks. Chad's face fell as he studied them closely. When Bryan turned back to them he noticed how his countenance had fallen. Slowly he turned back to view the figures. What was troubling him so greatly? After a few seconds he discovered the problem. In the hands of the workers were metal batons. These heavy clubs looked as if they could do nasty damage to solid concrete. So why were they carrying them when there were children around? Naturally his sceptical mind tried to explain away what was happening. Of course they weren't clubs. Logic dictates that they have to be batons for a relay race. What other explanation could there be? As he looked closely he saw their faces had hardened. No longer were they the loving people he presumed them to be. Instead he saw malice in their beings. From their eyes came rays of hatred directed at every child they could see.

"What's happening?" The anxious crowd began to mumble.

"I want to go home!" One ten year old squealed pitifully as the adults advanced towards them.

There seemed to be a collective realisation that something was wrong. Naturally people so young struggled to comprehend what was going on. Nonetheless, they backed away as the club-wielding brutes came towards them. Their minds refused to believe there was genuine spite in their actions. Surely this was some sort of prank. It wasn't as if such things don't happen. In a few minutes everyone would be laughing about how the organisers pulled the legs of every camper present. Presumably they wouldn't do the same thing with the girls. Boys were naturally resilient; they were capable of bouncing back from almost anything. Girls, on the other hand, were more like clay. Once marked, they tend to remain in that state. If this is a joke it would certainly find a warm reception amongst the young lads. Bryan shot a glance at the older boys standing together. Surprisingly their faces were just as distressed as those of the ten year olds. Normally the fellow was quite highly strung. Once he heard his teacher refer to him as neurotic to another member of staff. Looking the word up was a death sentence for their relationship. After realising what the comment implied, he found himself unable to bond with that person again. How could he knowing what was being said behind his back? Across the room he saw the same pair of boys he noticed earlier. Could they be brothers? It seemed probable given how they were practically inseparable.

Clement didn't know what to do as the boys were forced together. Like sardines they were packed tightly as they moved to get away from the hostile adults. Adam did his best to make room for his younger sibling. Whenever the lad looked up at him he could tell what he was thinking. This was not going to be a holiday they would remember fondly. His own facial expression didn't help. He had been there before; he knew exactly what to expect. Everything about him panicked the boy. Both eyes looked deeply tired. Now they were in the log cabin there was no turning back. They could not simply leave on one of the buses. By now the clueless drivers were long gone. Their only means of escape had casually driven away, not knowing the month the children were in for. Hidden by the worried chattering were the boy's laboured breaths. Something was certainly wrong. The theory that this was an illusion was rapidly disintegrating. This had gone on far too long already. Yet he didn't want to believe this was the case. His mind fought against the thought that he was in any sort of danger. Of course this was a joke. It just couldn't be true. For a second he believed these notions. But when he set eyes on the faces of the adults, it fell apart. There was no way they could fake the hatred they felt for the children. Not even actors in films demonstrated that level of skill. He didn't know what was happening here, but he didn't like it. Now he wished he had listened to his brother when he told him he wouldn't enjoy camp. Evidently he had been foolish not to take such wise advice. If events so far were anything to go by, he would be glad to go home. Four weeks couldn't roll past quickly enough for his liking.

"Are you okay?" Adam asked him, knowing the answer already.

"No," Clement responded with a heart-breaking tone.

"Don't worry," he told his brother. "You'll be fine if you just do what they tell you to."

For over ten minutes they were kept in their cramped conditions. There was almost no room to breath as they desperately waited for the joke to end. This was enough as far as they were concerned. It was time for them to reveal the punch-line. Sadly this didn't seem to be on the horizon. The faces of the adults hardened further when they studied the stressed children. Were these kids so weak that they couldn't take being a bit crowded? How would they ever cope if they rode a subway? People so pitifully insipid didn't deserve any happiness at all. Most of them had to fight for everything they ever had. Why should these kids be any different? Joy is not something handed out freely. Clement could tell exactly what the others were thinking. More than anything they wanted to be away from these people. When was the fun going to start? This could still be some sort of initiation. Things would change in an instant. The batons they held aloft would hang harmlessly at their sides. Hard faces would become grins as they enjoyed the trick they had played. Sadly this wasn't the case. He knew that their hostility was not an act. It would be better if they came to a collective agreement to fight back. Could they not see the danger they were in? Naturally their intentions were unknown to him. Even so, how could they be good? These were not the actions of decent human beings. When he looked at their weapons he wondered who would be struck first. Surely if the whole group attacked at once they would be able to get away. So many opponents would prove a challenge to even the best fighters. Deep down he knew this was not an option. They were kids; most were only ten. Strangely his thoughts drifted on to the girl's camp. Was this happening there? Briefly the boy pictured himself as a knight in shining armour, racing to protect the females. Worryingly it wasn't just the two premises that were in operation. His brother told him that most of the older boys went to other camps owned by the corporation. How many were suffering in the same way? Such a thought was horrifying to the boy. Something needed to be done about this. Had they gone mad?

"It'll be okay," his brother whispered to him.

Surprisingly he felt something wrap itself round his hand. When he looked down he saw Adam holding his hand. Judging by the look on his face it was not just for the younger lad's benefit. In many ways he was just as scared as Clement was. This was not a good sign. After a few minutes the men in the back began to speak. Unlike the others, they were unarmed. Why didn't the older boys attack them? If everyone charged together they would be swamped through sheer numbers. Regrettably he had a rather childlike concept of how easy victory would be in such a situation. He didn't take the electric gates into account. Even if they did escape, how were they going to get through them? Climbing certainly wasn't an option. The way they had been designed made attempts at scaling them almost impossible. As they started talking the room fell silent. Everyone was far too upset to risk provoking the adults further. Still, across the room he was sure he could hear someone crying. Hearing the sounds almost tore his heart in two. In time he would hear far more sobbing than he ever considered in his worst nightmares. This one noise turned his eyes scarlet. As they continued to speak it only got worse. What exactly was going to happen to them? In the brochures they were promised fun from the minute they arrived. So far this had bordered on torture. When he got home he would have a lot to tell his parents. Every vile act committed against them would be aired for anyone who cared to listen.

"Now you have changed, you will be taken to the camp," one of them said. "Your clothes will be kept in storage; you will collect them when you leave at the end of the holiday. It is best if you do what you are told. As we are not your parents, it doesn't matter to us if you are injured or not. We simply do not care about you."

This made Clement's heart miss a beat. How could anyone be so cruel? At the same time, he wondered if it was part of a trick. The brochure told him that first aid would be available if it was needed. One of his parents told him they had a duty of care over the children. If anything happened they could be sued for negligence. Also, he told them they would be taken to the camp. Surely they were already at the camp? Where did he think they were? This was enough to convince him that it was a joke. Flaws had become apparent in the charade. In school that is how the teachers tell if someone is lying. The accuracy of a story reflects how truthful it is. Now he had told them things that didn't make sense. That, in his mind, was enough for him to dismiss the whole thing. A smile instantly appeared on his face. Those around him, including his brother, looked terrified. Didn't they know that the whole thing was a lie? It had to be; such cruel treatment given earnestly would break the law. His eyes drifted back onto the man who was speaking. If he had gone into show business he would make a good actor. Without giving anything away he told lies that were almost perfectly plausible. Momentarily he stopped speaking, his eyes drifting over the silent crowd. Almost every pair of panicked eyes was fixed on him. Everything was going nicely from his perspective. Almost half of them looked as if they were about to burst into tears. The other half was so stunned by what was happening that they were numb. Their hearts were paralysed to ensure they didn't have a breakdown. One or two were crying; their cheeks streaked as they tried to comprehend what he was saying. From experience he knew they were not going to cause the adults any bother. These runts would do exactly what they were told for fear of repercussions.

"You will not enjoy this holiday, but you will not be harmed if you behave yourselves," he started once more. "If you try to keep out of our way, we will have no reason to punish you. However, the consequences of disobedience will be severe. If anyone tries to run while we are taking you to the camp, they will be beaten to the floor."

Upon hearing that, several groans erupted from the crowd. Was this what their parents paid for? Who would possibly send their children to such a terrible place? Some of them actually believed that their parents knew this would happen. It was written over their faces as they wished they had stayed at home. Was it that they were so cold they didn't care what happened to their offspring? Not even the worst people would allow their own flesh and blood to be subjected to this. If they found out what was going on they would summon the police in the flash. But this was a bit difficult for the ten year olds to understand. A few wondered if this was supposed to be a punishment. Perhaps their parents sent them here for their misbehaviour. But did they really deserve it? All little boys are mischievous; there is no escaping that. Paying to send them to a brutal world is not the answer to human nature. Bryan found the emotional change of the crowd incredibly distressing. Less than ten minutes ago they had been eager to arrive. Almost half a year had been spent looking forwards to this trip. They had been almost uncontrollable on the bus. Now they looked as if they wanted to crawl into a hole and die. Their once ecstatic faces had fallen considerably. When he saw someone crying he felt himself began to detach from the situation. This was far too much for him to handle. How are ten year olds supposed to deal with such aggression? These men were at least four times their age. There was no way they could defend themselves if attacked. It was the same as the times he had crushed woodlice in the garden. Did they honestly think anyone would come back next year after this? If this was revealed to be a joke, it would not be met with much laughter. Even so, they would be grateful if it could be resolved shortly. There was no need for any of the hatred directed towards them. Humour was capable of surviving without threats against relatively powerless people. They might as well go into a nursery with a loaded shotgun.

"You will not be playing games; you will be working. As long as you are willing to make a good effort, you will not be harmed. Refusal to work will be punished with violence. By now you are probably starting to understand that we are willing to use force against you. That's good; you must realise that we will treat you well if you are pleasant."

These last few statements caused the most distress. Could they honestly be running some sort of labour camp? If so, why hadn't anyone done anything about it? Bryan did not react to this in any way. He did not let his head slump in shame as the older boys did. Unlike the other ten year olds, he did not begin choking back tears. Instead he beamed at the man. There was no way this could be real. How could such an establishment run without anyone blowing the whistle on it? Ergo, this was merely some sort of trick. Pretty soon their situation would change; it had to. What he didn't realise is that fear is a powerful persuader. That is why terrorism is so popular in some parts of the world. People sit up and listen the moment violence is used. A similar process was happening here. These adults, who dwarfed the younger boys, were unconquerable foes who had to be treated with the same respect as a black widow sitting beneath the toilet seat. One of the boys close to him looked as if he was about to collapse. He could only have been eleven years old. That was far too young to deal with a situation someone four times his age would be unable to handle. Yet there he was, barely able to take in what was being said. How many hours had he spent thinking of the fun he would have? His home life wasn't that good; he deserved a break from the rows that gripped his family. Completely powerless to help himself, he broke down completely. Terrible sobs shook his upper body as he quickly marched towards hysteria. Coldly Bryan giggled at him. Is he really taking the threats seriously? Was he honestly that weak? Those around him couldn't believe he was laughing at such a time. To them he was nothing more than a bully. Nobody with a shred of decency in them would be able to mock a person in such a state.

"You will now be taken to the camp," the man spoke one last time before opening the back doors.

As far as the boy was concerned, this was the end of it. Any moment now he would reveal the joke he had played on them. In his mind there was no doubt at all that this was a misguided attempt at humour. Behind him the club-wielders advanced forwards. Those closest to them backed away in horror. What had seemed so paradisiacal now sickened them. Why couldn't they have just stayed at home? At least there they would be safe. There was no telling what these lunatics would do. Within seconds he felt the other children forcing him towards the rear doors. They didn't care that they were trampling on his feet. All they wanted was to avoid the dangerous workers quickly heading towards them. At first he thought he could take the joke. What harm would it do to them in the long run? Now he saw the fear in them, he knew things could turn ugly. If someone fell they wouldn't be able to get back up. Feet would trample them in a slow stampede of death. It would take a long time for them to perish; they might even live through it, enduring collapsed lungs and broken ribs. In all honesty he knew next to nothing about medicine. His only knowledge of these things came from the family's medical encyclopaedia. When he thought no-one was watching he flicked through it, devouring gruesome images of foul ailments. Privately he considered himself a mini-expert on such things. Yet if there ever was an emergency he would be powerless. A ten year old, whatever they had read, was not a doctor. For an eternity he was waiting to leave through the back doors. He certainly did not enjoy being forced up against others. The kids were desperate to get out. If they had to push each other out of the way to do so, then so be it. Somehow he managed to squeeze past a fatter boy next to the exit. Finally he was outside. No longer was he struggling to breath with the sheer weight of others crushing against him. Now they were outside they might reveal the trick they were playing. Naturally this had been a good way to forge links between the campers. Going through such an experience together would bond them for life.

"There's no way out!" Someone ahead of him shouted.

"Calm down!" An older boy told him firmly.

When he looked he recognised the pair immediately. Adam was holding Clement firmly by the shoulders. Both of them were crying, albeit for different reasons. The younger brother was desperate to get away. He knew staying where he was could get him killed. Even at that young age he knew the peril he was in. His older sibling felt as if he had failed them both. For three years he had been unable to stop coming. Why couldn't he summon the strength to make some sort of complaint to the authorities? His cowardice now meant his brother was also suffering. To him that meant he wasn't a good person. How could he be when he didn't do nearly enough to keep the lad safe? His failures meant an innocent child would be traumatised for life. But he could still make this right. As long as there was breath in his body he would defend the young man. If they wanted to harm him they would have to step over his corpse. Despite Clement's extremely high emotions, he was right. As soon as they left the log cabin they saw the additional workers. These people were also armed with truncheons. They too looked at the children as if they were scum from the bottom of a pond. What they found particularly alarming was that they were relatively normal people. Those who threatened them were the same folks they would see if they walked down a street. How could they do this to ten year olds? Didn't they have any morality at all? Two lines of them stretched from the rear doors to a gate on the other side of the field. Trapped in this formation were the terrified youths. Most of them were crying; the rest were too emotionally numb to move. Adam looked into his brothers eyes. It was clear that he thought he wasn't going to make it. He knew this was a bad sign. Those who survived the ordeal in one piece remained strong. They had to see the adults as the monsters they were. Nothing they would do could ever warrant a beating from people three times their size. To think otherwise was to succumb to almost total madness. These human beings were children, not workers. Having the older men tell them otherwise made no difference to this whatsoever. Sadly children are programmed from birth to listen to what seniors have to say. It would be hard for even the most rebellious camper not to internalise the horrific things that would soon happen to them.

"Get moving!" A twenty year old woman told those at the front as she opened the metal gates at the end of the field.

With that their fate was sealed. As soon as they entered the pathway there was no chance of escape. That said, it wasn't as if their hopes were justified beforehand. If anyone as much as looked at a guard the wrong way they would be beaten. None of the workers were fools; they knew that if all the children tried to run they probably wouldn't be able to maintain their formations. Of course, there was nowhere for them to go. There were fences all round the area; they would merely be running haphazardly until the last one received a smack to the back of the head. Reducing themselves to the levels of headless chickens would do them no good whatsoever. In no way would such a stand be successful. Ten year old boys playing with tin soldiers are not the generals they believe themselves to be. Bryan watched as the first of the kids were forced down a passage. It struck him as strange that they were doing this. Could it be that this wasn't a trick? Were they earnestly running some sort of labour camp? These thoughts lasted less than a few seconds. Such a notion was enough to make him laugh. It was a convincing joke; he had to give them that. Their persistence was more than admirable. More than likely this would reveal to be some sort of nature hike. Once they reached the summit of a draughty peak they would announce that they had fooled the campers in spectacular fashion. In small groups the boys began to trickle through the gates. This was nowhere near quick enough for the guard's liking. Shouts filled the air as they urged the juveniles on. Bryan was in no particular hurry to go anywhere. He knew this was all a wind-up. In a few hours, once they had their hike, it would be over. Still, he had no desire whatsoever to go walking. After such a long bus ride he was tired. One could not stay so excited all day without crashing afterwards. Furthermore, the walks mentioned in the brochure were supposed to be voluntary. His mother had told him that he didn't have to go anywhere if he didn't want to. Something he heard one of the older men say struck a cord with him. Failure to comply was apparently punishable by physical force. Perhaps it was time he put their joke to the test. Armed with a smile, he turned to face the worker on his left.

"I'm not going," he stated with an almost arrogant air. "I don't like walks. What are you going to do about it?"

Immediately the air changed. What he had done was something the adults would not simply forgive. He had been warned about the consequences of refusing to obey commands. In a split second all eyes were upon him. Crying children stopped their fearful sobbing. They were stunned that there was someone brave enough to stand up to the bullies. The older boys noticed the charge in the air building. At first they couldn't believe what had happened. Could this be happening? Was the smallest fish in the ocean going to take on a blue whale? Again they hung their heads. There would be enough violence later on for a lifetime. Why would they want to see a poor kid being beaten to a pulp? Surprisingly the consequences of his cheek weren't as severe as they thought they would be. If they did that they would be out cold for hours. Instead she merely gave the boy a tap on the arm. It wasn't a light blow by any stretch of the imagination. When it made contact with him he staggered momentarily. A pitifully cute yelp echoed through the field as he struggled to make sense of what was happening. Bryan simply couldn't believe that had happened. In shock he clutched his arm. Both eyes turned scarlet in seconds. Why had she done that? As he looked into her eyes he felt for the first time as if someone truly hated him. It wasn't nice at all. Never in his life had he experienced such loathing directed at his own self. This was something a ten year old couldn't handle. His belief that it was a joke flew straight out the window. That wasn't something any camp would allow. Feeling the pain, he was more than ready to accept the nightmare he had willingly rode into.

"I'll let that one slip because you're new here," she warned him with the menace of a charging lioness. "But if you ever say anything like that again, you'll wish you had never been born. We'll be keeping our eyes on you."

A tear rolled down his cheek. This couldn't be possible. Such a camp couldn't be allowed to operate. He watched with his screwed face as she pointed in the direction of the path. All around him the other children were silent. Now they knew the threat of violence was not empty. If they so much as stepped out of line they would be severely punished. Their worried faces seemed to make the guards happy. As every disturbed little boy went past, their smiles got bigger. Having power over someone else was addictive. Sadists are made; these monsters were the products of their own profession. They were vampires of emotions, feeding on the misery they caused those too young to possibly fight back. Worryingly they were in charge of the children for a month. There was no guarantee they would make it out alive. Naturally there would be a cover-up. Even under adult supervision kids are clumsy; they get up to mischief. The public would undoubtedly hear how the workers had done everything in their power to save the dead lad. His parents would probably thank them for their attentiveness in their son's final moments. All of this would be a lie. They would have beaten him to death, then intimidated the witnesses into keeping their mouths closed. After securing the body they could stage whatever accident they wanted. There was still a full month of this to go. How they would get through it remained to be seen.

Clement stayed close to Adam as they made their way up the path. Escape had truly been made impossible. Surrounding them on both sides were walls of rock. These ten-metre obstacles made climbing fanciful. Anyone who tried to do so would be scaling a surface as smooth as silk. By now it was pretty clear to him that his older brother had been through his before. Since he was thirteen, he must have done it three times. He knew exactly what to expect. So why hadn't he been honest with his parents? If he told them what had happened they would never have sent either of them here in the first place. Almost certainly they would have made a complaint to the authorities. Such actions could not go unpunished. There had to be laws preventing these camps from operating. In a way it was hard not to feel angry with the older boy. His inaction was the cause of his present suffering. Because of him he would have to take a month of torture. Of course, his experience was still useful. If he utilised what his brother knew he could do quite well. Clearly his sibling wanted to protect him as much as possible. Information was as valuable as gold in these sorts of situations. Yet the thought of even being around his sibling was almost sickening at the moment. What was going to happen to him over the next month? Tears streaked down his cheeks as he imagined the torture he would receive. This was all his brothers fault. It wouldn't be an exaggeration to say he hated him. Some of this emotion must have diffused into the air; Adam could almost sense the rage building in the smaller boy.

"I'm sorry you're going to have to go through all this," he told him cautiously. "But you'll get through it. The first week is always the hardest. After a while time will fly by. Before you know it you'll be home."

Clement slowly turned his head to look at his brother. No words could explain the negative feelings he harboured for him. In less tragic circumstances it would have been almost comical. A thirteen year old was almost shying away from a miniscule ten year old. Those around them could tell that he was seeing red. The boy was surely a bomb about to go off at any moment. When he finally blew they didn't want to be anywhere in the vicinity. Bryan was behind them, holding his wounded arm. Clement already knew enough about him to be put off. When everyone else feared for his lives, he smirked with the arrogance of a thousand dictators. If he wasn't so short he would have turned round to confront him. In his opinion the worker hadn't done enough to punish him for his comment. No other boy held himself in so high an esteem he could demand not to follow orders. He should consider himself extremely lucky he got off with a smack to the arm. If Clement had control of the baton he wouldn't get away so lightly. This sort of thinking shocked the boy. Normally he was such a nice person. Adults around him tended to enjoy his presence because of this quality. Now a fellow camper had turned him into something he despised. Adam kept turning to look at him. The tears streaked his face terribly. How was he going to cope with the next month if he couldn't take the initial shock? Others had already begun to emotionally detach from the situation. The workers had their bodies, but not their minds. These were the people who spent the whole of their time awake in a trance. As soon as they left they resumed normal functioning, the supposed holiday merely a blur in the memory. Naturally the boys were not psychologists. They could not put this mental state into words. Hurtfully they referred to them as 'zombies', pretending they didn't admire the way they were almost immune to the malicious acts of the guards. In front of them there was one such person. Clement noticed the stiff way he walked. It was as if he was deep in thought. No part of him registered the surrounding scenery. Why would they? From what they heard their parents had apparently agreed to send them to a glorified prison. Others would at least look at the walls of rock, even if it was a mere distraction from the death march. He didn't glance anywhere other than the floor. Something about his shoes must have amazed him. In the time it took to get to the camp he didn't look at anything else. Adam felt sorry for the boy. Those who set up the horrible place had robbed him of his humanity. While his body was there, his psyche had retreated into itself. Nobody knew if he would notice being speared with a drawing pin. If his own mother appeared to take him home he would look straight through her.

"He's going to fall flat on his face if he doesn't walk properly," Adam remarked to his brother as they both watched the child.

"Good," Clement coldly replied, not interested at all about the lad.

This shocked his brother. How could he speak so aloofly of someone in such a state? Essentially the boy was sleepwalking to the death of his innocence. Any reasonable person would surely be appalled by the spectacle. Sadly he didn't seem to care. After everything that had happened so far, he wasn't exactly to blame. Now he had to focus on keeping himself safe. A ten year old simply didn't have the capacity to empathise properly with another human being under such conditions. Adam swore to himself as he considered the coward he had become. There was a very good reason he hadn't stopped coming to the camp. Of course there was; why would anyone willingly agree to be subjected to terrible abuse? If he could he would just tell the young man the truth. But how could he when it would be so devastating? He wished he could reverse time with sheer will. Going back to meet himself three years earlier would be ideal. For weeks he begged his parents to send him to what he considered a utopia. Eventually they caved in; his nagging paid off. Unfortunately the reality hit him hard. When he got home he went to his room and cried. Neither of his parents could understand why he was so upset. For months he never smiled. How could he be happy when he had gone through so much? As time wore on he distanced himself from the events. They became akin to the nightmares he frequently suffered. Camp was a whole different reality from the world he normally inhabited. The second year he only needed a fortnight to get over it. By now his crude coping strategies had begun to pay off. Yet this didn't mean he wasn't upset as the summer rolled round once more. Last night his brother was wide awake for hours, only falling asleep when he burnt himself out. In the next room Adam couldn't sleep either. Only this was for a different reason; he knew what would happen. All he wanted was to stay at home and pretend he had never seen the poster for the camp to begin with. Regrettably that was only a dream. Deep down he knew he was stuck with this for years. They could only hope the guards wouldn't injure them too badly.

Finally they reached the real camp. This was where they would spend the next month. Two very large gates stood between them and the prison they would call home. At the top were dozens of coils of barbed wire. From the looks of things they could strip flesh from bone. Upon seeing them, the thirteen year old immediately felt sick. Memories flashed through his head as if they were photographs in a video. This was far too much for him. He wasn't strong enough to deal with the whirlwind in his head. Before he could do anything he found himself retching. Up ahead were those who had walked in front of them. As the gates were being opened they had collected at the entrance. Hearing him vomit, they turned to watch his stomach contents erupt from his mouth. Part of it went over the trousers of the boy they had seen. Only then did they realise just how badly damaged he was. A normal person would be inconsolable after being defiled in such a way. However, the lad didn't make a fuss of any kind. Instead he acted as if he thought someone had tapped him on the shoulder. His tired head casually turned to look behind him. Clement was finally able to feel something for him when he witnessed the shocking display. This fellow had done nothing wrong. So why had he been driven into this state? All sorts of things washed over him. Anger towards those who oppressed him filled his mind. It wasn't as if he could confide in his parents when he finally went home. How could he? Whatever stopped Adam spilling the beans would inevitably keep that camper's lips sealed as well. With a bit of luck they could change that. Whatever happened, he would reveal everything to anyone who would listen. Hopefully they would investigate his claims of mistreatment. Who could doubt his story if they saw the place themselves? No doubt they would have bruises if they were struck by the guards. Someone he showed them too would take them seriously. They had to; people couldn't all be as cold as those that led them here. Alongside him Adam retched for the final time. Bent over, with his hands on his knees, he looked much younger than he was. It was amazing how a little sickness took years off a person's age. One thing was certain to him. This lad was not his enemy. Those who should receive his hatred were wielding the clubs.

"What are we waiting for?" Clement asked as he joined the horde waiting to be let into the prison.

"They're waiting for the boss," he explained, not even wanting to think about such a man.

"Who?" His younger brother replied.

He never got an answer to his question; he didn't need one. As soon as the he spoke he saw the doors being pulled backwards from the other side. Some of the older boys looked as if they were going to faint. How could the year have gone so quickly? Once again they were back here, waiting for the abuse to begin. Adam wanted nothing more than to die. He couldn't face four weeks of hell. You would have to be a monster to enjoy what was in store for them. The boys watched cautiously as the gates revealed their home. What they saw made their eyes glisten. Wonderful log cabins were nowhere in sight. Apparently they would have to sleep in run-down brick huts. Although large, they didn't look comfortable in the slightest. These structures were the sorts of things you would see in third world countries. Inevitably they would turn out to be damp, draughty and generally miserable. Everything they could see made their hearts sink. Something awful must inhabit the ground; it would explain why there wasn't a patch of green anywhere. It was as if every plant within range had been poisoned by the collective suffering of the campers. A few of the boys backed away at the thought of this. Overhead the sun seemed to have deserted them. Obscured by clouds, its glow was barely strong enough to register on their systems. In front of them the three men told them to wait. Clement wanted to tear them limb from limb. How dare they do this? How dare they treat kids so poorly? Logically this wasn't an option. Even alone they would utterly defeat the boy in a fight. Six workers, all carrying nightsticks with them, would ward off even the most determined attacks. Up against ten year olds they were almost invincible. One of the cabins was different from the others. This one, although smaller, looked as if it was almost fit for service. From it came a man wearing a black suit. This fellow looked rather old even from a distance. As he slowly sauntered towards the gates they got a better look at him. Adam couldn't bear to set eyes on the figure. When he did so he considered all the heinous things that happened under his watch. It wasn't as if he could get away with merely letting these things happen. On many accounts he devised almost sadistic punishments for the children. That made him guiltier than anyone else working there. He was the nucleus of the whole operation; his shining light led others towards immorality.

"He looks about a hundred," Clement remarked as the man made his way towards the boys.

To them he didn't look that harmful. In his sixties, his greying hair disarmed them somewhat. He reminded many of them of their grandfathers. Physically he wasn't very impressive. A thin man of average height, he didn't look anywhere near as threatening as his armed guards. The three other men turned to converse with him once he was close enough. Speaking in hushed whispers, they obviously respected the gentleman. From the way they acted around him he was revered amongst his staff. Whatever the point of torturing the children was, he was surely leading them in the right direction. Clement thought about their manners in his presence. It put him in mind of royalty in medieval times. Could the building he emerged from be his private office? There was no doubt about it in his mind; this fellow was the boss. If anyone led the sadists in their horrid affairs, it was him. Yet none of the ten year olds had any idea what he was like. In time they would come to thoroughly despise the man. People in the street that bore a resemblance to him would make their fists curl at their sides. He would be the face of their nightmares; when he entered their minds they would grow quiet as they contemplated their darkest memories. Strangely there was no sign of this menace as he strolled towards the children. They could go as far as to say he looked peaceful. There was no difference between his manner and that of any other elderly person out for a stroll. Leaving the three men he had conversed with behind him, he spoke aloud to the children. His voice conveyed a great sense of authority. Although the older boys detested the sight of him, they couldn't help but feel respect as he spoke. This was something they hated. Wounding them was one thing; infiltrating their minds was quite another. Of course, he had taken this one step further with the guards. They had once been campers subjected to the same abuse they were about to go through. As they desperately sought approval from the workers, they slowly became them. Before they knew it they were being offered a job to work in the camps. Adam would never let something so horrible happen to him. He would rather die before he served the spiteful man set to poison the minds of every child around him.

"Welcome," he projected his voice through the forest. "I was hoping the advice my deputies had given you would be enough to keep you all in line." When he finished the sentence he looked around, as if peering into the souls of those present. "It has been brought to my attention that one of you said something incredibly disrespectful to one of my employees. Regrettably that necessitated the use of force. I presume we have shown you that obeying us is the best way to avoid punishments. I know who that person is, and if he does anything else today he will be facing far more serious consequences."

Somehow his eyes seemed to focus on Bryan. When he made eye contact he felt himself blush. Of course he had learnt his lesson from being struck. His arm wasn't really damaged in any way, but he had tasted the strength of the guards. The men were right when they had told them not to give the adults trouble. It was only his own arrogance that prevented him from seeing the situation for what it was. For that he had received his just rewards. As the leader looked away he seemed to snap from this spell for a moment. What had he been thinking? How could he have deserved what he received? He was only ten; did they expect boys so young to be the pinnacles of obedience? When he realised he had somehow betrayed himself he was rather sad. Was all this already starting to get to him? Could he be losing his mind after a few minutes? His thoughts began to drift to his home. If he hadn't caught the bus that morning he would be playing in the garden. Instead he wasn't sure when the next blow was going to come. Still, he did know it was coming. It was inevitable that he would find himself on the wrong side of a guard. For that he would be reprimanded without restraint. Yet there was one good thing; the leader didn't look at him again. Evidently he felt his warning had been enough to dissuade further comments. Ironically he was correct. Bryan was in no mood to challenge the workers. His arm throbbed constantly, despite his gentle rubbing. In his mind he wondered if it was broken. There was a small lump forming where he had been hit. What exactly did that mean? Others looking at him knew he regretted making those statements. Of course, they had no way of knowing that by the end of the month he would be sorry for far more than just that. At times like these he wished he had Jordon around to comfort him. But the boy was gone; there was no-one to help him through this difficult patch.

"You will be separated into three work groups. You will not be allowed to change group to be with your friends. You will sleep with your workmates in the same dormitory, but at mealtimes you will be able to mingle freely. Those of you that are twelve and above may be assigned various tasks. These will take into account what you have done in previous years. Does anyone have any questions?"

Somehow a boy at the front managed to raise his hand. From the looks of things he wouldn't make it through another hour. How he was supposed to last the full four weeks they didn't know. Bryan barely noticed the lad's predicament at all. Selfishly he thought of himself, ignoring those around him. Why wouldn't he? He was the one suffering. Thanks to the mistake of seeing a poster he was trapped in this place for a long time. For someone of his age a month was an eternity. There was no end in sight; he might as well have been given a life sentence. Such a thought made the tears flow faster. The atmosphere was so charged it could electrocute all those present. The boy didn't notice that; he barely cared if the other young man was punished or not. All he concerned himself with was getting out of here. Behind him the older boys knew the boss's question was rhetorical. If they actually did have any questions, it would be better to ask someone who had been there before. When the adults saw the fellow's arm they looked sceptical. Normally people learnt very quickly to keep their mouths shut and to do what they are told. It was no secret society around them was degenerating. People treated each other appalling these days. Thus it was no wonder they were challenged so directly. Fortunately for his administration the threat of corporal punishment remained a powerful persuader. Little could stand up to heavy blows from the workers' batons. For over a hundred years the strategy had worked perfectly. It would not fail now, despite the spirit of those opposing him. Still, he nodded at the boy. Fairness dictated that he should allow the person the chance to speak. At the very least he could have a private laugh later on.

"I- I," he started, his mouth unable to form the words. "I just want to go home."

His peers couldn't believe what he had just said. Was there something wrong with him? Did he honestly believe that someone could just leave by stating the desire to do so? Those standing next to him took a step backwards. He had just challenged the boss. They could only hope that God would have mercy upon his soul. For five seconds nothing happened. The shock of his statement stunned the crowd deeply. Tears constantly flowed down his cheeks. This was someone who mentally couldn't take the abuse. A lifetime of being wrapped in cotton wool had left him incredibly dependant. One of the reasons why his parents sent him there was to cut the apron strings a bit. After this they would probably be lucky if they still had a son to coddle. After a short period the man's face glowed bright red. How dare this thing speak so poorly to him? Didn't he realise that next to him he was barely a human being? Straight away he turned to his deputies. A series of whispers led one of them to advance towards the boy. In terror he could do nothing. Running wasn't an option. If he could get his muscles to work he wouldn't have anywhere to go. The workers would beat him to a pulp if he so much as turned to flee. Watching the man come towards him was horrifying. The enraged equivalent of a giant began to sprint towards him. A scream of heartbreaking alarm echoed through the forest as the man caught hold of the lad's arm. Spinning him round, he brought his other hand slamming down onto the boy's buttocks. For thirty seconds he continuously struck the youth. Incredulous stares came from the other campers as they watched the display. At first the male was shouting only when he was struck. By the end he was wailing constantly, only stopping to take breaths. Clement couldn't believe what he was seeing. His parents had spanked him in the past, but they had never done so with such ferocity. His victim wouldn't be able to sit down for a week. Next to him, his older brother thanked God that the chastisement wasn't far more serious than it was. Frankly the juvenile was getting off lightly. The fact he was only ten helped his case. An older boy would suffer more pain than he believed was possible. Bryan surprisingly noticed the torment he was experiencing. Coldly he was grateful he was not on the receiving end of it.

"That'll hurt in the morning," he whispered as he flinched repeatedly.

After the beating he spun the boy round. Now facing him head on, he saw the emotions on the boy's face. The deputy stared into his eyes for a moment. His victim was screaming apologies at him constantly. Mucous flowed from both nostrils, matching the tears that glided down his flushed face. When he noticed the state he was in he knew he had done his job properly. This kid was so much of a mess he wouldn't dare risk being hit again. More than likely he would be too afraid to complain if he was being eaten alive by a giant python. A twisted smile grew on the face of the employee. All the signs suggested that his work was done. Thirty seconds had crushed the boy's resistance completely. He had snapped his spirit as easily as he would break a matchstick. His target was too afraid to do anything other than mumble how sorry he was. That was all he said for over a minute. Strangely there was no anger in his mind. Self-preservation was all he pursued. What mattered other than being allowed to live? Yet subconsciously he despised this man more than anyone else in the world. He hated the hollow, frosty eyes with a vengeance. His misshapen nose would feel good in his hands if he ripped it off. His apologies only made the man's grin grow. To him he was a truly pathetic human being. At that age he would have escaped once he realised the camp wasn't the paradise he believed it to be. Humanity had fallen far compared to when he was a boy. Some of this hatred must have been sensed by the younger male. At the back of his mind he would love nothing more than to aim a fist at his protruding stomach. There had to be some law against treating children in such a way. He couldn't just be allowed to do what he had done. Even if he had significant awareness of these thoughts, he wouldn't have said anything. Merely asking a question was enough to leave his flesh red raw. How would they react if he commented on their bullying? He didn't have the strength to stand up to them, either mentally or physically. Ultimately it was far better if he kept his mouth shut and followed instructions. That was the best thing the workers had said so far. It was advice he really ought to have taken.

"You having to see that was unfortunate," he told the campers, once again staring at the boy. "I believe he has learnt his lesson. Just try and stay out of our way," he added, his eyes studying the face of the wounded lad. "Now, if you'll excuse me, I have to return to my office. My deputies will assign you to your groups."

With that he turned round and walked back the way he came. Clement was amazed that such a seemingly nice person could authorise something so terrible. Indeed, the fellow was a gentleman of the highest order. In conversation he was flawless; his voice revealed the wonderful private education he must have received. His mannerisms were perfectly refined. You would not see the thuggish, arrogant swaggers of scum that the children encountered in their estates. Instead he was as graceful as a bird of prey gliding through the air. So why had he decided to run such a camp? Surely if he had gone to private school he would have the contacts to earn far more than most. There was no need to torture children. Of course, the answers were not known to anyone around him. Not even his deputies knew the reasons why he had taken this dark path. Most likely they would be taken to his grave. Certainly the kids were clueless as they tried to get over what they had just seen. More than one sobbed hysterically at the sight of the beating. They were united as one against the employees. His pain was surely their pain. Bryan was the only one who wasn't deeply disturbed by the terrible event. From his perspective he couldn't see the point. A different incentive to make friends began to grow within him. Having people around him meant there were others to soak up some of the blows. Their presence could be the difference between one smack and fifty. He looked on as one of the men drew a folded piece of paper from his pocket. As he unfolded it they could see a list of names on the back. Adam desperately wanted to be with his brother. He needed him around; who else would show him the ropes? If there was an incident he could try to negotiate with the workers for a lesser punishment. More than anyone else he knew the boy was weak. It wasn't just his role as an intercessor that he had to fulfil. Bullying between campers was rife. There was so much hatred for the guards that the only way for some to remain sane was to unload it onto the others around them. That wouldn't end well for someone as small as Clement. Yet there wasn't any particular reason to believe they would be split up. Generally siblings were kept together in groups. This was a rare act of mercy none of the older boys could understand. Even friends were occasionally allocated the same work detail. Perhaps it was because the boss wasn't a complete monster at heart. Alternatively, he didn't want to break the spirit of the children so badly that they couldn't work. Why would he do something that could damage the initiative?

"Calum Geraint; group one," he read from the list. "Alan Lloyd; group two, Nicky Davidson; group one."

This went on for roughly ten minutes. Adam was incredibly relieved to discover that he was in the same quarters as his brother. That meant he would be there when they were sleeping, too. A hard day's work was a catalyst for abuse amongst the boys. This way he would be able to guide Clement through the month without him suffering too badly. He couldn't control the guards, but he could make sure the other slaves stayed away from him. When he considered this he almost withdrew the word. Slavery seemed a rather harsh description. He didn't enjoy the thought of what it implied. But he couldn't disagree that it was the truth. For the next four weeks they were unpaid workers, acting against their will. They would be beaten for refusal to comply with orders. How could it not be slavery? Quickly he tried to distract himself from this. Upsetting himself further would be of no benefit whatsoever. A single sentence from the man was enough to send the children marching towards the brick buildings. It was odd that they decided to use full names rather than imprinting numbers onto the outfits. With a little imagination it was as if they were humanising the young men. Alternatively, perhaps something within the employees remembered what a camp was supposed to be like. Almost certainly they had attended one when they were children. It was not a great leap to believe they wanted to keep some parts of it intact. This might be a hellhole in the middle of the forest, but there was nothing to be gained from depersonalising the victims further. None of this occurred to the boys as they feared what would happen next. What work would they be doing? Nobody spoke as they made their way towards their collective cells. Once they were inside they might be able to ask the older boys. Having been there before, if anyone knew it would be them. But they didn't dare speak until they were out of earshot. How could they be sure a single word wouldn't lead to a beating? The leader told them that punishments would stem from disobedience. Whether or not he seriously believed this, it was clear that the guards were looking for an excuse. Even a dirty look could be deliberately misconstrued as justification for their bloodlust. How anyone could be so cruel simply boggled the mind. In a way it was tragic that these people could only satisfy their emotional needs with sadism.

"If anyone picks on you, let me know," Adam whispered cautiously into Clement's ear.

"I will," he replied, hoping his brother wouldn't say anything else until they were inside.

The buildings looked even worse from up close. From appearances a strong breeze could be enough to knock them down. There would come a time when they would wish they would, provided they were in it when it happened. Adam knew that this desperation point would hit his brother sooner or later. When it did, he needed to be there for him. How would he get through it without his sibling there to protect him? If anything happened to the lad he would never forgive himself. For the rest of his life he would know that he was responsible for his brother's misery. Of course, his cowardice had already sealed his fate in this respect. Yet he could ensure that he suffered as little as possible throughout the period. If he had a good first year, he might survive the next several. The boys seemed slightly reluctant to enter the building once they reached it. It was as if some malevolent force would ensnare them forever if they dared cross the threshold. Sadly they couldn't remain outside forever. The thought of the beating given to the young man was still fresh in their minds. To resist the authority of the guards after witnessing such a thing was pure madness. Gingerly they began to take their first steps into the building. What they saw was enough to reduce grown men to tears. Their quarters lacked beds of any kind. The walls and ceiling had been speedily whitewashed; perhaps the adults wanted to hide the fact that they could collapse at any moment. A few light bulbs hung down from the ceiling, resembling vines that someone could swing from. There were no lampshades of any kind. Whoever wired them up considered functionality thousands of times more important than aesthetics. Most worrying was the complete lack of furniture. The ten year olds had been expecting camping beds, perhaps with cheap tables to put things on. No such things had been provided for them. Rather than sleeping in separate beds, they would be lying directly on the cold concrete floor. It would surely be freezing when night fell.

"You'll be cramped when you go to bed," Adam warned the boys close by. "Unless you can fight for a space you'll be choking," he told them with a tone that made it clear he had endured great torment in previous years.

What he said was true; they would feel like they were suffocating at times. Cost was one reason why they didn't provide beds. Money could be saved through cramming the children into a few buildings. Who cared if sardines had more room? They were there to work, not to have fun. Part of their motives might be based in sadism. There was no such thing as personal space under these conditions. Having others intrude into their beings in an intimate way would keep the lads on edge constantly. The result was that they would be desperate to get out by sunrise. Once the doors were opened they would be eager to start work immediately. Clement tried to find somewhere he could sleep. His brother was right in saying there would be no room. On his left was a fourteen year old, his bulging stomach betraying his eating habits. To his right was another ten year old, clutching something in the pockets of his uniform. The look on his face made it very clear he would rather be having his teeth drilled than be squashed to death. His eyes made it seem as if he wasn't there at all. Emotionally he was absent, as the camper they had seen earlier had been. Even so, there were flickers of normality there. When they made contact with Clement they began to glisten. There was only one way they would get through this; together. Although they were not related at all, they were brothers united against the adults. Sadly the fellow wasn't up for fighting at all. Regardless of how ill-advised a rebellion would be, it was completely off the table considering the state everyone else seemed to be in. Surely if they attacked together they might be able to overwhelm the guards for a brief period. That would give someone enough time to climb the fences. Immediately the youth realised the flaw in his plan. Anyone going over the walls would face the barbed wire. That stuff might just be lethal. If it severed an artery they could bleed to death in minutes. Before he could think of a solution he felt the fourteen year old slam his hand into his arm. Straight away he turned to look at the teenager. What was going on? Had he somehow read his thoughts and discovered his desires to escape? He listened as the boy began to speak. When he did so his double chin moved in an almost comical fashion.

"Shift over now, I've got no room!" He told his younger peer, greedily consuming space for himself.

"I can't," Clement replied, already touching the side of the boy to his right.

"I said move!" He shouted with pure anger in his eyes.

Immediately the young man tried to shift over. Sadly this was easier said than done. He made an effort to scoot over, although he only shifted a centimetre at most. There simply wasn't anywhere to move into. They were stuck where they were. Nervously he turned to the older male. This had the potential to turn very ugly. How was he going to defend himself against the bully? Not for the first time he lamented having ever come to this place. If he had to risk a fight with someone four years older than him, he would rather sleep outside. At least that way he would have as much room as he wanted. Although he couldn't give the boy space, surely he could understand he was trying. Of course, this wasn't enough for the fellow. Clement turned to look at him, a dark glare aimed squarely at his young face. This person must be fifteen stone at least. Perhaps if he tried loosing weight he might find the cramped conditions easier to deal with. You could get about three ten year olds in the area he currently occupied. He didn't particularly enjoy the thought of having to see this person on a regular basis. The fact he would be sleeping next to him for a month was even more infuriating. The final straw came when the boy placed his hand on the younger lad's arm again. This time he shoved the male as hard as he could away from him. Next to him, the other camper scrambled towards the wall, unwilling to get drawn into a fight. He had seen enough violence to know he wouldn't be getting into trouble that month. Whatever his feelings on the matter were, he was not going to comment on it.

"I said move your arse!" He spoke slowly with a smug tone.

This was enough for the boy to spring into action. Being civil to the bully hadn't worked at all. Somehow he felt entitled to treat those younger than him in whatever way he saw fit. If the obese aggressor wanted to survive the holiday he would have to change his ways. Clement saw red as he recovered from being assaulted. His parents were to blame for this. They had tried to make him happy by giving him whatever he wanted. Their son had grown spoilt, demanding that every need was immediately attended to. His poor parents probably put up with him, but he certainly wouldn't. Momentarily the lad attempted to control himself. Inside his chest his heart pounded furiously. His hands curled into fists as he threw himself to his feet. Logically he wouldn't have much of a chance in a fight. Still, irrational impulses drove him towards violence. When the attacker saw the state the boy was in he panicked for a moment. In a fight both people were punished. The adults didn't care who started it. If he didn't calm down they could both end up being smacked. But he still considered himself right. Someone his age needed more room than a ten year old did. Couldn't he see that this is the case? It wasn't right that the boy had to be squashed against someone on his side just to sleep; yet there was no alternative. Getting into a fight wouldn't help anyone. It would just make everything worse in the long run.

"Calm down, mate!" He urged the boy, but to no avail.

"Don't you dare touch me again!" Clement screamed at the top of his voice. "If you went on a diet you might not be so bloody fat!"

The boy felt his own anger levels rise at that point. In school he was frequently teased because of his physical condition. Although he would never admit it, the name-calling broke his heart. There was little he could do about that. His teachers would seldom reprimand the popular students for anything. Even so, a ten year old wouldn't put up much of a fight against him. Does he honestly think he wants to sleep next to someone so young? Judging by the look of him he still wets the bed. Who could possibly want to be around such a child? Adam was following the events closely. He knew the older lad had a predisposition towards violence. Last year he made an eleven year old eat dirt when he wouldn't give him his lunch. He stood up, ready to step in if things took a dark turn. Surprisingly his brother appeared confident. It was hard not to feel a little pride for such a small person taking on a large teenager. At the same time he felt terrified for him. He knew that the older boys tended to look after themselves. They could gang up on the fellow if he wasn't careful. Clement attempted to give the young man a shove. Unfortunately he was too weak to have any sort of real effect. Without a wrecking ball he didn't really stand much of a chance. Before he knew it, Adam found himself running over to the pair. Both of them glared into each others eyes. Neither would risk face by backing down. Whoever gave up would be considered an easy target for the next month.

"Graham, leave it!" He told the teenager, placing his hands of his shoulders.

"Why should I?! I'm going to break his nose!" He screamed back, taking a step towards Clement.

"Come on then, fat boy!" The ten year old shouted, followed by giggles from the other campers.

Graham fired both his arms out in unison. When they touched the smaller male's chest he was thrust backwards. Adam was powerless to help as his sibling skidded painfully across the concrete floor. As he did so he cried out, the rough surface almost grating his skin. After a few seconds he came to a stop. Sadly the damage had already been done. Somehow he managed to flip himself onto his stomach. That was when his older brother caught a glimpse of the wounds. Part of his uniform had torn from the forces exerted on it. Many patches of blood had formed, most of which were growing quickly. Immediately Adam turned to face his peer. There was absolutely no way he was going to get away with this. An adult in the outside world would be sent to prison for that. Why should he get off the hook? Without saying a word he raised his fist. Drawing it backwards, he launched the missile straight towards the camper's face. For a split second there was a moment of panic in his targets eyes. He was a coward; he only picked on little children because he didn't have the courage to go for anyone else. Now he was going to be punished for what he had done. When he made contact with the boy he watched him stagger backwards. One of his hands came up to clutch his aching chin. His eyes were jammed shut, as if trying to cope with the pain he had been burdened with. Adam had no idea what was going to happen next. Hopefully this would be the end of the whole affair. However, he didn't believe this would be the case. Graham was far too petty to let such a thing slide. After thirty seconds he let his hands drop to his sides. Looking at the boy that had hit him, he made it clear that there was more to follow. Of course, he wasn't going to get into a fist-fight with someone as strong as him. Deep down he knew he wasn't strong. A ten year old he could overpower; it was a different matter entirely with a boy of thirteen.

"I'll get you back for that!" He warned Adam, before turning to Clement. "You'd better watch your back!"

"If you touch him, I'll make you wish you were never born," the amateur boxer replied with an acidic tone.

Ultimately he wasn't afraid of this boy. He didn't want to get into a brawl with anyone, but he would if necessary. To protect himself and his brother he would gladly lay into such a foul human being. The fact he was bigger didn't matter at all. Nobody had the right to threaten another human being in such a way. Graham was obviously angry with his attacker. How could he not be when he had just been assaulted? Both sides considered themselves right. If the lad had just moved when he asked him to there wouldn't have been a problem. Unfortunately for them he was quite longsuffering when he needed to be. After all, revenge is a dish best served cold. When he tasted his blood in his mouth he began to consider ways to get them back. Even he wasn't stupid enough to know he couldn't win a fight with the others. But his time would come. When the older brother's back was turned he would get even with the little boy. The fact they had to sleep alongside each other was a plus. Perhaps he could pretend to make friends with him; after that whatever he did would truly hurt. To his horror he realised this wasn't going to be an option. How could it be? At all times he would be escorted around by Adam. There wouldn't be a moment when he wasn't there to intervene. Thus the long game wouldn't really work. It would be far better to try to get someone to distract Adam for him. That way he could access the boy unchecked. He would make sure he got equal with him for the fat comments. In his own head he was tormented with a poor body image. What good would such hurtful remarks do him? If he felt he could lose weight he would have done so already.

"Don't worry about him, he's just a twat," the older boy told his sibling gently.

"Thanks," Clement whispered, more grateful for his assistance than he cared to let on.

Graham looked as if he could swing for anyone when he saw the brotherly love. As an only child he would never have that sort of relationship. In terms of friends he was almost a pariah. The only positive relationships he had were with his parents. Yet he had spoilt it by making them comply with his excessive demands. That tore him apart slightly when he considered it. They were the people who would love him no matter what. Rather than treat them with respect he was compelled to view them as living vending machines. Whatever he asked for he got. That was certainly not the way things should be. But he didn't know how to change it. He was stuck in this poisonous mindset. In typical teenage fashion, because he was miserable everyone around him had to be as well. The last part he would never admit to himself. If he saw his true soul, tainted by all the misdeeds he had committed, he would surely lose his mind. Subconsciously he knew he wasn't a good person. So why couldn't he stop? One thing was certain; neither of the brothers would get away with what they had done. Maybe it wasn't him with the problem. Perhaps it was the attitudes of everyone around him that needed to change. If they weren't so judgemental he might stand a chance of obtaining a few friends. This was the real tragedy of the situation; he couldn't see that it was him with the problem. For that reason he might never be happy.

"I'll get you back for that!" He seemed to scream with the facial expression he directed at the ten year old.

Bryan had slightly better luck in settling into his new accommodation. Seeing his quarters came as a terrible shock to him. He had no idea how he was supposed to live in such conditions. Yet he was realistic in some ways. Although he had no idea the camp would be this bad, he did know the sorts of things people do when they are camping. Sleeping on the floor was ill-advised, but certainly not uncommon. Many chose to sleep beneath the stars on a clear night. Certainly they deserve a medal for their outstanding bravery. Somehow he found a place to sleep without the aid of an older brother. It was by no means an ideal situation. He would have to sleep on his side; even then he would be touching those either side of him. Nonetheless, it was only as good as he made it. If he had a terrible attitude he would find the whole experience exhausting. His attempts to befriend those around him didn't work that well. They were far too upset over the whole ordeal to exchange pleasantries. Still, they didn't insult him when he introduced himself. It was fairly clear they simply had too much on their minds to be sociable. Bryan was, for the most part, acceptant of this. How could he not be when he hadn't uttered a word after being struck? Gingerly he clutched his wounded arm. The throbbing was worse than any pain he had ever experienced before in his life. Grazing a knee was nothing compared to the ache that gripped his beaten limb.

"Come outside now!" One of the workers shouted at the children from the doorway, his baton held aloft.

Begrudgingly the boys made their way towards him. Of course, they would never reveal these feelings. The fellow saw nothing but fearful obedience as they trundled across the floor. This was good from his perspective. It told him they were more than willing to follow the orders given to them. Occasionally he had a twinge of guilt over what he was doing. Was it right that he should be treating others this way? After all, he had hated having to come to this place every year, as if he was making some dark pilgrimage. Unfortunately for his victims these thoughts were swiftly buried. His own twisted logic told him he was morally correct. What made these children think they were somehow about physical punishment? As a child he had been struck by the guards of his day. Why should these kids be immune to character-building experiences? In less than twenty seconds the shack was void of life. Standing around on the bare earth, the young men didn't know what to expect. Perhaps they would be tortured for the amusement of the employees. Such an idea was enough to make them want to cry. Distressingly no tears flowed from their eyes. How could they when they had shed so many already? They were well past wanting to go home. Now they merely desired nightfall so they could retire to bed. That was not exactly an ideal solution. Sleeping in such conditions would be a challenge anyway. Every movement of those around you would jolt you back from the verge of sleep. Under the threat of torture it was almost impossible. They would lie awake all night picturing the horrors that would await them the next day. Frankly that should be the least of their concerns. There was still half a day left for them to suffer through. They had been inducted into the camp; now it was time for them to start to work.

"Take off that hat now!" One of the guards shouted, attracting the attention of the whole crowd.

When they heard it they turned immediately. It was quite clear that the punishment for disobedience was physical harm. Yet they couldn't stop looking at the slightly chubby, relatively harmless little boy. Maybe subconsciously they wanted to remind themselves of the rules. Evidently it was in their best interests to follow them. His only crime had apparently been to wear a backwards-facing baseball cap. There was a logo on the front that those around him struggled to recognise. In terror the lad did nothing. How could he when he knew what was coming? The poor fellow was scared stiff by the abusive adult. Nervously his eyes darted at his two school friends either side of him. In return they silently offered comfort. That was the best they could do given the circumstances. If they could they would defend him in a fight. Sadly that was out of the question given the size and the age of the aggressor. The female worker turned to look at her colleagues. These people were driving her onwards, urging her to reprimand him for his transgression. As she was new she didn't feel quite up to that yet. To compromise she repeated her order. There was a chance he didn't fully understand what she had said. Many of the boys she saw were so lost in their own thoughts that they could walk straight off a cliff. She was under no delusion that she would enjoy the camp if she was in their shoes. Indeed, she certainly didn't when she was a child. But while they were there they would follow orders. She had to when she was younger; why shouldn't they?

"Miss," the friend to his left began to speak. "His dad got it for him before he died."

The mere mention of such a tragedy was enough to make the male bow his head. Pain generated by the incident had yet to fade. Healing would take a lot longer than a single year. One of the reasons why he had come was to try to escape the rut his family had entered. In good faith his mother had sent him there. She believed making new friends would help him move on. Ironically she was successful. The fear of being beaten to a pulp had just about consumed his whole mind. He had his friend to thank for raking the matter up again. Still, he couldn't blame him for doing so. What he did was a declaration to the world that he truly cared about his chum. By doing so he risked being assaulted himself. That hadn't mattered to him at all. How could it? He wasn't going to watch him being attacked without doing everything in his power to stop it. But would the explanation be enough? Something that meant so much to him couldn't be taken away. The lad would never recover from such a thing. Everywhere he went he took it with him. His mother had told him to leave it at home. A precious item shouldn't be carried where it might be left behind. Regrettably he had ignored her advice. It wasn't that he didn't trust what she was saying; he simply couldn't do without it. Now he might not have anything at all. The woman did appear to soften a little when she processed the information given to her. A small part of her soul melted, visible through her eyes for the world to see. From the look she gave the boy she was sorry she had ever brought it up. What harm was a hat going to do them? Having it around might even help the boy to work. Surely if she turned a blind eye once it wouldn't be held against her. Her colleagues clearly didn't agree with her. They hadn't told him he could keep the hat on him. When had they told the children that they could keep their headgear on them? They would overlook her inaction as she was new to her role. In future she would have to be far more careful if she wanted a share of the camp's profits.

"You heard what she said!" A worker shouted, walking over to stand alongside her. "Take that off now or you will get a smack!"

The poor lad didn't particularly care about that. He wanted the garment more than anything. It was, perhaps, the only piece of his father left around. How could he stop wearing it just because he had been threatened? Tears flowed swiftly down his cheeks as he stared at his oppressors. To a reasonable person he would appear heartbreaking. Nobody could stand to see a child in such a state. The female looked as if she was about to cave in. It was, after all, just a hat. Couldn't he keep it in his pocket? In contrast her male colleague was indignant over the matter. This was totally unacceptable. He had disobeyed a direct order from a person of authority. As far as he was concerned there was only one way to sort this out. In a rage he took a step towards the boy. People didn't have the respect they once did. These children would have received the cane frequently if they had been born three decades ago. Unofficially corporal punishment was still on the menu. He was about to find out that what he had done was not tolerable. As soon as he took as step forwards the boy flinched. He didn't want to be hurt for his mistake. It wasn't as if he had done anything terribly wrong. These people clearly need to see a doctor. They shouldn't be treating others in such a fashion. In his mind he pictured himself being beaten. Less than half an hour ago he had seen someone being spanked just for daring to ask if he could go home. That would just have to be the case for him. Nobody had the right to tell him he couldn't have something so precious. As the man approached, his resolve faltered. His heart pounded as he began to turn to run. Surely there was somewhere he could hide to get away from all this. Unfortunately he didn't take a single step before the hand of the guard was upon him. So this was it. He was going to be tortured for nothing. Whatever they did to his body was irrelevant. He needed the hat; he was going to keep it.

"Leave me alone!" He screamed at the top of his voice. "Get off me!"

"Shut your mouth," the man replied harshly as he grabbed the boy's other shoulder.

"I said leave me alone!" He shouted back, fighting against the man with all the strength he could muster.

The guard was certainly not going to stand for such cheek. It was about time these kids learnt just who was in charge. While they were in the camp they had no control over their bodies. They would be assaulted for whatever reason the leadership felt necessary. If they didn't like it there was absolutely nothing they could do. As hard as he could he threw the lad to the floor. The other children looked on in horror as their friend slid across the bare soil. Before he came to a stop he tried to get up. There was no way he could win a fight with an adult. Fleeing was the only viable course of action he had. Miraculously his hat remained on his head. Seemingly his father was still with him despite the barrier of death. In less than a second the guard was upon him. Bryan winced as the juvenile was dragged to his feet. He was crying hysterically, thrashing out as if he was being hanged. What he was saying made no sense at all. By now the guard felt he had punished the boy enough. When he threw him to the ground again he was merely being sadistic. As he felt himself falling he screamed in horror. There was something terribly wrong with these people. Not just the workers; the children as well. How could they stand by and do nothing while he was so badly abused? At that moment he wished a hole in the ground would swallow the place. None of them deserved to live after what they had done to him. There were plenty of decent people who had died; why should they remain alive? The way he felt he could easily smash the head of his attacker with a brick. When he tried to stand the second time he felt his hat slip off his head. When it did so his heart missed a beat. This meant so much to him. Whatever happened he had to pick it up again.

"Not so fast!" He shouted to his victim as he began to bend.

"Get off it now!" The teary ten year old cried out as he saw the foot of the worker crush it.

His eyes were wide open as he quickly looked up at the male. Slowly he drew his baton from his belt. There was a time for physical violence, just as there was for a little understanding. Cautiously the young man thought about what he should do. He knew he couldn't win a fight. What had just happened proved that beyond all doubt. Even so, he cared about the item more than anything else in the world. If he couldn't have it he would fall to pieces. He knew he couldn't wear it anymore. He would have to keep it hidden in his clothes. That way he could rub it whenever he felt nervous about the nightmare he was in. Ironically if he did that he would never have both hands free again. Strangely there was no longer any hatred in the eyes of the adult. Naturally he looked as if he resented the boy, but he didn't appear to want to cause anymore damage. After twenty seconds the man pulled his foot away. The hat was lying there, caked in mud. Seeing it in such a state sent the kid into shock. His most treasured possession was filthy, having been trodden into the dirt. Even if he wanted to wear it again he couldn't. In terms of hygiene it was certainly not fit for purpose. In a way the man looked almost sorry for him. Even he had to admit that he got caught up in the moment. In no way had he meant to destroy the object. He only wanted the boy to respect the authority he was under. If he had taken it off when asked he wouldn't have been thrown into the mud.

"Stand up," he told the lad with surprisingly little malice.

He did as he was told. There was nothing to be gained in resisting the man. His property was still on the floor. In all honesty he was too afraid to pick it up. His aggressor studied him closely. Although there was an abundance of dirt on his clothes, he was not wounded. Not the slightest trickle of blood flowed from his skin. That was something that calmed the man slightly. They had to report serious wounds to the boss before treating them. The fact he was alright would save him a lot of bother. While there might be some bruising, he would live. With a nod he signalled for the boy to pick up his hat. Cautiously he did so, reaching for it as if it was a grenade about to go off. He couldn't understand why the punishment was so mild. Shouldn't he have been thrown into the dirt half a dozen times? He wasn't even bleeding from the onslaught he had taken. There was definitely something wrong. For all he knew, part two of the attack could be about to start. His bemusement only increased when he caught hold of the soiled garment. If someone wanted to lash out, now would be the time to do it. So why wasn't he beating the boy furiously? When he stood up again his eyes were wide open. Every bone in his body anticipated an attack. Surely something else was going to happen. After a few seconds the man began to speak. When he did so everyone listened to him. How could they not? Any advice given could mean the difference between being beaten and left alone.

"I hope I don't have to do that again," he warned the fellow earnestly. "We're not going to take it off you, but make sure we don't see it again."

With that he turned to walk back towards the other guards. None of the children could understand his mercy. One minute they were spanking a boy for asking to go home. His flesh was probably red raw after what they had done to him. The next they were allowing someone to keep an item that was a clear violation of the rules. Although it possessed great sentimental value, it should never have been worn in the camp. Honestly something so precious should never leave his house. What if he left it somewhere accidentally? He would never be able to forgive himself for such a tragedy. This dawned on him too as he considered how close he came to never being able to wear it again. If he ever managed to get home it would not leave the house again. When he realised what he was thinking he zoned out a little. Would he get home? He wasn't the only one to wonder if this month would go on forever. Perhaps they would never be allowed to leave. Maybe those ensnared by the guards were imprisoned forever. Of course, this wasn't the case. Any of the older boys could tell him that the reality was much more horrifying. Spending the rest of their lives there would be beneficial. Eventually they would adjust to constant torment. Their minds would be able to deal with the trauma. Instead they were released to live their lives for eleven months. After that they had to return once more. Just as they get past the abuse they are thrust back into the midst of it again. Going back to their normal lives from this prison is incredibly difficult. At home, people care about them when they are sick. Teachers in their schools would drag them from the path of an oncoming vehicle. They are given sufficient love to become well-adjusted adults. Here, the opposite is true. The only thing stopping them from killing the campers is the hard work that would go into covering up the incident. Slaying them in cold blood is fine, but for the guards it was a major headache. Anyway, why should they kill them if they are going to form the workforce? These kids have value in the form of unpaid labourers. Now it was time for them to get to work.

"You will head towards that building," one of the workers told the group, pointing towards the one of three large buildings.

None of them knew what to expect when he said that. By now they knew enough not to disobey commands. But their fear made them hesitate momentarily. What was in there waiting for them? All sorts of things ran through their head as they anticipated the worst. For all they knew there could be someone in there waiting to beat them to death. Still, there was nothing they could to stop themselves from ambling towards it. The very sight of the batons was enough to drive them forwards. How could they say no when they risked serious harm? The punishment for noncompliance was severe pain. At the back of their minds they knew there was a risk of death. Even at that young age they understood the danger to themselves in refusing to obey commands. But they couldn't do anything to help themselves. If they tried to refuse they would be beaten. That said, if they so much as looked at a guard in the wrong way they would be spanked. It was as if they were trying to tiptoe past a sleeping lion. One wrong move could end their lives. Everything they might have done would never come to fruition. All that promise would be thrown away just because they begged their parents to send them to camp. Thus it came as no surprise when they found themselves congregating outside the building. Despite the horrors that could await them, following instructions had become an irresistible impulse.

"I see you are learning to do as you are told," one of the workers complemented them with a sadistic smile as he opened he door to the shack.

Straight away they were ordered inside. None of them wanted to go. There was no way of telling what was waiting for them. At this point they wouldn't put it past the leaders to have several rather hungry tigers in there. Seemingly no task was beyond the means of the cruel management. The boy who was just thrown to the ground didn't care what they had in store for him. Frankly he was so glad he could keep his hat that anything else was irrelevant. How could it be when his most treasured possession was safely within his grasp? When they saw what was in the room they were bemused. Contrary to what they imagined, there was nothing that could directly be used for torture. Arranged in an obsessively precise fashion were several old wooden tables. Looking at them allowed the children to catch a glimpse of suffering they could not handle. Every scratch and blemish was an expression of the hell former campers had been through. Sitting menacingly on each of the tables was a sewing machine. Small baskets made of dull blue plastic had been placed next to them. What was the point of all this? Why go to such extreme lengths just to scare the children? Slowly it dawned on them that this was why they were here. A month of torture was inherently pointless. There was only so much emotional gratification the guards could gain from abusing the youngsters. By making them work they could humiliate them far more than they could otherwise. Furthermore, they could make things the leaders could sell. That would surely be more profitable than simply running a summer camp.

"You will be shown exactly what to do," a voice called out from the doorway.

When they turned to look they saw one of the boss' deputies. For the first time the middle-aged man looked rather upset. Glancing around at the machines, his eyes betrayed his inner emotions. The workers were once campers who had been offered jobs in the vile establishment. Many years ago this fellow had been in their situation. Of course, the children could not understand why he looked so lost when he saw a particular machine. How could they know that decades ago he had sat there for the first time? He too had endured the abuse of the guards of his day. Yet this did not excuse the fact he was proliferating the torment. If anything it made him guiltier. Clearly he remembered his time as a victim, despising every moment he had to spend in the care of the workers. So why was he unable to break the cycle? Once he became an adult he would have the credibility to make a complaint to the authorities. Instead he had chosen to believe the lies of the leader. Why should he make a fuss when he could earn easy money by taking his frustration out on someone else? By the time he came of age he was so twisted his moral compass had snapped in half. Desperate to find somewhere he belonged, he chose the easy option. It wasn't exactly his fault; where else could he work given the emotional baggage weighing him down? Swiftly he recovered his composure. Seeing the interior of the building for the first time after eleven months had brought back some bad memories. Repressing them once more, he began to speak again.

"Every day you will work here, making leather handbags. Some campers from previous years will be on hand to assist you. If you listen to them you will do well. If not, you will suffer the consequences. I am sure I don't need to tell you that missing the mark will not be pleasant." By now his composure was once again concrete. "Your work will be interspaced with meals; supper is scheduled for eight tonight. That gives you seven hours to build up an appetite."

With that he turned and left. Secretly he hated the place he was trapped in. How could he be expected to go to the camp every year when it made him so miserable? Seeing the place he had to toil at for a month was enough to make him want to vomit. Fortunately his presence wasn't even required. The workers were more than capable of running things in his absence. They would show the new recruits what to do. If the children failed they knew how to punish them. Everything could run smoothly without him being there. Anyway, he had paperwork to sort out. There were several orders for the items his workforce produced. Unless he could ensure the desired productivity was feasible, his head would be for the chop. The boss would cut him off as a surgeon would a gangrenous limb. Why keep someone on the payroll if they weren't up to the task? A saucepan with a broken handle would find itself in the bin rather rapidly. Not even staff members were immune to this sort of treatment. Yet there was every hope he would manage the sweatshop properly. In three decades he had not failed to do so. Surely this year would not be the exception. By now the kids had witnessed a glimpse of the power the guards had over them. That was normally enough to keep them in line. As he walked back to his private quarters he heard the heavy door being pushed shut. Those youngsters were not leaving until it was time to fill their stomachs. They would not enjoy the labour required of them, but they would be grateful they were not in the first group. He pictured himself in their shoes for a moment. Many years ago he had stood in front of the guards as a nervous ten year old. It had been his first trip away from home without his parents. Naturally he expected to have a fun-filled summer. Sadly those fantasies remained exactly that. Not once did they materialise into reality. Never did he make true friends. The boys he associated himself with did so out of habit. In a place like this, familiarity does not breed contempt. The stability of a routine is often the difference between sanity and utter madness. After all, who wouldn't go a little crazy in a work camp? As he walked away he tried to suppress the innocence of the lad he had been at the time. No good could come from dwelling in the past.

    Clement's trip to his work building seemed rather less stressful than Bryan's. There was something different about the adults attending to his group. While they were very harsh in speech, their voices were not as saturated with hatred as they normally were. Adam remained by his brother's side constantly. He knew exactly what was going to happen if the boy's products weren't up to scratch. Still, there was nothing he could do to stop a beating. Interfering with discipline was a good way to get killed. As much as he would welcome an escape from the torment, he would rather return home at the end of the month. He didn't want to give the boss the sadistic pleasure that would come from knowing he got away with murder. Even so, he could comfort his sibling. A few kind words could make all the difference in these sorts of situations. When the older male looked around he noticed Graham was glaring. That was always a bad sign. Not once in his life had he ever forgiven anyone. Perhaps it was beyond his emotional capacity. Adam didn't care; he just wanted him to leave his little brother alone. Part of it could stem from jealousy. Clement's brother was given the position of night time helper. In the evenings he made sure the children in his group brushed their teeth. He was also supposed to intimidate the lads. Logically he wasn't going to do this. As long as he wouldn't get in trouble himself he was willing to let the younger boys get things past the radar. Graham clearly wanted his role. He was the sort of monster who would make up lies about others to satisfy his own lust for inflicting pain. Perhaps that was why he hadn't received the role. The guards had to punish the children when they deserved it, not to satisfy their own pleasure. It was clear in the eyes of the adults that they were praying for some minor transgression on behalf of the kids. That meant they could deal out all the torment they desired. However, none of them would actively lie about the youngsters. There was simply no need; left to their own devices, ten year olds are going to make mistakes.

    "You'll have to work," the older boy told his brother as they waited outside their work building. "But, what you'll be doing is quite easy. Just listen to what the guards say."

    Neither of them felt particularly comfortable outside the run-down structure. Their labour would be mind-numbingly boring at times, but not difficult. He was rather fortunate in being allocated to the least strenuous of the three departments. Being assigned to the first was a nightmare. Officially it was the recycling centre. The camp bought bags of rubbish to recover anything if value. Scrap metal sells for a great deal in the realm, as did used plastics. The boys were forced to search for these amongst decaying remnants of food. Apparently the smell was enough to make them retch. Hauling bags was also strenuous; by the end of the day they were too fatigued to do anything but sleep. Still, there were benefits to an intensive regime. A quick look at the older boys revealed just how muscular they became. At fourteen they could tackle players twice their age on the rugby fields. Adam studied the worried face of his sibling. There was enough fear in his eyes to fill the oceans. Slowly he placed a hand on his shoulder. His touch appeared to comfort the boy. It was as if some energy flowed from his arm, filling the whole body of the younger male. Clement tried to smile back, although a grimace was all he could muster. Truly he feared for the young man's safety. How much more of this could he stand? Adam knew there was enough fight in the lad to get him through this dark month. If he could just hold himself together he would emerge a stronger person. Experiences of this kind change people. When he returned to his normal life he would have a whole new perspective of things. What was a long wait in a queue if he didn't have to fear being beaten? Homework seemed a trivial request next to the stress of being cocooned by those around you while sleeping. His mind would explode in size; life would be far more manageable with this increased capacity.

"Will I be alright?" Clement asked his brother, his tone pitiful.

"Sure," Adam lied through his teeth, pulling the ten year old in for a hug.

Why couldn't he find the strength to tell the boy the truth? While he would benefit in some ways from the experience, not all changes would be for the better. He wouldn't be able to talk to anyone about the nightmare he had been through. Every bad memory would remain inside him, corroding his soul as if acid had been poured onto his heart. It was certain that his brother would be struck during the month. Everyone was for some folderol reason or another. Whenever he closed his eyes he would see the limb or the baton approaching to strike his flesh. People around him wouldn't understand why he went from bubbly to quiet in a split second. Most likely these so-called holidays would leave him a miserable human being for some time. Fortunately the human brain has an amazing ability to recover. As soon as the final summer of hell ended he would begin his recovery. It would take some time, but he would become a much happier person. The problems would only come if he was offered a job as a worker. Those who found themselves compelled to accept would never be unchained. They would voluntary enslave themselves to the boss who had ordered their own torture. These brainwashed individuals were just as much victims as the children they assaulted. Luckily he wouldn't have to worry about that for some time. For now it was best to focus on getting his brother through the first workday. After that they could think about the future.

"Do your best," he urged Clement with an expression of pure panic. "If you try hard they wouldn't beat you."

He was hugging the smaller fellow more tightly now. The chance he would be stolen from him was next to nothing. In sixty years they had only had eight deaths across all the camps. Even so, he couldn't help but feel as if this could be the last chance they had to cuddle. At the sound of the workers barking orders they began to shuffle into the building. As with Bryan's station, this one also had tables arranged in a precise formation. There was something eerie about how similar each desk was. All sorts of materials covered them; tubes of glitter, sachets of sequins, feathers and glue. So great was the order that it bordered on the deranged. It wasn't that the desks had these things on them. Rather, it was as if someone had taken a ruler and measured precisely how far apart these things should be from each other. They might as well have reproduced a photograph. When the children saw this they didn't know what to think. Was this the work they would have to do? It seemed more likely that they were going to start a craft session. More than one of them wondered if what they had seen was a trick. Their memories of the other children being assaulted began to waver. Their minds tried to convince them the whole thing was a joke. How could it not be? They wouldn't be allowed to operate an establishment centred on abuse. Surely this was where the boss was going to reveal that they were the victims of an elaborate hoax. Those around them didn't share this belief. They knew that the torment was real. Still, they couldn't explain the somewhat light toil asked of them. What could they do with the items on the desks that would be so strenuous? As soon as the last one was inside, one of the leader's deputy's began to speak from the doorway.

"First of all, you're to call me 'Sir'. You've all been very lucky in being selected for this group," he started, his tone surprisingly harsh. "Since you don't know what is going to happen, I will explain it to you. You will be decorating photo frames, using the items on the desks. If your work is subpar, you will be beaten. You will work until we call you for supper. Any resistance will be punished severely. I will leave you in the capable hands of my employees. I will be back to check on your progress, so do not disappoint me."

With that he turned to leave. The children didn't doubt what he had said. Their task was so easy that it almost insulted the workers to have to entertain it. Unfortunately, there was a market for this sort of thing. People want unique decorations they can boast about. Such things can fetch high prices among certain social circles. Naturally Adam was thankful the managers had placed Clement in the same group as him. There was nothing inherently dangerous about what they would be doing. That was something to be thankful for. A nasty looking male stepped forwards. Around twenty, he appeared to be in charge of the six other workers present. How many people did the leader think he needed to keep control of ten year olds? Most of them were not going to be based there permanently. Instead they were going to do other things; over half of them would leave to prepare the next meal. Those that remained didn't even need their batons to inflict serious injuries. The male that took a large step forwards was surely a bodybuilder. Wherever Clement looked he had muscles bulging through his clothes. In his mind he pictured the man flexing, causing his garments to split around him. Logic dictated that this was a very dangerous individual. In terms of strength he was a giant, but that wasn't enough on its own. What worried the lad was his facial expression. His eyes fired hatred at the youngsters. Clement's observations made him think the fellow lacked a soul. There was no conscience he could see. It was as if it had been replaced with bile. Adam wouldn't have been surprised if his brother had suggested it to him. Years of brainwashing from the guards had moulded the being into a creature of hate. He was more of a Rottweiler than a human being.

"Listen, I'm not going to repeat myself for you," he spat at the kids. "Take a seat around a desk. You have ten seconds," he looked sadistically at his voice. "Anyone standing after that will be spanked."

Immediately the shack became a hive of activity. The boys scrambled over each other to sit down. Adam caught hold of his brother's hand. As quickly as he could he dragged the younger child towards a workstation. So great was the fear that the guard had to shout his countdown over the noise of the lads. Nobody wanted to be on the receiving end of a beating. For that reason they did everything in their power to reach a free space. They shoved each other and knocked some off their seats to ensure their own safety. With a cruel grin the male watched their frenzied behaviour. His group was desperate to follow their commands. This was exactly what he wanted. He could have some fun with youths in this sort of emotional state. If he told them to fight to the death with knives they probably would. Proudly he watched as the boys tore their social bonds apart to secure a place. Any friendships they had built so far he had knocked down. Isolated individuals were much easier to control than a cohesive group. Everything was going well until he saw what Adam was doing. He had placed Clement at a desk in the second row, with himself at the table to his left. A twelve year old tried to force him from his spot. His older brother was upon him in a flash. Delivering a punch to his stomach, he drove the other boy away. When he turned round a ten year old was in his seat. A single glance from the teenager was enough to send him packing. Finally he ended the countdown. Ten seconds was enough to get all but three of the boys organised. As quickly as humanly possible they rushed towards the remaining desks. There was no way the adult was going to let them avoid punishment. Why should they respect him if his threats are as empty as flowerpots?

"You three, come here!" He bellowed at the top of his voice.

When they heard him they almost jumped out of their skins. They knew they had been caught out. If they had been a little more aggressive they might just have made it. Why hadn't they just fought harder for their spots? Slowly they began to amble towards the male. Two of them were ten, the other twelve. The adult viewed them in a rather strange light. They were the inferior competitors that needed to be shown the consequences of failure. Who knows, they might become better people because of it. Their slow saunter was not going to save them. Every slow, ginger step they took only increased his rage. This scum wasn't going to get away with trying to delay their punishments. For that they were going to suffer deeply. With a command he got them to speed up. By the time they congregated in front of him they were almost running. He hadn't told them it was a race, but they did seem to compete against each other. This was exactly what he desired. Already they were developing the sort of spirits they needed to survive in the camp. By the time they left their whole personalities would change. As he looked into their eyes he saw the fear he had caused. He fed on this, drawing their terror in like a sponge. To say it was a source of emotional gratification would be an understatement. Although he had been employed for only a few years, already he was exactly the sort of sadist the boss was looking for. That was why he had risen through the ranks so readily. As the boys grew older, their capacity for roles was assessed. Some couldn't control the urge to beat the children senseless. They never received any sort of position of authority. Certainly they would never have an offer of a job. Others resisted the programming the camp installed upon them. Despite years of abuse they could not bring themselves to strike innocent kids. Again, these were useless to the management. What they needed were people that could hold themselves back when necessary, while feeling comfortable in distributing punishments. In the case of this fellow he was more effective than most. He knew what he could get away with. His mind possessed some sort of code telling him exactly what would get through to the right youngster. That was a gift the leadership would be foolish to let slip past them. At twelve he had the role of a watchman, his gifts better served outside production. That was rare to say the least. Usually fifteen year olds were the youngest to be removed from mainstream duties.

"We're sorry, Sir," one of them whimpered, his pleading drawing the attention of the male.

When he heard the twelve year old he almost laughed. This child was totally pathetic in his opinion. Someone so weak barely deserved to be in the boy's camp. He ought to march him down to the girl's section where he belonged. A frown grew on his face when he realised he had just insulted the girls. Surprisingly they were some of the toughest people he had ever met. It was interesting how the females coped with the camp's abuse better than the males. He certainly wouldn't like to come up against one of the female workers in a fight. Without warning he sent his open palm swinging through the air. The boy was not going to get away with this weakness. When he slapped the male there was a collective gasp from the crowd. Sounds of flesh hitting flesh echoed through the building as the kid staggered backwards. His legs desperately tried to keep him upright, adjusting his balance as best they could. Unfortunately for him it wasn't enough to keep him from tumbling. Before he knew what was happening he was lying on his back. One side of his face was numb as the blow registered on his system. The two ten year olds took a step backwards in horror. They certainly didn't want to be on the receiving end of one of those slaps. Logically it would be wise not to provoke the man further. He was clearly mentally unbalanced. How could someone so mad be allowed anywhere near children? Tears streaked the faces of the pair as they waited for their own beatings to follow. Why had they ever come to this place? They would have been much better off staying at home. That way their parents would have saved money. Neither of them would have been separated from their friends. They could have been playing in their gardens now. Instead they were waiting for whatever torment they were facing to be unleashed upon them. The lunatic turned to face them. It was obvious from his eyes that he had enjoyed that. Surely this was no human being. His countenance held such fury that he looked demonic. Both of them had seen enough not to disobey an order again. This display was enough to convince them that compliance was their best option.

"I take it you two have learnt your lesson," he told them firmly, picturing himself slapping their fearful faces.

"We have, Sir!" They bellowed in unison.

"Then find a seat quickly!" He balled at the pair as they scrambled to the free desks.

"As for you," he looked at the boy he had stunned, still lying on the floor. "I suggest you do the same before I spank you!"

The boy was not quite as speedy as he normally would be in getting up. Placing a hand on one of the tables, he just about managed to pull himself up. The others implored him with their eyes to make haste. Seeing someone take abuse was never a pleasant experience. It didn't matter that they were not the ones on the receiving end of it. When he had been struck, everyone in the room had felt it. His abuser followed him with his eyes as he stumbled to the last remaining free spot at the back. As he passed his fellow campers they retreated into their seats slightly. None of them could bear another second in this nightmare. Anything that reminded them of what they had seen was automatically labelled as negative in their minds. That included the fellow they pitied greatly. Clement couldn't even bear to look at him as he passed by. Really he ought to be doing something. The workers could only treat them in such a fashion if they accepted it. If they all turned against the guards they could change things. Corporal punishment could be taken off the menu altogether. However, the boy had to admit he was a coward. When he saw the lad he let down he realised how spineless he truly was. He didn't dare glance at him lest he made eye contact. That would leave him a hysterical wreck. It was only wishful thinking that was holding him together presently. If that dissolved everything would spill out. The dam wall would disintegrate, leaving millions of gallons of water with nowhere to go but downhill. Adam turned to look at his younger brother. A small smile was offered, but Clement couldn't raise his head in his direction. He could feel his eyes upon him perfectly well. Still, he couldn't respond to this at all. Seeing a friendly face when he had so much hostility directed at his own heart would crush him. He didn't consider himself worthy of love at all. In his own eyes he was barely a human being.

"Now, we'll have a practice run at producing a sellable object this time," the abusive adult announced to his terrified captive audience. "It's perfectly simple; you will each be given a plain wooden picture frame. Using the decorations provided you will have five minutes to decorate it as best you can. Remember, we're not looking for uniform items. Each of our products has a unique touch, so don't just copy what everyone else is doing. There is no right or wrong, just original."

When he spoke this time his voice sounded surprisingly softer. What they didn't know was that this was something he felt very passionate about. The deputy in charge of Bryan's sweatshop couldn't bear to be in the building. Curiously, he actually enjoyed seeing where he used to work years ago. This camp made him who he was today. In his twisted psyche he was actually glad he had endured the torment. Without it he wouldn't be such a strong human being. He hoped that one day the boys would thank him for their experiences. Having been there less than an hour, they had already seen more bile than most do in their lifetime. That would surely toughen them up. He would make decent people out of them yet. Sadly he was aware that he was dealing with clinically ungrateful children. They would never offer him anything but foul language if he met them on the street. So far that had only happened once. The thirteen year old he encountered had tried to cross the street to avoid him. Regrettably his muscles refused to function. He was just left staring at the man he ought to be thanking. He noticed Graham getting up to hand out the wooden frames. There was no glass in them yet; that was done by the older boys. In no event was he going to let ten year olds play with such a dangerous material. That was like hiring a shark as a children's swimming instructor. It would only end with bloodshed. Knowing his luck they would attempt some sort of juvenile revolution. Naturally it would fail. Those instigating it would wish they had never been born. Even so, it could put their workforce at a disadvantage for a few days. That was not going to happen while there was breath in his body. One day he hoped to become the leader of this camp. Such a disaster was not going to stand in his way.

"If, for some strange reason, you have any questions, we'll answer them. Although I don't see how even ten year olds could be confused about what you have to do." His voice once again reassured the group that he totally despised the children in his care.

Clement waited patiently as the overweight teenager panted his way around the workstations. If he was in a classroom he would conveniently forget to give the boy one. Unfortunately that sort of behaviour wasn't tolerated by the guards. They would not stand for anything that upset the group's productivity. What went on outside the work buildings was their own business. Inside them there was no room for messing around. Thus he found himself placing one down in front of his new enemy. It was no secret that he hated the lad. With regret he had to admit that his victimisation would have to wait until their next meal. His target noticed there was a strange air to the fellow's movements. This was due to the fear that he would receive a beating. Emotional torment had all but turned his muscles to stone. Even seventeen year olds were eligible for spankings. The man in charge of them would not think twice about clubbing him in the side with a nightstick. When he glanced over his shoulder he saw the adult staring at him. Lions give their prey similar looks before breaking into a run. Seeing such a horrible expression almost made him drop the remaining picture frames he was carrying. As his grip weakened his heart missed a beat. An act that threatened to disrupt the work schedule was punishable by physical force. Something that actually will cause a commotion would bring about far greater reprimands. There was no way he could allow even a single one of them to fall. If they broke he could be eating soil for months. Luckily for him they hadn't fallen to a noticeable degree. Merely strengthening his grip brought the items to an immediate halt. His heart pounded in his chest as he contemplated his near miss. That was far too close a call for him to risk another glance at the leader. As he continued walking he felt rather lightheaded. Adrenaline continued to flood his system, his complexion taking on a white hue. Yet he could still feel the eyes of the man pecking him to death. Perhaps he had read the fatter male's thoughts. Maybe it was a slight change in his body language that revealed the averted accident. Either way, he picked up on it somehow. Through mysterious means he could tell that the boy had just about avoided a severe beating.

"Careful with those," he smugly told the boy, his heart beating faster than ever.

With great speed he handed out the last few frames. Finally he could go back to his seat. Since he had not been given a job as a watchman he was going to spend another year labouring. He couldn't exactly complain; the products were incredibly simple to produce. However, after several hours it did get boring. It wasn't as if he could even take a break for a few minutes. The only acceptable reasons to stop working were death and to eat. Thinking about food made his stomach rumble. Amazingly the meals were just about the only good thing in the camp. Unlike everything else they were actually up to standards. Whenever he went home after his holiday he always weighed himself. Last year he put on five pounds, something his classmates were very quick to point out. Clement watched him waddle over to his desk. With so much to worry about he really didn't need a sulky teenager added to the list. He knew Adam would protect him if the boy so much as gave him a dirty look. Still, he knew it made sense if the children became friends. In these places alliances were more important than ever. If they wanted to make a stand against beatings they would have to form a cohesive unit. A group of unruly children attacking as individuals was a recipe for a disaster. Slowly he lowered his head to look at the picture frame in front of him. In itself it was nothing special; he doubted it cost the organisation more than twenty pence to buy in bulk. Gently he picked it up in his hands. The square structure was about the same size as an A5 sheet of paper. It was just the sort of thing you would use to hold pictures in on your bedside cabinet. Perhaps if he ever had a holiday in a normal camp he would be able to keep the photos safe in one of these. Horrifying he realised he might not get a decent break until he reached eighteen. Only then could he be free of this awful place. Momentarily he thought tears were going to form in his eyes again. Bizarrely the urge to sob dissipated as soon as it arrived. How could such a place be allowed to run? Why hadn't it been shut down years ago? At the back of his mind he knew he stood a chance of getting through it. This was his brother's fourth experience. Thrice in the past he managed to make it through to the other end. Surely it was just a matter of waiting. A month was not an infinite unit of time. If he maintained the right attitude he would be back at home before he knew it.

"Remember; use the paintbrush in front of you to cover the wood in glue first. Stir it occasionally to make sure it doesn't dry out," the leader instructed the children with startling tenderness.

Clement knew he was dealing with an unbalanced person. Logically anyone willing to work in this place had a screw missing. Only then did he realise how deeply the man's problems ran. Once minute he was slapping a relatively defenceless twelve year old across the face, the next he was the caring teacher. Never before did the lad fear him as much. Someone thoroughly wicked was perhaps less dangerous than a person prone to such severe mood swings. There was no telling what would happen if the man had a bad spell while at the hands of a baton. That was probably how people died. Gingerly he reached for a large pot on the table. Others were already coating the wood in glue, so he had to get started. Five minutes was far too little time to do everything they needed to. With trembling hands he unscrewed the lid. The paintbrush shook as he dipped it into the mixture. A strange smell met his nostrils when he withdrew the tool. He recalled visiting a friend's house when his older brother was assembling a model plane. Recalling a time when he was happy helped. Waves of ice-cold water soothed the raging fires of terror that threatened to incinerate his soul. Thinking of his chum made his problems seem more distant. He wished he could immerse himself fully in the memory. If he did that he might be able to push away reality forever. Was living in the past any worse than the hell his parents had paid for him to be in? At least if he ended up in a madhouse he wouldn't be in physical danger. Sadly he found his problems returning. With a vengeance they reclaimed the land they had temporarily lost. So great was the torment that he gasped. He hadn't noticed the several large droplets of glue falling from the brush. Setting eyes on them almost made him faint. What would be the punishment for this transgression?

"Come on." He urged himself firmly.

As quickly as he could he ran the paintbrush over the wood. By now his brother was already sprinkling glitter around. In a different setting this could be a lovely activity. He knew his mother would love to have such an item. She would compliment him on it whenever they were both in her bedroom. Knowing that he had made something she could store a treasured photograph in would make her year. Eventually he would grow too old to take more than a passing pride in it. When that day came she would stop bringing it up. But until then she would milk it for everything it had. Even so, that was a scenario that would never play out. These products fetched too high a price for the management to let the children taken specimens home. Anyway, it would raise suspicions if the youngsters claimed to have made items purchasable in stores. How would the administration explain that away? Clement didn't dare think about it too much. His life could depend on doing well on this assessment. If he failed he might not be able to sit down for a week. It took less than twenty seconds to give the wood a sticky layer. By the time he had finished his hands were covered in the stuff. Absent-mindedly he grasped a tube of glitter. When he wrenched the lid off he sent half its contents flying into the air. Those behind him gasped when they saw the cloud catching the light. All sorts of colours illuminated the ether, turning his desk into a disco. Immediately the boy tried to focus on damage limitation. Spilling glitter wasn't necessary a death sentence. As long as he could still use it he would surely avoid being reprimanded.

"Sweep it with your hand," Adam encouraged him when he noticed his brother's predicament.

He didn't need to be told twice. Cupping his hand, he set about collecting the spilt decorations. Although he was trembling he managed this without much difficulty. In his mind he was praying that nobody would report him to the guards. Once he had a mound of glitter he took a pinch between his fingers. As his hands were covered it glue they sparkled beneath the lights. Swiftly he let the material drop gently onto the wood. Again and again he did this, until he had something that looked reasonably pretty. If his mother saw it he knew she would love it. Unfortunately her opinion was irrelevant at the moment. Only the viewpoint of the guards carried any weight. Would they honestly value his creation? He could do little more than hope as his time ran out. So this was it, the moment that would decide if he would be assaulted. The leader stepped forwards, his eyes radiating sadism. If they fired heat he would incinerate half the camp. Behind him some of the guards slipped away. They had to go to prepare dinner for the children. Half of them remained, however. Their batons hung at their sides, ready to cave in the skull of any child who tried to attack them. Clement wondered what he would do if he got hold of one himself. It wouldn't be a pretty outcome. A ten year old wasn't really a match for a man in his early twenties. Before he could land a single blow he would be beaten to the floor. Attempting to start a revolution would see him in his grave rather quickly. This was behaviour that had to be punishable by death. Letting the rioters live would give the next potential resisters hope.

"Stop working!" His voice filled the air, causing every child to freeze. "Your work will now be assessed."

Slowly he walked towards the first of the desks. This one belonged to a twelve year old that shook when the man started to stroll in his direction. He had worked quite hard on the item. Having previous experience had helped dramatically. What he had produced was of the same quality as in previous years. Thus it came as no surprise when the man turned to look at his neighbour. When he did so he sighed heavily. The ten year old had never attempted anything like this before. Under the pressure his brain had turned to mush. All he had done is sprinkle some glitter in one or two places. He hadn't even coated the whole thing in glue. This was certainly not going to pass inspection. With two fingers he picked the horrid mess up. His facial expression was neutral as he did so. This gave the fellow a glimmer of optimism. Perhaps he had just done enough to scrape by. Unfortunately the man was a deceptive fellow. His features hardened in a single second. Turning, he flung the object as hard as he could at the wall. The poor lad watched as his efforts shattered. The sound it made caused him to jump in his seat. What would happen to him now? His heart pounded as the attacker turned back to face him. There was so much hatred in his eyes that he looked monstrous. Surely no human being had ever harnessed such pure rage before. Even the children in the back were terrified. He was a volcano about to erupt. They could only hope his fury wouldn't consume them as well.

"Sir," he started to say, his whole body consumed by a tremor.

He didn't get to say another word. The hand of the man wrapped itself round the boy's throat. With a small amount of pressure he stopped the youngster from breathing. One of his own arms came up to defend him. His relatively tiny fingers gripped the guard's wrist. As hard as he could he tried to yank the man off him. Why had he ever asked to come to this place? It was a nightmare. As long as he lived he would never come back. That was, of course, if he wasn't strangled to death. The man lowered his head to stare into the lad's eyes. In one way this was more terrifying that the fact he couldn't breathe. With all the strength he could muster he tore at the man's arm. His eyes were wide open as he stared at his attacker. Every attempt to draw breath failed. The choking sounds that filled the room drove his comrades to tears. They could be next. After he killed the boy he could suffocate them, too. The terror was indescribable as they waited to see if their friend lived or died. Their hearts were full of dread as they willed the lad to overcome his adversary. Unfortunately there wouldn't be enough strength in seven of his clones to free him from the lunatic. His tongue eased from his mouth as his head began to spin. Still the fellow did not relent in his attack. Only when he felt the kid's strength fade did he release him. Immediately the youth drew breath. His chest heaved as he took as much of the stale air into his body as possible. There were marks around his neck from where he had been gripped. Tears flowed from his eyes as he sobbed in fear. That was the worst thing that had ever happened to him. If he lived to be a hundred he would never forget it. Surprisingly he didn't hate his abuser. How could he feel anger when so much fear clouded his mind? After seven deep breaths he began to grow more lucid. The darkness his mind slipped into retreated. Clement couldn't believe what he had just seen. Spanking a child was one thing. It would likely not kill the person. Strangulation was another matter entirely. His hand could have crushed his windpipe. If he cut off an artery the boy could have been dead in seconds. How could someone do such a thing? He daren't move as the man callously moved on to the next person. The camper he had just attacked let his head rest in his hands. His shoulders rose and fell as he sobbed bitterly. When was this nightmare going to end? He had only been there an hour or so. Already he was sick to death of the place.

"He'll be okay," Adam whispered to his younger brother, not quite believing it himself.

Bryan had not been so lucky in his work group assignment. He was undertaking work that required more effort than Clement, but he was still fortunate. The boy could have been placed in the other building. There he would have to participate in real work. He would sweat all day long, manual labour leaving him exhausted. As it happened he would not have to do anything so strenuous. Their guard was not as sadistic as the one Clement had to put up with. Even so, he was far from a warm hearted individual. When they entered the room they had been allowed to take seats in their own time. However, the ginger haired male would not give them an easy ride. Bryan was sitting directly in front of the thirty year old as he began to speak. With his former best friend nowhere in sight he felt rather alone. Still, he couldn't casually chat to relieve his anxiety anyway. He had no idea what to expect. All he knew was that sewing was involved. That wouldn't be so difficult; he was sure he would pick it up. The leader seemed strangely peaceful as he spoke to them. His cheeks were covered in freckles, as if someone had decorated him with brown glitter. His short hair had been gelled up, giving him the appearance of a hedgehog. This would have amused the lad if he saw him in the street. Unfortunately he couldn't even smile knowing he would risk a beating. He cradled his pulsating limb, still in agony after a single strike. Yet he had faith that it would get better. If he was broken he wouldn't be able to move it at all. While his flesh ached, it remained fully functional. There was nothing to do but wait for time to heal it.

"You may call me Mr Evans," the man introduced himself with a calming tone. "As long as you try you will do well here. We will not tolerate any slacking, though. You will be wondering what you have to do here. Using the sewing machines in front of you, you will be making bags for us to sell." Bryan noticed that every syllable was perfectly pronounced. "The punishments for lack of effort will be severe. If you work hard you will be left alone. But we will come down like a tonne of bricks on anyone that thinks they can fob us off with shoddy goods."

When he finished the last sentence his face hardened for a moment. This was obviously a man who valued hard work. This would be admirable if he wasn't torturing children for money. The boy found himself drawn to the man's eyes. They were much warmer than those of his underlings behind him. Maybe he could be reasoned with. There was a chance Bryan could show him the error of his ways. If he could do that he could arrange for the police to be called. The authorities would take his cooperation into account when deciding his fate. Surely this plan was something to put aside for later on. If he was granted a private audience with the manager he could try to bring him round to his way of thinking. Never did it occur to him that this wouldn't work. Why would he consider such a possibility? Wasn't he smarter than those around him? Wasn't he mature for his age? By this logic he should be running the country. Arrogance would be his undoing. He honestly thought he could get the children out of this nightmare. Still, it wasn't fair to judge him too harshly. What ten year old didn't think he would change the world? He continued to listen as the man announced his plans for them. Apparently they would get the chance to practice making a bag. He gesticulated to a fifteen year old in the second row. The male stood up as a basket of cloth was handed to him. Bryan barely noticed him handing out the blue leather. He couldn't take his eyes off Mr Evans. When he looked into them he found his self slipping away. It was as if nothing existed but the fellow in front of him. There was almost no reaction when the teenager placed some of the material in front of him. Although the leader was thirty, his eyes looked much younger. If he had to guess he would place him at seventeen.

"Don't worry about not knowing how to sew," he told the group. "I will walk you through everything. All you have to do is listen and follow my instructions. On average it should take you fifteen minutes to make one bag. The older boys can do it in ten, but you shouldn't worry about matching them. It's better to spend a few minutes more than rush and make something we can't sell."

Bryan became totally fixated on his eyes. How could such a kind-hearted man have been caught up in a wicked venture? At that moment it was hard for the lad to judge him at all. He knew he was supposed to oppose the guards. They stood for everything that was wrong with the world. But how could he despise this man? Every movement he made was incredibly graceful. Radiating peace, he soothed the mind of the entranced male. Deep within him stirred a desire to make the best product he could. That would surely earn the gent's respect. At no point did the boy wonder if this was exactly what he wanted. All three of the leaders had their ways of achieving obedience. Clement's supervisor used cruelty to get what he wanted. This worker decided long ago that a pleasant nature could be far more effective. The more sadistic his underlings, the more effective the strategy became. He would be the one person who didn't shout or abuse the kids. In return they would grow rather fond of him. His methods had been questioned at first by those above him. However, his results spoke for themselves. As long as productivity remained sky-high he could do whatever he wanted. At the end of the day the goal was to make as much money as possible. Anything that fulfilled that ambition was to be supported fully. Beneath the surface he was incredibly loathsome of the boys in his care. As far as he was concerned they were little runts. Secretly he felt the same way towards his workers. All of them had been his slaves in the past. When he looked at them he still saw the pathetic prepubescents too timid to breathe. That said, their service beneath him had salved his opinion of them somewhat. Every year he saw them more and more as human beings. There would come a time when the images he had of them from years gone by would be a distant memory.

"Once everyone has enough fabric for one bag I will show you what to do. You will be shown how to cut and stitch it, so if you don't have any experience it won't matter. I know you are going to pick it up quickly. You don't look like the horrid lot we usually have to deal with."

This made Bryan giggle slightly. Praise from this man had assumed a golden hue. He was exactly the sort of person who should be in charge. Unknown to them, he was a master of emotional manipulation. There was nothing he couldn't get the boys to do if he so desired. At the moment he had them eating out of the palm of his hand. Tomorrow he might encourage them to kill each other. Without them realising he had mentally attached strings to their limbs. Now he could hover above them at will; his loyal puppets. Turning them into his toys was an incredibly powerful experience. Behind his tranquil eyes he was bursting with energy. If he wired himself into the electrical system he could power the whole realm for centuries. His heart was floating in a mixture of determination and euphoria. In his experience nothing compared to the thrill of hypnotising others. Bryan was not as strong as he thought he was. He could not tell that his conscious mind was being altered. Indeed, his subconscious being was changing. When he went home he would think of the leader when he was having a bad day. If a teacher shouted at him he would slowly close his eyes. Instantly he would be back in the workroom, the wonderful manager standing over him. Lacking the intellectual might to resist such alterations to his soul, Bryan was just as besotted with the adult as the others. This was exactly what the mental sculptor wanted. He knew that the best way to enslave people was to bring them over to his side. In society there are others like him. Some politicians were able to do this to whole nations, getting into power and starting wars. In their paths they left nothing but destruction. Fortunately for the country the man wasn't interested in wide-scale leadership. He had a nice job where he could flex his skills upon a captive audience. That was more than enough for him. His morals might be dubious, but he was certainly not a megalomaniac.

"Oh good," he spoke when he saw that the last person had received their fabric, "now we can begin." It was impossible for even the most bitter of campers to hate him when they heard his peaceful tone. "I really enjoy teaching you children how to sew. I always say that to master a skill you have to pass it on."

Without them realising, the atmosphere in the room had become almost insufferable peaceful. A sense of bliss had descended upon the hearts of the workforce. Even the other workers found it hard to scowl when they felt the primordial glee wash over them. The hearts of his victims contained not a single atom of hostility. Now Mr Evans knew his work was done. Looking into their eyes, he could tell he had totally enslaved their will. Naturally they would retain full autonomy. However, he would flex his control whenever he thought he needed to get something done. It was hard to believe that he discovered this ability when he was only eight. In attempting to get out of trouble at school he found he could lie perfectly to the break time supervisors. An incident that should have resulted in his exclusion was mitigated to a minor telling off. Other than being told to stay away from the other pupil, not further action was taken. It was then that he began to improve his abilities. By the time he was eighteen he could get others to do whatever he wanted. Thus it was no wonder the head of the camp decided to offer him a job. Their thinking was that if he could manipulate campers as easily as he could his peers, they were on to a winner. Within three years he was the deputy to the person who used to occupy his role. Now he was in charge of a whole work group. Logically he had his sights set on other positions. In five years time he hoped to be a deputy of the camp's leader, before he took the latter role for himself. A long time ago he had vowed to end up on the board of directors. If his career continued the way it had done he would make it.

"True," Bryan whispered, agreeing totally with the fellow.

"As you can see, the fabric comes in rectangles. You will need to make handles for them out of the smaller strips we have given you, and sew on the internal pocket. The colour of the fabric might vary from day to day, but the design remains the same. Some of the older boys will iron logos onto the side of them when you have finished," he mentioned, glancing over at three seventeen year olds standing at the back. "You don't want them to receive a bad bag, do you?" He asked them to generate guilt within their hearts.

"No, Mr Evans," they collectively replied as soon as he finished speaking.

"I know you don't; you're good boys."

Every face in the room wore a smile as they revelled in his compliment. It struck them as odd how he could contrast with the other adults so strongly. They looked as if they wanted to beat the children to death for no reason most of the time. This fellow was clearly a good man. He would never arrange for them to come to harm. In no way did he belong in such a terrible establishment. Since he was so nice to them it was only fair they were nice to him. They were going to make the best bags they possibly could. That way they would make the most pleasant worker in the place happy. He deserved that for his kindness, surely. This sort of thinking was exactly what the man wanted. Without their knowledge he had carved out these twisted thought processes within them. With their unknowing permission he was going to let them grow in strength. By the time they left they would be coming up to him for cuddles. Mr Evans didn't mind such things; a happy workforce was an efficient workforce. The sadism of his colleagues only generated obedience through terror. He made them want to work hard. This was something they had yet to get to grips with. For the rest of their lives these children would recall him fondly. Frankly he didn't care if they did or they didn't, provided they don't blame him for their abuse. If this venture was exposed there would be mass arrests. In court his solicitors could argue that he had been brainwashed, and that he had treated those in his care well. The prosecutors would struggle to find something they could charge him with, let alone convict him of. In this way he was smarter than the other two leaders. Where they ran marathons he would not take a step. Instead, like a spider in its web, he would control everything from the shadows.

"Now, I want you to try making the straps for the bag. What you need to do is fold over one of the strips, as I have done," he told them, showing them with a piece of fabric he pulled from the pocket of his black trousers.

Bryan did as he was told. He didn't know why he had to show them this. All they had to do was fold over a piece of cloth. It wasn't as if they were doing anything terribly advanced. Once he had done it he waited further instructions. A quick glance over at others revealed that they hadn't made the two halves completely parallel. Within him grew the desire to correct them. He would have done so with some satisfaction if his throbbing arm hadn't stopped him. His injury reminded him of the consequences talking could bring. Even though he knew Mr Evans wouldn't strike him for it, he didn't want to risk further pain. Thus he kept his mouth firmly shut, despite the mental itch growing in intensity. Fortunately it passed the moment the man began to speak once more. Whenever he spoke the boys gave him their full attention. They would do so anyway; making the best bags they could was necessary to avoid corporal punishment. However, their minds were enslaved to the man. His control meant that when he began talking they listened, almost mesmerised. Like flies to a toffee they were stuck to him. He knew this was the case. When he looked into their eyes he saw how deeply his programming was already running. By the end of the week they would have no will left to resist him. He could tell them to slaughter each other if he desired. Nothing he asked of them would seem worth less than the hassle of doing it. The boys felt lucky to have received such a kind-hearted manager. Everyone else they had met so far had been violent bullies. This fellow treated them as they deserved. With him they were human beings; with the others they were animals to be beaten.

"On the floor, beneath your desks, are the pedals that operate the sowing machines. Place the folded strap beneath the needle, and try to sow in a straight line down one side. Take your time," he told them gently.

They did as they were told. Bryan held the halves together so they did not shift. Making sure they were perfectly parallel, he pushed the pedal down with his foot. Immediately the needle descended, stitching together the two halves. He almost giggled as he saw his creation coming together. There was something nice about this sort of thing. Someone might one day love his bag. They would find it becoming ingrained into their lives. Without their bag they might feel lost. Of course, they wouldn't know it, but a little part of him would live with them for as long as they owned it. Perhaps one day he might even walk past the new owner in the street. He could look at them and think, proudly, that their beloved possession was made with his hands. Moving the strap along, he continued to stitch the left side. The black thread matched the dark blue fabric nicely. Unless you looked closely you wouldn't notice it was there. The end product was one that looked as if there wasn't a single piece of thread in it. Such things were rather fashionable these days. It took less than ten seconds to finish joining one side together. When he reached the end of the material he looked at what he had created. It wasn't a terrible piece of work. The line was very nearly straight. Unfortunately the straps hadn't been completely parallel. He cursed himself when he realised his mistake. How could he have been so negligent? His face hardened when he considered the consequences. There was no way they could sell this now. Because of his carelessness he had cost the nice man money. In this emotional state he couldn't help but look at what others had done. When he saw their efforts he felt better about his own. While his was slightly askew, the work of some was abysmal. Not only were their straps not worthy of sale; they were also monstrosities. They hadn't taken the time to try to efficiently line the fabric up. He watched as they desperately tried to pull apart what they had done. A twisted smile grew on his face as he took pride in his own efforts. Having never used a sowing machine before, he hadn't done too badly. The next strap he made would be much better. As far as the other lads were concerned, their situations were hopeless.

"How are we getting on?" Mr Evans asked, studying his workforce with the eyes of a patient father.

"I've gone wrong," someone at the back shouted; his voice slightly fearful of repercussions.

"Me too," the fellow alongside Bryan whimpered.

"Don't worry, this is only a practice run," the man replied softly. "As long as you tried your best I'm happy. Use the scissors in front of you to cut the threads and try again. If you think your strap is fine, go ahead and stitch the other side. After that my workers will come round and assess your work."

The way he spoke filled them with confidence. He was not like the others, who would trample them into the dust. This fellow appeared to genuinely care for them. They had no way of knowing that this was only a well-crafted persona. Beneath the surface he was angry at them for spoiling the fabric straps. As these things cost money, there were only so many times he could let them practice. If they didn't pick it up soon he would have to allow his underlings to use force. Naturally he wouldn't let the children overhear him doing so. He had created a system where he could do so with a simple set of gesticulations. His workers were on the lookout for this sign. That meant they could have fun with the boys. In their minds they were desperate for the youngsters to drive him to authorise violence. Superficially he would have to condemn it, of course. He would even hug the young men to help them through the dark spell. That was something that would open their hearts even further to him. If he didn't have complete control already, he would after that. Some of the other managers were a bit jealous of his productivity records. How could they not be when he was the most successful of all of them? How he obtained the figures wasn't exactly a secret. They knew his methods perfectly. Sadly, they were unable to comprehend why the children preferred it. Some of the children grew so attached to them man that they would even protect him from rioters. That had happened once or twice in the past. Through their violence, the other managers had managed to avoid rebellions for the most part. Certainly there was some low level resistance. But these battles were over in less than a minute. The fear they had of the men paralysed them in combat. Their underlings could them slash through the lines of their enemies. In no time at all the errant children were on the floor, the punishment for their disobedience underway. In their opinion, a constant and extreme threat of peril was the only way to keep people in line. Their minds simply lacked the ability to maintain the facade Mr Evans put up. In other words, they were sociopaths, but he was a psychopath. He knew exactly which strings to pull at the right time to maximise results. They could simply flex their muscles and hope for the best.

"This going really well," Bryan thought to himself, feeling much better about his work product than he had done moments ago.

He carefully cut the piece of thread with the scissors, releasing the strap from the machine. Gently he placed the top right hand side beneath the needle. In moments he was stitching away, the air filled with the sounds of the motor. Those around him couldn't believe he had picked it up so easily. With fabric he was surely a natural. The leader hadn't noticed yet, but he would when he began his rounds. The second time he got the line much straighter than it was. When he reached the end of the fabric he stopped, cutting the thread once more. Finally he had finished his first piece of work. Picking it up, he definitely saw an improvement the second time. While the two halves weren't exactly parallel, they weren't far off. It was certainly passable, if not exactly sellable. But, as Mr Evans had announced, this was only a practice run. As far as he was concerned, the next strap he made would be perfect. His face was consumed with a grin as he waited for the others to finish. An overwhelming feeling of euphoria appeared in his chest as he sat back in his chair. Never before had he felt so happy. He had done something that would please the cordial manager. This meant that even if there was a slight chance he would beat them, he would evade it. There was nothing to do but wait as those around him struggled to finish what they had started. He noticed that his neighbours were looking at him. Their faces revealed exactly what they were thinking. Was he really only ten? Could he be eleven? If he was he would have done this last year. If he wasn't, he surely sewed at home. Both of these conclusions were totally incorrect. Until five minutes ago he had never even touched a sewing machine. The only difference between him and them was that he had listened to what had been said. He had paid attention to the demonstration given. When the man had folded his fabric strip he had joined the corners together. Bryan had done that, even if they hadn't stayed together when he was sowing them.

"You have one minute left before we will come round and check your work," he heard Mr Evans urging them.

Some began to groan when they heard this. Bryan saw the workers behind the man scowl. Other managers would never put up with this sort of cheek. Those that moaned would be beaten senseless. Fortunately their boss had more sense than to do this. He also understood what their complaints meant. Their protests were a sign of frustration at not meeting his targets. One day his workers might understand that it was far more efficient to make the boys want to work for him than through fear of him. This lack of insight was one of the reasons why he couldn't stand the guards. At times he wanted to disarm them and knock some sense into them with their own weapons. It wasn't as if he couldn't do it. He was probably stronger than the whole rabble put together. Although the children knew him as a perfectly amiable fellow, he certainly was not defenceless. If he wanted to he could break the necks of everyone in the room. He would be out of a job, but he didn't lack the strength to do so. It never ceased to amaze him how good he was at masking his emotions. Nobody guessed that behind his smiling face he was fantasising about going on a killing spree. If people caught a glimpse into his mind they would run in terror. People would rather throw themselves at incoming traffic than walk past him on the street. At least the vehicles did not inherently wish them harm. With outwardly friendly eyes he glanced at his watch. There were ten seconds left before he would begin his inspection. Some of the boys were still working frantically to please him. This was exactly what he wanted. These boys felt guilty for every wrong stitch they made. Their loyalty was to him, not to themselves. If he threatened them at every turn they would develop a subconscious desire to snub him. Thanks to his methods he had a room full of workers willingly enslaving themselves to him.

"Times up," he announced lovingly. "I'll come round to check on your work. I don't want you to panic. This is a chance for you to improve yourselves. Your parents will be proud of you when you go home. You'll be able to fix your own clothes. The other parents will marvel at how mature you are."

This seemed to placate the youths somewhat. They began to picture themselves being praised for their sewing abilities. That was a further incentive to do well at what they were tasked with. If they could make sellable items they would never be stuck for things to give their relatives. Whenever a birthday came up they could just ask for some fabric. Their mothers' heads would explode when they see the bags their beloved sons had made them. Unlike those in Clement's group, the boys did not tremble when they saw him advancing towards them. Instead they relaxed, knowing that perhaps the only sane man in the camp was alongside them. If one of the workers tried to attack them, they could see him stepping in. Such a person would not stand back and let the children in his care suffer abuse. Of course, this image was of his making. It was what he had wanted them to believe. In reality there were circumstances where he would quietly arrange for the kids to come to harm. However, afterwards he would rebuke the person strongly. While doing so he could cradle the terrified camper. He would remain there for as long as it took the boy to emotionally get back on his feet. When that happened, the bond between them would be stronger than ever. They would see him as their hero, protecting them from the monsters. That was good; it meant they would work their fingers to the bone for him. That sort of mentality could never come from the constant threat of violence. That method could get very good results, but they would never be as good as those he achieved. It was worth being thought of as mad when he received his share of the profits. He had caught a glimpse of the checks given to the other managers. His salary was, in the worst year yet, twice as high as theirs. Long ago he asked his own boss to keep his commission a secret. Nobody liked to hear that they didn't compare to their colleagues. Truly he didn't care if they hated him. Still, it was logical to keep in their good books. No good could come from making enemies of the other supervisors.

"I'm going to make him proud of me," Bryan reassured himself, inspecting his work once more.

Chapter two

Clement had dreaded the moment the man would reach him. So far all but twelve had produced something worthy of sale. Even so, the leader did not exactly state his pride in their efforts. He deliberately made them think they were only just acceptable. Regardless of how good they were, he never gave them a single compliment. Some pieces were brilliant; he had to work hard to suppress a smile of satisfaction when he saw them. Mr Evans, his colleague, believes that becoming an emotional puppet master is the best way to increase productivity. This fellow was the opposite. In his opinion, only through coldness could the children be inspired to work harder. If they thought that what they were producing wasn't good enough, they would inevitably put more effort into their labour. That was his method; Mr Evans was, of course, free to run his own building in whatever way he desired. But nobody could deny that his group was a profitable venture. At the end of the month the managers are given checks for their share of the profits. So far his had been enough to live very comfortably for the rest of the year. The mark-ups on the items must have been extreme. Fortunately, the demand for their products never seemed to decrease. Online sales were higher than ever. Everyone had to have one of their handmade picture frames. They were truly adorable; reviewers often stated that they could almost believe they had been made by real children. Reading such things always made the man smile. If they knew how their beloved items were actually made they would be horrified. How many beatings would have to be dished out so they could have their prized frame?

Clement wondered if what he had produced was worthy of sale. Looking down at it, he saw that the red glitter was uniform. Not one sliver of wood had been left uncovered. Around the edges he had also scattered a few silver sequins. He would buy it in the shops if he was looking for such a thing. A few heavy steps brought the man directly in front of his table. He could barely raise his head to stare at the man's mouth. Glancing into his eyes would utterly destroy him. How could he come face to face with a monster? He relaxed a little when Adam's work had been declared passable. That was all anyone got for their efforts. The fact no-one had been told their work was good hadn't escaped his notice. Not even the fifteen year olds had been able to elicit such a comment from him. Either his standards were impossibly high, or he had decided that the slightest hint of flattery would go straight to their heads. Every step he took made the boy tremble. This was it; the next few seconds would decide if he was almost strangled to death. The man had inflicted some horrible punishments on the boys in his care. Clement found one incident particularly horrific. One boy had been punched to the floor, the crying boy left writhing. How could an adult do such a thing to a ten year old boy? It simply boggled the mind to wonder how he slept at night. His heart missed a beat when the man stopped in front of him. If he could he would stand up as fast as he could. Both legs would pound fiercely, carrying him miles away from his tormentor. He wouldn't stop until he found someone else or collapsed from exhaustion. Sadly he doubted he could even move an inch. His fear was so great he could barely breathe. Every muscle in his body turned to stone as he waited to hear his fate. Slowly the man exhaled, the warm air blowing eerily across the lad's face.

"Acceptable," the man stated with the slightest hint of a sneer. "Good use of contrasting colours."

Clement immediately looked up, making eye contact. Was that a compliment? Had the man just applauded his work? Adam turned to his younger brother. When their eyes met they offered each other slight grins. The older boy couldn't believe it. It was a rare occurrence when someone dragged a positive statement from him. Exactly how he had pulled it off he didn't know. That said, as this was only the first attempt, he would need to keep up this standard for the rest of the month. At no point could he afford to let the bar slip. To do so would make things very unpleasant for him. The other campers were surprised that he had earned much-coveted praise. What did he know that they didn't? Could he be a relative of the manager? That couldn't be the case. No sane person would allow a member of their family to come here. Regrettably they could only conclude that the man wasn't sane. He had to be totally barking mad to work in such a place. At the back of their minds another thought began to stir. Lunacy was definitely one possibility. Another was that he was one of the most evil people in the whole realm. Even a mental patient would surely know that harming children for no reason was unacceptable. A person malicious to their decaying core would not care one way or the other. Obviously he was earning money from this scheme. As long as that continued to be the case, why should he mind how it comes about? To this man the means are irrelevant as long as the end is satisfactory. Clement almost caught a glimpse of the man's darkness as he felt his breath across his face. While the air was warm, it carried with it a certain sensation. It was as if thousands of microscopic icicles were dancing across his skin. He wouldn't have minded if it had merely tickled. It was the feeling of it tainting his soul that almost drove him over the edge. If he hadn't feared the man he would have wiped his face with his shirt. This simply wasn't an option with him hovering above his desk. Despite the man's frosty demeanour, he didn't hang around for long after his inspection. The supervisor stepped towards the next desk before the boy knew it. Clement was almost disappointed by the anticlimax. Was this it? Had all the energy he spent on fear been wasted? Logically he wasn't ungrateful for the divine mercy bestowed upon him. He simply wished he hadn't made a fool out of himself by harbouring such terror.

"Alright for a first go," he heard the man comment on his neighbour's work. "Next time try to do better than a five year old would."

When Clement heard this he felt slightly smug. Not even the teenagers had received a word of compliment. He had been lucky enough to actually receive a kind statement from the fellow. With this in mind it was hard not to take the high-ground overlooking his peers. Compared to them he was standing on the top of a castle tower. They were in the moat, drowning in the stress the camp generated within them. Even so, he promised himself he would remember which side he was on. He didn't dare allow himself to think of the man as a friend. It would betray the children he had seen being beaten. Whatever this man told him, he was still an enemy. Nobody that assaulted children could ever be on cordial terms with the boy. He didn't realise that the manager didn't care whether or not the youngster desired warm relations with him. As long as he was prepared to work he could want to dress him in a tutu. Naturally he would find it strange, but as long as it didn't interfere with his toiling he didn't care. People would think whatever twisted things they wanted to. He had no control over that aspect of their psyche, so why should it bother him? Adam squirmed in his seat as he looked at the boy lying on the floor. More than anything he wanted to go over there, to help him up. By nature he was a caring soul that desired nothing more than to help those around him. It hurt him to see a person in so much pain. In one way he pitied the horrid workers. This was true regardless of the foul treatment they subjected him to. Clearly they were dangerous, deranged individuals. When they were away for the camp for eleven months, people must notice how odd they are. Why hadn't anyone tried to get medical attention for their defects?

"Sorry, kid," he whispered almost silently as he watched him hold his aching face.

"At least that's not me!" Clement thought to himself, eager to find a silver lining behind the abuse.

"Are you going to litter my floor all day?" The man turned to look at the child he had assaulted.

Somehow the male was able to sit up. He wasn't able to jump to his feet. His head was still spinning after the shock of the impact. Nevertheless, he knew he had to get up. What would he do if he didn't return to his seat? Frankly he couldn't understand why he had done that. The harsh comment itself would have been enough to correct his lack of effort. There had been no need for additional torment. Clement could have cleared the matter up in only a few words. This man was a sadist. He derived pleasure from inflicting pain on others. Such people should be avoided at all costs. The fact every person in charge of them was the same was terrifying. When Clement stopped to think about it he could feel himself slipping away. Why would he want to remain sane when his life could end at any time? It would be much easier to lose himself in a dark corner of his mind. That way he wouldn't have to think about the lunatics ready to beat him to a bloody pulp whenever they fancied. Sadly he knew this would do him no good. He couldn't join the legions of the boys that ambled through their newfound hell. When they had walked here he had seen the boy in front of him, his entire being having receded to the safety of his subconscious. That was no way to live. Evidently the only way to avoid punishment was to work hard and not cause trouble. How could he fulfil these criteria if he was a zombie? Even so, the concept of escaping his current situation was attractive. Switching to autopilot until the month ended had to be better than enduring the constant barrage of fear that came his way. Cautiously he turned to his older brother. Somehow he had managed to survive three summers here without resorting to such extreme measures. There had to be some trick to it that he was missing. What could it be? As hard as he tried he couldn't think of this solution. Maybe when he had a chance he could ask him. There wasn't a clock in sight in the building. How long had they been there? When would they be released for dinner? Honestly he had no idea how much time had passed. Perhaps an hour had slipped by already. Potentially he had been there less than ten minutes. This lack of awareness was truly infuriating. Not being able to quantify how much torture remained was worse than the dread the manager produced within him. Presumably this was why they had neglected to provide a timepiece in the first place.

"Get up!" The man barked at the child once more.

Holding onto his overturned chair, the lad just about managed to drag himself to his feet. Swiftly he placed the seat back into position. He half-sat half-collapsed onto it. While his face was rather sore, he would live to be struck another day. Tears flowed down his streaked face. They were so scarlet he looked as if he was having an allergic reaction. Clement found his eyes glued to him as he leant forwards. Placing his head in his hands, he looked as if he had been pushed to the absolute limit. If he had access to a weapon he would probably end his life. Adam picked up on this too. So far there hadn't been a suicide in any of the camps. That was hard to believe, given the treatment they received daily. It was easy to understand why a camper would desire death. For children a month could be an eternity. Trying to get through four weeks of hell was akin to crossing the desert without as much as a bottle of water. Adam knew that the trick was to take it one minute at a time. Every second that passed was one more behind them. Before they knew it they would be about to depart for home on the buses. Clement turned to face towards the front. All these thoughts about suicide would do him no good whatsoever. While he was intelligent, a ten year old had no real concept of the finality of death. For him an eternity was no longer than the distance between one week and the next. Nonetheless, he didn't enjoy thinking about harming himself. Even in these dire times he would cling to life with everything he had. Repeating the supervisor's compliment in his head helped drive away these awful feelings. Graham was sitting in the front, doing his best not to let the gravity of the situation get the best of him. The lad could take pleasure in knowing that the fat teenager had not been praised. All he got was the usual comment; that his work was passable. For him to receive a positive word was surely a sign that he was a skilled worker.

"With a lot more effort you'll make a better worker than a paperweight," he heard the man shout at someone behind him.

He heard the sound of a fist meeting flesh as he began to turn his head. Immediately he stopped. Did he really want to see chid abuse? Wasn't it bad enough it was going on without him turning it into a spectacle? With his head facing forwards he resigned himself to listening passively to it. There was nothing he could do except hope the bullying would stop soon. Alongside him his brother glanced tentatively at the boy. Considering this was his first time he was holding up rather well. Where he found such fortitude was a mystery. When he was ten he was hysterical when he saw the way the other boys were being treated. Of course, this attracted the attention of the madman. Before he knew it he was being slammed into a wall while the aggressor screamed in his face. He remembered begging himself to stop sobbing. As far as he was concerned it might be the only way to stay alive. Somehow he had regained his composure. Yet he never again found it within him to truly release his feelings. Even when he was at home he found it hard to blow off steam while others were around. It was as if the man frozen his heart when he had him up against the wall. Perhaps one day he would meet a nice girl to thaw him out again. Until that day he would just have to live with what he had. A fleeting look over his shoulder revealed that the man was coming to the end of his inspection. When he did so he caught a glimpse of one of the worst sights he had ever encountered. Many dozens of traumatised children looked back at him. Their faces implored someone to burst in through the door to rescue them. Their wide eyes looked as if they would burst. These were not people who would grow up emotionally healthy. That was, of course, if they managed to survive the month. From what he could tell, quite a few weren't sure they wanted to live another hour.

Bryan was not scared of his inspection at all. In fact he was grateful for an opportunity to show off his handiwork. It wasn't often he got a chance to demonstrate clear superiority over his peers. This occasion was surely to be cherished. Mr Evans didn't bother assaulting the children who didn't meet his standards. Why would he need to when he had infiltrated his workers minds? Comments he made to those who fell short of expectations were rather subtle in nature. Superficially they commended the children for what they had done. Yet in no uncertain terms he told them to work harder. Not one of them realised that if they stripped away the top layers, his words were devastating. No-one in the room noticed that he told one boy that his monstrosity was worse than setting eyes on his mother. Why would they when an adult would have to hear the statement a hundred times before suspecting he had actually insulted them? That was one of the man's finest qualities. His intelligence allowed him to get away with some outrageous things. In the past he had got a ten year old to attack the teenager next to him for no reason at all. The subtext of his speech convinced a deep portion of his brain that he could win such a fight. It didn't matter that the peaceful young man he targeted wouldn't hurt a fly. The coward was probably out there somewhere, scratching his head as to why the prepubescent next to him had suddenly gone mad. This was why he loved words. They were better than fear ever could be at manipulating people. Due to his natural charm he was never short of romantic partners. The other managers couldn't understand why the female workers flocked to him in droves. Oddly the conquest was more fun than the subsequent relationship. Many times he found he simply got bored once the fun of the chase was over.

"Not bad," he softly told the boy next to Bryan. "Try to tone down the homemade feel the next time you use my resources. Your mother might be proud of this, but anyone else's might have a few words forming in the back of their minds. On the whole you've got the idea there. It's a good piece of work, but you just need to try a little harder next time," he slipped in one obvious statement to disguise the thousand subliminal ones he had fired at the other males.

"Thank you, Sir," the boy replied as the man walked slowly towards Bryan.

When he looked at the child he didn't know what to expect. There was something in his eyes that told the adult he thought highly of himself. The rigid way he held himself didn't help this effect. Still, there was no fear there as he approached. This was exactly what he wanted. No terror meant he was a friend to the boys. They would see him as a surrogate father; someone to look up to. As long as they did this they would want to work hard for him. Unfortunately the effect was not strong enough in itself. That was why the subconscious emotional blackmail in his speech was necessary. With the addition of a strong contrast from just about everyone else working in the camp, he had winning trio of factors. This was how he managed to obtain such wonderful results. Other leaders marvelled at how he was so efficient. They criticised his methods in their ignorance. If they knew how much he earned they would gang up on him in jealousy. He was much smarter than they would ever be. He knew they were monsters kept in check only by a sense of camaraderie. In his pocket he kept a pen knife. If he ever needed to fight against his own colleagues he would slaughter the rest of the staff. After draining the business accounts he would disappear without a trace. Thinking of this made him zone out for a split second. Luckily he was back before he knew it. Surprisingly he saw a rather good strap. Laid out in front of him was a remarkable effort for a ten year old. Normally it took three or four goes before they could make someone half decent. He was to be commended for his success. This did generate a small amount of anger within him. If this boy could do it first time round, why couldn't the others? If he didn't have to keep up the con he would have gone mad with the children. Chairs would have been thrown around like cannonballs as he terrorised the incompetent juveniles. Sadly they were of value as a workforce. He couldn't do anything that would disable them as money makers. It would be far better if they invented machines to do these sorts of things for them. Unfortunately no microchips could replicate the creativity of the human brain. Maybe one day there would be automated production lines that could generate totally unique items. With regret he had to acknowledge that he was stuck with the youths. His customers wanted the personalised feel that only humans could bring.

"That is really good," he told the boy, genuinely surprised. "If you keep this up you might just be offered a job when you are eighteen. It's early days yet, but if you can do that without any previous experience you should go far."

It was obvious, even to the children, that Bryan's work was remarkable. Naturally he picked up on it. He was a sponge for compliments. The fact those in front of him hadn't received such open praise only strengthened this effect. Next to him, the fellow he openly criticised glared at him. To earn good comments from this man was as wonderful as striking oil. He had created a type of craving within the members of his workforce. Whenever he directed positive attention towards them they lapped it up. The fact he had spoken so nicely and so simply to this individual was almost infuriating. Surely he must have been taught to sew at home. How else could he have got it right first time? It didn't occur to the envious bunch that he had merely listened and acted rationally. If they had given what they were doing a little forethought they would have been commended equally. Instead they had let their nerves cloud their thinking. To be fair, it wasn't exactly their fault. It wasn't often that adults brutally beat children in front of them. Bryan's trick was tuning out such things. By throwing himself into his work he had the perfect escape from the misery surrounding him. For another ten seconds Mr Evans stood in front of him. Picturing himself slaughtering the staff and running off with the millions the camp held threatened to push him over the edge. He was not on the same wavelength as everyone else. He could not delude himself into thinking he wasn't a monster. As long as he didn't give into these impulses he had an easy means of earning money. Still, he could make an infinitely greater amount if he put his plan into action. Before he could get carried away he buried these notions. They would do him no good in the long run. As soon as he started taking his colleagues out they would summon reinforcements. He would be shot by the overall camp manager before he had removed a third of the workers.

"Nice job, kid," he told him before moving on to the next person.

Bryan listened to his reviews of the others' straps as the inspection went on. All of them received kind words; he was able to pick up on the open criticism the fellow rarely gave. Unfortunately the subliminal programming flew straight over the juvenile's head. He wasn't smart enough to pick up on such things. So far the man had only met one adult in his life that could see straight through him. An old woman he used to live next door to could tell he was a dangerous human being. That was only because her murderer son was also a psychopath. Fortunately for him she was also a bitter drunk. Those who were taken in by his charm didn't believe a word she said. How could they when the man they had seen was so polite and friendly? Just in case someone believed her, he thought it best to shut her up. Time, however, did it for him. When he went round her house he found her lying dead on the floor. To avoid suspicion he called an ambulance. Cardiac arrest took her after twenty years of intermittent alcoholism. Ultimately there hadn't been a need for him to lift a finger. In one way he was glad he didn't have to dirty his hands. In another he was almost angry she had denied him the thrill of ending her life. It would amaze anyone listening to his thoughts that he could hold such concepts in his head while not even showing a flicker of them on his face. To the children he was a smiling, amiable figure. None of them would ever know that at the same time he was grinning he was picturing the woman he almost killed. He didn't mind having these images in his head, but he didn't want anyone else to know about them. Common sense told him they would react in terror if they saw his true self. Who had heard of someone moving towards a person with his condition? They would sooner run towards a crowd of smallpox patients. At least with them they might dodge infection and live. To them a psychopath was nothing more than a person with insatiable bloodlust. In reality they are more like sharks. There is so much more to them than just murder. Unfortunately, sharks can be studied from points of relative safety. Usually these people would only find out a person has his condition when they are about to perish. They know they have to work hard to screen the reality of themselves from others.

"If you tried any harder you would be putting in some effort," the man told the last fellow whose work he checked. "I like the use of the feather; it reminds me of something I made when I was half your age. On the whole it's a reasonable attempt. Next time try to make sure more of the glitter gets on the frame than on the table," he let loose a somewhat less subtle string of pseudo-compliments.

Clement had been left reeling from the compliment. He had no way of knowing that this was part of the leader's manipulation. Mr Evans was not the only one who could reduce his workers to clay in his hands. The brothers' supervisor was also a puppet-master, albeit using the strings of fear. It was good to try to split the children into smaller groups. As one cohesive unit they could cause trouble for him. However, if they turned on each other they would lack the strength to pose any credible threat to his underlings. This was why he had given the boy praise. The others would wonder why he, in particular, was the only one to receive such a nice comment. As he was a very aggressive person in the minds of the children, anything that wasn't direct abuse was surely a boon from his own twisted mind. They would see that he had been complimented, while others had been left as traumatised as death row prisoners hearing their gaolers' boots. Clement, unlike Bryan, did not struggle with an extremely high opinion of himself. In terms of self-esteem he was quite healthy, but he did not have a superiority complex. Nonetheless, it was pleasant to not have aggression directed towards him for a few moments. While awaiting further instructions he wore a grin that stretched from ear to ear. The fact he had not even been insulted was almost unbelievable in his mind. Obviously God must be smiling down at him from heaven. Adam was pleased that his sibling hadn't been on the receiving end of corporal punishment. Most newcomers are assaulted in the first week.

Ten year olds are not generally known for their expertise in dodging trouble. Some of them believed that acting cute would tug at the heart strings of the wardens. Unfortunately this was just not the case. It might work with a reasonable older boy given a position of minor authority, but against the adults it was worse than useless. Those who would respond positively to it were weeded out. Not until the bottom of the barrel had been scraped to the floor beneath would they consider taking such a person on. The natural attributes desired in the workers were in contrast to those held by decent individuals. Most of the adults who saw the campers' almost grotesque attempts at charm cultivated a barely hidden desire to strike them in the face.

"Right," the man said once his inspection was complete. "That was, in all honesty, disappointing. I hope you'll all work harder next time. Except of course, you," he stated while looking directly at Clement. "Somehow a ten year old who hasn't even hit puberty managed to put a fourteen year old to shame!" He spat at Graham, his voice so saturated with bile that the air suddenly felt staler.

"Sorry, Sir," the chubby teenager managed to whimper back at him.

"Well done," Adam thought to himself, giving his younger brother a friendly smile.

Neither of them guessed that this flattery was merely part of the fellow's plan. By giving a select few special treatment he could cleave his work group in half. People would inevitably resent those who were held favourably, even if the indignation was clearly done for appearance purposes. Their juvenile brains were incapable of leaping as much as a single step ahead of him. He was the knight on the chessboard, constantly able to weave around the pawns trying to catch him up. As children there was only so much they could pick on, regardless of their level of intellect. They simply hadn't lived; they hadn't experienced manipulation, so didn't recognise it when it hit them squarely on the jaw. However, there was something special about Clement. For a first attempt it was quite good. If he could keep that level of quality up he should have no problems in the future. Perhaps, if their psychological programming took root within him, he might be offered a job when he turned eighteen. But that was so far off it was beyond the horizon. Maybe his product was the result of beginner's luck. When he decorated three or four frames to such a high standard there would be room for comment. He could tell that the comments he had made were having the desired effects. Those behind Clement glared at him intently. Why should he be the only one not to receive abuse? What advantage did he have that they didn't? Meanwhile, the fat boy he scolded was barely able to lift his head to look at the man. His words evidently had left a mark on him. But he would recover with time. One thing he had learned during his career at the camp was that children were incredibly resilient. Although they could go down like lead balloons, they soon sprung back up. Sometimes he could see it in their eyes. It was as if some spark within their souls reignited. Even a friendly pair of eyes making contact with their own could be enough to get the fire going once more.

"Since most of you didn't meet my standards, we will have another practice run," he told the boys with malice as clear as the nose on his face. "Graham, you need the exercise, so you can hand out the next lot."

This last statement was met with giggles from the younger boys. At that age they seemed not to understand empathy. Putting themselves in his place was hard for them. If they could see how destructive their sniggering was they would never have done it. The wounded male stood quickly to avoid a further telling-off. He had taken enough jokes about his weight for one day. Never before had he felt so embarrassed about his own body. When he was at home his mother always made him feel better about himself. She seemed to know instinctively when he was in need of a confidence boost. A good hug with some tender words never failed to do the trick. Upon coming home from school he almost ran up to greet her, even though he was a teenager. He had never understood why people of his age seem to go off their parents. Did the presence of hormones in their blood hide the fact she carried him for nine months? Did it undo the love she had shown him, even when he didn't deserve it? One of the workers looked disgusted as she handed him the second box of frames. To her he was living filth; she couldn't have made it any more obvious if she tried. A six foot neon sign would have been less direct than her body language. Frankly he didn't care about her opinion of him. She was a child abuser, the worst kind of human being. In his order of criminals she was below a murderer. If a person kills another they only offend once. What she was doing ruined the lives of innocent minors year after year. There was surely a special place in hell for sinners of her magnitude. The fact she was able to judge him at all was mindboggling.

"Try and waddle a little faster!" He told the boy as he handed out the objects.

More than anything he wanted to throw the wooden frames to the floor. Nothing would give him greater pleasure than picking up a chair and hurling it at the man's head. He didn't care if he had to throw the occupant to the floor. As long as he caved the aggressor's skull in he could throw the camper as well. Somehow he managed to keep his cool. Without explanation he managed to continue placing the blank timber canvasses in front of the campers. Still, internally he was raging. A mercury thermometer would squeal in protest if it was placed next to him. Surely there was enough heat coming from his face to boil an egg. Those who looked up at him saw how red he had gone. They knew better than to laugh when they saw the look in his eyes. Emotionally he was rapidly approaching crisis point. In this state he was a stick of dynamite waiting to be lit. None of them wanted to be the one to strike the match. Furthermore, they felt sorry for him. Finally they realised that their giggling had damaged him further. Almost all of them had witnessed bullying while at school. Thanks to the child obesity epidemic, many of them had been picked on because of their own weight. The scars from the vicious taunts were still fresh in their minds. They hadn't enjoyed being singled out for such a minor flaw as their size. Why had they made someone else feel so bad about their own condition? The manager detected the boy's stress levels rather swiftly. Having a fight with someone while work was in session was never a good idea. Naturally there was no chance he could defeat him, even if his workers didn't get involved. Even so, he had to draw a line when it came to provoking fear. He wanted nothing more than absolute terror at the sight of him. This was necessary to encourage them to try their best while toiling. However, he didn't want to inspire enough dread to cause them to run upon setting eyes on him. As time went by he had gained a perfect ability to gage the fear of the masses. To him it was clear that a fight with Graham would be the straw that broke the camel's back.

Clement found it difficult to remain so happy when he saw how distressed the older boy was. A glance into his eyes as he handed out the frames revealed the inner turmoil the man had stirred up. Although the teenager had picked on him previously, he didn't enjoy seeing someone upset. How could he be cheerful when another sentient being looked so distraught? This was one thing that could always be said of the boy; he was empathetic. For that reason he would never receive an offer of employment from the company. They would see that he didn't have the heart to mistreat others. Neither violence nor subtle manipulation would enable him to carry out such a role. In a word, he was useless to them. That was not to say that they couldn't benefit from his skills while he was a camper. During the summers of his youth his sole purpose in life would be to churn out as many of the products as he could. That would be his reason for existing. As long as he worked at maximum efficiency he would never be beaten. The guards would even look out for him. There was no sense in letting one of their best workers suffer unnecessarily. As long as he didn't let his behaviour or his effort slip, he would sail through his time in their care. Adam knew this, even if his brother didn't. Provided the lad could keep up his good work he was on easy street. If he told his sibling he would be relieved to know the adults would afford him protection. However, it wouldn't remove the emotional burden he felt for Graham. Never before had he seen a person in such a state. It was worse than any sort of spanking the man could have given him. Seeing the older male melted his heart. Any frostiness he held towards him sublimed after they made eye contact. Before he knew it the smile on his face had also vanished. All he could think of was the poor fellow who had received the worst torment yet. Although there were no wounds visible to the naked eye, that didn't mean he wasn't bleeding to death. If the manager had used a knife there would be a corpse littering the floor.

"Poor kid," he thought to himself as he followed the youngster around the room.

"That's it," the adult surprisingly complimented the lad, "keep up that pace."

Suddenly the boy found himself looking at the man. That was, perhaps, an attempt at kindness by the monster. His capacity for detecting the emotions of others came in handy once again. The distance between the two didn't matter. He was fully aware that the camper was haemorrhaging. To him it was as conspicuous as the person himself. A few seconds after he spoke he felt the boy starting to piece himself back together. While it would take a few hours for him to return to his usual self, he would live. A depressed worker was better than one in the throes of a mental breakdown. Graham seemed to speed up as the fact he had been praised sunk in. By the time he finished handing out the frames he appeared much better. His eyes still contained more pain than was bearable to an onlooker. Nevertheless, he wasn't drowning in his own despair. Surely once they started working he would forget his troubles. There was no foreseeable reason for them to get any worse. He was good at decorating; only once had he ever been beaten by a guard. A few minutes of work would take his mind off the anguish completely. Momentarily the man felt a slight pang of guilt in his twisted psyche. Unfortunately it was gone in less than a split second. Before it reached the surface it boiled to nothing. The sadism surrounding it corroded the emotion out of existence. He may as well have poured acid on it. He wasn't even aware of the alien sensation as he wondered what new torment he could cook up for the children.

"You did well in the end," he told Graham, making Clement feel a little less special.

The boy wasn't too bothered about someone else receiving flattery. His reward had been given to him. Of all the boys in the room, he had been the only one whose work had been considered good. That was more than enough to keep a smile on his face. Everyone in the room could feel the tension between the teenager and the manager. Witnessing terrible abuse had given them the ability to sense danger. They were deer in a forest clearing, reacting to the slightest noise in the undergrowth. However, there was hope in their hearts that things would work themselves out. Their relationship might be a volcano about to erupt, but the lad was piecing himself back together. The few kind words from the normally monstrous supervisor had done their job with expert precision. No surgeon could ever heal in the same way as the human tongue. Language could wound a person and suture their injuries the next. Yet the male could not forget the hurtful comments that had been made previously. They were always at the back of his mind. Quite how the man could say such things to a child was beyond him. Clement didn't understand it either. He was surely a man with some sort of chemical imbalance in his brain. What other explanation could there be? Whatever the cause of his problems, the fact remained that he was a dangerous individual. Clement might feel more comfortable around him now, but he was still capable of great sadism. Somewhere during the man's development a cog must have fallen out of place. He knew he would do well to keep in his good books. That was why it was crucial he tried his best while working. A few years ago, Adam had discovered that the hard way. Clement clearly had some talent for artistic pursuits. He would be a fool not to use the opportunity to develop these skills further. Perhaps the seed of a career would be planted within his soul. It was certainly possible; many of the boys went on to enter a field similar to the work they were assigned to in the camp. Why shouldn't they obtain a job they know they can do well? Certainly this was too far off in the future for the lad to consider. For the time being he was content to sit around, waiting for the next set of instructions to be given.

Chapter three

Bryan barely noticed time passing as he cracked on with the rest of the bag. Mr Evans had been impressed with both straps he had created. As far as he was concerned there was a genuine aptitude for the task in the child. For a ten year old, being complimented so openly was a wonderful experience. His comments went straight to his head, as if a bicycle pump had been taken to his ego. For an already self-satisfied person this was not entirely positive. He was on top of the world as he laid his finished product in front of him. The manager's tricks had worked well on the group. Subtle manipulation had increased the quality of their work exponentially. By the time they finished the first bag he had almost made them extensions of his own body. When he gave them instructions they listened intently, almost mesmerized by his charm. Their love for him was so great that they obeyed his commands without question. Why shouldn't they? This fellow was by far the kindest person in the camp, if not the whole realm. How he ended up working in such a horrible place was utterly beyond them. Not even Bryan was immune to his puppetry. There was nothing he wouldn't do for the supervisor. If he was asked to kill his own mother, he would do so with regret, but he would still follow the instruction. It was fortunate, then, that the man had no reason to tell the children to kill each other. Slaughtering his workforce was not a good way to impress the higher management. Most of the youths had managed to produce something on the cusp of being sellable. They took in every word as he told them how to change the thread spindles inside the machines. When he described the process of removing stitches they were almost hypnotised. If they could step outside their bodies they would be shocked to see themselves. Perhaps some part of them knew they were willingly enslaving themselves. If that was the case, the notion was held in check by the fear they had of physical punishment. Nobody wanted to take a beating, or even see one being given to another camper.

"You're all such good kids," he told them, leaving the group almost purring. "I know we are going to get on well together. Just make sure you try your hardest while you are working."

When they heard this they felt almost guilty. Within them stemmed shame for their perceived prior lack of determination. This was the best person they could hope to have in charge of them. How could they not do everything in their power to make him happy? The concept of slacking off seemed slightly deviant. If they didn't pull their weight they could be sent to another work building. That would mean labour that was far harder than what they were doing at the moment. Their new keeper would surely beat them senseless. Did they honestly want that? They would have to be insane to desire such a thing. Thus it was best if they did as the man bid them. By working their fingers to the bone they would ensure they would not have to toil ten times harder in another shack. Their physical safety might depend on maintaining the smile on the adult's face. Not sweating to keep the ends of his lips turned upwards was sheer lunacy. One source of concern was the uncertainty facing their schedule. None of them knew what was in store for them as the day progressed. All they knew was that they would receive a meal later on that evening. Would the food be edible? The ten year olds sat fearful as they imagined themselves eating the worst things known to man. Perhaps they would be presented with a plateful of writhing maggots. Who could tell if they would even get crockery? It wasn't unfeasible to picture their group having to eat out of a trough. That was exactly the sort of thing the guards would do to humiliate the boys. Yet they couldn't see Mr Evans doing that to them. He was obviously a decent human being. There was no way he would allow the other adults to treat them so poorly. Thinking of him made the fear retreat from their conscious minds. To them he was a hero; they would undoubtedly rely on him for their safekeeping for the rest of the month. Truly they had been blessed to be under his care. One or two of them wondered if he would find out about any abuse going on during dinner. If the others strove the keep him away from the dining hall he wouldn't pick up on their mistreatment. Contrary to their views, the reality was quite shocking. He didn't care about any of the children as long as they worked hard and kept their mouths shut. As long as those two criteria were met they could be forced to eat standing on their heads.

"You're work is very nearly there," he told the children, lying through his teeth. "I just need you to work a little harder in our next practice run."

With his hands he gesticulated for them to start working once more. It was pleasant for them to be in his company. One of his smiles could melt all the glaciers in the world. For impressionable ten year olds he was one of the best people they had ever met. Not even the older boys were able to see through his act. Not even his underlings could dissolve the front to get to the real man underneath. A man who can fool the entire establishment was bound to get to the top. That was his opinion, anyway. To his superiors he was far too soft on the kids. They preferred direct violence as they knew it achieved good results. Frankly they couldn't understand how he was doing so well without threatening the children. From his point of view that was probably a good thing. If the others tried it there would be many grotesque caricatures of him operating all over the place. The children would not be fooled by him for a second. His skills came from a mixture of psychopathy and a lifetime of practise. He didn't get where he was today by deciding to wear a mask one morning. They would be better off sticking to their own methods. Those strategies worked perfectly well for them, even if they couldn't match his results. Why change what worked already? Bryan, despite his preconceived superiority, hadn't been able to avoid the man's manipulation. Like a black hole he had sucked in the will of everyone around him. From inside his cosmic tar pit he could pull their strings at will. The youths he studied intently were no longer fully autonomous units. Willingly they had let him enslave them. He was the only person they had met who hadn't treated them with revulsion since they got there. Emotionally they threw themselves at him. Now they would suffer for their errors.

"I can't do it," one of the ten year olds at the back sighed in exasperation, "it's too hard. I'm sorry, I've let you down."

Mr Evans looked at the boy the moment he began speaking. His eyes were scarlet, releasing tears which flowed down his rosy cheeks. When he realised he was crying he wiped them away. No male enjoyed emasculating himself in front of others, even at that age. This spectacle was good news for the manager. Now he had a guarantee that his tactics had worked on at least one of them. Until now there was no way to be certain that they weren't just doing what he asked them out of kindness. For someone to cry when they considered their work a failure was a sign of a deep emotional connection. The only logical thing for the supervisor to do was deepen this bond. By fertilising the link between them he could make the vines in the boy's heart stronger. In silence he walked over to the boy. The others round him knew that if it was any other worker he would leave the room in pieces. This was an opportunity to see if the man was as kind as he appeared to be. There was no menace in him at all as he strolled towards the depressed boy. Quite how anyone could constantly be so calm was a bit strange to the lads. Even the best people in their lives occasionally had off moments. This man seemed to lack any sort of capacity for aggression. Even so, they weren't complaining. They were fortunate to have received such a gracious instructor. Perhaps at the back of their minds was the thought that they could take advantage of him. Someone so nice wouldn't do anything if they slacked off. Mr Evans knew that they would probably try this. That was why he kept his underlings around rather than dismissing them. While he would condemn their violence, he would secretly authorise force against the children. Anyone caught not pulling their weight would answer to a baton smashing into their flesh. When he reached the camper he leant over his desk. Warm, inviting eyes met those of the youngster as he wiped away some more tears.

"Yes you can," he whispered to him in the most comforting tone he could muster. "In all the years I've worked here I've never met someone who couldn't do it. You have to have faith in yourself."

The boy managed to smile when he heard those words. He didn't quite believe them, but there was something in the way the man spoke that soothed the tumult in his soul. How could anyone resist those eyes? He found himself being drawn to them. Whenever he looked away he found his gaze drifting back to where it had been. It was possible that this was one of the nicest people he had ever met. In reality this wasn't the case. His pleasant nature was little more than a charade designed to hypnotise the children into serving him. Those around him fell into his trap. He had been careful in speaking just loud enough for the others to tune into the conversation. There was no doubt about it in their minds; he was genuinely amiable. Swiftly the adult stood upright once more. Confident that he had done his job, he turned to walk towards the front of the building. When he saw his workers he got a shock. The children might love him, but the other adults were staring daggers. Who was this person who thought he could treat the kids nicely? What good could possibly come from that? It wasn't as if those above them even seemed to notice the problem. Whenever they made a complaint they were told the matter would be investigated. Yet nothing ever seemed to be done. Mr Evans could tell them exactly why this was the case. When they considered his productivity they couldn't turn round and tell him to change his system of control. In response to their scowls he fired a sweet grin in their direction. In one way he hated his colleagues more than he did the children. They weren't stupid, but they did seem to lack the spark that would allow them to comprehend emotional manipulation. Frankly he found their lust for violence rather lowbrow. Upon seeing his smile they wanted to club him to death. One of them could have his role. They would surely do a much better job than he could ever do. Sometimes the sight of him was enough to make them desire a revolution. Beating him into submission with their nightsticks would surely be a pleasant experience. They had no way of knowing that he would welcome such a challenge to his leadership. In combat he was far stronger than any of them. He could take the whole platoon out while avoiding every single blow they sent his way. The children would surely be his for life. To destroy their enemies would earn him a place in their hearts forever.

Bryan had pumped out his second back much quicker than he had the first. This time he wasn't held back by the pauses he had to take. The others needed to work step-by-step, receiving instructions from Mr Evans. He took great pride in the fact he didn't need such things. Before the others had started stitching the main section together he was attaching the pocket. Their instructor noticed his progress. Out of the corner of his eye he kept close watch on the ten year old. His speed wasn't quite the same as that of the older boys, but he was still shockingly efficient. While his colleagues fumbled somewhat, he was flying through the whole exercise. Never before had he seen such raw talent for such labour. There was every chance this fellow juvenile could be offered a job when he turned eighteen. In less than ten minutes he had completed the task. He was ready to start the next one; he could have done if he had been given more material. Losing himself in sewing made him forget about the throbbing in his arm. By now it had became slightly swollen. The underlying bone hadn't been damaged, but it would be quite painful for the next few days. Being able to tune it out was a massive help to him. Patiently he waited while the man counted down the clock to the next inspection. By the time everyone was up to the required standard there would be nothing holding him back. When he ran out of fabric he could simply raise his hand to receive more. Those who were less competent at stitching would not be able to influence his productivity.

"I see you have all finished," he announced after half an hour, "that was much quicker than our first go," he told them with feigned pride. "I'll come round again and make sure you know exactly how you can improve. But from what I can see you've all done really well."

Bryan braced himself for another compliment from the adult. Praise from the man felt wonderful. He pushed himself to work harder just so he could see his splendid smile. What he had said was essentially true. He only had his eyesight to go on so far, but the overall quality had shot up now they knew what they were doing. His words of comfort to the nervous boy at the back seemed to have done the trick. No longer was he nervously chewing his bottom lip. His eyes showed a sense of confidence they had lacked previously. Still, only time would tell if the items were worthy of sale. Their clientele expected the bags to look as if they were homemade. However, that did not mean they would tolerate slapdash products. There had to be a fine balance between the desired appearance and the skill utilised. As he sauntered to the first boy he felt the positive atmosphere that had filled the room. His underlings behind him couldn't stand such a thing. They hated the fact he was being nice to the children. The climate in the building should be one of sheer dread. His presence should make the children tremble. When they considered the vista in from of them they struggled to believe the scene. He might as well have been leading an arts and crafts section in an actual camp. Their superiors would hear of this; he would not get away with what he has done. The sight of the kids grinning maniacally inspired urges within them to charge forwards. Nothing would give them greater pleasure than to wipe the looks off their faces with their clubs. Unfortunately that wasn't an option. He would have them reported for using violence for no reason. Sadism was tolerated extremely well by the upper management. They could go as far as to say it was encouraged. Yet without even the slightest justification it went down poorly. A guard could hit a camper for whistling while in the work buildings. Strangely they couldn't do so for smiling. Hitting children that were doing what they were supposed to would reduce productivity. That was something that would bring their bosses down on them like a tonne of bricks. Thus they resigned themselves to glaring at the children, hoping the hearts of the youths would suddenly stop. Dead youngsters had to be better than happy ones.

"Very good; a definite improvement," Bryan heard him telling a twelve year old, struggling to contain his excitement for his own feedback.

If time flew by for Bryan, it dragged on for Clement. Never before had he felt so anxious for the clock to speed up. The man overseeing their work was certainly a lunatic. When he started his second inspection there was a tangible sense of collective dread. The children were desperate for him to announce they could take a break for dinner. At the same time they wanted the seconds to grind to a halt. Who in their right mind would want this madman to take a look at their work? Even so, the extreme violence he used appeared to have worked. Clement's eyes were fixed on the first boy who had been strangled earlier on. His whole body was shaking as he anticipated even worse torment than before. He had to admit to himself that he had tried a lot harder this time. The torture he had been subjected to was something he never wanted to experience again. Merely picturing the man's fingers wrapping themselves round his throat was enough to make him tremble. The adult could see that this was the case. Purposefully he stared at the object on the lad's table. For thirty seconds he remained where he was, dragging out the assessment for all it was worth. Every moment seemed like an eternity as the youth waited for the abuse to begin. This time he had made sure there was an even coating of glitter on the wood. He had also used sequins to try to make it look as pretty as possible. So why was the adult taking so long? Couldn't he see that not knowing if he was going to be assaulted was the worst horror of all? In the end the man could only conclude that his work was worthy of sale. It was not the best thing he had ever seen in his life, but it was a start. Someone would be happy to have it sitting in their bedroom. Obviously he had no desire to let the boy know how good his work was. Here there could be no room for such thing as good effort. What mattered was whether or not something could be sent to a shop. A customer didn't care if a person had tried their best. Only the overall quality would get them to part with their money.

"Try a little harder next time," he told the lad, suddenly staring up into his eyes.

"Yes, Sir," the child just about managed to croak back to him.

Slowly he walked towards the next desk. The atmosphere in the room was unbearable as they waited to hear their fates. There was, however, a great sense of relief within the first camper. Somehow he had managed to avoid a beating. That was a surely a bigger achievement than the product in front of him. The man's underlings had no qualms with his methods. To them he was doing exactly what he ought to. In their opinions violence was the only way to get people to do anything. These kids would do a lot more through threats than they would ever do through Mr Evan's soft approach. There was a sense of pride in the man as he made his way around the room. So far nobody had been struck this time round. What they had seen had been enough to inspire them to work their fingers to the bone. Clement was relieved that he hadn't witnessed any more violence. Although it hadn't been directed against his person, he couldn't bear to see others being hurt in such a way. That fellow ought to be in prison for what he had done to the kids. Frankly he couldn't understand why this camp had managed to run for so long. Why hadn't someone said anything to their parents? One call to the police could shut the whole operation down. Even an anonymous tip could do it. So why hadn't they? Debating the issue in his mind distracted him from the progress the man was making. By the time he reached Clement he was so deep in thought he wouldn't have noticed a bomb going off. However, the man's voice was far more powerful than any supernova in the heavens. Hearing him speaking would revive ancient mummies. There was a moment of sheer panic when he realised the adult was standing directly in front of him. As fast as he could he looked down at the item in front of him. It was better than his first attempt. Since that one had been passable, this frame would surely earn a compliment from him.

"Good," the male stated before walking to the next desk.

Clement couldn't believe that was all he got. Previously he had received praise for his use of different colours. Why hadn't he received more than a single word? He had no way of getting inside the mind of the sadist. This was a person that enjoyed inflicting severe pain on relatively helpless individuals. How could any sane human empathise with such a being? As far as the man was concerned, producing something worthy of sale was what they were supposed to be doing. Who ever heard of someone being flattered for following the rules? They were in the wrong place if they expected commendation for adhering to byelaws. Despite some disappointment, he was awfully glad he hadn't been wounded. If the man wanted to he could snap the boy's neck. The very fact he was still alive meant he owed a lot to the fellow's self-restraint. Clearly he despised children with all his heart. It was nothing short of a miracle that he hadn't attacked the group with a chair by now. Feeling deflated, the boy rested his head in his hands. Logically what he had done was worthy of admiration. He had pulled out all the stops to try to impress the supervisor. Rather than acknowledge his efforts he had fobbed him off. Adam could sense hostility in his younger brother's body language. More than anything he wanted the boy to take control of his emotions. One wrong glance could be enough to receive a vicious spanking. He would do well to distance himself from the whole sordid affair. What good would feelings do him in a place of this calibre? They only caused you harm in the long run. Relying on autopilot was a very successful strategy for getting through the month of hell. Unfortunately it left you open to the brainwashing of the guards. Those that switched themselves off tended to be offered positions when they come of age.

"But at least I didn't get strangled," he told himself quietly, realising too late that he was whispering what he was thinking.

Immediately he threw his head sideways to look at the man. Had he heard him? It wasn't as if he had spoken at a normal volume. Yet the room was as quiet as a grave. You could hear the wheezes of the workers at the front of the building. There was certainly something about scared children that seemed to excite them. Quite what it was the young man didn't know. Frankly he considered them strange for even accepting a position in such a deranged institution. When he set his gaze upon the manager he did so fearfully. He didn't know what to do for the best. Perhaps he should run for his life. There was no telling what the madman would do if he thought someone was being cheeky. Alongside him his older brother skilfully detected the change in his body language. Having not heard what Clement had said, he had no idea why he was acting so peculiarly. From the reaction of his peers he was reassured nobody had heard the statement. Whenever someone set an adult off, there was a distinct change in the atmosphere. It was as if the anticipation of abuse gave the air an electric charge. That would certainly explain why all the heads in the room turned at such occasions. Yet this was not the case after his transgression. Seemingly his utterance had slipped past the notice of the terrified children. Even so, this was no guarantee that the man hadn't heard it. Maybe by letting him think he had got away with it he could make the punishment far more severe. Revenge is, after all, a dish best served cold. It wasn't impossible that the man would wait until they were about to have their food. By this point the lad would be pleased his misdemeanour hadn't reached the supervisor's ears. Suddenly being subjected to an attack would wipe the smile off his face for a long time. After that he would be infinitely more careful about every glance he made. Something he wouldn't consider bad behaviour might come back to haunt him later on.

"What's happening to me?" He thought to himself when he noticed the direction his thoughts had taken.

He seemed to have forgotten that the man was simply that; a human being. He had no magical powers to harm the boy. His hearing wasn't able to pick up every hoarse whisper vaguely mentioning him. If he let the man become a monster to him he was giving up without a fight. Whatever happened he had to stay strong. Unfortunately he lacked the maturity to realise that the compliments he had been given were a system of control. Why was he trying to seek this person's approval? There was no doubt in his mind that the worker was a beast that enjoyed causing people harm. So what was so good about praise from a man of that calibre? Perhaps he would discover this when he got a bit older. If he survived the month in one piece he would have plenty of time to dwell on his experiences. At the moment he wasn't sure if he wanted to wait for the four weeks to end. He was more than wiling to find a corner he could curl up and die in. All he wanted was to go home. If he could escape the camp he wouldn't tell anyone what went on there. As time went by he would forget he had ever attended the horrible place. A month was a long time for a ten year old. It stretched out in front of him as an infinite journey. With no end in sight it wasn't unreasonable for him to want to give up. All this dreaming of death made him happy in a strange sort of way. He wasn't going to pretend he enjoyed picturing his demise, but it seemed to be an escape from the terrible reality. Within seconds he was wrenched from his reverie. The man's furious shouts brought every pair of eyes in the room flying over to him. Terrified, the campers watched as the adult punched a thirteen year old in the stomach. Adam flinched as the lad hit the floor. When was this madness going to end? When was someone going to do something about this bullying?

"This is just as bad as your first attempt!" He spat at the youth as he curled up on the floor.

Clement looked at the sobbing boy. He wasn't exactly small for his age. His wiry pubescent muscles betrayed the fact he visited the gym occasionally. Still, what could someone so young do against a person almost twice his age? It was pitiful to watch the juvenile athlete writhe in agony.

Luckily there was a desk screening his face from Clement's vista. That was for the best in the long run. If he saw the boy's eyes he wouldn't sleep for a fortnight. They were those of a person enduring unbearable torment. He had come under attack in just about every way possible. An ordeal of that nature was bound to be reflected in his countenance. But what he saw told him everything he needed to know. His pain must have been unimaginable. Who in their right mind could say the lad had a chance against the aggressor? Those who did see his face quickly turned away. Nobody could stand to see anyone in such distress. The fact it was a child made everything a thousand times worse. Once again the reality of the situation hit them. Next time it could be one of them on the receiving end of the blow. This man had more power over them than anyone else they had ever met before. Their relatives wouldn't dream of hurting them because of their psychological bonds. Teachers couldn't even spank them for fear of losing their jobs. Yet this man knew exactly what he could get away with. Without any sort of conscience he was able to unleash his primordial hate on the next generation. Clement found an urge growing within him. His whole body ached for him to run as fast as he could towards the door. If he could just get outside he might stand a chance of climbing the fence. His mind wasn't bothered by the barbed wire standing between him and freedom. All he wanted was to escape the creature that seemed content to beat youngsters to the ground. To his horror he saw the adult squatting next to the kid.

"Get up!" He bellowed into the juvenile's face.

"Please, Sir!" The victim tried to reason with the adult.

"Get up now or your stomach will be the least of your worries!" His screams were enough to make the hairs on Clement's neck stand on edge.

"Please," the boy desperately choked out once more.

There was no way the man was going to put up with this sort of attitude. Obviously the other workers hadn't done nearly enough to show the campers that they were in charge. While they were on the premises they were going to do what they were told. If they had to inflict pain on their wards, so be it. Before the lad could react he had been scooped up. All the hours he had spent working out came to nothing as the manager strove to teach him a lesson. No feeble protests from the youth would save him now. As hard as he could he threw the youngster towards one of his peers. The ten year old balled in shock as the bulk of his comrade slammed into his chest. Adam could barely watch as they both tumbled to the floor. Somehow the table managed to avoid tumbling over. Clement wondered if even it feared the man's wrath. Apparently neither man, beast nor furniture dared cross the path of the lunatic. For some reason the boys couldn't peel their eyes from the scene. What they were witnessing was one of the most terrifying events of their lives. So why couldn't they bear to look at anything else? The brothers studied the mass of limbs carefully. The ten year old was still moving. With all his strength he frantically tried to crawl from under the other boy. Was the original target even breathing? It was easy to jump to conclusions given how emotionally charged the atmosphere was. More than half the group had tears pouring from their eyes. Nobody could stand to be in the building a second longer. Yet if they even stood up the underlings would pounce of them. They remained close to the door for a good reason. If the kids saw a chance to flee they would be gone in a heartbeat.

"Stamp on his back!" The man ordered the younger male as he struggled to stand.

"Sir, I- I can't do that," he wheezed, just about managing to lever himself upright.

"Did you not hear me?!" His response was so loud it would have shaken the windows if they had any.

Pitifully the lad appeared to debate what to do. His face made it clear there was a struggle raging in his psyche. His whole body ached from what he had just been through. Yet there was still plenty of room for more pain. If he hurt the teenager he could avoid being wounded himself. Who knew what the retribution for insubordination would be? The events of the past few minutes told him there was no limit to what the manager was prepared to do. Anything could happen if he didn't comply with the instruction. At the same time, his parents had raised him well. How could he hurt another human being? Would he want the fellow to stamp on him if the roles were reversed? Doing what was asked of him would conflict with just about every principle instilled within him. Ultimately he did nothing. With a slightly pathetic expression he chewed his bottom lip as he stood over his fallen ally. Sluggishly the beaten boy began to try to get up. A collective sigh of relief emanated from the other campers. They were lucky the fellow was so consumed by his prey that he didn't notice it. Clement wondered if he would see someone coming up to him with a chair. Could escape really be that simple? Was a strike to the back of the head enough to release them from their torment? For a moment he thought that was the answer. If the pair of brothers could get close enough to him they could disable the threat. Before they knew it they would surely be joined by the others. Only the oldest boys would help at first. Yet it would be minutes before the whole work group was giving him a taste of his own medicine. In his enthusiasm he forgot the guards stationed at the only exit. If they saw anything suspicious they would charge forwards in the blink of an eye. There were only a handful of them, but they were fully grown adults. Even without the batons the children would struggle to defeat them. How was a ten year old boy supposed to gain the upper hand in such a situation? In less than thirty seconds they would leave half the boys sprawled on the floor. The others would gravitate towards the back of the room. That would give the workers enough time to send for reinforcements.

"I said stamp on his back!" He told the boy, leaping forwards with his fist raised.

The sight of the psychopath looming over him did the trick. All notions of morality were thrown out as pure terror took control of the lad. Before he could stop himself he jumped on the groaning male. There was a sadistic smile on the face of the man as he heard the wheezing of his victim. Turning innocent kids into monsters was something he always found pleasurable. His novice looked down at the boy he had hurt in the name of self-preservation. It took a few moments for what he had done to register on his system. Beneath his feet was a human being in need of help. Instead of standing up for himself he had been bullied into inflicting further pain. Yet he didn't dare move a muscle. He had done more than the man had asked of him. Rather than simply stamp on him with one foot he had almost crushed the lad's ribcage. The battered youngster did his best to raise his head. Any more punishment would render him unconscious. Satisfied he had taught the kid a lesson, he told the younger male to step off him. With the expression of a deer caught in headlights he did as he was told. After seeing the mess he had made of the teenager he wasn't going to risk being wounded himself. Who knew if the fellow would even live through the night? To someone so young it was strange to think that life could come to an end. Obviously he knew that death was imminent for every human being, but picturing the youth as a corpse was a queer activity. How could someone who had just been so full of life have their whole existence snuffed out so easily? If this whole affair had taught him one thing it was that people are fragile. His juvenile muscles hadn't done him any good against his attacker. He didn't even have a chance to defend himself. Adam would have loved to have joined in. If he could he would have been by the boys' side, making sure the monster got what was coming to him. Unfortunately this was nothing more than a heroic reverie. Clement was correct when he considered the immense punishment such an uprising would generate. Perhaps the guards would arrange for one of the children to be executed. For years afterwards the stories would percolate with every new batch of prisoners. Everyone who came through the gates would hear of the time they were forced to watch one of their peers being killed. That would send a powerful message of compliance to the youngsters. From it would stem a powerful new means of control that didn't seem to have been used before. Why give the monster the idea of utilising such a thing? Even considering the possibility seemed to be tempting fate. They wouldn't put it past him to have a machine capable of reading their thoughts. Seemingly nothing was beyond the terrible people working here.

"Help him up," he urged the ten year old through gritted teeth.

The younger boy did as he was told. With both hands on the lad's arm he managed to pull him upright. Clement wondered if the initial shock was worse than the injuries inflicted. Nobody had expected him to be thrown through the air in such a way. Certainly the prepubescent hadn't listed human torpedoes amongst the horrors he could encounter during the month. The others were still terrified of what was going to happen next. Perhaps the worst thing of all was the erratic nature of the manager. They couldn't tell when he was going to explode next. Now they understood how geologists feel when trying to predict volcanic eruptions. Only there was some semblance of warning with the latter hazard. There was usually time to at least seek shelter before the worst of the event hit. In the work building there was nothing they could do to defend themselves against the adult. Hiding under their desks wasn't going to do the trick. He would beat them for cowardice just to rub salt in their wounds. Most of the youngsters wouldn't be able to act anyway. Fear tended to paralyse the muscles when it reached certain levels. Seeing the horrific abuse unfold in front of them had turned those present to statues. As time went by the victim appeared to recover from the trauma. His pained face was dripping blood from one nostril. One of his hands gripped his aching stomach. When he limped back to his desk his gait suggested he was in agony. A tear rolled down Clement's cheek as he watched him hobble. An adult had done that to him; he hadn't simply tripped on the playground. Merely registering this truth was difficult. Logically he couldn't deny it. What had transpired had been witnessed with his own eyes. Yet he didn't want to admit he was around such a person. This madman was going to kill someone one day. Whatever happened he had to be stopped. If they could get him on his own they could take him hostage. The underlings wouldn't be able to help or they would hurt him as badly as he had hurt their friend. Potentially they could even escape by taking him captive. Leaving the awful place forever was certainly a nice thought.

"Let that be a lesson to all of you!" He shouted so loudly he caused the whole congregation to jump. "If you don't want to work, we'll beat you until you change your attitude!"

There could be no doubt that he meant it. They knew exactly what sort of a man he was. He took delight in hurting those weaker than him. Where was the incentive for him to change his ways. Clement wondered if he had children of his own at home. Would his wife have any idea what went on in his work? Naturally he would do everything in his power to avoid spilling the beans. Who would stay with him knowing the abuse he dished out so freely? Adam had often asked himself this question. He only had to spend one month of the year in the camp. His children had him for the remaining eleven. If he did have any kids, they must be so frightened to live with him. He would run away as soon as he could walk if he had to share a house with this lunatic. Closing his eyes, he caught a glimpse of his parents. He knew that they didn't have a clue what was going on here. As soon as he got home he would change that. Every detail of the horrid affair would come pouring from his mouth. It didn't matter if they refused to believe his story at first. He would keep pestering them until they saw the truth in what he was saying. The thought of making sure nobody would suffer this torment again warmed his heart. For the first time in a while he saw a future where he might just be able to get through the four weeks of hell. To do so would require a lot of strength; far more than a ten year old normally has inside him. But nothing except survival was adequate. If he excelled at his job he would get an easy ride to the end of the month. Only then could he convince his guardians of what was going on in the foul place. Thus he resigned himself to waiting out the period until he could report the psychopaths for their transgressions. They were not going to get away with what they had done. It would be best for them if they killed him outright. Nothing else would stop him from becoming of the architect of their downfall.

Time was stolen from Bryan with neither his knowledge nor permission. To demonstrate his skills to Mr Evans he worked solidly through the afternoon. Surprisingly the children picked up the skills necessary to make the bags within a few attempts. By the fourth demonstration they were ready to work on their own. Whenever they finished a bag they would place it in the basket on the table. When their supplies of fabric had been expended they simply raised their hand to receive more. Bryan couldn't believe how enjoyable the task was. He thought the month would be a nightmare given what he had seen so far. Yet the labour expected of him was highly agreeable. He wouldn't mind if he eventually found a job doing this sort of thing. There was pleasure to be gained in knowing he took to it like a bird to the air. Others in the room still struggled on their eighth attempt; he had mastered the task on his second. What they were producing was still worthy of sale, but to him he was certainly the elite. This was further proof of his superiority. What other evidence was needed to corroborate the notion? Currently his output was matching those of the sixteen year olds. They had presumably been doing this for over half a decade. He had only started it a few hours ago, yet he could easily keep up with them. This had not escaped the attention of Mr Evans. One of his roles was to scout for talent. As far as he was concerned he had found some. If he could keep this up he might just earn a few pennies as an incentive to try as hard next year.

"Are you enjoying this?" The supervisor asked the lad quietly.

"Yes, Sir," he replied truthfully. "I didn't know how much fun you could have sewing until I came here."

"It's nice you're enjoying yourself," the man told him pleasantly. "Keep up the good work."

Those working around him could see how well he was doing. Deep within them stirred a few pangs of jealousy. How could he be doing so well? Surely he had only started that morning. How old was he? It wasn't as if he had been here last year. They would have remembered him if he had. Still, there was every chance it was beginner's luck. Once the long work days got to him he would realise it wasn't much fun. Working from dusk to dawn wasn't good for adults. A ten year old would be a zombie by the end of the first week. Sadly they didn't know the boy very well. He could fall asleep anywhere as soon as his head touched his pillow. After only a few hours his batteries were fully recharged. His father often called him a puppy for this reason. When he was younger they used to make him run around in the garden to burn off energy before bed. Logically this limitless liveliness helped when it came to repetitive work. After a while he got into a lovely routine. For several hours he lost himself in his work, forgetting there was even danger in the camp. The throbbing in his arm subsided completely as he retreated into his own mind. Regrettably he couldn't work forever. There came a point when a worker entered the building. Whispering something into Mr Evans' ear, she left as he began to speak. This building was a haven for those lucky enough to use it. They knew the manager wasn't going to let anything bad happen to them. This did not mean peril didn't lurk behind every corner, however. Those who had been there for a year knew the other work groups resented them. They were envious of the nice man who didn't use corporal punishment. More than anything they wished they could be transferred to his department. Since that was not an option, the best they could do was settle for bullying those fortunate enough to have him.

"Excuse me," he announced to the group, "dinner is about to be served. Please leave your work and make your way outside."

Bryan groaned when he heard the news. What they had been doing was fun. Why did they have to stop now? It seemed a cruel trick in a way, even though he was about to be given a meal. The ten year olds didn't know what to expect. They hadn't forgotten that the workers were inherently psychotic. Who could tell what they were going to be served? Perhaps they would find rabbit droppings in their stew. Their water could be saturated with the hottest chilly powder they could find. Silently they contemplated what would happen to them. There was nothing they could do except wait to see the events unfold. Part of them knew they could report any such trouble to Mr Evans. Such a nice man wouldn't want them to go hungry if it could be avoided. Those in the other buildings would be desperate to get away from their cruel supervisors. Mr Evans had succeeded in cultivating a group of people that actually wanted to work for him. Some of them would be begging for overtime towards the end. Deep down the children knew they were better off where they were then outside the shack. For that reason they rose from their desks slowly. Why couldn't they just have another hour with him? Presumably they would go straight back to work after their dinner. Despite their reluctance to leave they knew they had to do as they were told. Many of them were still not convinced he wouldn't lash out if they pushed him too much. He would have to work hard to bring these critics round. After a week it would become apparent that no amount of pushing on their part could ruffle his feathers. However, this didn't mean he would tolerate any sort of cheek. One barely noticeable gesture to his underlings would result in the errant child being beaten. Superficially he would condemn the act, hiding his satisfaction behind his face of stone.

"It has been a pleasure to work with such nice young men," the man told them as they marched through the door in single file. "I'm looking forwards to seeing you all again tomorrow."

This statement made Bryan stop dead in his tracks. The person walking behind him crashed into his back. Could it be true? Could they be going straight to bed after their dinner? Someone to his rear shouted for him to start walking again. Slowly he did so, wondering what the rest of the evening would have in store for him. Collecting outside, the group waited for one of the guards to lead them towards the dining hall. It was surprising how much of the day had passed them by. None of them had the bravery to wear their watches, but it had to be about eight pm. Midges were circulating overhead, drawn out of hiding by the fading warmth. In the distance the first crimson streaks of a sunset began to filter through the trees. If abuse was banned this could be quite a nice place. As it was summer there was enough daylight left to see clearly. Those around him began to move, their stomachs grumbling through hunger. It was then that Bryan realised how famished he was. His work consumed so much of his attention that he hadn't noticed the void in his abdomen. As much as he wanted to keep working, he could eat quite a large meal. He could only hope that the food would be decent. He recalled his earlier misgivings about the dinner they would receive. None of the ten year olds knew what sort of tricks the cooks would play on them. Perhaps there would be razor blades in the pudding. Maybe they would be given bread and water. Ironically he realised a diet fit for slaves would be suitable in their situation. When he approached the cafeteria he saw that it was the least dilapidated of all the buildings. It was by no means perfect, however. Many decades of decay had removed whatever glory it might have once possessed. Cracks stretched from the foundations to the fragile-looking roof. There were spaces where the brickwork appeared to have crumbled. Was this the result of natural weathering? Or was it where campers had been slammed into the wall years ago? Such a thought was enough to make the lad frightened. A quick look around didn't fill him with confidence. Mr Evans was nowhere in sight. The protector of the children had vanished without a trace. Who would protect them if he had gone? His arm started throbbing as the inhabitants of the other buildings began to appear. This could be very bad for him. If there was a fight he had no-one to rally to his defence.

***

"How was that for you?" Adam asked Clement, wondering if he had escaped the shift in a good emotional state.

"How do you think it was?!" His younger brother replied quietly as they made their way towards the dining hall. "That guy's a lunatic!"

Adam's heart almost missed a beat when he heard his comment. Did he honestly think it was a good idea to say such things this openly? There were plenty of snitches around to pass such insults back to the staff members. His sibling would be wise to keep his criticism to himself. Even so, he did have a point. He had often wondered what was wrong with the people working in the camp. A psychologist could write a textbook based on the scum on the payroll. When they were told to leave the building there had almost been a stampede. Nobody could get away from the vile manager quick enough. This hadn't escaped his attention. By now they feared his wrath so much that a single glare got them all to slow down. There was no need for him to make any more verbal threats. The children had seen enough to know he was far stronger than they were put together. Hurling the youngster through the air had been a good move. His wards were too afraid to cough loudly for fear of setting him off. Adam sensed that his brother was similar to him; neither of them fell under the man's spell. Many of the males started to feel as if the abuse was their fault. He had set up the trauma to inspire feelings of inadequacy within them. These subtle nudges were just enough for them to wonder if they really were to blame for what was happening to them. Neither of them brothers subscribed to this nonsense, however. They could see that there was no justification whatsoever for what he was doing to them. Not even murder would warrant torture on such an extreme level. The problem lay with the aggressor. He had to be some sort of psychopath. It certainly wasn't normal for someone to enjoy tormenting kids. Clement had thought about what he would do when he got home. Spilling the beans to his parents was just one part of his plan. He would draw a picture of the man to stick on his wall. Whenever he was having a bad day he would fill the image with pins. That would relieve stress faster than any rubber ball ever could.

"Nobody is to steal food from anyone else," a woman in her young twenties shouted to the congregation in front of the doors. "If you are caught stealing food you won't be eating again for three days."

Clement couldn't believe what he was hearing. Could this be true? Would they actually starve the children? Suddenly he realised what he was thinking. How could he doubt that they would do something so cruel? Of course they would deny their prisoners food. Believing it was an empty threat was surely a sign he was losing his mind. Since he had come to the camp he found his outlook on life growing far more cynical. That word wasn't in his juvenile vocabulary, but he couldn't deny that he no longer considered people inherently good. It was as if a veil had been lifted from his eyes. For the first time he could look at a person and see the horrible things they might be capable of. To a therapist this certainly wouldn't come as a shock. Being placed in a corrosive environment was bound to steal away his innocence. How could he remain in a child-like state when there were kids being physically bullied around him? No longer did he see adults as caregivers and protectors. Instead he was beginning to grow distrustful of them. Currently an adult entering his vista was enough to make him break out in a cold sweat. Workers in close proximity in the camp meant danger. With hindsight he knew this moment would come. There would naturally come a day when this revelation dawned on him. Everyone had a moment when they saw some people as malicious. Even so, he wished it could have been delayed a little while. Prior to coming to the camp the realm had appeared so wonderful. Now it was a stinking cesspit threatening to consume his very soul if he wasn't careful.

"Don't even take something from a plate that's been left on its own," Adam carefully whispered to his brother.

"You are to go in there and sit down. We will bring the plates out to you," the woman added, giving Adam a sour expression. "We don't care if the work groups mingle," she told them with a weary tone. "Just don't come running to us if you get bullied because of it."

With that she pushed the door to the dining hall open. Immediately a pleasant smell hit their nostrils. A wave of stomach rumbles followed. All the hours they had spent working had generated a massive collective appetite. This was their chance to satiate themselves. They couldn't get up in the middle of the night for a Satsuma. If they didn't gorge themselves now they would have to wait until breakfast the next morning. That said, eating was always difficult at first. How could anyone stuff their faces after what they had seen? The torment of their peers was enough to drive everyone off food for life. Still, failure to eat at least half their meal was punishable with a beating. Ultimately this camp was a business, regardless of how crooked it was. Providing meals came at a cost to the organisation. Food wasted was money that could be spent on other things. Swiftly the group made its way through the entrance. Bryan couldn't wait to start his meal. It was a shame they weren't going back to work afterwards. Even so, there was a whole month ahead of them in which to toil. If he could dodge the guards he could have quite a nice time. Already he knew what he could make his parents for Christmas. Politely he ducked past someone to enter the hall. The smell of the food made his mouth salivate greatly. If he didn't keep his lips together he would dribble down his shirt. There was quite a lot of choice as to where he could sit. Wooden benches had been pulled up to tables of the same material. Looking to his left, he saw Jordan throwing one of his legs over the seat. Lowering himself down onto it, he raised his leg so both feet were on the same side. There were other boys around him. One of them was a rather dishevelled looking teenager. From appearances Bryan would say he was around fifteen. Why was it that all the older boys seem to work out? The muscles of the lad looked as if they would burst through his sleeves. If he had bothered asking he might know that such tissues normally grew in puberty. Also, it was wise to bulk up as much as possible. A good body might not offer protection against the nightsticks of their keepers, but against other campers they were a godsend. On either side of his former friend were other ten year olds. Perhaps the boy had agreed to keep an eye on them. A cohesive network was a logical way of evading bullies. Who would attack the three prepubescents knowing they had a fifteen year old ready to beat them to a pulp?

"Jordan!" Bryan called out, hoping he could join their group.

His former friend turned to look at him. Sighing tiredly, the boy refocused himself on the conversation. The lad couldn't believe what he had just seen. Was his chum refusing to even acknowledge his existence? This was something he was not going to stand for. In school he was always the person Jordan turned to for help with work. Had he forgotten everything he had done for him? It was then that the pieces of the puzzle finally slipped into place. Maybe they had been friends a long time ago. Something they had in common years ago had brought them together. Whatever that was, it had fizzled out almost as soon as it had started. They only hung around after that because Jordan had no-one else to talk to. Once he discovered he was good at sports he had joined the afterschool teams. Now he had friends of his own he didn't need Bryan tagging along with him. However, he had taken advantage of the boy's brain. Either through stupidity or general laziness, he couldn't complete his class work most of the time. That was why he continued to sit by the boy in lessons. Who else would put up with him essentially asking to do his work for him? This was something that could not carry on. More anger than the boy had ever experienced before rose to the surface of his mind. His psyche boiled as he saw red. If hatred was heat he would incinerate the whole building. He didn't care that there were three others ready to defend the shallow boy. All he wanted was to make the user bleed. He was nothing more than an academic parasite. Now it was time to rinse his hair through with delousing shampoo. He would not suck any more of his blood. This he would be certain of, even if it was because the older boy stopped his heart.

"You are the worst human being I have ever met!" He screamed at Jordan at the top of his voice. "I wish you were dead!" He began to charge towards his enemy.

It didn't matter that every pair of eyes in the room were on him. All he wanted was to smash the lad's head in. How dare he treat him so poorly? Some of his anger was directed at himself. How could he have been so blind? The kid had only got away with it because he let him. It wasn't just the guards he hated. His former friend would go straight at the top of his hit list. His target didn't know what was happening. No part of him could comprehend why he was being bellowed at. This was surely a sign of his poor character. Not once did he stop to review the morality of what he was doing. Why shouldn't he cheat on his work at school? The boy had never stood up to him before. School was something he had to go to. If he could he would never set foot in one again. Bryan didn't have the best foresight in the world. While this was true, Jordan's was a thousand times worse. This awful boy was going to get what was coming to him. The ten year olds either side of him didn't know what to do. Should they defend their new comrade? It would be strange not to given the lunatic staggering towards them. In a rage he caught hold of Jordan's neck. They would be scraping him off the floor by the time he had finished. The fifteen year old took a back seat for the moment. Fighting in the dining hall was frowned upon by the guards. If he got involved he would be punished as well. The target was still ignorant of why the pest had grabbed him. How could someone without a scrap of morality know the difference between right and wrong?

"All these years you've been using me!" He screamed in the boy's face.

"What are you talking about?" Jordan responded flippantly, not willing to entertain the idea that he had done anything wrong whatsoever.

"You pretend to be my friend so I'll do your work for you in school. But the moment someone you really like comes along I can go to hell!"

Was this it? Was this the reason why the lad was so upset? From deep within the male a ruffle of laughter burst from his mouth. Of course he had pretended to enjoy his company. As long as he kept up the false friendship he had an easy ride in lessons. Was the dummy only just figuring this out? For years he had been manipulating the boy. He enjoyed his help in classes, but outside the school they certainly were not close. To Jordan the boy was just a nuisance. Why did he even take school seriously? Kicking a ball around was far more enjoyable than completing homework. Bryan's glare was met by a nasty grin. The sight of him smiling broke down a wall in the smarter boy. How dare he do this to him? No longer would he let himself be used by the kid. When their next report cards were issued there would be a big drop in Jordan's grades. No further help would be given in any way. He would rather be beaten than answer another simple question for the abuser. But it wasn't even for him to let the lad fail in life. When the internal wall broke a primordial rage consumed him. His other hand curled into a fist. As hard as he could he sent it flying towards the face of the stupid aspiring athlete. A mighty gasp filled the air as the victim was knocked backwards. By now the guards were taking note of what was going on. They weren't about to jump in yet. It was better to let the males injure each other a little than stop their brawl straight away. Jordan couldn't believe the boy had hit him. Normally he was a pushover in every respect. Merely pretending to be friendly unlocked the door to his heart. Evidently his academic slave was rebelling against him. He would not enjoy the repercussions spawned from his disobedience.

"Do your own work!" He shouted at the male, bashing him again between the eyes.

"No, you're going to do it for me!" Jordan screamed, pushing the boy away. "I'm going to mess around and you're going to do whatever I say!" He answered back with venom.

This was a struggle that was too good for the others to miss. Bryan was fighting for control of his soul. If he didn't make a stand now people would be picking on him for the rest of his life. Jordan realised the danger he was in. No longer was pseudo-companionship going to be enough to secure the boy's help. If he wanted to retain power over the lad, he was going to have to use force. Bryan felt disgusted by his target's statement. Who was this ape that thought he could do this to him? By the time this was over he would tremble at the sight of his victim. Another slam to Jordan's face sent his head flying backwards into the bench. The fifteen year old struggled to suppress a smile. For a small child he was doing quite well. Sheer anger fuelled his assault on the lad. Unfortunately his enemy could harness his own rage. With both hands he pushed the aggressor away. Bryan briefly wondered if he had made a mistake. It would have been better to sabotage his adversary. By giving him the wrong answers he could ensure his target's downfall. It was the lust to spill blood that had taken over him. Hopefully it would be enough for him to overcome the threat to his sanity. If he let him get away with his actions he would go mad. Never would he have a scrap of respect for himself. Defeating the idiot was the only way he could regain his self-worth.

"When we go back to school you're going to do everything for me. I'm going to sit back and let you do my work!" Jordan instructed him, hoping he could scare the male into backing down.

Sadly for him there was no way this would work. Why should he fear Jordan? This boy couldn't answer the simplest questions in class. He knew nothing about the world. Why should he get an easy ride through the sweat of his victims? As hard as he could he slammed his leg into the boy's stomach. For a moment the target looked confused. Never before had Bryan been in a fight. The thought of him getting into a scuffle was almost laughable. Yet here he was, delivering great pain to his emotional captor. The guards began to charge over towards the boys. Another kick made Jordan cry out in pain. By the third attack there were tears in his eyes. Bryan's cheeks were also streaked. However, he was joyous that an enemy had fallen. Of course he could defeat the parasite in a scrap. He was better than just about everyone in the room. His aptitude for the work asked of him more than demonstrated this. He caught hold of the boy's neck. As hard as he could he began to squeeze with both hands. Jordan stuck his tongue out, his stinking breath unable to drive the foe away. The two ten year olds either side of him contemplated coming to Jordan's defence. But how could they? They would have to be mad to interfere with such a feral person. A great smile grew on the face of the fifteen year old. This was the kind of person that would do well in life. Now he would be able to identify bullies in his life. They weren't always the brute beating people smaller than them. Some, like Jordan, delighted in infiltrating their minds. Hopefully he would be able to deal with such people when he met them. Ironically he couldn't see through Mr Evan's facade. With a bit of luck he would understand why he had to do what he did. Unless he took care of Jordan he would be suffering his entire life. That was something he simply couldn't allow.

"That's enough!" A nineteen year old bellowed, dragging the boy away from the vanquished foe. "I can't believe you did that!"

"Help me!" Jordan pleaded, revealing the coward he truly was. "Spank him for hitting me."

"Don't act as if you didn't deserve it," another worker told him, looking at the sobbing lad with disgust.

He grabbed the supposed victim's arm as hard as he could. With a great level of force he tore him from the bench. His face was screwed in pain as he was pulled to the centre of the room. There was nothing they hated more than a spineless camper. He was going to be punished for the weakness he had showed. Fighting was one thing, but lacking a gut was another. If he was going to break the rules of the camp he should at least be masculine enough to take responsibility for what he had done. The nineteen year old restrained Bryan as best he could. The boy's chest heaved as adrenaline kicked his system into overdrive. It was lucky the adults had arrived when they did. He could happily beat the bully to death without losing a night's sleep over it. Bryan didn't realise how much trouble the pair of them could have got into. As it happens, the first week the guards are usually fairly lenient on troublemaking. However, their grace would not last forever. There would come a time when they would be locked in the coal shed all night for misbehaviour in the dining hall. Fortunately the workers had decided to be merciful on them. Bryan was knocked forwards in shock as a baton was rammed into his back. Before he knew what was happening he was lying flat on his face. Jordan giggled sadistically at the sight of his fallen aggressor. His sobbing had worked; they had seen him as the victim in all of this. Misdeeds have a way of catching up with people. As he sneered, Jordan too was struck from behind. Before he had started to fall he was hit again for good measure. Bryan shouldn't have attacked him, but his supposed victim was worse. Spinelessness was something the adults couldn't stand. Ironically they didn't much care for recklessness, either. Whatever position the lads took they couldn't win.

"Sorry, Sir," Bryan managed to speak as he struggled to his feet.

"You will not fight in here!" The nineteen year old that hit him screamed in his face.

"Yes, Sir," the child replied, hurrying to find a seat amongst his peers.

"As for you," he spoke aloud, turning to Jordan. "I'm not going to pretend I didn't enjoy my colleague doing that to you. What's this I hear about you forcing him to do your work in school for you?"

Jordan managed to struggle onto his knees. There wasn't a great deal wrong with him. Still, at home he often acted worse than he was. He had learnt a long time ago that it got the attention he craved from his parents. Frankly he was surprised the worker had brought up the issue. As far as he was concerned, nothing they did in class had any relevance in his future life. He would rather have a football match than sit through maths. So what if he got someone else to do the work for him? Wasn't that a sign that he was intelligent? Surely by outsourcing work he had demonstrated superiority over those who struggled through it alone. Unfortunately for him, the staff had a strong mindset against this sort of thing. Everyone had to pull their weight or the system would grind to a halt. The nineteen year old knew the fellow had the potential to become a pain in his rear end. Unless it was sorted out now it could influence his work group's productivity. There stirred within him a desire to punish the lad more strongly than he ever would Bryan. At least he had the guts to admit his misdemeanour and apologise for it. Jordan seemed happy to play the goat, feigning great injury to gain sympathy. It was obvious to him that there was nothing wrong with this lad. Those who were seriously injured withdrew totally from the world. They entered a state of mind where they wouldn't notice being bayoneted through their feet. Some of them even pretend to carry on as normal. They would crawl away from the guards, desperate to find a place a shelter. Never had he witnessed one putting on a show in the same way as Jordan. He had, however, seen such amateur dramatics on sports pitches. The fellow hadn't responded to the adult's enquiry. Cautiously he leant over him, hoping the lad wouldn't try to earn a reputation for himself by assaulting a worker. If he did that he would spend the rest of the fortnight in the coal shed.

"Answer me!" The employee bellowed, putting an end to the theatrics immediately.

"So what if I make him do my work? What's it got to do with you?" Jordan replied with an obnoxious tone.

Instantly the whole room fell silent. Previously there had been a constant exchange of hushed whispers. Now the only sound was of breathing. Even the stupidest of the children knew he had made a big mistake in being so rude to the nineteen year old. Clement sighed when he realised he was going to witness another beating. This one could be serious; the prepubescent had directly confronted the fellow. He was looking at more than just a spanking for sloppy labour. Discipline was essential to the running of the camp. Anything that threatened that would be slashed and burnt. Nervously he began to expect the worst. Surely they would want to make an example of the boy. The other adults in the room were grinning maniacally as they waited for their colleague's response. Adam would agree with his younger brother's conclusion if he heard it. Fights between young males are bound to happen. Normally a single strike was enough to bring them back under control. This was something else entirely. Every so often a particularly foolish person decides to challenge the staff. These occasions were an opportunity for them to show the others just where a sassy mouth would get them. Bryan secretly hoped the man would assault his friend. For too long he had allowed him to get away with some shocking abuse. It was only fair he received a taste of his own medicine. Although he didn't show any emotion on his face, he was looking forwards to witnessing his chastisement. If he could freely express himself he would be egging the man on with everything he had. Mentally he was urging the man to punch him straight in the face. Hopefully there would be some permanent damage by the time he had finished. His own muscles were fairly limited in strength; a nineteen year old was infinitely stronger than him. Bryan wanted the lad to see the fruits of his labour whenever he looked in the mirror. For the rest of his life he would wonder why he had crossed paths with a superior being. Part of him wondered if these thoughts were appropriate. However, what Jordan had done was totally unacceptable. Pretending to be someone's friend to manipulate them was horrible. He had preyed upon a lonely child, providing company to hide his true agenda. Now retribution would hopefully be extracted from him.

"Shall I tell you what you are?" He asked the boy, effortlessly dragging him to his feet with one arm.

"Get your hands off me!" Jordan suddenly screamed, slamming his hands into the adult.

Those in the room knew something bad was going to happen. Although the nineteen year old hadn't even staggered, he had just been assaulted. Cheek was a very severe offence in the eyes of the management. Assaulting a member of staff was far worse. Blood would surely be spilt before the day was over. The older boys had seen it all before. Some charlatan often believed he could take on a member of staff. Usually it was these people who ended up having nervous breakdowns. The guards would make things so difficult for these people that their very souls began to ache. This boy would learn very quickly how things worked around here. Unless he submitted himself to the rules he would begin to rue the day his mother expelled him from her womb. The nineteen year old grabbed him tightly with the other hand. His fingers clutched his flesh so tightly that his knuckles turned white. There was a strange smile on the man's face. It seemed to convey so many things to the outside world. Of course, there was a malicious element to it. The child was in for a great deal of pain. However, so many other thoughts were visible to those who could stand to look at it. Once upon a time he had been in the same situation as Jordan. As a ten year old he had been a terrible bully. His teachers, unwilling to spank a juvenile, had almost given up on him as an incorrigible thug. His rough background followed him wherever he went. Even twelve year olds respected him as someone not to be crossed. For a prepubescent that was quite an exhilarating feeling. Knowing that little kids cried at the sight of him was more power than someone of his age could possibly comprehend. He considered himself to be the king of the world in those days. Luckily for him he couldn't continue along this path. Where would it get him, in the end? The boys he used to associate with weren't as lucky as him. They couldn't change their ways; as a consequence they are now the underclass in their town. These wastes of space were in youth prisons before they could legally learn to drive. Yet he was fortunate; his parents won some money on a scratch-card. They could afford to send him to this very camp when he was just ten. At first he pushed the other campers around a bit. The proudest moment in his life was getting a thirteen year old to step backwards in fear. Sadly his reign as a tyrant came abruptly to an end. The guards gave him more discipline in one hour than he had received in a decade. Several hard spankings planted the seeds of a conscience in his young psyche. Now he had a good job, a girlfriend and a nice house. Hopefully he could turn this boy's life round as well.

"You are just the worst form of life," he spoke to him with a perturbingly calm voice. "You are a sickening parasite that should be bitten in half."

Jordan hated being spoken to in this way. Why wasn't the man letting go of him? Surely he had suffered enough already. Did he want him to leave Bryan alone? He would gladly do so as long as he could go back to where he was sitting. Nobody had ever stood up to him like this before. Frankly he hated it. How dare this man treat him in such a way? If he wanted he could get him arrested for what he was doing. Striking a child was unacceptable in modern society. Picturing the man in handcuffs was enough to make the corners of his lips rise. That was exactly what he would do. Once the police found out what had happened to him there would be many arrests. The camp would be shut down. This bloke would be sorry he had ever laid a finger on him. Sadly the older male didn't need to worry about the authorities. He could do just about whatever he wanted to. If he killed the lad he would merely get a telling off from the upper management. The sight of this lower life form grinning drove him over the edge. Drawing his arm back, his fingers curled to make a fist. Jordan was far too slow-witted to foresee what was about to happen. He felt the punch explode across his face as the adult released his grip. Why would he want to be in contact with a maggot for a moment more than he had to be? His victim yelped as he was thrown backwards. What had just happened? His feeble intellect registered that he had been hit far later than Bryan's would have. The original assailant would have stood and clapped if he hadn't feared further punishment. What he was seeing had made his year. It was as if a deep itch had been scratched.

"If you smile at me again you'll be in real trouble!" He bellowed at the sobbing lad.

This time his crying was real. There could be no doubt that such a strong blow had shaken him deeply. Naturally this was exactly what he had wanted. Only through pain could people improve themselves. Without a need to do so their subconscious minds rejected the change. Who would leave a fertile valley without a motive? However, it would empty rather quickly if a pride of lions was introduced to the pastures. People would be tripping each other up to ensure they were not leapt upon. Now he had given the male a chance to change. Hopefully the other workers would give him similar treatment if they saw him misbehaving. Maybe the lesson he had taught him would be enough for him to straighten himself out. Frankly the man didn't care one way or the other. He had no interest at all in the boy's future as long as he didn't play up while he was at camp. Jordan pulled his hand away from his face cautiously. He had no way of knowing if there would be further blows. Still he hadn't grasped that he wouldn't be able to stop them. In his mind he was more than capable of taking out the nineteen year old. The first time he had merely been taken by surprise. As quickly as he could he struggled onto his knees. With one hand he reached for the man's thigh. This was the biggest mistake of his life. His target fired his knee upwards with the force of a charging horse. As soon as it made contact with Jordan's face he was knocked onto his back. Another groan filled the air as the lad came to terms with his second failure. It was obvious to everyone present that the kid was fighting a lost cause. He was almost a decade older than the child. In terms of strength Jordan couldn't hope to match the older male. Nonetheless, his stupidity kept him going. If he could just get back onto his feet he would be in a better position to launch an attack. The adult watched him trying to stand with amusement. Blood was flowing from his lacerated lips. His legs appeared so shaky that exhaling would knock him over. Bryan was thoroughly enjoying the spectacle. He knew his friend was the bluntest knife in the draw, but until now he hadn't realised just how idiotic he was. Was he seriously trying to take out someone four times his size? There was no way he could possibly win. David slew Goliath with the aid of God's grace. Jordan had no-one behind him but his own shadow.

"Is he seriously going to attack him again?" Clement whispered to Adam, unable to look away from the pair.

"I hope not. This time he won't show any mercy to him."

Adam was completely correct in his statement. Previously the man had been playing with the boy. He was a cat toying with a mouse before delivering the fatal bite. Now that time had come. With a clenched fist he hit the lad as hard as he could between the eyes. This time there wasn't a pained cry. His target flew through the air as his attacker looked on with a proud smile. He could take pleasure in demonstrating his strength to the children. Some of the more muscular teenagers envied the might he could muster. Certainly this camper would learn his lesson. Attacking a guard was one of the worst offences a child could commit. If it happened again he would ensure the boy was scarred for life. That would be a fitting punishment for a truly vile human being. Bryan tried his best to bury a laugh when he saw the way the boy landed. It was as if someone had dumped a mannequin on the floor. Other than his giggling the room was deathly silent. The adult punched the air enthusiastically. He was pleased he could send a ten year old fifteen feet through the air. Clement couldn't help but notice the child laughing. How could he do something so cruel? They weren't friends, granted, but this was a human being. He was laughing at a person beating a defenceless prepubescent for entertainment. A look of anger grew on his face. Everyone else was sitting perfectly still, not wanting to attract the attention of the guards. However, this young man was cackling sadistically at the sight of the boy being harmed. Adam could sense tension coming from his younger brother. Even so, he couldn't look away from the lad lying on the floor. His arms were sprawled as if he was directing air traffic. The only sign of life was the constant heaving of his chest. It was a miracle no permanent damage had been done. Luckily the guards had been trained to injure the children superficially. Never would they break someone's nose. That could require surgery to correct. Leaving bruises was fine as long as the underlying bones weren't fractured. Jordan might have a black eye for a few days, but otherwise he would be fine. When he regained consciousness he would demonstrate newfound respect for those in authority. The sight of the guards would be enough to make him want to vomit. After the salvo he had taken there would be no question of further attacks on guards.

"Well, I hope this has been a lesson for all of you. If you want to misbehave, go ahead. Just don't complain when you end up like him!" The nineteen year old announced to the stunned congregation.

"I know I won't," Bryan whispered to the people next to him, smiling after the evening's show.

Clement couldn't believe what he had just seen. Strangling a child for a while was bad enough. Beating them to unconsciousness was quite another. This was, perhaps, the worst thing he had seen since arriving in the horrible place. Suddenly he wondered if any of this was real. Could the bus have crashed on the way there? Was this hell? It certainly wouldn't surprise him if this turned out to be the case. If it was true, the guards were surely demons. At first he wasn't serious about the concept. Yet he couldn't doubt that the adults seemed to live to cause those weaker than them harm. What else would fallen angels spend their time doing? With wide eyes he stared at the floor. Adam wondered what was wrong with him. Even so, he didn't dare speak until the atmosphere of the room had changed. The worst time to do anything was after a violent chastisement. That was when the workers were more likely to attack again to satisfy their bloodlust. The thought of them being in Hades was terrifying to him. What could they have done to earn a place there? Adam grew increasingly concerned as the seconds went on. His brother went pale as he contemplated the eternity he would have to spend in this place. More than anything he wanted to ask the boy what was wrong. But how could he? Talking might make him the next person to be beaten. He had more sense than Jordan ever would have. Anything that minimised the risk of being assaulted had to be done. Yet there came a point when he couldn't bear his sibling's pain any longer. The need to discover the source of the problem outweighed the risk of being targeted by the abusive guards.

"Are you alright?" He asked the younger camper, eager to help him overcome what was troubling him.

"Is this hell? Am I dead?" Clement quietly responded, as despondent as it is possible for a person to be.

Adam was dumbstruck when he heard the question. When he had come here for the first time he had asked it himself. Seemingly everyone that passes through the gates has a similar moment during the first week. There came a point when the abuse drove them to rock bottom. Their emotional state couldn't get any lower if the weight of a galaxy was placed upon it. It was surprising that his normally upbeat brother had reached this point so quickly. Yet even the darkest night was not completely void of light. Regardless of how long he remained depressed, there was nowhere to go except upwards. Within a few days he would see how good his home was relative to this place. Time passing would give him a new appreciation of how lovely his life was. By the time he left he would be more optimistic and content than ever before. It wasn't hard to see why he would think this was hell. Non-one could doubt that it was a good physical representation of the spiritual place. But they had the option of leaving once the month was over. The guards, while inconceivably cruel, were only human beings. They were not servants of God that had fallen from grace. Although the summer heat made things uncomfortable, their skin would not burn off. The food, if they ever got it, would hit the spot exactly. No-one would have to eat rotting meat while they were on the grounds. Adam's stomach rumbled when he thought of the meal they were going to have. Perhaps the food was the only good thing in the place. After half a minute he realised he hadn't answered the question. Leaning forwards, he whispered into the boy's ear.

"No, you're okay. What you need to remember is that this won't last forever. We're all going home once the month ends. Just try to keep your head down until them."

A few seconds later the boy seemed to perk up a bit. He was pleased to see this slight improvement in his sibling's condition. Honestly the worst thing he had encountered so far was the low moods of his relative. What they did to him was irrelevant as long as his brother escaped the ordeal undamaged. From the rear room the first plates of food were brought out. Hungrily the crowd began to chat amongst itself. Amazingly Jordan hadn't been moved. The nineteen year old had coldly left him where he had fallen. What good would moving him do? He needed to constantly remind the campers what would happen if they messed around. Clement turned his head slowly to view the meal. What he saw did look appetising. Large plates of sausages, beans and mash were pilled sky-high. A great deal of chatting filled the air as they struggled to contain their excitement. Part of them wanted to get the food down their throats as much as possible. Another section of their psyche feared that it had been sabotaged. If the nineteen year old offered them a sweet, who in their right mind would accept it? For all they knew the food had been poisoned. Thus many of them appeared apprehensive as the plates were placed in front of them. Another pair of workers handed out plastic cutlery. None of the guards would trust the children with metal instruments. Giving oppressed people the means to stage a rebellion was generally a bad idea. However, these plastic tools were so cheap they would shatter upon contact with human flesh. Thus any uprising based around them would fail catastrophically. Bryan was certainly going to enjoy the meal once it arrived. Normally he would worry about the older boys taking his food. Fortunately for him this was strictly prohibited by the guards. Anyway, the servings were far larger than he could hope to finish. If they wanted to pick at his scraps they were more than welcome. Yet more workers brought glasses of milk out to everyone. They were a bit surprised that the meal was so wholesome. Surely bread and water would be better for keeping the boys down and in their place.

"They like to fatten you up," Adam told his brother nonchalantly. "Don't be surprised if you put on weight while you're here."

"Why?" Clement wondered, genuinely confused.

"I think they want parents to get their children back looking healthy. Plus if they feed us properly we heal quicker."

This gave the younger sibling something to think about. Not being of great stature, he couldn't possibly consume the whole offering. Yet he feared what would happen if he left even a crumb. Surely they would punish him for perceived ingratitude. This notion generated a new wave of fear within him. If he hadn't been so hungry it would have driven him even further into the pit of despair. Fortunately the hole in his stomach consumed the resulting terror. Clearly he wouldn't get another chance to eat until tomorrow morning. It was best for him if he devoured the whole thing. Feeling sick was worth not having to spend all night hungry. Within a few minutes every child in the room had a meal in front of them. As quickly as possible they gobbled down the food. Being young males, the table manners left a little to be desired. Nobody minded what everyone else was doing. Somehow the kitchen staff had produced truly wonderful food. The idea that the camp was hell quickly departed the boy's mind. Still, a new thought entered him. Surely providing food of this quality generated a paradox. He understood why they did it, but wouldn't less palatable substances fulfil the sadistic desires of the workers? If they wanted to keep the lads healthy they could just give them a vitamin pill. Naturally it would be cheaper than granting the boys a bounty. Could it be that the slight subconscious guilt for what they were doing led to this practice? Or was it that they knew the children could only take so much torment before their minds snapped? How would they explain a camp full of insane individuals? With this in mind it was no wonder they went to such trouble. Mealtimes would surely become a refuge for those who otherwise struggled through the days.

"Eat your food," Adam told him as he tucked into his own dinner.

Clement grasped the plastic knife loosely in one hand. He didn't trust himself to try to stab himself to death with it. Taking a look over his shoulder, he once again set eyes upon Jordan. He didn't know anything about the original fight. Everything came from abuse hurled in the midst of an argument. Who could say if the comments made were accurate? It seemed to slip his notice that the unconscious male admitted it was true. All he could think about was what the nineteen year old had done to him. Evidently there was bullying going on between the campers. Even so, that didn't justify an adult sending a child flying into the air. Gingerly he scooped some of the mashed potato up with his cutlery. Part of him wanted to hurl the plate as far away from him as he could. The guards were exceptionally cruel; you would have to be mad not to see their sadistic tendencies. So how could he be sure the food wasn't poisoned? He hadn't seen it being prepared. Thus he had no way of knowing if he should consume the offering. Still, everyone else seemed to be fine with it. Even his older brother merrily chewed away next to him. After several hours of work they were all famished. It wasn't unreasonable that they would eat anything placed in front of them. Before he could talk himself out of it he placed the morsel into his mouth. To his surprise he found the taste wonderful. Truly this was a delectable meal. His taste buds could pick up the butter that had been mixed into it. His stomach growled as it sensed it was about to be filled. Picking up the plastic knife with his other hand, he cut off a large piece of sausage. In less than twenty seconds it had disappeared down his gullet. Alongside him his brother smiled when he heard his satisfied groaning. Shockingly he had to admit that this food could be better than the stuff he got at home. Clement couldn't believe that something so good could come out of a nightmare. Those around him looked on as he stuffed his mouth to bursting point. Like a hamster he filled his cheeks, gobbling down the wholesome serving without a care for his table manners. It wasn't long before his psyche buried the torment he had suffered. So far neither of the siblings had been attacked. As he wasn't in immediate danger there was nothing wrong with turning his anxiety levels back to nought. In his chest his heartbeat slowed. This was the first time he had truly forgotten the hell he had found himself in.

"You enjoyed that," Adam commented sweetly as the boy finished scraping his plate clean.

"Yes," he spoke with a mouthful of food, not caring about social conventions.

As soon as he swallowed he gripped his glass of milk tightly. A nice drink would make the heaven of the meal complete. In less than thirty seconds he poured it all down his throat. The room had become slightly hot. A partially chilled beverage hit the spot nicely. Placing the cold cup against his sweaty forehead, he wondered what the rest of the evening had in store for them. Hopefully they wouldn't have to go to bed straight away. Although he was no longer fearful, he didn't think he could sleep. When he glanced around the room he caught a glimpse of Graham. Surely he hadn't forgotten the horrible comments about his weight that afternoon. There were no prizes for guessing who would end up bearing the brunt of his rage. That was the problem with bullies; they always go for those smaller than them. Heroes, ironically, do the opposite. He hadn't abandoned the vow he had made while working. If it cost him his life he would make sure this place was shut down. Briefly he considered the attention he would get when the story broke in the papers. Everyone would know about him and what he went through. He would become a household name overnight. Not just him, but everyone who had ever struggled through the month of depravity. He had no doubt there would be several arrests. Would he have to give evidence in their trials? Suddenly his confidence stepped away from him. How could he face all those people? At home he had seen documentaries based around courtrooms. Everyone gets pecked to death by the eyes of the officials. Those in the galleries fired a constant salvo blasting the witnesses to atoms. It wouldn't just be a friendly barrister interviewing him. The defence would get a chance to attack him at their leisure. How was a child supposed to deal with that? He might be young, but Clement was no fool. Taking this matter to the police would be emotionally scarring. What happened here would earn him a reputation for life. Never again would he get a chance to be his normal self. For the rest of his life he would be known as a survivor of horrid abuse. He would have grown a little sad if it wasn't for the noises behind him.

"He's waking up!" Someone shouted, causing him to turn his head.

Immediately he fixed his eyes on Jordan. Who else could he have been talking about? Exactly why he looked he didn't know. Seeing him in such a pitiful state was yet another image to fuel his nightmares. The wounded youngster was very groggy after the mighty blows he had taken. At first he could do little more than slowly move his head. Blood from his split lips had collected on the floor. By now it had started to dry. There would a crimson stain marking the battle the next day. The boy who had fought him originally was spellbound by the sight. A chance to see his abuser in this condition was a gift. The guards had, unknowingly, blessed him when they disciplined him. There was a look of twisted pleasure in Bryan's eyes. Clearly he was hoping more torment was coming his enemy's way. The whole world could see the disgusting desire imprinted on his face. It was at this point that Clement decided he didn't like either of them. Jordan was a bully, but he didn't deserve to be beaten so badly. Bryan wasn't much better despite being a victim. Couldn't he just be satisfied that the mistreatment was going to stop? He certainly didn't have to enjoy watching the punishment so much. Anyone who would wish this on a peer was not right in the head. The fact there had been bad feelings between them didn't excuse his malicious expectations. Seeing the look on his face was almost enough to make him vomit. Narrowing his eyes at the boy, he looked down at the victim. None of the guards had come over to ensure he was alright. It was as if he had been thrown into a well; afterwards he was on his own. Opening his eyes, he tried to look around. This was awful in Clement's opinion. Someone ought to help him from the floor. Staring at him was only going to make the situation worse. He didn't doubt that some cared enough to try to help him stand. But what could they do with the adults around? Nobody could tell what the erratic workers were going to do next. Perhaps they would be beaten simply for standing up. As much as they wanted to provide assistance, how could they when the stakes were so high? Selfishly they thought of themselves before they considered the comfort of the boy. What good would their intentions do them if they ended up lying next to him? Maybe the adults would take their help as a sign of collaboration with a troublemaker. That would go down as well as a spoonful of volcanic lava.

"I know you want to help him," Adam whispered into his ear, "I want to go over there as well. But here you can't help other people. They'll hit you just for looking at them the wrong way. It's best if you try to tune out your emotions. That way they can't hurt you."

Clement couldn't believe what he had just heard. Could he be serious? Was becoming a zombie the best way to deal with his problems? More than ever he hated the camp. At every turn it seemed to throw up new ways to torment him. If he had a gun he would kill all the workers in a heartbeat. Bryan's laugh caught his attention. How could this be true? Were his injured adversary's attempts to sit up comical to him? The lad studied the drowsy boy closely. He could only guess what sort of pain he was in. Still none of the guards had come over to see if he was alright. A deep itch to go over there grew within him. As the seconds passed it grew in intensity. His body ached as he powerlessly watched the child fail to prop himself up. Why was everyone chatting when they should be doing something about this? He refused to believe that a rebellion wasn't the answer. Of course, he hated violence with a passion. Nonetheless he clung to the opinion that they could succeed as a group.

Together they could overpower the guards. Stealing their batons, the older boys could mount a real strike against any reinforcements that arrived. Wasn't that worth attempting? Moments later he hung his head in shame. He was nothing more than a coward. Someone would need to lead by example. If one person appeared to be successful others would follow. He was smart enough to know that individual wasn't him. If Adam joined him they would still fail miserably. Not even the muscular teenagers at the opposite end of the room would stand much of a chance. How could they last long when so many factors were against them? In terms of passion for brawls they were ants next to the staff. Being vastly outnumbered would hamper even the most determined of rioters. Too many nightsticks would come from all directions, beating the juvenile body builders to a pulp. They would be scraping their remains off the floor with a shovel. Either that or they would strip them naked and tie them up outside for the elements to claim. Clement tried to imagine what that would be like. For three days they would be there, dying of thirst, having everyone stare at their bodies. That hell was surely infinitely worse than enduring the rest of the month. It wouldn't be nice for anyone else to see either. Knowing the guards, they would leave the bodies out to rot. Anyone who even thought about fighting the workers would smell the consequences of such action. The notion would be crushed as soon as if appeared within their minds.

"Help me," he thought he heard Jordan whisper.

That was the snapping point for him. There came a time when adding a single straw would supposedly break a camel's back. Hearing the plea was enough for the lad to throw himself into action. Everyone else could do what they wanted. If they were too spineless to make a stand that was their problem. But he had to live with himself once his imprisonment ended. That meant he couldn't sit back and do nothing while another sentient being was in need. What sort of person would that make him? Until they day he died he wouldn't be able to get the thought out of his head. What was life if his own skull wasn't a nice place to inhabit? How would he go on living when this situation would show him exactly the sort of person he was? Thus there was only one possible cause of action. Purposefully he threw himself upright. None of the adults had said anything to them about walking around. The directions given only concerned stealing food. Presumably they could change seats as long as they didn't cause trouble. Bryan seemed to have evaded further punishment somehow. Logically Clement couldn't know the true motive. However, standing by his mistake appeared to have played some role. It wasn't inconceivable that the guards would admire his courage. By going over to the boy's side he was showing real bravery. Even a dullard would pick up on the instability of the adults' tempers. Doing anything required great faith that they would not be singled out for abuse. Frankly Clement didn't care if he got a smacked bottom. All he wanted to do was help Jordan. Would they appreciate camaraderie? He could only hope they would. If this isn't the case he wouldn't be able to sit properly for a week.

"Wait!" Adam cried out, noticing his brother was charging towards the troubled lad.

Unfortunately it was too late for him to catch hold of his sibling's arm. A great feeling of panic tore through his heart as his fingers hit thin air. What was wrong with him? Hadn't he listened to anything he had said? This wasn't the sort of place for altruism. Drawing attention to yourself is a bad idea. Doing so to help the fallen was an even worse move. The guards were dogs chewing over bones. Reaching down to take it from them was not recommended. Yet there was no way his brother was going to be bitten. Not while there was breath in his body would he sit idle. As fast as he could he threw himself to his feet. The madman had decided to intervene despite his advice. They would just have to deal with the consequences together. Like lightning across the sky the ten year old reached the boy. Bending over him, he put on the most sympathetic look he could muster. He didn't know much about first aid. Certainly there was no way of tending to his wounds medically. Even so, being helped to a seat was a start. He would feel better once he had some food inside his stomach. He didn't notice Adam coming up behind him. This wasn't a good sign. Luckily he didn't mean the younger male any harm. The same could not be said for the guards. When Jordan saw his expression his features hardened. Despite having been beaten with venom he retained his despicable attitude. Clement didn't grasp the look at first. Was it a symptom of the pain he was in? Other than offer more comfort he didn't know what else he could do.

"Get away from me, freak!" He managed to choke out, bitter over what had happened to him.

"What are you playing at?!" Adam wondered loudly, earning scowls from the workers. "Get back over there now!"

"You're not right in the head," Clement told the victim with a remarkably neutral tone. "I tried to help you."

"I don't need your bloody help!" He spat back at the boy, causing the onlookers to whisper.

"Were you trying to help him?" The nineteen year old shouted from across the room, bemused.

"Yes, Sir," the young man did his best to appear as polite as possible.

"Why?" A woman next to him asked.

"He asked for it. I heard him from where I was sitting."

Immediately the atmosphere changed in the dining hall. Terror overcame the poor lad. What was he thinking when he set off on this foolhardy venture? The so-called victim was nothing more than a bully. Some would say he didn't receive enough of a punishment for what he had done to the other camper. It would have been in his best interests to do nothing. Why should he care about what happened to scum? Evidently he was going to suffer a nasty assault for his actions. Altruism doesn't benefit the person showing it, but he was going to be worse off than ever. He was just about coping with the emotional turmoil as it is. How was he supposed to carry on after the man had finished with him? He didn't see Jordan staring daggers at him. If he did he would begin to doubt whether it was worth helping anyone. This day had taught him that people are not inherently good. Obviously he knew that some were capable of terrible things, but until today he believed people had a kernel of goodness in their souls. Obviously this was a misgiving. Now he had seen what people are really like. Often he had argued with his brother at home. Currently he was wondering why, given how nice he was. It could be worse; he could have Graham or Jordan as siblings. Neither of them deserved his company. They both attacked those weaker than them to hide the selves they couldn't stand. Frankly he had more important things to worry about at the moment. Avoiding a beating was right at the top of his list. Unless he could explain that he hadn't wanted to cause trouble he could end up in a worse state than Jordan. The adults were piranhas; once they tasted blood they bit deeper and deeper. Attacking the camper had given the nineteen year old a taste of the fun sadism brings. Clement trembled slightly as the man approached. A tear flowed down his cheek as he pictured what would happen to him. If he had seen Bryan he would have noticed him watching intently. In his somewhat sinister mind he thanked the camp for the mealtime entertainment. Adam was too busy to notice the boy baying for his brother's blood. His heart was pounding so fiercely he feared it would cut out completely. Every instinct in his body was screaming at him to do something. This was his younger brother. If anything happened to him he would never forgive himself. But what could he do? He wasn't strong enough to take on the man. Even if he scored a victory the others would descend on him. Their batons would beat the resistance from him in seconds.

"I don't know why you're wasting your time with him," he told the lad, truly curious as to why he had answered the call for help. "You seem like a good kid. Why are you associating yourself with scum? He's not worth the concrete he's lying on. You'd be better off helping a cockroach. At least they aren't parasites!"

"Shut your mouth!" Jordan screamed at the adult, desperate to stop the abuse.

Adam thanked God for the youngster's comment. In an instant the attention of the whole room was back on the wounded boy. Clement had no idea what he should do. As a morally upright person he knew he should try to help the endangered fellow. Even so, human selflessness does have its limits. A ten year old could not stand up to a man nearing twenty. This worker would crush him as an insect if he so much as frowned at him. He stood observing the teenage psychopath, wondering if there was anything at all he could do. Unfortunately he could only conclude that there wasn't. Adam mentally urged his brother to back away from the injured male. A nuclear bomb kills everything within a portion of its blast radius. He didn't want the man to turn on Clement once he had finished with Jordan. Bryan watched things unfold with a pleased grin. Hearing the comment lowered the bully in his estimation. It wasn't a secret to him that Jordan was thick. Yet, until now he didn't realise just how stupid he was. He had no way of fighting the adult or evading his attacks, so why provoke him further? For a moment he thought of the lad's mother. That woman had spoilt him rotten, giving him unwarranted compliments constantly. Her puckered lips must never have stopped giving him praise for nothing. With a wave of his hand the man told Clement to sit down. Relieved, Adam watched as the youth hurried back to his seat. He wasn't going to pretend the boy hadn't earned what was coming to him. Jordan must be an idiot if he didn't realise he had risked a lot by walking over to tend to him. His response was to throw the assistance back in his face. Although he hated the endemic violence, he couldn't say it wasn't gratuitous given the boy's sharp tongue.

"What did you say to me you little bastard!" He asked the boy, leaning over his face.

The brothers watched as the young man's face changed its expression. A strange mixture of vexation and perturbation consumed his countenance. Finally the peril he was in dawned on him. One thing was certain in Adam's mind; he was in for more torment than he had ever faced in his life. Cheek was the one thing the guards would not tolerate. Campers were expected to be respectful at all times. Evidently that was too hard for the chimp to understand. Clement nonchalantly studied the scene in front of him. The gears in Jordan's head were turning very slowly. From his body language it was obvious he was thinking of a plan. Bryan picked up on this as well. How could the bully possibly fight back? He couldn't even sit up after the first salvo. The second one would be much longer than the first. Clearly this was a male that was slow on the uptake. He needed to be taught a much harder lesson so the penny would drop into place. Why had the lad given him such a horrid instruction? It wasn't as if he was going to do anything else to the boy. If he had kept his mouth shut he simply would have intimidated him with a grimace. Now he was going to have to teach him to think before he speaks. However, he wasn't exactly complaining. Amongst the staff he was known as a man with a great thirst for combat. His dream was to find a child who could match him in combat. Perhaps one of the muscular seventeen year olds could just about spar with him. Still, most of them were doing their best to be considered for a job. It wouldn't be in their best interests to do anything to queer their chances. Usually it was only those who thought they could do better elsewhere that gave him hassle. Despite desiring someone who could fight back, punishing the children did help him to keep his fists sharp. When he was fifteen he won a boxing tournament for under eighteen year olds. In his final match he came up against a lad who had a few days left before he legally became an adult. The doctors told his adversary afterwards that his nose might never be the same again. Since then the guard was looking to relive that day of glory. As he could not find someone willing to have a proper fight with him, this brat would have to do.

"I asked you what you said!" He shouted at the lad before spitting on his tear-streaked face.

A few groans of disgust filled the air. Fortunately the adult didn't hear them. His attention was focused solely on the urchin littering his floor. Jordan quickly wiped away the saliva. He couldn't understand why the man had done it. How dare he do something so horrible to him? If he wanted to do that he would have to deal with the consequences. A determined look greeted the man as he awaited a reply. The ten year old wasn't going to waste his breath on his attacker. He was going to make him wish he had never been born. His mother constantly told him how strong he was getting. This creature of hate was going to go down begging for mercy. Mentally he pictured himself standing over the unconscious attacker. Sadly he didn't quite know how he was going to manifest the image in reality. Even so, adrenaline continued to flood his system. The picture in his psyche refused to let him admit he was up the creek without a paddle. Common sense would tell him to embark on a mission of damage limitation. He should beg for mercy with everything he had. Wasn't he injured enough yet for his liking? What could he possibly achieve by continuing this foolhardy venture? His lack of intelligence could lead him to a brutal death. The upper management frowned upon killing the campers, but they didn't prohibit it completely. Sometimes sacrificing one was essential as an example to the many. Adam found himself wishing that this wouldn't be the case here. He hated the boy for rebuking his brother's help. Still, he didn't want to see someone die in front of him.

"What did you say?!" He bellowed in the boy's face as loudly as possible.

Bryan hoped he would provoke the man further. He would be lying if he said he didn't enjoy what was happening. The amount of odium he had in his heart for Jordan could fill an ocean. It didn't matter that his back ached after being struck with a baton. The fight was worth it just to see his foe vanquished. This had been a long time coming. If the boy lived to the end of the month he wouldn't be so tough anymore. No longer would he bother his former friend. One punch could put a stop to that straight away. How could he have been so blind in the past? Why hadn't he seen the manipulation he had been exposed to? He found himself wanting for an explanation as to why he went along with it. Perhaps, since he found schoolwork so easy, he had felt compelled to do someone else's for them. Fortunately he had passed the tapeworm in his stool. Never again would he have to complete the ape's worksheets for him. His easy ride was over; now he would have to struggle through it on his own. If he knew him as well as he thought he did he would surely fail miserably. Bryan watched as a flame in the boy's eyes died out. The image he held of him emerging victorious had finally crumbled to dust. After all this time he realised he was in great trouble. Unless he could get away from the adult he was finished. Nervously he glanced over at Clement. Adam watched as he implored the boy to help him. Clement's heart melted when he saw the look. A wave of sympathy washed away the abhorrence he had for him. Adam placed his hand on his sibling's knee. There was no way he was going to go over there. If he did he might be an only child by the time the sun rose tomorrow. Luckily for him there was no need for physical restraint. His sibling had the presence of mind to see there was nothing he could do. If he threw himself into battle he would be defeated in seconds. What could he do against a muscular nineteen year old? His previous brush with the adult was enough for him to control his desire to help. He was sorry he couldn't assist him, but that didn't change the fact he couldn't. Jordan seemed to realise that he wasn't prepared to intervene. The last horse had crossed the line; he knew he was on his own.

"I'll tell you what you said," he spat the words out with disgust. "You told me to shut my mouth, didn't you?"

"Yes," he found himself whispering, lacking the courage to speak properly.

"Yes what!" The aggressor screamed in anger.

This truly was a rude boy. First of all he gives an adult a command. As if this wasn't bad enough, it was one laden with brazen cheek. How his parents could have brought up such an animal was beyond him. To make things worse, he had refused to answer the question. Yet more cowardice had emanated from his crude mind. Finally he had spoken to him without the proper form of address. Campers are to refer to adults by their titles. Did he honestly need to tell the fellow this? Or was he so stupid he couldn't handle anything other than monosyllabic responses? He wouldn't be surprised if the boy's intelligence was so low he needed help stringing together more than one word. To correct the boy he punched him straight in the stomach. Winding him, he watched as the boy struggled for breath. Both his hands clutched his aching stomach. He hadn't just given him a light tap; this was as hard as he would hit another grown man. Thus it was no wonder he curled up onto his side. The pain stemming from the blow must be unbearable. If he wasn't struggling to horde the air he would be balling his lungs out. Clement watched as the juvenile delinquent lost control of his bladder. Half the room giggled as his trousers incorporated a rapidly growing wet patch. His abuser laughed as he stared into the lad's eyes. Never before had he seen such a look of humiliation. The other males were laughing their heads off at him. Some were slapping themselves on the back as they watched the sobbing boy. How could this have happened to him? Jordan swore at himself for being so stupid. Why couldn't he have just kept his mouth shut?

"I think we'd better get you some nappies," he told the ten year old with a patronising tone. "I hope you're potty trained, otherwise the boys you're sleeping next to won't be too happy."

"I'm not sleeping next to him now," Clement thought he could hear someone whisper behind him.

"You're going to be sleeping in the coal shed tonight," he told the boy with a menacing tone.

The boys stared as the frightened child was dragged from the floor by his wrist. His muscles were so weak he could barely walk. His captor didn't care about this in the slightest. After a few steps he simply dragged his prey across the floor. He groaned pitifully as the rough concrete began to graze his flesh. More than anything he wanted to get away from the adult. To his horror he realised there was nothing he could do. Finally he had seen the error of his ways. These guards were in a position of authority over him. If he didn't do what they told him to he would have to suffer the consequences. He supposed that meant he would also have to show them some respect. These concepts seemed so foreign to him. At home he was the respected one. His mother did everything for him so he could enjoy his life. If he was rude he wouldn't be told off for it. Now his cheek could earn him a horrible assault. His whole body ached from the onslaught he had taken. Obviously he couldn't beat the nineteen year old in a fight. To maintain his inflated ego his psyche manipulated the situation in his head. Could he emerge victorious from a brawl with the madman? Naturally he would have to wait for his wounds to heal first, but he certainly had a chance. His conscious mind told him the problem was the element of surprise the adult had over him. If they had been fighting properly he would have caused him as much damage as he had taken. That had to be the case; the alternative was unthinkable. If he took the situation at face value he could only conclude that he was a bad kid worthy of such treatment. After all, he had been bullying Bryan for years. Once again his pride prevented him from drawing a meaningful conclusion. Of course this scenario was not true. He was not at fault here. The man who hit him was a lunatic. As for bullying Bryan, the lad was happy to be used. Not once had he told him that if he didn't do his work he would bash him. Thus he couldn't possibly have been picking on the lad. The only explanation for everything was that his former friend was as crooked as the adults running the camp. They had probably arranged this torment between themselves just to hurt a decent human being. Bryan was giggling as the injured male was dragged from the dining hall. Some of the older boys had been forced to spend the night in the coal shed when they were his age. Jordan would not enjoy the damp darkness one bit. He would be hysterical by the time morning came round. Without food or warm clothes he would be thrown into the chamber until it was time to start work again the next day. One night of that was enough to straighten out the worst campers. Self-professed 'bad-boys' came out whimpering, their tough masks slipping after the nightmare they had been thrust into. Compared to the makeshift cell the rest of the camp was better than the outside world. At least when they were working they had warmth, light and air; when they were in solitary confinement they were cut off from the rest of the universe. Not even the other poor prisoners were around to keep them company. That was why the management encouraged the use of it. Surely such treatment would cure Jordan's bad attitude permanently.

"Please don't put me in the coal shed," he managed to choke out, barely audible over the sound of chatting.

"Shut up!" His aggressor ordered him through gritted teeth.

Adam waited a few minutes until things had calmed down. Holding his second glass of milk, he turned to face his younger brother. What he had done was rather noble. If it had happened on the playground he would be commending him for bravery. However, more peril lurked in this camp than anywhere else in their home town. If he wasn't careful he would be spanked to within an inch of his life. Couldn't he see that he had jeopardised his safety by running over to assist Jordan? If he couldn't get him to understand the risks of such acts he would struggle to keep his sibling safe. Both of them needed to get to the end of the month in one piece. Clement wasn't helping matters at all by adopting such a reckless mindset. He was not under the delusion that children are stupid, just as he didn't consider those in history less intelligent than himself. Even so, some concepts seemed lost on children. How could a ten year old fully comprehend death? Adam believed in the afterlife, but he wasn't ready to say goodbye to Clement yet. He also didn't want to see his closest friend beaten to a pulp for no reason. If he so much as caught a glimpse of the gruesome scene he would never get it out of his head. Also, just out of general compassion he had to make this boy see sense. If he died his parents would do their best to console their remaining son. Yet at the back of their minds they would always wonder why it happened. Why hadn't his older brother been looking out for him? To them if he had done his job properly he would still be alive. Shockingly he noticed the shoddy service he had given his sibling so far. If he hadn't been so negligent the ten year old would never have set foot in the camp. He would have done everything in his power to stop Clement from going through the same horrors he had. There was no way to opt out now. Both of them were trapped in the system until they turned eighteen.

"I can't believe you tried to help him," Adam spoke with a thoughtful voice. "You shouldn't have done that."

"I know," the youngster replied regretfully. "He didn't appreciate it at all. I could have been spanked for doing that."

For a moment there was silence between them. Maybe the experience had done Adam's work for him. He appeared to recognise the mistake he had made. Shamefully he had to admit that his brother had done the right thing. Trying to help was the only morally justifiable action they could take. Still, it didn't change the fact that it was too risky to attempt. The bloodthirsty guards would strike someone just for giving them a dirty look. If the nineteen year old hadn't felt such hatred for the juvenile bully he would have turned on Clement. They had to be grateful for the lad's ability to horde negative emotions. Without his magnetic attraction consuming the adult's attention the other prepubescent would have been in the firing line. It is funny how tunnel vision can be an active form of defence at times. By now both of them were ready for bed. Everything they had seen that day had drained them of their energy. Clement could happily nod off where he was sitting. It was probably best not to, however. If he entered slumber now he might be pounced upon by the hostile workers. What lion could resist attacking a sleeping calf? On the other hand, he had faith that his older brother would wake him if a guard took interest in him. Although he was only thirteen, Adam was someone he could always rely on to protect him. Never did it occur to him that he should have done more to prevent him from coming. Potentially the thought was there in the depths of his soul. Even if it was, what good would considering it do? They needed each other to survive the four weeks of misery ahead of them. Squabbling over nothing was a sure-fire way of bringing everything crashing down upon their heads. For that reason he would never even entertain the concept. Maybe it was the younger boy that was in the wrong. Adam had protested when he had been told Clement would be coming along that summer. If he had listened to him he would never have experienced the terror that constantly lingered in his brain. Carefully he placed his arm round his chum's neck.

"You're good to me," he told Adam out of nowhere, eager to strengthen the friendship they had.

"Are you his boyfriend?" Someone laughed when they saw the brothers hugging each other.

"Hello Rory," the older youth responded playfully as his brother broke away from him.

"Hello," the boy responded with a smile. "Seriously though, are you two going out together?"

Clement studied the rude male in front of him. From what he had said he already knew they wouldn't get along. Judging by appearances he was the same age as Adam. However, this boy was much bigger. There was easily half a foot between them. His muscles were also bigger than some lads nearing sixteen. Clearly this was a boy that enjoyed lifting weights. Why couldn't he go and do some push ups in the corner? Frankly he didn't care what he did as long as he walked away from them. His appearance seemed to please his brother. Both of them wore large smiles as they marvelled at how much they had grown in the past year. This was the age where they started to have growth spurts. How could it come as a surprise to them that they were getting bigger? Suddenly Clement felt himself fading into the background. He listened passively as the two friends reacquainted with each other. There was obviously some connection between the pair. While he was upset he had been forgotten, he couldn't deny that the young man was making his brother happy. For the first time since they had arrived Adam truly came out of his shell. He wasn't in their work group; Clement didn't recognise him at all. He doubted the adolescent was merely a late arrival. Who would come to such a place if they had missed the bus? Only a lunatic would desire such an environment if they had any choice whatsoever.

"Is this your brother?" Rory asked ten minutes into the conversation. "You didn't tell me he was so small. Is he even old enough to be here?"

The subject of these comments immediately began to blush. Normally being short didn't matter to him. As his mother often said, there would come a time when he would shoot up. Being smaller than his peers at ten did not mean things would stay this way for the rest of his life. Regardless of what the future held, he didn't appreciate being spoken about in such a way. Rory might as well have been talking about a dog. Clement turned to look at the pair. Although he was listening to what was being said, he wasn't enjoying taking a back seat. Any moment now they would be told to return to their dormitories to get ready for bed. The time they spent chatting could have been used to impart words of advice. Sleeping in such close contact with Graham wouldn't be a pleasant experience. There would undoubtedly be harsh words between them. The older boy's hateful tongue was bound to cause problems. Maybe fists would fly before the lights went out. If that happened he needed to know his sibling would have his back. There certainly wasn't time to waste discussing his spatial dimensions. Adam casually nodded, confirming that they were related. His friend seemed hesitant to believe he was ten. While his physical appearance was youthful, as soon as he opened his mouth there was no doubt as to his intelligence. Rory was somewhat apologetic for the fact his brother had been lured into their nightmare. There was no way anyone he knew would set foot in such a place. Some had tried to get as many new recruits as possible to sign up for the camp. When the new arrivals were presented to the guards they had tried to use their services as a bargaining tool for being sent home. Unfortunately things don't work like that. They were only appreciative of the new prisoners insofar as they could increase their bank balances. Those who attempted to strike a deal were usually given even worse tasks to perform. After all, they had as good as tried to escape by merely suggesting they should be spared the month of hell. It didn't matter one way or another if they did bring more people to the settlement.

"He's old enough. Did you see him trying to help that kid?" Adam wondered, seemingly mocking his brother's compassionate side.

"I am here you know," he told them with a slightly sassy tone.

"I know," Rory answered, ignoring the lad's statement. "You need to talk to him about that. He's going to learn very quickly that he shouldn't interfere with punishments."

"I think he gets that now," his older sibling replied sadly. "I just hope he doesn't get us both into trouble. I worry about him all the time."

"As I said, he'll learn," the other thirteen year old stated with a remarkable coldness in his tone.

"Dinner is over," a female guard bellowed from the entrance. "Lights out is in half an hour. Your work groups will all be provided with a few toothbrushes to share, as well as some paste. Everything you need to do must be done in these thirty minutes. If you don't use the toilet you'll have to wait until morning."

"Looks like we need to get moving," Adam told Rory, extending his fist for his friend to bump.

"See you later," the lad responded, clearly pleased to have caught up with his friend.

"Nice to meet you," Clement told him politely as they stood to go about their business.

Chapter four

The wind down to bed wasn't as much of a struggle as Clement imagined it would be. By this point the older boys were incredibly tired. Most of them were tense knowing there were another four weeks of hell coming. All they wanted was to put their heads down to sleep. The younger boys would eventually understand that slumber was an escape from the torment they suffered during every waking moment. When they drifted off they were no longer imprisoned in the work camp. Their bodies remained where they were, but their souls were free to visit other places. One of the sweetest joys in prison life was to be free from shackles in a dream. It didn't matter that they had to wake in the morning and go through another day of labour. All they cared about was liberating their spirits for a while. Adam had been appointed as a night-time warden. His duty was to ensure the younger boys got ready for bed and didn't cause trouble. Yet he wasn't exactly needed in this capacity. The other teenagers were ready to step in if they saw fit. Their sole desire currently was to retreat from the world into their own minds. As soon as their heads hit the pillow they would be unconscious. Anything that delayed their transition was to be removed at once. That included errant children messing round. Clement was a bit nauseated by the thought of group toothbrushes. His mother had packed his own utensils in his back. Could he ask a guard to retrieve them for him? If only he had his luggage he wouldn't have to touch the communal facility. How the older campers could use it without question he didn't know. It had yet to dawn on him that there were worse things out there than germs. That was true despite what he had seen that day. As his brother presented it to him he almost gagged. Was there a piece of food stuck between the bristles? Part of him knew it wouldn't kill him. The rest of his being couldn't get over the disgust of the concept. Adam was extremely fatigued after the ordeal he had been through. He wanted nothing more than to get through this as painlessly and as quickly as possible.

"Just use it," he ordered him, thrusting it into his hand.

"What if I don't want to?" Clement replied swiftly, hating touching the handle.

"You won't have to worry about the guards," he sighed tiredly. "They don't care if you brush your teeth or not. Some of them will enjoy picturing you having your cavities drilled. But I do," his tone became harder along with his expression. "If you don't brush your teeth now I'll hit you myself!"

Suddenly the lad felt rather afraid. At home they often had confrontations of this sort. More than once their parents had to break up wrestling matches. Still, he had never feared his brother. If he wanted to he could break the child's nose. Previously he had no desire to do so. He could hit him for control of the remote without inflicting serious harm. This situation was different. When he looked into his sibling's eyes there was a strange emotion behind them. Could it be that he hated him in a way? This was the first time he had tagged along with his brother. It couldn't be easy having a prepubescent getting in his way. All the time he had to worry about what was going to happen to him. In return he was unable to socialise properly with his friends. How could he have been so blind? Earlier on, when the two boys had fought, he got the impression that Jordan had manipulated Bryan. If he knew the background of the brawl he would have known this was true. Yet Clement had been tricked in the same way. All day his brother had fought hard to fight the resentment he harboured for his sibling. For the first time he wondered if he ought to dissociate from him. Quickly he wrapped his fingers round the handle. It wasn't wise to make his only ally even angrier. So many dangers lurked behind every corner that he wouldn't survive without Adam's protection. No longer did he care about the sickening state of the brush. He only wanted to avoid his one friend's ire.

"Okay," he tearfully responded as his brother squeezed a sphere of toothpaste onto the brush.

Clement realised how much he valued his brother's friendship. Without him there was no-one round to protect him from the guards. If he hadn't stepped in earlier on he would have been attacked by Graham. Selfishly he concluded that he had to keep the relationship cordial. If things turned sour between them he was out in the cold. There wouldn't be any more helpful advice coming. His bodyguard would depart, leaving him to the mercy of anyone who fancied striking the short kid. Rory was accurate when he commented on his stature. In no way was he able to stand up for himself in a fight. Even other ten year olds would slaughter him if it came to combat. His only defence was to use his wits to keep out of trouble. It wasn't pleasant for him to exist in such a parasitic state. Knowing he was giving his brother nothing in return was almost heartbreaking for him. How could he judge Jordan's transgressions if he had committed them himself? But what did he have to offer his sibling? He could give him nothing in exchange for protection. Ignorant of a solution to his conundrum, he settled for following his instructions. As he brushed his teeth he could almost sense the bitter rage radiating from Adam's body. It was incredibly unpleasant to know that his only friend was secretly wishing harm upon him. More than ever he felt utterly powerless about this situation. While toiling he could avoid punishment by trying his best. How could he control what someone else was thinking? In silence he brushed his teeth, spitting the paste out into the sink. After wiping his mouth with the back of his hand he offered his former friend a weak smile. Adam didn't return it at all. He saw it as clearly as Clement could see the hatred in his relative's eyes. Yet the corners of his lips didn't twist in the slightest. He couldn't be bothered to even feign a grin. Instead he merely gestured for the boy to head for bed.

"Hurry up!" He heard his brother growl to the next boy in the queue.

On the verge of crying he hurried back towards their dormitory. He was ashamed to shed tears n such circumstances. If only he had listened to the lad's protests he would never have set foot in this horrible place. Perhaps if he was smarter he wouldn't have been so stubborn. He had to come here, falling for the brochure that promised a summer he would never forget. In his mind he pictured what he would be doing if he was at home. Most likely he would be curled up with a book. His parents would be cuddling each other on the couch. In the background the television would be playing some video he had no interest in. That image broke the dam wall keeping his tears back. Before he could take another breath they were flowing down his cheeks. In seconds he almost doubled over, his chest heaving as he sobbed. In emotional agony he ambled towards the shack. After a few seconds he stopped. He knew he couldn't let the others see him in this condition. He took enough abuse merely for being smaller than his peers. How would they react when they saw him blubbering? Quickly he walked to the side of the building. In the distance the sunset was blazing a beautiful red. Not even the beauty of nature could wipe away the pain he was in. Being in such a terrible place was alright provided he still had his brother. Now he felt as if he was alone in the world. His parents might as well be dead. What good could they do him when he was totally isolated from the rest of the universe? Once he was out of sight he lost all control of himself. Every ounce of emotion poured from the reservoir. Such a tidal wave could wipe out whole cities. His eyes were scarlet as he held his streaked face. How could this camp exist? Why hadn't it been shut down? Earlier on he had vowed to go to the police when he returned home. It dawned on him that he might never leave. The month stretched to infinity. Never would he walk through the intimidating gates that stood between him and freedom. Even if he did it wouldn't matter. This institute would hold him prisoner for life. How could he forget everything he had seen? Whenever he closed his eyes he would see the horrific images flashing before his eyes. Such a thing would cost him his sanity long before his broken heart proved terminal.

    His legs began to give way beneath him. Before he could collapse he slid onto his posterior. Why couldn't he go home? No child deserved to go through this sort of thing. It wouldn't be right to treat adults in such a way. Not even prisoners are given this torment. Ironically prisons are obligated to provide conditions superior to those in the camp. In the realm they are given free dental hygiene products. They don't have to share them between themselves. No felon had to worry about contracting a disease from their brushes. Clement had no way of knowing if he would end up with some horrible condition. Yet this was nothing in comparison to the threat of violence. Being spanked at home paled with the mere thought of corporal punishment here. Jordan had been beaten half to death by the guard. He could have died if he had hit his head on the floor. Now he was locked up in the coal shed until morning. At least Clement had been given a chance to eat. For about three minutes he sat crying where no-one could see him. In the distance he could hear the girl's camp. A few sounds carried by the wind found their way to him. Focusing his mind on deciphering the sounds slowly stopped his weeping. Clearly he had to wait until he patched himself back together before he could let anyone see him. Even he would consider himself weak if he looked in the mirror. In no way was it correct, but boys tend to carve out a pecking order. Logically there was nothing to be gained from etching out a place at the bottom. As he choked out his last sob he wiped his tired eyes. Finally he was where he needed to be. Sadly while he retreated into his psyche he hadn't noticed someone spying on him. Slowly turning his head, he caught a glimpse of the last person he would want to see. His eyes widened as Graham began to smile. Clement couldn't believe his luck. Could this day get any worse? Evidently fate had more torture stored up for him before he could go to sleep. His first thought was to summon Adam. Who else could deal with a fourteen year old? Other than him, who would want to help him? Everyone else seemed to have made friends. They had their own groups that looked out for each other. What did he have? Because he was shadowed by his brother he hadn't even tried to make friends. There would be time for him to consider this later on. For now he had to deal with Graham.

    "What are you crying for?" The larger boy asked him in a mocking tone. "Do you think anyone cares about you?"

    "Shut up!" Clement shouted, begging more than insulting.

    "I saw how your brother treated you. He hates you now. You haven't got anyone!"

    "I said shut up!"

    "Why? What are you going to do?"

    He couldn't bear to be treated in such a way. Part of him expected Adam to appear to deal with the obese terror. With regret he concluded that the fellow was correct. He was on his own. His brother was away helping the younger boys to bed. If he wanted his foe to be quiet he would have to do it himself. There was no way he could take any more abuse that night. If one more insult came his way he would run amok. No-one would be spared their share of his pain. Before he could lose his mind he began to run. Graham looked intrigued as the child sped towards him. Clement pumped his legs as hard as he could. Faster than a charging buffalo he appeared in front of his victim. This boy wasn't going to get away with his comments. He couldn't take on the guards in a fight. Whenever he saw them torturing the campers he knew he should step in. If he did they would crush him underfoot. However, this lad he might just manage to defeat. All the rage that had been building was about to explode. Maybe the older boy could tell he was a being on the brink of losing his sanity. Even if he didn't notice it he didn't look happy. Clement punched him in the stomach as hard as he could. Relatively speaking it was a fairly soft hit. Regardless of his strength he caused the boy to wheeze slightly. Before Graham could retaliate he kicked him between the legs. There was a pained look on his face as the male kicked him again. This time his victim dropped onto his knees. The younger man realised he had hurt his opponent. A smile gripped his features as he threw a punch to his head. Another kick to the stomach followed. After this barrage the teenager didn't look so ready to insult him. There was a slight trickle of blood flowing from one of his nostrils. His stomach ached from where he had been struck. Worst of all was the pain in his testicles. How could a ten year old inflict such a sensation? He would claw at his face if it would ease his suffering.

"Don't speak to me like that!" He ordered the fatter lad, noticing a tear rolling down his cheek. "How embarrassing," he continued, "a teenager beaten by someone who isn't even in secondary school yet!"

It was the laughter that hit Graham's nerve. If word of his defeat got out he would be a figure of fun until he turned eighteen. Fortunately there was time for him to claw back a victory. One of his hands grabbed Clement's upper arm. Straight away the boy tried to jerk himself free. With all his might he punched the fat boy between the eyes. His knuckles hurt as the blow knocked his opponent's head back. Desperately he tried to get away from the male. What good would it do him to hang around? Attacking him in the first place was foolish. He had to sleep next to him. In less than half an hour he would have the cover of darkness to launch an attack. Leaving would be the worst thing he could do. It would be far better to continue beating him. Teaching his adversary a lesson he would never forget was the only way he could avoid retaliation. One blow to the nose caused the other nostril to ooze blood. He brought his fist down again. Graham looked slightly dazed as the kicks slammed into his stomach. For three minutes he pounded the boy with all he had. The fact he was still gripping his arm didn't matter. What could he do if he kept the pressure up? There was a strange sense of satisfaction in pummelling his target. Firstly he was rubbing cream on a festering insect bite. Secondly, he had done it without any help from Adam. Wherever he was, he hoped his older brother was happy. Finally he had shown the world he didn't need his assistance. Hopefully news of the fight would inspire him to loosen the lead a bit. He didn't need to be watched quite so closely. Adam could go off and talk to his friends if he wanted. Adrenaline had saturated Clement's mind as he stood over his prey. Graham emitted an agonised groan as he gripped his aching bollocks. He looked up, setting eyes upon Clement's glare. That look told the bully everything he needed to know. There was nothing he could do but try to get along with the kid. If he didn't he would get another kick between the legs. A bleeding nose was nothing on the grand scheme of things. Regrettably the family jewels were another matter entirely. Although he hated the boy with all his heart, he didn't want to continue fighting. Clement smiled maniacally as he walked away from the teenager.

"Don't talk to me again!" He shouted back, leaving him to nurse his wounds.

For the first time since he arrived he was truly happy. Somehow he had managed to score a point against a vile human being. Every punch he threw had erased part of his stress. The kicks had chipped away at the tiles of sorrow within his heart. Now, sauntering into the dormitory, not a flicker of torment burdened his sweaty brow. Certainly he had aged a few years in less than five minutes. His body language was much more confident than before. Anyone would think he was a completely different person. At the back of his mind he knew Graham probably wouldn't leave it there. At some point in the future there would be retaliation for what he had done. For his own peace of mind he would attack the child. Nobody could be defeated by someone so much younger than them without starting to brood. His pride would drive him into a scrap with the fellow. If he was older he would realise that a bad scuffle was the least of his concerns. There was a lot he could do to sabotage his work product. If he had half a brain he would use the workers to do his job for him. If he injured the prepubescent he would get in trouble. Engineering a situation where the adults would punish him would be far more effective. But for the moment Clement was content to simply enjoy his victory. Currently his priority was to get some sleep if he could. With a bit of luck the room wouldn't be too cold overnight. All those bodies would surely heat the room to a small degree. If not, he could always use Graham's flab as a blanket. This thought would be enough to bring a smile to his face for some time to come.

Without further hesitation he entered the chamber. Presumably he would have to sleep in his work clothes. Thinking about that eroded his joy slightly. At home his mother warmed his pyjamas on the radiator. Not once had he gone to bed cold. Instead of fresh, clean garments he was stuck in his sweaty uniform. But did that matter in the grand scheme of things? One of his enemies had been defeated. As far as he was concerned he had scored a great victory against the camp. Nothing could be allowed to take this feeling from him. He didn't know when he would happy again. Thus upon obtaining some cheer he held it within in. In a way it shielded him against further emotional injury. Although it had only been a day, he had endured enough pain to last him a lifetime. The thought of taking any more knocks was unfathomable to him. Even so, he knew he had a long way to go before his journey was over. When he boarded the bus home at the end of the month he would jeer with everything he had. For the next eleven months he would live as if he only had one day left. Before he knew it he would be back in the camp. The horrors he thought he had escaped would be waiting there for him. Another four weeks were stretched out in front of him, but the reality was that he would be here until he turned eighteen. He could even be taken on as an employee. Perhaps the camp would keep him captive for the rest of his life. Fortunately he was too young to conceive such a notion. Ignorance truly is bliss; maybe it was for the best that he didn't consider this future. On the other hand, forewarned is forearmed. Potentially if he took steps now he could stop himself being chained to the institute until the day he died. Money he received would be drenched in the blood of innocent children. Any enjoyment would be through torturing individuals too feeble to fight back. Sickeningly they would manipulate his mind so he didn't care about these things. Over the years they would turn him into a sociopath capable of deriving pleasure from sadism. So far his brother had managed to resist their programming. But he was changing. His soul had been cracked; water was leaking through these breaches. Surely it was a matter of time before he was beating youngsters for the adrenaline rush. Hopefully he would be taken up to heaven before he could sign a contract with the camp. Wasn't it better to be dead than play a role in the deviancy of the management? There would be time for him to worry about such things in a few years. At the moment he was happy to sleep off the enormous dinner he had just consumed. He had to get some rest; tomorrow was going to be a long day.

Bryan had just about managed to clean his teeth. Exactly how he had been able to touch the communal item he didn't know. Yet he was in no hurry to earn another punishment. Twice that day he had been struck with the batons. His back ached from where he had been hit. The blow he took to his arm had yielded a large bruise. In a way he was grateful for the discomfort. Whenever he wanted to do something questionable it made him think twice. At least some good had come from these terrible experiences. Anyway, he couldn't say he hadn't deserved the first assault. What he had said to the woman was worthy of correcting. Being hit in the back was a small price to pray for being able to sort out Jordan. When he thought of the boy his heart was consumed by hatred. Never before had he had such a relationship with someone. Strangely he couldn't say it was unpleasant. When the feelings of rage entered him he felt truly alive. There was a glimmer in his eyes that had never graced him before. Could it be that a little violence was good for a man? Certainly he considered himself unchained from something. His heart, now drifting free, was ready to anchor onto more mature pursuits. His soul had aged a great deal since he had arrived. It was a shame his exterior didn't match his mind. A teenager in a prepubescent's body couldn't have a great deal of fun. If he was just a few years older he would have a smashing time at the camp. All sorts of wonderful notions flowed through his psyche. Now the concept of fighting didn't appear alien. It was a phenomenon he could freely partake in if he so desired. If he had the strength to do so he could take on the adults. Once he stole a baton he could smash them to pieces. For their abuse they would pay dearly. Nothing would stop him as he ran rampant through the premises. Before the management knew it they would have to refill every position going. Their previous employees would presumably be dumped in a ditch like rats.

He couldn't pretend that he didn't enjoy what his former friend had been through. Jordan had shown his true colours. Perhaps at no time during their association had they been on cordial terms. Clearly he saw the fellow as nothing more than a ticket to easy street. Without him doing the boy's work he would actually have to grow a brain cell. That period in his life was over. Never again would he allow himself to be manipulated in such a way. He sincerely hoped that being in the coal shed was the worst experience of his life. If it wasn't he would be grateful to supply one. Picturing beating the child to submission brought a smile to his face. More bliss adorned his countenance than ever before. His features were stretched to breaking point as his emotions ran riot in his soul. A curious thought entered his mind. It wasn't a secret that he didn't have any friends. Maybe there was a reason for this. Jordan had been using him for years. Could he have kept people away from him? Parasites do tend to defend their monopolies. In case anyone pointed out what was going on he couldn't allow Bryan to have any friends. What would he do if his tactics were revealed? That was why he had tried to fight back in the dining hall. It wasn't that he was defending himself. What he said made this crystal clear. He knew he was stuck if Bryan refused to help him in the classroom. Now he had lost the one lifeline he had. Imagining how the teachers would react to his academic freefall was powerful. He felt drunk as he walked towards his dormitory. There was no need for him to worry about bullying now. The evening entertainment had shown the camp he could fight back if necessary. Generally speaking it was the passive kids that tended to be picked on. This he knew from personal experience. Until half an hour ago he had been the passive child. That chapter in his life had been buried by the new one. Nobody was going to mess with him in the future. Anyone who tried would ride straight into a wall of spears. For the time being he satisfied himself with his fantasies.

"It's been nice meeting you," he heard someone speak as he plotted Jordan's downfall.

A thought entered the boy's mind. This could be a chance to make a new friend. Perhaps his theory that Jordan was the problem was correct. If it was he could have many new chums by the time he left camp. Having other kids to talk to would be a boon during the harsh treatment they would inevitably experience. Bryan wondered how many the adults would allow him to have. The workers surely knew they had to keep the children in small social groups. If one became too large they would have to break them up. Large cohesive units are more likely to rebel than smaller, frightened parties. Even so, it couldn't hurt him to practice sociality. He didn't want to spend the rest of his life a self-made pariah. Briefly he observed the scene in front of him. A boy was standing next to the fence that divided the two halves of the camp. They were on the male side; the other person was on the girls'. He struggled to make out who she was. Certainly he had never seen her before when he glanced across to their area. She had ginger hair that stretched down to her hips. It was far too long for a girl of ten. How she could stand having it was utterly beyond the lad. He began to grow agitated when his grew past two inches. He smiled when he saw them together. Before he came here he read about summer romances. Hopefully these two would be able to see each other again. If they were particularly lucky they would meet outside the camp. No guards or barriers would be able to stand in their way then. Bryan remained where he was as the youngster waved to the female. When he turned round they made eye contact. He smiled friendlily, although the stranger appeared wary. What would this kid do now he knew he had been talking to a girl? He could run straight to an adult. As far as he knew, nobody had said anything about talking to them through the fence. But what if that was a serious transgression? He could end up in the coal shed as well. As he studied Bryan's face he recognised where he had seen him before. This was the boy who had been fighting in the dining hall. Did he want to attack him? If he did he would have to fight back. You don't get any respect unless you put up a fight.

"Don't worry, I'm not going to cause trouble," Bryan reassured him politely. "I think you like her."

"Not so loud!" His new friend began to panic. "Don't let anyone hear us!"

"I'm Bryan," he told him as he walked over.

"Victor," the stranger told him, slightly unsure about the situation.

There was something about Bryan's demeanour that told him he shouldn't worry. If he wanted to get him in trouble he would have started hollering straight away. Instead he chose to go to the trouble of introducing himself. Why would he do that if he was out to harm him? Even so, he didn't trust anything around him. To do so was madness given the cruelty of the workers. They would beat someone for looking at them. Getting close to a stranger could only mean pain. Still, he managed to return Bryan's smile. He hadn't made many friends that day either. Perhaps he could keep the boy company. His new friend was glad he grinned warmly. Neither of them seemed to be particularly well endowed with comrades. It made sense for them to talk to each other. Victor was the same age as Bryan. Both of them looked as if they had taken more torment in one day than they had done in their whole lives. Their eyes showed great weariness as they studied each other. There were marks around Victor's neck where a worker had tried to strangle him. He had avoided this punishment from the manager of his work group. However, he had refused to brush his teeth with the shared toothbrush. As he was the first one in the queue a passing adult had decided to make an example of him. He thought he was going to die when he struggled desperately for breath. If the torturer had made a mistake he might have accidentally killed him. Never again did he want to experience something so horrible. For the rest of the month he would do whatever was asked of him without question. It was better to use a communal toothbrush than lose his life. His smile ran away from his face when he considered how close he came to death. Bryan noticed his change of mood. Terrible things had happened to him too.

"I hate this place," he told Victor, suddenly unable to make eye contact.

"So do I," his friend replied with a forlorn tone.

"What group are you in?" Bryan asked him, not wanting to go to bed just yet.

"I have to sort through rubbish," his face revealed his disgust. "They actually tell us we're helping the environment by recycling!"

"I sew bags. The man who runs it is the best person I've ever met. He doesn't beat us or anything," Bryan began to drift off as he thought of Mr Evans.

"Are you joking? The bastard running my group threw someone across the room! How did you get so lucky?"

"No, he's actually quite nice. I suppose it's the luck of the draw. Did he really throw someone across the room?" Bryan was astonished by this part of his statement.

"Yes," Victor sighed with a fearful expression. "Just thinking about it makes me sweat. He's completely round the twist."

"Boys!" Someone shouted from behind them.

Immediately Bryan turned to look at the figure. Who were they? If they were an adult there was no telling what would happen. Perhaps they would be beaten as punishment for not going straight to bed. Maybe they would simply be told off. After all, no-one had said they had to go straight to bed. They had done their teeth. Did it matter if they waited a little bit before lying down in the cramped conditions? When they saw the person they relaxed slightly. It wasn't a psychopathic guard itching to draw blood from innocent children; it was a fellow camper. From the looks of things he was around fifteen years of age. His protruding stomach was counteracted by obvious musculature in his arms. If he lost weight he could have quite a nice body. His strong, rugby player's frame appeared threatening at first. Indeed, he was quite angry when he caught them by the fence. Bryan was hoping he wouldn't be spanked for this. Twice he had received blows from batons. The adrenaline from the fight had dissipated while he had been chatting. Some more entered his system, but he didn't feel the effects. He just wanted to curl into a ball and die. Finally he had found someone who appreciates him for who he is. Now the camp was poised to torture them for daring to befriend each other. Strangely the teenager didn't call for an adult as he could have done. Victor noticed he wasn't carrying any sort of weapon on him. Neither of his arms ended in a lethal looking nightstick. He hadn't tucked it into his belt either. Lacking a weapon was a good sign. However, he could still beat them to within an inch of his life. Punches could destroy their faces before they had even hit puberty. Kicks could leave them haemorrhaging internally. Bryan knew they shouldn't celebrate yet. Being abused by a camper was worse than chastisement from a worker. At least the latter knew what would cause lasting damage. They didn't want to suffer for the rest of their lives because a brainless athlete decided to take them on himself.

"Go to bed. I don't want an adult to find you. You could get in trouble for being here," his deep voice filled the air, relieving the boys massively.

"Yes, Sir," they responded in unison, walking away from the fence.

"I don't like hitting children myself," he told them as they hurried towards their dormitories, "but I'll have to get a worker if I see you there again."

Victor hurried off to his building. Bryan, waving goodbye to him, entered his. Secretly he was over the moon. Although he was large enough to break their necks, he was a gentle giant. The older boy had not been brainwashed to enjoy sadistic behaviour. There could be no doubt that physically he was capable of disciplining them severely. However, he would not do so while an ounce of his being remained. He vowed not to accept an offer of a job when he turned eighteen. If they strove to employ him he would have to turn it down. When he considered this he knew it wouldn't be as easy as saying no. People came back year after year for a reason. Some were forced into jobs they despised for the same cause. It broke his heart to picture himself having to assault young children. No amount of money could ever erase the guilt he would feel for such things. If he was forced into a position he knew he would only have one way out. His life had gone south the moment he had arrived here as a ten year old. Only death would spare him from hating himself for all time. Yet death could be a wonderful opportunity. His faith would get him to heaven. Meeting his maker had to be better than hanging on to hurt others. If one child was spared pain through his sacrifice, he knew it would be worth it. A tear formed in his eye as he turned back to patrol between the dormitories. In a short period of time he would put his head down himself. Entering a gentle slumber was the only time he was ever at peace. At the depths of his mind he envied the two children. They had their whole lives in front of them. He knew exactly what his future would be. Unless he hit the road when he left school he would be forced to beat kids for a living. If he didn't end up in jail or dead he would have to live a lie. His work would have to remain a secret from the girl he chose to spend the rest of his life with. Not even his children would find out his secret on his deathbed. How could they cope knowing that they had been raised with the profits of slaughter? In silence he disappeared between two buildings. Part of this was his duties as a watchman. Another motive was that he couldn't bear to let anyone see him cry.

Bryan didn't want to go to sleep. Surprisingly the worst day of his life had also been the best. His back ached from where he had been struck. When he bent over to lie down, a twinge went up his whole arm. Twice he had been beaten with batons. Both times he had deserved them entirely. However, as bad as witnessing all the abuse was, the day did have several beautiful moments. Of all the horrible people in the camp, the man chosen to watch over them was wonderful. Mr Evans had put on a mask that had fooled the normally superior young man. To him he was one of the best people he had ever met. Beneath the surface he was a psychopath just waiting for an excuse to disembowel the children he hated. Jordan had been exposed as the academic parasite he was. Seeing the nineteen year old beating the lad to submission was wonderful. Somewhere out there he was suffering in the coal shed. Knowing he was alone in the darkness must be awful. Bryan couldn't pretend he hadn't brought the whole thing on himself. Freeing himself from that bully was one of his greatest achievements. He had to be right to fight him; an adult agreeing with him confirmed it. Meeting Victor had been more than pleasant. Their conversation had gone well. Perhaps the lad would have a new friend by the time he left. The fact they hadn't even been slapped by the older boy who discovered them was the icing on the cake. Most important of all, he had showed the world he was a great person. By keeping up with the teenagers in the work group he had demonstrated superiority. Nobody could doubt that he was an intellectual heavyweight. By the time he left he hoped to produce more bags than any of the other campers. Mr Evans would congratulate him as he surpassed the historical record he presumed they held for such things. He was lying face up on the cold concrete when a guard stood in the doorway.

"Lights out in two minutes," he told them with a firm tone. "You'll be chained in here, so if you need the toilet you're stuck. If there's a fire we'll come and let you out. Good night girls," he told them sneeringly.

With a laugh he closed the heavy metal door. So many people were in such cramped conditions that already the air was growing stale. Bryan barely noticed what had been said. He was happier now than he had ever been in his life. Who knew that good could come from being at an appalling place? Perhaps there was a little light at the end of the tunnel after all. All around him he could hear the sound of sniffling. Almost everyone else wished they had passed away in their sleep that morning. Death had to be better than a month of torment. What lay in front of them would scar them for life. Afterwards they would never be the same people again. Events happening around them would remain with them until the day they died. Knowing their luck they would carry their bad memories into the afterlife. Could anything be worse than floating around the camp for eternity, lamenting having ever seen the advert? Such a fate didn't bear thinking about. Within a minute many of the lads were crying openly. At first it was just the ten year olds. This was the first time most of them had endured anything truly bad. It was too much for their young minds to comprehend. Their only protection mechanism was to let the emotions pour out before they corroded their souls like acid. Within five minutes the noise was almost deafening. Even the older boys added their voices to the cacophony. None of them wanted to be there. Not even those who had been brainwashed found their experience pleasant. They wanted to be at home with their families. Although their lives weren't perfect, they were much better than this. Anything was preferential to this constant nightmare. In the other tents the other boys were also crying. When the lights went out the reality of the situation hit them. Many of them were aching from the punishments dished out to them. One or two were still bleeding from the wounds inflicted by the guards. How could they stand another hour in this place?

The air in the room was suffocating after a while. They were getting enough oxygen, but without adequate circulation it became stuffy almost immediately after closing the door. Their hearts desired an end to their torment. What had they done to deserve a month in this place? In previous lives they must have been truly awful people. What other explanation would do as to why this camp operated? The workers were very clever in their tactics. Making their victims believe they were responsible for the abuse was a great victory. Most of the boys couldn't help but believe they had brought it on themselves. At their ages it hadn't dawned on them that some people were just evil. The fault didn't lie with them; it was with those that dispensed such discipline. These monsters enjoyed tormenting children for pleasure and profit. To satisfy their lust for gold they gathered wealth on the backs of innocents. To feed their troubled souls they spilt the blood of those too feeble to fight back. Bryan was the only one in the room who didn't join in their collective sobbing. Frankly he couldn't understand why they were doing it. Of course the camp wasn't perfect. There were facets of its existence that he couldn't stand. But was it so bad that they had to pour their eyes out as a group? Here an individual could shine if they chose to. As long as they kept out of trouble there was nothing to fear. Generally he found that the best way to do this is to do what you are told when you are told to do it. Who could find fault with them if they followed this advice? He didn't seem to understand that not everyone is cut out for the work on offer. He was lucky in that sewing seemed right for him. This didn't mean that it was the correct path for everyone else. With a superior grin he closed his eyes to sleep. As the minutes went by the sobbing grew quieter. Members of the night chorus drifted off, the terrible memories the last thing they saw before they entered slumber. Secretly

Bryan couldn't wait for the next day to begin. There was a whole day of work ahead of him tomorrow. He had another chance to show the other kids just how good he was.

Clement had slightly more trouble before bed. Bryan's group had been placated by Mr Evans throughout the day. They were less likely to misbehave through fear of letting them down. Their group's manager was the worst person most of them had met in their lives. One or two of them had witnessed domestic violence in the past. This was a different sort of fear. Their siblings and parents pursued a revolting brand of discipline. It wasn't right that they had to see such things at their ages. However, the erring relatives at least had a link preventing serious harm from being caused. Their supervisor didn't have that. He only cared about them in the same way he cared about ants in the grass. If he wanted to he could kill them in a heartbeat. Perhaps he would play with them momentarily. Even if he did his curiosity would soon wane. Before they knew it they would feel his boots crushing them into the soil. Behind his abusive countenance must have been a truly wicked heart. Clement wondered how he viewed the children as he sat in the dormitory. Did he look upon them as human beings? He couldn't; if he did he wouldn't be able to beat them so savagely. Yet if he saw them as animals he would at least know harming such things is incorrect. Either he didn't agree with this or he saw them in the same light as pebbles. Who cared if a stone shattered after being thrown? It was of no consequence to anything in his life. Likewise, would his feathers be ruffled if one of his campers was killed in cold blood? His older brother would be able to answer that. Their manager's concern would only be raised if profits were reduced. The management would freely allow a slaughter if it wouldn't impact the production of stock. If they could bring the corpses back to life afterwards they could kill the kids as many times as they wanted. It was an unspoken truth that murders had occurred in the camp's history. Not even the older boys talked about it openly, though. They preferred to dwell under the delusion that the guards would stop when the beatings had gone too far.

"I'm sorry for what I said," he heard his sibling speaking.

When he raised his head Adam was standing there, his eyes glistening. Graham had not yet returned from the side of the building. Had he gone too far with his retribution? Maybe a single blow would have been enough to ward off further confrontations. This train of thought derailed when he saw his brother. He seemed genuinely apologetic for the threats he had made. But what consolation was that? If he hadn't meant it why had he said it? For the first time in his life Adam had made him truly fear for his safety. This was more than just young men disagreeing. It would be obvious to the worst dullard that he had been deadly serious. If he hadn't brushed his teeth with the horrible utensil he would have been punched. Ultimately he could do nothing more than stare into his brothers eyes. The look on his face told Adam exactly what he needed to know. Could the ten year old forgive him for what he had said? He had been given a minor position by the guards. If he lost control he would be removed from it and punished. Being stripped of a role was a terrible fate. When he was eleven he had seen a thirteen year old in his current position almost cause a riot. Because he refused to rule with an iron fist the guards had to crush the petty uprising. As a result he was publically beaten. The workers had shouted all sorts of horrible things as he was beaten before the whole camp population. After his spanking he had been locked in the coal shed for three days. At the end of it he was a nervous wreck. Adam had wondered if sorting through rubbish on a daily basis was enough of a punishment. He is still around today, a damaged teenager that badly needed to escape the jaws of the organisation. Adam had no ambition to let his life follow the same path. Was Clement old enough to understand why he had to make such a horrible threat? He was exhausted after the day's trials. All he wanted was to go to sleep. It would be nice if he could do so on cordial terms with his relative.

"Please hear me out," he implored his brother with scarlet eyes. "I have a job to do. You have to listen to me or I have to punish you. I can't give you special treatment because you're family."

Clement did listen to what he had to say. Frankly he didn't think much of his explanation. All day he had done nothing but give him special treatment. It was rather foolish to think it wouldn't be the same just because he was on duty. He could have at least arranged for him to use the brush first. That way it wouldn't matter if it was a shared possession. His teeth would be the first one it touched. Yet he couldn't even do that. Why should he forgive him? Clement didn't want to think about the whole affair now. His head was thumping through terror and fatigue. Perhaps if he lived through the night he would be in a better position to think. Adam remained where he was, inspecting the boy's face. Any sign things were warming between them would satisfy his itch. The boy did give him a weak smile. While it didn't reach his eyes, the older male could tell himself whatever he wanted. With a grin of his own the teenager went over to his own spot. Already the smell of sweat was making the air incredibly unpleasant. It was a terrible shame that the shack lacked windows. Only the open door provided a small breeze to relieve their suffering. Clement wasn't looking forwards to going to sleep. Graham would surely use his slumber as an opportunity to cause him harm. If he dropped off he could wake up being hit in the face. Perhaps the fatter boy would strangle the life out of him. Such a thought left his eyes as wide as caverns. Picturing what would happen to him was almost too much for his mind to deal with. While he was conscious he could at least try to take evasive action. But what could he do while he was asleep? If he lost consciousness he would be a sitting duck for anyone that wants to have a go. Taking on a fourteen year old would be difficult enough in ideal conditions. How could he do it when the odds were against him? His brother had told him previously that it would be pitch black. In such conditions he wouldn't stand a chance.

"I'll be over here if you need me," he waved to him before sitting down close by.

Clement lay on his back, not wanting to go to sleep for fear of what might happen to him. He turned his head when Graham entered. Briefly he considered leaping to his feet. The boy looked rather heavy on his feet as he waddled through the doorway. The look he gave the lad made it clear retribution for the attack was inevitable. Swallowing heavily, the boy glanced over at his brother. Naturally if he needed to he could call Adam over. Yet he didn't want to until it became necessary. Perhaps he wouldn't have to even if it came to a fight. Previously he had defeated the teenager using just his four limbs. Graham didn't take his glaring eyes off the youngster as he passed. Touching his genatalia through his pants, he carried on walking straight past him. Clement had no idea what was going on as his enemy looked around the room. There was just enough space for him to squeeze his bulk in to rest between two boys at the far end of the room. Immediately a smile broke out on his face. Could he have defeated the foe? It seemed he was determined to avoid him. Finally he might have accomplished something in the camp by himself. He had shown the world that he didn't need his sibling to do everything for him. That was probably for the best in the long run. Adam was more than willing to do anything within his power. Almost certainly he would wrestle a crocodile if one leapt at him. Unfortunately the kid was smart enough to know that this wasn't the way to do things. Unless he could become self-reliant he would never learn to cope with the horrors that faced him. What would he do when his brother became too old to attend? He would be on his own with no skills whatsoever. That must be how pets feel when they are abandoned by their owners. Lying on his back with his eyes open, he listened as a guard told them they would be locked in overnight. Somehow that comforted and worried him at the same time. He was relieved that nothing could get in to harm them. However, there was plenty of danger inside. Angry, frightened boys competing for space was bound to generate friction. Sadly the air was as explosive as gunpowder. One young man rubbing another up the wrong way could lead to a mass brawl. It didn't occur to him that they would be in total darkness. When Adam told him this before he simply presumed it would be akin to a starless sky. Yet they wouldn't even be able to make out the outlines of objects. If someone waved a hand a centimetre from their faces they would be none the wiser. When the lights did go out a few children began crying. Their wails were deliberately muffled, as if they didn't want anyone to hear them sobbing. Clement's heart almost broke when he realised why. It wasn't just so the others wouldn't consider them weak. They didn't dare make a sound in case an adult entered to beat them for it. Was this the effect the guards had on them? These boys were crying their eyes out. They wanted to go home where they felt safe. These individuals wanted a cuddle from their mothers. Surely that would make everything alright. It was as if they could go on as long as they could see one friendly familiar face.

"Stop crying you babies!" An older boy shouted from close to the entrance.

"Leave them alone!" Someone else bellowed, incensed by the callous remark.

Clement didn't know what to make of the whole situation. The sudden loss of light left him a little confused. For some reason he had expected the transition to occur slowly. Exactly why this was the case he didn't know. Like everything else around him it was a crude and nasty process. Closing his eyes, he prayed for something to come along to spare them further torment. It didn't have to be anything big as long as they could escape from the clutches of the guards. Strangely the youth no longer felt tired. Perhaps it was the excitement of the unfamiliar surroundings. Maybe it was the anxiety for the day that lay ahead of them. Either way, he seemed as fully charged as ever. As he lay there worrying he found himself thinking of their parents. Perhaps the biggest irony was that they were probably picturing the boys having the times of their lives away from home. Every year when Adam came home he had pretended to be happy. For weeks he had gone on about the fun things he had done. It dawned on the lad that these stories were all lies. But why had he told them? Clement couldn't understand why he hadn't been honest about the camp. If he had come clean about the whole thing they might have gone to the police. Come to think of it, why hadn't anyone done that? This establishment must have been running for years. How could nobody have breathed a word about what was going on? It wasn't a case of children not being believed. If this was true there would still be rumours of what was going on. Playground stories tend to be exaggerated, but there is often a kernel of truth at their core. He hadn't even heard one of these tales. What would cause everyone to remain silent when a single word could change the outcome of their lives? He had yet to learn to truth of this. It was a secret that would make him keep his mouth shut as well. This horror lay in store for him for when the so-called holiday drew to a close. After a surprisingly short period of time the boy did manage to sleep. His subconscious mind couldn't bear to keep him in the awful place a moment longer. Thus it came as no surprise when he dozed off for the night. Unfortunately the depths of his psyche couldn't protect him from the torment the following day had in store for him.

Part two

Chapter five

Nobody knew what was happening when the building was suddenly flooded with light. Their slumber made them feel as if only a few seconds had passed. Sadly this was not the case. The refreshing sleep had gone on for as long as the guards were willing to allow it. Now the campers had received eight hours it was time for them to eat and return to work. Adam wondered if anyone ever got used to being bathed in light so unexpectedly. Even at the end of the month it came as a great shock to the system. That was probably why the guards used it. There were other means of rousing them that were just as effective. However, this system caused them discomfort when it was used. As long as it satisfied that criterion it could be two elephants banging together symbols with their trunks. Only two things mattered to the management; sadism and profits. He sat upright, wiping the sleep from his eyes. Looking across at his younger brother, the lad looked reasonably well rested. Ironically he had slept less than he would do at home. Their mother tucked him in at nine, returning at half seven so she could serve him his breakfast. It was such a shame they were separated from her. Such a lovely woman would take on all the guards with her bare hands if her precious sons could escape into the woods. Alas, she was nowhere in sight. They couldn't even receive a hug or be told that everything would be alright. Waking up in these squalid conditions was enough to make the teenager wonder if anything would ever be alright again. It was hard to see how he could survive coming here for another five years. That said, after the first month he thought the same thing about the following year. In one way he was a prisoner sentenced to spend his adolescence in misery. He wished the same lunatic judge hadn't got to his brother as well. It wasn't right that any of them had to go through this. Even so, he felt particularly outraged when he viewed his apprehensive brother wipe a tear from his eyes. As he studied the ten year old he heard the chain on the outside door being removed. In less than twenty seconds it fell to the floor. Immediately afterwards the door was flung open. Standing behind was it was the nineteen year old worker who dealt with Jordan the previous evening.

"Hello girls," the worker told them with malice in his voice. "I hope you all slept well. Get up, breakfast's in thirty minutes."

Quickly the boys began to get up from the cold concrete floor. The air had become choking overnight. Flooding the room with mustard gas wouldn't make much of a difference. While asleep they had sweat buckets, turning the air into a pungent cocktail of different odours. More than one sported wet trousers. These ten year olds did their best to hide where they had lost control of their bladders. Seeing others laugh at them inspired a deep seething within Clement. How could they be so cruel? These older boys must have wet themselves during nightmares when they were younger. Didn't they take enough abuse from the people running this place? Why did they have to pour petrol onto the fire? If they banded together they could bring about change. Instead they kept themselves in hell because they couldn't be bothered to get along. A seventeen year old walked out of the building, returning to announce that they had half an hour to brush their teeth. Thinking of the horrible instrument made the child shudder. That thought was perhaps worse than the danger of being spanked. At least he had some control over punishments. If he did what he was told he wouldn't be struck. However, that toothbrush would not change if he lived a perfect life. He would still feel its worn bristles and taste a thousand mouths before him. How anyone could take such an assault on the mind he didn't know. Merely thinking about it was enough to make him gag. What amazed him was how quickly the camp got to work attacking its inmates. He had only been awake for two minutes yet he was fearful for his life. Who knew what germs were lurking on it? Not all of the campers looked in the best of health. Coughs and sneezes can infect whole rooms of people; toothbrushes surely are more dangerous. By the end of the month the guards would have to fill wheelbarrows to transport the used tissues. That was, of course, if the management cared enough to provide them. Perhaps it would leave them covered in their own waste. Why did they care if it didn't influence their own profitability? Provided their products weren't soiled they would house the camp in a sewer.

"Alright?" Adam asked his brother, suddenly appearing beside him.

"Sure," Clement grumbled, as sleepy as it was humanly possibly to be.

Somehow he was lucid enough to stagger out of the building. Boys from the other two dormitories were doing the same. Not one of them looked happy to be awake. How could they when they knew what lay ahead of them? Hopefully today there would be less violence than before. After the previous day's torment they all knew what to do when it came to work. They could crack on and forget all about the horrors that lurked behind every corner. Slowly he made his way towards the tooth cleaning stations. They reminded of something he had seen in a Victorian painting; dirty people living in poverty pumping water from a communal outside tap. The only difference was that in his case the outlet seemed rather modern. It was by no means clean, but it wasn't smeared with faeces. People looked at the kid as he hobbled along. To them he must have resembled the young boy he had walked behind on the way to the camp. That fellow had retreated into his own mind as a way of dealing with the stress. Presumably he was even worse, given the fact he was dragging his feet. More than once he almost ended up lying flat on his face. Adam wasn't on duty in the mornings, so a black haired teenager handed him the shared toothbrush. Perhaps it was a blessing that he wasn't too in touch with reality. As he was not thinking clearly he wasn't worried about the germs that would soon inhabit his mouth. The older male gave him a slightly concerned look as he squeezed a globe of paste onto the old bristles. Dipping it into a glass of water, he quickly began scrubbing. Behind him a few others had already began to gather. By the time he had finished, the whole dormitory was queuing up to attend to their oral hygiene. Starting the day in this fashion was totally alien to the lad. Normally he was greeted by breakfast, followed by a cuddle from his mother. Sadly there were no hugs coming for a long time. The only shot he had at getting one was if his sibling was willing. Knowing him, he would refuse to save face in front of the others.

"Are you okay?" The older boy asked him as he handed the toothbrush back.

"Fine," he replied solemnly, spitting into a basin at his feet.

Wondering where to go next, he began to walk towards the dining hall. Where else could he go? The dormitory would yield nothing of interest to him. Certainly he wasn't going to go to the labour shacks yet. The less time he spent in there the better. That left the cafeteria the only viable destination. Fortunately by this point he had woken a little. Lucid enough to start to truly notice what was going on around him, he studied the faces passing by. One or two of them he recognised from yesterday. However, what snapped him out of the stupor was seeing the boy who had been fighting the previous evening. Bryan jogged merrily towards the same place as him. He looked perfectly content to be starting a new day in this prison. So great was his bemusement that he was stopped dead in his tracks. What was he so cheerful about? Did he know something they didn't? Swiftly he continued his journey. The smell of breakfast hit him as soon as he entered the building. Although it was summer, the sun hadn't yet made the morning air comfortably warm. By comparison the building was hot enough to fry an egg. Smelling the food made his mouth salivate. Swallowing it, he sat down in roughly the same place he occupied before. How much time had passed since the guard had unlocked the door? It had to have been a good five minutes. That meant he would have to wait a long time before the plates would start coming through the doors at the back. Even so, it was nice just to sit somewhere quiet. As he was alone with his thoughts he wondered what had happened to Jordan. That poor boy had been left in the coal shed overnight. Amazingly as he tried to imagine these conditions he saw a worker dragging him into the building. His eyes were scarlet from where he had been crying. His previously spotless uniform was covered in black dust. This horrible substance had not spared a single surface. His skin was barely visible beneath it; his face made him look as if he just emerged from a mine. It would have been comical if he didn't have to be held up by the adult.

"I hope you learnt your lesson," the woman escorting him spoke loudly. "If you try to fight back again you'll be in there for a week!"

"Yes, miss," he replied with a wavering tone.

What horrors had be been subjected to while in there? He had no doubt that the disused cell would be crawling with insects. Maybe a rat or two had taken up residence in the dilapidated construct. Being alone with these things must have been terrible. All night he would have stayed awake, listening to them moving in the darkness. The fact he hadn't lost his mind completely had to be an act of divine will. Clement followed him closely as he was helped into a seat. His face was bruised heavily from the onslaught he had taken the previous night. Quite a lot of it was from the blows the guards had dished out. However, a great deal was his sparring partner's handiwork. Bryan had done that to him. This was the same boy who had laughed when his victim had been beaten by the guard. Remembering he was in the same room, he turned to see what the lad was doing. With one hand over his mouth he was doing his best to suppress laughter. How anyone could be so cold he had no idea. Scowling at the lad, he watched as the female walked away from him. Breathing seemed to be a considerable effort. With each inhalation he grimaced slightly. His bruised chest must have been giving him no end of discomfort. A few more campers walked into the building. These older boys took one look at Jordan before starting to laugh. Clement frowned at them as well. What was it about this place that made them so sadistic? Could it be that children tend to mirror the behaviour of the adults in their lives? It wouldn't surprise him if this was true. These kids were probably perfectly normal in the outside world. When they come here for the month they found themselves unknowingly copying the workers.

"What was it like in there?!" Bryan shouted to his victim once the female was out of earshot.

"Awful," the lad managed to whimper in response.

"Leave him alone!" Clement shouted, standing as the rage began to bubble through to the surface. "What's wrong with you?!"

"I think you'll find he deserved everything he got," Bryan flippantly told him, throwing a dark stare in his direction.

The boy feared where this was going. If he wasn't careful he would end up in a fight himself. Perhaps they would throw the pair of them into the coal shed. Picturing such a punishment was enough to make him sit down. How could he risk aggravating the adults when they were desperate for an excuse to draw blood? He might as well throw himself amidst a den of wild lions. Still, he couldn't help but loathe Bryan. Hadn't he scored enough of a victory yet? When would he call it a day? Would he desecrate his foe's corpse? Growing up in a loving home, these feelings of rage were new to him. Naturally he had been angry with others before, but this was the first time he wanted to kill someone. If he could he would ram the boy's head through the glass screen of a television set. Picturing such a fate befalling the male was strangely satisfying. At this point he realised why Bryan was being so cruel. By extension he was aware why people do bad things. The secret is that it's fun. Such a revelation made him want to run to the most remote location he could find. What hope was there for humanity if torturing others was pleasurable? No wonder society was crumbling as time marched on. In another few generations they might be watching people fight to the death for entertainment. He sat in silence until breakfast arrived. All around him people were talking but he barely heard a word they said. Clement merely stared at the same patch of concrete for the best part of half an hour. Adam had gone to sit by his friends. Nearby he was telling Rory some sort of crude joke. Although he was certainly the more moral person, Bryan was definitely having more fun. Every so often he glanced at the youth, seeing him talking to someone. How he wished he had someone to chat with. With a sigh he resigned himself to solitude as the first plates were carried from the kitchen.

"I can't believe we didn't meet sooner," Bryan told the boy he met last night.
"Me too," the lad responded swiftly. "We have so much in common."
Truly the pair seemed as if they had been made for each other. As they chatted they found they enjoyed the same things. In terms of interests they were almost identical. While their exteriors differed, in minds they were incredibly similar. This was why the juvenile had been so happy when Clement had seen him. As soon as he woke up he wondered how he was going to find his associate again. Although they weren't in the same dormitories, they could bond over meals. The guards didn't care if work groups mingled while eating. As long as order was maintained they could arrange themselves according to the ages of their dogs' aunts. Both of them enjoyed the same detective stories. Time flew by as they discussed the latest instalments of the novels. For the first time he felt himself blend in with the others. No longer was he sitting on his own, waiting for the time to pass. If someone looked at them they would see two children talking pleasantly. Focusing on these things prevented their minds from panicking over the day ahead. Yesterday they had only worked in the afternoon. Now they had a full day ahead of them, punctuated only by a meal. How they would get through that is anyone's guess. What they did was as boring as anything, even if approached with the right attitude. By the time lunch was served they would be pulling their hair out. A worker placed a fried breakfast in front of Bryan. The sudden movement before his eyes made him jump a little. When he woke up his back was aching a little. His arm had a bruise larger than any he had experienced in the past. For a few minutes he was a bit worried. It wasn't a pretty sight; someone actually gasped when they saw it. However, it wasn't going to kill him. His arm couldn't be broken or he wouldn't be able to move it.

"Thank you," he told the woman as she placed another plate down for the person next to him.
Smelling the food was lovely. It reminded him just how hungry he was. Tempted to pick at it, he managed to wait as plastic cutlery was handed out. What was the point of risking punishment? The management obviously believed the children should be provided with knives and forks. Who could guarantee him that they wouldn't hit him for using his fingers? Probably this was his paranoia, but he feared the batons enough to keep his urges under control. Victor noticed that the smile had run from the lad's face. Immediately he attempted to restore it to its rightful position. A massive friendly grin caused Bryan's lips to curl upwards once more. His friend was happy as well. Last night he met a nice girl the same age as him. She seemed interested in him, even if they had only spoken for ten

minutes. Hopefully he could attract her attention again tonight. He was grateful that his new friend hadn't told anyone what he had been doing. They were lucky the older boy had found them rather than a guard. If an adult had come across them they would have got a baton across their rear ends. Wincing from the thought, he began to speak about the latest book he had read. The other male listened, glancing over his shoulder at Clement. What was his problem? Why was he just staring at them? It was sad that he didn't have any friends. Although judging by the way he had spoken to him earlier, it was perhaps not surprising he was alone. Who would want to spend their time with someone who shouts across the room in such a way? There was a very good reason why he had taunted Jordan. That parasite had sucked his blood for years. Was Clement going to chastise a bird for ridding itself of a tick? Jordan deserved everything he had got. Frankly he was getting off lightly by Bryan's standards. If it was up to him he would have left him in the coal shed for the rest of the month.

"It was alright," he replied, starting his own evaluation of the book. "I've only got halfway through it so don't ruin the ending for me," he added quickly, not wanting to lose the element of surprise.

"You seen a little distracted," Victor told him, finishing the last of his breakfast.

"I'm sorry, I don't like that kid staring at us," he replied, pointing at Clement as if he was a voyeur in the bushes.

"Do you fancy me or something?" He asked the onlooker, his face harder than a diamond.

"What? Why can't you keep your mouth shut?" Adam's brother responded tiredly.

A fight was the last thing he wanted. Seeing no end in sight, he was wondering how he was going to flee the camp. It was a coincidence that his eyes had become fixated on the pair. Unfortunately he hadn't come up with an escape plan that would work. Indeed, absconding seemed impossible in his opinion. You can't hop the fence; you would be cut to pieces by the razor wire. Regrettably getting away from the nightmare was something he simply couldn't do. He was stuck in it until time decided he had endured enough torment. Only then would the camp regurgitate him into the real world. By then there might only be a shell remaining. Everything that made him unique could be stripped away by the brutal regime. A potentially wonderful life would be snatched from him. Greatness could be replaced with utter insanity. Dealing with that was difficult enough. He wasn't going to take abuse from this kid. Standing, he gave him the worst look he had ever fired at someone. Adam turned his head, his mouth hanging open when he saw the look on his brother's face. It was as if a monster had replaced his sibling. The sweet young man had been replaced by a creature of darkness. In a way he was absolutely correct. This place had plucked his innocence from him. While he was still a child, he would never again be the same person. Adam followed his line of sight back to Bryan. Was this lad causing problems again? How could someone who looked so nice stir up so much bad feeling? He wasn't going to get away with it. If he wanted to attack his brother he would have to go through him. Immediately he threw himself to his feet. In Bryan's heart hatred burnt for Clement. Everything that had happened had turned his emotions against the boy who had been staring at him. The two boys walked towards each other, hatred burning in their eyes. Adam watched cautiously, knowing that the guards would punish them both. An urge to protect his brother rose within him. Some little kid wasn't going to harm his sibling. Rory pounded the table eagerly in anticipation of the brawl. Clement didn't care if he spent a week in the coal shed. All he wanted was to teach the smug brat a little respect. One of the adults handing out glasses of water studied the pair. Bryan had struck her as controlled in the past. The other lad hadn't given anyone any problems so far. He was normally so quiet you could forget he was around. While this was true, Bryan wasn't going to get away with everything he had done. His attitude would change or things would get very ugly very fast.

"What is your problem?" He asked Clement, his voice as saturated with hate as the guards'.

"Me? You insulted him after everything he's been through!" The lad screamed while pointing at Jordan.

"Calm down," Adam warned him, feeling the atmosphere becoming increasingly charged.

"I deserve to! Do you have any idea what he did to me?!"

"Whatever he's done, it doesn't give you the right to attack him!"

Bryan couldn't control himself any longer. Until yesterday he hadn't been in a fight in his life. Hitting his bully had opened a door within his soul. This passageway spewed nothing but bloodlust into his soul. Something was awakened within him when he rained blows down on his target. Whatever he tried he could not excise the urge to take others on. The adrenaline rush had already become an addiction. Since he couldn't spill any more of Jordan's blood, this boy would have to do. Clement's mind was split in half as he studied his opponent up close. Logically it was a bad idea as he was smaller than his opponent. But he refused to allow himself to be intimidated. Deep within his soul he knew what he was doing was right. It might not be the best option, but it was justifiable. This puerile prepubescent had no manners whatsoever. Peering behind the lad, Victor looked ready to step in. Evidently it would become two against two. Even so, this had to be done. There was a limit to what he was prepared to take. If he didn't do something he would have to look at the arrogant smile every day until he died. His psyche would always taunt him with it. Not a day would go by where he didn't ask himself why he stood back and let him get away with such cruelty. If the boy wanted to use his sharp tongue he was welcome to. He couldn't complain when Clement turned round and yanked it from his cavernous mouth.

Part of him couldn't believe what he was doing. Regardless of how much he despised Bryan, he was a living being. His mind wandered to the fight with Graham the previous evening. He had turned into a wild beast with murder on his mind. This was totally out of character. Was this what the camp did to people? Before he came he had been a strong pacifist. By the time he left he could be a homicidal maniac. This part of his psyche was eclipsed by the rest. Adrenaline flooded his system as he prepared for a fight. Adam studied his sibling with amazement. Was this the same boy who complained whenever a spider was killed? How could he have degenerated so quickly? From the look on his face he was baying for his enemy's blood. Honestly he had no idea what to do. This could be the start of independence for him. If he proved to himself that he didn't need help he could break his reliance on the older boy. Even so, his protection instincts compelled him to step in. By now the boys were standing close enough to strike. The guards looked on, waiting for them to injure each other. They would only interfere when one of them got the upper hand. Until then they were content for the lads to tear chunks out of each other. Most eyes in the room were on the pair. It was always the same when conflict broke out. These vultures couldn't wait for blood to spill. In the camp it was just about the only fun they got. They didn't even have a ball to kick around when they weren't working. With impatience they waited for the first blow to be launched. Ironically the older boys were the ones who didn't get into scraps. Most of them knew it wouldn't do them any good. All they wanted was a nice easy month before they could go home. The younger boys had to learn the hard way that fist fights were harmful to all concerned. It was unusual to have such young looking juveniles take aggressive action. Neither of them was as large as their peers. People of their stature normally do everything they can to blend into their surroundings. However, these boys were anything but timid. Something big must have happened to cause them to confront each other in such a way.

"Are you going to apologise for bullying him?" Clement asked, nodding in Jordan's direction.

"He bullied me!" Bryan screamed, slapping the other boy across the face in blind rage.

Clement wasn't going to stand for this. He barely felt the blow as adrenaline drove him to full power. One of his hands curled into a fist. As hard as he could he flung it at the boy's nose. When it struck there was a strange squelching sound. The cocky lad staggered backwards in shock. Before he could recover he was kicked in the abdomen. Adam's mouth hung open as he watched the events unfold. How was his brother so strong? He didn't know what to make of the scene. Again Clement hit him in the face. This time the lad fought back. A punch of his own exploded across his target's face. There were huge smiles on the face of the workers. It was almost cute how they were trying to batter each other to death. The force of the blow knocked Clement for six. This hadn't been a good idea. Even so, he couldn't back down now. Everyone would think he was a coward if he walked away. Only by struggling on could he maintain some semblance of respect. Bryan had developed a taste for violence. Last night had been wonderful as he pounded Jordan to the ground. The familiar adrenaline rush led him to shove his opponent backwards. Clement did his utmost to remain upright. But what could he do? At first he staggered before turning and falling flat on his face. When he tumbled downwards he heard Bryan cheering. Did this mean he had won? Some of the other campers booed when they realised it was over. They were hoping for far more of a show. Remarkably there wasn't any reason why he couldn't continue. Although his face was grazed, he wasn't really injured. As he tried to stand he heard someone rushing over to him. In his mind he started to panic. That had to be the guards ready to spank him for fighting. Any moment now he would feel a baton slamming into his flesh. For some time to come he would feel a dull ache, reminding him not to brawl again. However, the feet weren't coming towards him. Instead they reached the lad who had sent him reeling. It had to be his brother. Who else would come to rescue him?

"Come here you little runt!" He heard him shout.

Bryan didn't know what to do. The thirteen year old caught hold of his victim by the scruff of his knack. The crowd suddenly cheered as they realised the action was only just beginning. How dare this little boy attack his sibling? Rage evaporated from his pores as he punched the kid in the stomach. If he wanted to fight anyone he could fight him. Clement managed to turn over to study the scene. It wasn't exactly fair that Adam was bigger than Bryan. Still, he wasn't going to pretend he didn't enjoy him springing to his defence. He had never seen such fury in the teenager before. It was much stronger than the previous evening when he had threatened him into using the toothbrush. This time there was a real danger that he would grind someone's skull into the dirt. Bryan threw a useless punch towards Adam's shoulder. So weak was the force that the older boy didn't even flinch. With his knee he sent the boy flying backwards. The brothers watched as the pest slammed into the table behind him. By now the guards had started to walk over. It was time for everyone to have one more glass of water before the morning shift. They hoped there wouldn't be any further trouble. Really their fears were misgivings. The ten year old didn't want to continue the brawl. Against Clement he had emerged victorious. However, the teenager was unstoppable. How could he take on such a strong opponent? He hadn't even hit puberty yet. Luckily for him he knew when to call it a day. Adam helped his relative up from the ground. There was still a great deal of shock in the older lad's eyes. No part of him could believe that the battle had occurred in the first place. His brother was the last person who would get involved in a skirmish.

"What's going on here?" The female guards who had brought Jordan in asked.

"Nothing, Miss," Adam started to speak. "I just had to take care of some business."

"Really?" She wondered, studying the two ten year olds carefully. "Is there going to be any more fighting?"

"No, Miss," Clement replied respectfully as he got to his feet.

"That's goof to hear," she stated with a tone that made it clear she would spank them if they continued.

"He started it," Bryan told her, his fists clenched at his sides.

"Is there going to be any more fighting?!" She raised her voice at the angry boy.

"That depends on whether or not he'll stop being weird," Bryan choked out, his heart pounding in his head.

"If there is any more fighting you'll get my baton across your backside," she warned him firmly. "All three of you; drink another glass of water and sit down!"

Clement didn't need to be told twice. Bryan stared at him as he ambled over to where his brother had been sitting. They did so in silence, not willing to risk saying something that could be misinterpreted. A glare from the woman caused the bitter male to take a seat. He gripped the glass of water in front of him so tightly his knuckles turned white. There was no reason why he should end up in trouble. That kid obviously had something wrong with him. He had been minding his own business. Why should he be the one to bear the brunt of the woman's discontent? Nothing about the camp made sense. At least he had Victor to vent his frustrations to. In silence he seethed, not taking his eyes off the brothers for one second. This was not the last they would hear of the matter. There would be other fights. First of all he would get the younger brat. Once he had destroyed him he would leave his brother begging for mercy. That would be his purpose while he was in the camp. By the time they left they would be running from him. His new friend didn't know whether it was worth continuing the relationship. This boy was clearly very troubled. Two days in a row he had got into a fight. His mother had warned him not to associate himself with such people. Now he could see she was right. If he wasn't careful he would end up a yob.

"I can't believe you did that," Adam told Clement with a bemused tone. "You should have just ignored him."

"Yes, you wouldn't have needed your brother to come charging in to help you," Rory joked at the child's expense.

"I didn't need him!" The ten year old almost shouted to drown out the sniggers. "I was about to get up anyway."

"He's never going to learn to defend himself if you fight his battles for him," another teenager intruded his way into the conversation.

"You're right," Adam whispered, staring down at the empty plate in front of him. "You have to be more careful," he told the boy sadly. "You could have been beaten for that."

"I had everything under control!" Clement insisted through gritted teeth. "I wouldn't let him get the better of me."

Suddenly he wondered for whose benefit he had made that last comment. Did he have everything under his control? He defeated Graham last night. That lad was several years older than Bryan. How could he take on a fourteen year old but not someone his own age? His enemy was not the only one left a little confused by the incident. Hopefully there would be another brawl. If it was away from the adults he would not hold back. Everything he had he would fire at the youngster. By the time it was over there would be blood spilt. Currently he found himself a little hesitant in thanking Adam for what he had done. Clearly his heart had been in the right place. But Rory was right; he would never become independent if there was always a guiding hand around. The best thing he could have done is leave the pair alone. That would have allowed Clement to get up. Once he was on his feet he could do to Bryan what he had done to Graham. After all, the fat boy had been compelled to find a new place to sleep once he had sorted him out. There was every chance he would have made his adversary pay for the blows he had launched against him. Glancing at Bryan, he saw that blood was flowing from one of his nostrils. He quickly looked aware, his glare far too much for him to bear. There was nothing to do but drink and wait for the shift to start. Picturing himself working sent shivers down his spine. Their horrific supervisor made him more scared than he had ever been in his life. What if he messed up one of the photo frames? He could be strangled by one of his powerful hands. Such a thought made him tremble slightly. The boy wanted time to slow down to delay the start of the nightmare. Perhaps if he concentrated hard enough he could make the seconds stop ticking by. This meal could drag on for eternity; the hours spent working permanently kept at bay. Unfortunately this was not an option for a mortal being. Before he knew it he was filing back into the work building. Dread almost made him retch as he sat at his desk. Evidently the camp still had a full tank of terror to pump into its prisoners. The sight of the psychopath in charge of the group was enough to make his heart pound. However, the worst factor was the feeling that the nightmare was just warming up. He couldn't shake the feeling that what he had seen was only the beginning.

Bryan's fear dissipated the moment he set eyes on Mr Evans. How could anyone retain such a horrid feeling in the presence of someone so nice? In seconds he found himself reverting to his usual polite self. Feelings of rage were soon forgotten as he found the station he had been working at yesterday. Those around him were also eager to get started. Unlike the other staff members they viewed him as a decent human being. If they knew the truth they would be horrified. Certainly Bryan had no idea that lurking behind his nonchalant grin was the heart of a psychopath. He wouldn't hesitate to kill them if they turned against him. The only difference between him and the other adults was that he kept his rage veiled. He despised the kids he oversaw with all his heart. As far as he was concerned they were the scum of the earth. Prior to their arrival he had set out enough fabric for ten bags at every table. That should keep them busy for around ninety minutes. The children entering the shack saw a warm, welcoming figure. Behind his mask he was seething. It was as if the youngsters emitted a chemical that made him see red. Fortunately he was smart enough to keep control of himself. If he unleashed the anger he held within his heart he would slaughter everyone in sight. That simply wouldn't do in the eyes of the management. Who would complete the orders for bags if the slaves were being buried in open graves? They would sack him on the spot for misconduct. Even so, he found happiness in picturing a cavern being filled with their corpses. Such a powerful emotion filtered through his system in seconds. It contributed to the look of cheer adorning his pseudo-pleasant face.

"Good morning," he announced with a powerful voice, "I hope you all have a good night's sleep. Today you will be making bags again. I know smart people like you will remember the steps I showed you from yesterday. Just in case you can't, raise your hand once you start and I will send one of the senior campers to demonstrate it again."

As he studied the crowd he saw nothing but smiles. These kids had fallen for his act perfectly. Now they were under the impression that his building was a safe haven from the dangers of the premises. Nothing could be further from the truth. If they rubbed him up the wrong way he would make sure they suffered the consequences. It never ceased to amaze him how easily he could put people under his spell. There must be something about his demeanour that made people pour their souls out for him. Wiping his feet on their very beings, he had burrowed into their hearts. For the rest of their lives they would remember the nice man somehow working in the worst place imaginable. The true nature of his actions was a secret he would evidently take to his grave. A quick glimpse at his voice informed him of their early arrival. There were still five minutes to go before they were supposed to start the morning shift. In the other work groups they would do their best to turn up dead on time. A minute early was sixty seconds of abuse they could avoid. Being one minute late was grounds for a hard slap across the face. However, his wards had decided it was in their best interests to get started as soon as possible. With full stomachs they had wandered to his cabin. Who was he to stop them from beginning early? If they wanted to work he wasn't going to crush their ambition. Quickly he announced how long they would have to work before lunch. Four hours stood between them and their next meal. Some looked disappointed when they realised they didn't have longer to work. To them they were perfectly safe where they were. Surely a man of Mr Evans' calibre wouldn't let the baton-wielding guards anywhere near them. If they thought that they were more stupid than they looked. If he was so nice why wasn't he working somewhere else? Why wouldn't he run a mile from this place when he realised what was happening. Most importantly, why hadn't he tried to help them escape? These questions would have dawned on them the night before if he hadn't left them spellbound. Another word told the kids to crack on with the task at hand. Immediately they began to finish the bags they had started the previous evening. When he gazed at them he saw nothing but happiness. These youths were content to their core. This is exactly what he wanted. Prisoners who are satisfied in their surroundings don't cause trouble. As long as he could extend his tendrils into their brains he wouldn't have any trouble. The same couldn't be said for the other groups. Their leaders were as harsh as a hundred Antarctic winters hitting at once. It wouldn't be long before the children became desperate enough to try to flee.

Bryan was exceedingly joyful as he began work on a bag. Having finished the one already there promptly, he was one of the few who had started a fresh one. So far he had excelled at sewing. If he could keep his productivity up there wouldn't be any problems. He would sail through the month if he continued to take pleasure from the labour. Few others around him enjoyed what they did. They were glad they weren't given anything more strenuous, but it did get tedious after a while. Naturally they would never say anything to the supervisor. Such a nice man didn't deserve to be spoken back to. If they upset him he might turn into another bully. As long as he remained sweet there was nothing to fear. Thus the juveniles worked as hard as they could. Not one of them dared to give the slightest hint of trouble. Obviously the man had done his work. He could sit back while his unwitting servants played directly into his hands. Bryan, despite his air of superiority, was not immune to his manipulation. If anything, he had fallen into the trap deeper than anyone else. Victor was in a different group, so the only person he had to impress was Mr Evans. Perhaps if he befriended him he could further show his superiority over the others. To them he thoroughly enjoyed the presence of the campers. Certainly he was not the person who would have favourites. However, Bryan couldn't help but hope he would be the exception. There was only one thing that would ever make him come back to this place again. He was looking in the child's direction as he thought of him. Mr Evans had already become a hero figure in his heart. Similar processes were happening in the people around him. They all wanted this man to become their best friend. However, this was yet another trap. Anything that was rare had value. If he played hard to get it would make the kids desire him more.

"I'll be your favourite by the time I go home," Bryan whispered as he started sewing the handle of his third bag of the day.

Clement's day certainly didn't start as well as Bryan's. Why did he have to be stuck with such a horrible supervisor? Who would let this man anywhere near children? Whoever ran the camp belonged in a lunatic asylum. There was no excuse for the unparalleled cruelty this fellow had shown the previous evening. Adam once again took a seat next to his brother. Nobody could stop trembling as they looked into his sadistic eyes. They were black holes that stole all traces of happiness from the hearts of those staring into them. The younger boys shook the most as they waited for the horrors to come. Most of the older campers were able to get away with merely a slight tremor. Even so, this was all an act. Beneath the surface they were just as terrified as the ten year olds. They would move less if they were leaves in a hurricane. Never would they forget the look on his face as he studied them. It was the same glare a lion gave a gazelle before sinking its teeth into its neck. To him they were nothing more than prey. If he wanted he could have them all executed. Knowing him, he would probably do so just for fun. Every time they stepped into the work building they couldn't tell if they would ever leave. Of course, their bodies would have to be removed for disposal, but their souls would have departed. Adam had been careful to make sure they had entered a few minutes before the whistle was blown from the dining hall. That was the sound that told them they had sixty seconds to get to their work buildings. It didn't matter if they were sitting down on the toilet when they heard it. If they weren't there within that time frame they would get a nightstick across their buttocks. The manager had been a little surprised to see them arrive so early. A teacher at school would have welcomed their enthusiasm. Unfortunately nothing seemed to be enough to please this man. He looked at them with a face full of contempt. They might as well have smeared faeces over the walls. A cold glance was exactly what Adam had hoped for. Surely it was better they were pecked to death by his eyes than spanked for being late. What good would come from sinking lower in this man's expectations? Neither brother knew if there was a single name in his good books. It was as if the whole of the human population had become his enemy. In a way they were absolutely correct. His sociopathic tendencies formed an invisible social barrier between him and everyone else. If they knew this they still wouldn't pity him. Feeling alienated was no excuse for hurting those too weak to fight back. What he was doing was unforgiveable.

"Get to work," he told them in a terse manner, his voice harsh. "If I see any of you slacking there will be trouble."

Those cold words were enough to inspire a flurry of activity. A man of his madness was not to be messed with. There was no limit to the amount of pain he could deliver to them. If he wanted he could have them beaten to death by his guards. Thus it made perfect sense to do as he bid them. Looking down at their tables, they saw several wooden frames stacked for them to work on. Presumably they would have to pump out the products as quickly as they possibly could. The older boys could tell them that meeting the quota wasn't enough. If one person could complete three times that amount, why couldn't the others? His disturbing gaze fell upon several of them as they began to spread the glue over the wood. Although they didn't dare look up, they could feel him drilling into their souls. For that reason they were driven to put their all into their work. Why had he looked at them? Was he dissatisfied with the speed they were going at? Just in case this was true they did everything in their power to hurry up. Of course, they couldn't rush what they were doing. Bad workmanship had got several members of the group assaulted yesterday. He had hurled one boy at another in rage. Anything within their power to placate him was more than worth doing. After all, if they held a stick of dynamite they wouldn't hold it over a stove. Why was lighting the manager's fuse anything other than insanity? Clement managed to coat his first frame with a layer of glue in less than a minute. He found it was easy to do once he got into the habit. By the time his body brushed the timber instinctively he was good to go. Cautiously he checked to make sure the glue was evenly distributed. No part of him wished to provoke the man's wrath. Against Bryan his older brother was incredibly helpful. However, there was nothing he could do to intervene if a guard attacked him. Jordan had spent a night in the coal shed for merely pushing an employee. Adam would end up in serious trouble if he jumped in to save his sibling. As much as he would want to assist him, he could do nothing more than pray that the man was merciful. What else could he do?

"Try to vary the colours of the glitter you use," he heard the supervisor speaking.

Out of curiosity he raised his head. The psychopath was performing an inspection. Merely seeing him there made his heart miss a beat. That was a sneaky punch to the campers' guts. Without announcing it he had started to walk around the tables. Suddenly the youth began to panic. What if his work wasn't good enough? What if he was strangled to death by one of his menacing gloved hands? He wouldn't put it past the fellow to have claws underneath them. Someone as evil as him had to be some sort of monster. Surely people weren't as bad as him. They couldn't be, could they? Quickly he realised what he was thinking. Was this what the man had done to him? This male had no power to hurt him other than that of a human being. He wasn't going to extend his jaw to swallow the juvenile whole. The campers needn't fear being speared by a tail sprouting from the back of his jacket. This creature, regardless of how horrible he was, was only a man. Thus if he kept his cool he could try to avoid the terror of merely being in the same room as him. With a stony gaze he walked across the room. As he did so he inspected the work of the boys to his side. So far what he had seen must have been satisfactory. He would never say it, but he had to be pleased with what they were doing. When he passed an older boy Clement was sure he saw a little nod. Perhaps some subconscious emotion had manifested itself in his body language. Picturing the manager as a normal human being helped his anxiety a great deal. Naturally the same person who beat children also sat down to watch television. Without warning a small giggle erupted from his throat. Imagining him reaching through the television set to strangle an actor was too humorous for him to avoid laughing. Immediately his brother threw him a look of fear. If there was one thing the man despised it was happiness amongst his workers. It was a symptom that his methods weren't working. As best he could he tried to carry on. Maybe the fellow hadn't heard the unintended chuckle. If he didn't act any differently he might get away with it.

Sadly there wasn't much time before his theory would be put to the test. In less than twenty seconds he began to walk down their row. This was it; this was the moment where he would find out if he would be punished. A quick glance at his sibling revealed a strange tenseness in him. He must be wishing for the same thing as Clement. Neither of them wanted him to get in trouble for it. Nobody deserved to be assaulted just for giggling. What sort of nightmare had he walked into? Prisoners on death row got to express themselves freely. He was just an innocent child. What had he done to deserve his incarceration in this gaol? There was no time to debate the issue. His potential executioner was strolling towards him. So far he had made three of the frames. How long had they been at work? It couldn't have been longer than ten minutes. His level of productivity had to be worthy of some level of protection. Since when was it a good idea to beat your best workers? The tension was unbearable as he awaited his fate. Time seemed to slow down as he drew nearer. It almost mocked him as it cruelly prolonged his terror. Every step he took grew more spaced out. By the time he reached Clement's table an eternity passed between the footfalls. Waiting was the worst part of the torment. He wished the man would just get it over with. He couldn't stand not knowing if he would be viciously attacked. Eventually the man reached him. Clement did his best not to look up. If he made eye contact with him he would burst into tears. Nothing in the institute was enjoyable. The food would be good if there wasn't so much violence. It was as if the children used mealtimes as an excuse to skirmish.

"Please keep on walking," he begged the man in his mind.

For a second he looked as if he was going to follow his pleas. Then, without warning, he stopped in front of him. The boy couldn't believe his luck. His heart pounded in his chest with such fury it almost exploded through his ribcage. What was going to happen to him? Was he going to be beaten with a baton? There were several workers milling around that would oblige such a request. Would he hurl him across the room as if he was a sentient shot-put? Perhaps he would imply lift him off the ground with a hand around his neck. Picturing himself being suffocated in such a way was one of the worst moments of his life. Never before had he felt such horror. Witnessing it being done to someone was bad, but this was a thousand times worse. If he even thought he was going to suffer such a fate he was going to run. It didn't matter if they locked him in the coal shed for the rest of the month. He would either escape from the camp or die trying. Fear caused his mind to underestimate the difficulty he would have in doing so. The razor wire that stood between him and freedom became nothing more than a minor hurdle. As long as he was careful he considered himself fully able to climb over it. He was probably safer trying to fight the man directly. At least that way the whole group could rally behind him. Clement fought desperately to keep tears from forming in his eyes. The adults punished weakness when they saw it. Crying was certain to result in a slap across the face. Inside his chest his heart was ready to burst. How it managed to beat so quickly he didn't know. He was sure he could feel it in his head. Presumably it was counting down the seconds until he died.

"You managed to produce three frames in ten minutes?" He asked the lad, his voice betraying his surprise.

"Yes, Sir," he choked out while praying the quality was up to standards.

"Keep up the good work," he told the lad as he studied the products drying on the edge of his table.

There was something different about his demeanour after he had visited Clement. As he completed the rest of his inspection he didn't seem quite so harsh. Frankly he came across as a little distant when he told a boy in the back row to get a move on. As soon as the man walked on from his station he felt a wave of relief gripping his body. It was a tsunami that tore the layers of fear to shreds. Evidently he must be doing something right. To make the man show anything other than anger was a huge achievement. He had just won the lottery of the institution. Alongside him his brother was beaming with joy. Watching his brother being beaten mercilessly was the worst form of torture. Luckily the ten year old was skilled enough to impress the fellow. Even if he did hear the laugh, he wasn't going to punish him now. What sense was there in attacking your best workers? For the rest of the morning the boy inhabited a sweet reverie. For the first time since he arrived he wasn't afraid. Why should he be? His manager kept looking at him, assessing how he was getting on. Every time he did so the scowl on his face grew weaker. Perhaps the man genuinely valued him as a worker. It wasn't every day a new recruit could keep pace with the oldest boys. Time flew by as he completed his work instinctively. No longer did he need to run through everything in his head. Toiling for him was simply a matter of switching to autopilot. He remained in this curious state until the fellow announced it was time for lunch. At first Clement believed it was some sort of trick. Surely he was telling them they could leave as some sort of prank. As soon as they stood up to walk out he would correct himself, stating that they still had an hour to go. That had to be it; the hours couldn't have flown past that quickly.

"Hurry up!" He told them, urging them out so he could have his own lunch.

One of the workers opened the door with his typical sour look. Adam turned to his brother, thoroughly amazed that he had completed so many frames. Clement barely even noticed what he had been doing. His subconscious mind worked on them while his higher faculties explored the cosmos from inside his skull. At one point he was sure he was picturing himself skydiving. Where had that come from? Nothing around him felt real. It was as if he had been unwittingly teleported into the future. If that was the case he wished they would finish the job and project him to the end of the month. He was prepared to settle for being dropped outside the walls. Either way he didn't care; he would be out of the nightmare. When he regained his lucidity the gravity of the situation caught up with him. All the torment he had endured slammed into him as if he had been hit by a car. Suddenly he found himself struggling to draw breath. It wasn't surprisingly his mind had retreated into himself. His psyche had created a place where he could be happy. Now he was paying for his escape. Seemingly the camp treated all evasive action taken against it equally. It didn't matter if a camper fled psychologically or physically. In both circumstances they were reminded that the hell they were in could not be dodged. Clement was more aware than ever that he was trapped in a nightmare world. Still, his stomach grumbling drove him onwards. He might not be happy in his surroundings, but he could at least satiate himself. A nice meal would take care of the hunger that had crept up on him. His brother walked alongside him in silence. He didn't need to say a word to convey the fact he was overjoyed. Somehow the lad had become one of the most productive members of the group. It didn't bother Adam that his younger brother had outpaced him. He was just glad neither of them had been assaulted. That was the one thing that he truly feared in the camp. Bullies he could take on without many problems. Bryan had learnt that the hard way. However, the one thing he had no control over were the actions of the guards. They could chastise the pair as severely as they wanted without fear of retaliation. Such a thought was enough to chill the thirteen year old to his bones.

"I thought you were a goner back there for a moment," he told Clement while smiling contently. "How did you get so good at decorating?"

"I don't know," the juvenile replied softly. "When I giggled I imagined myself being throttled. How can he be allowed to get away with that? Why hasn't anyone reported this place?" He whispered these sentences for fear of summoning a raging employee.

There was a pause before Adam responded. No part of him wanted to acknowledge the truth. It was something they boy didn't need to know until he had to. What good could come from stripping yet more of his innocence away? People who attend the camps tend to grow up quickly. As children they arrive; as adults they leave. It wasn't a good transformation, however. Most of those forced to attend spend the best part of a decade getting over the trauma it causes. Yet they could never truly forget the memories of the abuse. Not one day would go by without some sort of flashback. The horrors would remain with them for the rest of their lives. Their experiences became forced into the background. At no point did they disappear completely. As a barrister would put it; you can't unring a bell. Even so, the peals of even the largest chimes eventually stop swinging. If the campers reached a hundred they would still be trapped in the institute. Once it caught you in its grip it swallowed you. You might be able to see the outside world, but it would never regurgitate its prey. It hurt Adam to know what his brother would be stuck here until he turned eighteen. Even then there was no guarantee he wouldn't be offered a job. It was likely this would happen, given the prowess he showed for his duties. Accepting the position of night-time helper was a terrible betrayal of his comrades. If he had the strength he would have told them exactly what they could do with their role. He wanted no part of the operation. Perhaps if he had the aptitude for tactics he could organise the older boys into a legion with which to strike the guards. If everyone fought their hardest they might be able to get to freedom. Sadly this ambition was just that. Any success over the employees in combat would be reported at once. While they tried to open the gates they would be swamped by fighters brought in from the other premises. There would be hell to pay for their actions. It dawned on him that he hadn't answered his younger sibling's question. Once again the cold sweat the answer generated gripped him. There was no way he was spilling the beans. He wasn't sure his sanity could bear to think about it.

"I'll tell you later," he just about managed to whimper as a response. "Let's get some food."

"I want a word with you!" The pair heard someone shouting as they were about to enter the dining hall.

Recognising the voice, they sighed heavily. What was wrong with this boy? Why did he think he could shove everyone around? Clement didn't want any unpleasant business to lower his mood. Running on autopilot had allowed his mind to recuperate from the deep tiredness that came with trauma. Buoyed up avoiding a punishment, he felt as if he could take on anything. The cruel manager had either not noticed him laughing or hadn't want to spoil his productivity. Either way, he had got away with giggling. Surely this meant his luck was changing. This lad wasn't going to enjoy any sort of victory over him. It was bad enough he considered himself victorious after that morning's incident. If Adam hadn't interfered he would have got back up. His full rage would have been unloaded on his enemy. Bryan wouldn't have stood a chance. There was still time for him to do this, however. When he started beating his foe he would unleash all the anger over his current situation. There was an awfully lot of it collecting at the bottom of his soul. He would be a fool not to use the opportunity to empty the tank. If he didn't it would begin to eat away at him. His soul would be corroded from the inside. He didn't want to end up like some of the older boys. Although they acted normal, you could tell that they were dead inside. The spark of life within them had been extinguished. They never found a way to come to terms with their incarceration in this horrible place. It is as if their souls have been carved out with a rusty blade. The festering wounds would probably never get a chance to heal. By the time they fully matured they would be broken men. There was no way he would let that happen to him. If beating this fellow to the ground would protect his psyche, so be it.

"Do you know I got told off because of you? If you stop being such a freak you might actually have friends!" The hostile youth marched up to the younger brother. "Why don't we have a proper fight? You're brother can stay out of this."

"Scram!" Adam shouted in his face with a venomous tone.

Bryan looked a little perturbed by the order. Nevertheless, he didn't back down. How could he when he had promised himself a victory? Clement could picture him brooding silently, chewing the brawl over in his head. What was going on inside the lad's skull? It was obvious he considered himself superior to everyone else. This would certainly explain the dirty looks he gave everyone around him. Yet he could see nothing about him that would grant him such a position. There was no doubt the boy was bright, but he certainly wasn't exceptional. Most likely he had been buttered up by his parents all his life. They had fed him compliments almost every waking moment. A deep loathing of this fellow stirred within him. Naturally he didn't care for him before. Even so, it dawned on him that he truly despised the camper. Those who knew him were aware that he tried to see the best in people. Yet Bryan seemed rotten down to the core. Was there a little good in him? If so he had buried it beneath miles of odium. Frankly he wasn't surprised that Jordan had been bullying him. Why did someone as repulsive as him deserve to be happy? Adam sighed heavily at the thought of having to intervene again. This didn't escape Clement's notice. It was obvious that he resented having to step in all the time. Rory approached from behind, sensing that something was wrong. A smile quickly broke out on his face when he realised there was going to be a fight.

"I know you have to help him. Do you wipe his bum, too?" He joked, earning a scowl from the older boy.

"I bet he does," Bryan laughed along. "This kid probably can't even tie his own shoelaces!"

"Shut your mouth!" Clement screamed as anger swelled within him.

"Make me!" The other ten year old responded with an infuriating sneer.

"Go away," Adam implored the child tiredly. "Just have your lunch and be quiet."

"No, I think I'd rather take your brother on again. He's so weak I could do it with a single hand."

"You can't fault his logic," Rory chuckled when he heard the insult.

"I'll show you how strong I am, shall I?" Clement shouted as he saw red.

With his blood boiling he stepped forwards. One of his hands curled into a fist before his target could draw breath. In an instant it had collided with the bully's face. The arrogant lad turned as he fell, ending up flat on his face. A smile grew within the aggressor. Surely this had showed him not to throw insults around in such a fashion. To his surprise the victim quickly got to his feet. Shaking himself, blood poured from his split lip. Yet there wasn't a sign of defeat in him. If anything he had just made his opponent angrier. Now there was no way the hostilities were going to end. He had simply shifted things up a gear. Before he knew what was happening Bryan was upon him. The older boys watched as Clement was kicked in the stomach. In their previous fight he had enjoyed the support of his brother. Now the boy was standing back, allowing things to unfold. Why wasn't he throwing himself into combat? A glance in his direction revealed exactly what he was thinking. Shame mixed with embarrassment adorned the teenager's face. Regardless of how much he wanted to intervene, he couldn't. Rory's words had taken root within him. Of course, the lad was right. He was doing far too much for his sibling. Suddenly he felt so alone. Without assurance Adam would protect him he felt weaker than he had ever done before. Even so, he was far from beaten. He threw another punch in his foe's direction. This one knocked Bryan back slightly. Before he could recover he kicked him squarely between the legs. Rory's eyes were wide open as Clement threw his final punch. Knocking the ten year old to the floor, he stood over him menacingly. He realised he had been wrong about this boy. He wasn't weak at all. Having been given a chance to shine he had emerged victorious. Adam was grinning from ear to ear as he observed the boys. His brother delivered a kick to the boy as he curled up into a ball. The look on Bryan's face was one of shock. How had this happened? How could he have vanquished him? Fortunately he wasn't severely injured. His body was aching, but he would live. Clement wondered if this would be the end of the violence. Graham hadn't come near him since the fight last night. Perhaps Bryan would finally get the message that he wasn't to be messed with.

"Wow," Rory mumbled with a look of amazement.

"That was awesome!" Adam whispered, scarcely able to take in what had happened.

"Let's get some grub," Clement declared before walking into the dining hall.

They couldn't believe the fight had taken place. It might as well have occurred in a dream. Certainly it had the characteristics of one. The events reassured Adam that he didn't have to constantly support his brother. That was exactly what he desired. Now he could go off with his friends without having to worry about the child. Yet this had actually happened. There was no need to doubt if he had defeated his enemy. It was as real as the nightmare they had found themselves in. In silence they strolled into the building. Clement was sitting in a different spot. In front of him a male worker was pouring him a glass of water. Sitting a little way along the table, they watched as a large bowl of salad was handed to him. With a look of hunger he began to tear into it. So much adrenaline flooded his system than he could probably eat the plastic plate as well. He would need all his strength to survive in the camp. Eagerly he spooned mouthful after mouthful down his throat. Through combat he had built up quite an appetite. Not once did he worry about Bryan. Why should he? That boy was an incorrigible bully. He deserved everything he got. Frankly he was getting off lightly with such a punishment. If it was up to him he would never dare glance in Clement's direction again. Bryan was truly a waste of air. Ironically he was glad the kid came to the camp. If he was here he was surely suffering. There was no need for him to do anything else. All that was required was for the system to do its job. Already he had been beaten by the guards. After their first fight he had almost been spanked by a worker. Such a person would inevitably get in trouble. There was nothing to do except wait for his mouth to betray him. When that time came he prayed he would be there to watch the spanking. If anyone else was chastised like that he would feel terrified. Should Bryan endure it he would have to fight to prevent himself from cheering.

"Look who's here!" He heard Rory shout as Bryan hobbled into the shack.

Clement was barely paying attention to anything around him. By now he was throwing back a glass of water. Still, his eyes lazily shifted in the direction of the door. That was when he witnessed his vanquished foe. The lad was staggering forwards, the pain in his genatalia agonising. This was not really surprisingly; he had used as much force as he would to dent steel. There was something strange about his face. Blood was pouring from his lip. Those who saw him seemed to take pity of the youth. These people had obviously no clue as to the nature of his soul. If they could see him in his true form he would be a monstrous creature. His spirit would be torn apart from years of being bathed in his own hatred. His expression was one of immense discomfort. Clement couldn't help but feel a sense of pride when he saw it. Nobody deserved pain more than him. Since he didn't dare insult the guards in his own mind while they are around, the juvenile would have to do. Bryan's eyes scoured the room, presumably looking for Victor. When his aggressor entered his vista he almost recoiled. He took this as a sign that his aggression had done its job. Hopefully he would stay away from him now he had proved himself a competent opponent. Naturally he couldn't access the boy's thoughts. If he could he wouldn't be able to believe them. This fellow might have been knocked back, but he hadn't been defeated. As far as he was concerned it was one all. There would be another battle. This time he would be ready for Clement. While the unsuspecting camper finished his water he began to plan his revenge. Logically he would have to have help. If he could persuade Victor to support him they could beat the lad into submission. First of all he would have to convince his friend that it was a good idea. Gingerly he turned to the ten year old sitting opposite him.

"Are you okay?" He asked the wounded male, wondering if he had been set upon by the adults.

"I fought the runt," he told him, gesticulating to Clement. "We're going to teach him a lesson," he announced confidently, even if his body didn't agree. "He will regret the day he crossed me."

Victor's eyes seemed to sharpen when he heard that. Did he just say that they would teach him a lesson? He couldn't possibly expect him to risk punishment from the guards. So far he had managed to avoid them. Not once had he felt a baton slamming into his flesh. That was exactly the way he wanted to stay. Yet he supposed he did owe the boy a favour. He hadn't reported him for talking to the girl last night. When he thought of her the real world grew more distant. Why should he live in it when he could inhabit his fantasies? In his mind he was sitting on a beach with her next to him. They held hands as the sun barraged them with its warm rays. Now that was a place he dwell in forever. The sound of his chum speaking shattered the illusion. It dissolved before his eyes as if it was a reel of film catching fire. Once again anchored back in reality, he was forced to listen to what Bryan was saying. Frankly he had no problems with Clement whatsoever. Why did the lad even care about him? For a fleeting moment he wondered if he should associate himself with this fellow. He felt as if he was leading him down a dark alley. Stepping in if a camper attacked him was one thing. Bryan was talking about ambushing him that night. Pretending to agree, the boy nodded along to everything he said. Secretly he wondered if he could go and sit with a nice looking group of boys further along the table. What was there to keep the bond between them alive? His friend was a bully, even thought he had fought Jordan because of it. Twice he had come very close to being assaulted by the guards. Remaining of cordial terms with him was akin to lighting a stick of dynamite in his throat. Unless he was very careful the lad would take both of them down. He didn't trust the employees to not bury them both alive in the forest. After all, why shouldn't they look out for their own interests? The adults had all the power on the premises. Any opinions to the contrary surely stemmed from illusions.

"I think we should arm ourselves," Bryan stated coldly.

This made Victor wince when he thought about it. There and then he decided he would have nothing more to do with the lad. He was obviously disturbed; that was obvious going by his disposition towards violence. Certainly he was no normal. How could he be when he talking about using weapons against another human being? This wasn't a case of him lashing out in anger. He was methodically planning the downfall of another person. His eyes were wide open as he studied the lunatic. Potentially he was more dangerous than any of the guards. At least they had profit as the centre of their activities. This fellow was out to cause harm for its own sake. There really was no justification for persecuting Clement. There were more than enough people for him to befriend. They weren't even in the same work group. Frankly if he doesn't like him he shouldn't be seeking him out. To avoid incurring his wrath he pretended to agree with his plan. Of course, there was no way he would actually go along with it. If he wanted to beat his foe to death he was on his own. Perhaps he should even let an adult know what was happening. Nobody could doubt the experiences had pushed this boy over the edge. When he looked into Bryan's eyes there was a tangible madness that terrified his former friend. Yet he hadn't always been this way. Before coming to the camp he had been superior, but not aggressive. He would be the last person you would expect to take such extreme measures. Evidently the camp had split his psyche in half. If would certainly explain why his grip on reality was so weak. Suddenly the boy felt afraid for his own safety. If he outright refused to keep him company he would turn on him. At the same time he couldn't beat up another camper. He saw no reason to even talk to Clement. More than anything he wished he could wake up in his bed at home. There he didn't have to worry about insane children tearing chunks out of each other.

"Are you being serious? Can't you just leave him alone?" Victor found the strength to confront the juvenile delinquent.

"Do you have any idea what he has done to me? He's a bully," Bryan told him, more for his own assurances than for his friend's benefit. "Why, are you feeling sort for him?"

The air between them became charged in an instant. Narrowing his eyes, the psychotic child appeared to be assessing his friend. Was this boy going to support him in combat? If not there would be repercussions. He had kept Victor's secret. Not one word about him talking to the girl had left his mouth. Now he was asking for a little help to do what he had to. What was so wrong about calling on an associate for a favour? Afraid for his own safety, the boy shrugged a response. He had absolutely no reason to hate Clement. It didn't matter if he was a bully or not. Bryan hadn't been a perfect individual from what he had seen. Maybe there was some way he could talk his friend into abandoning his plans. They could still look out for each other. If one of them was attacked the other could rally to his defence. There was absolutely nothing wrong in this. But what he couldn't do was let the lad talk him into doing something terrible. If he decided to carry out his plans he would not be part of the bloodlust. How could he live with himself knowing he had caused someone serious harm? What would the guards do to him if they discovered he was part of the plot? Struggling to regain his composure, he made himself look as strong as possible. He wasn't Bryan's property; he couldn't be ordered to do anything. Not helping him commit an assault was different from not being friends with him. Ironically he found himself despising the lad. He had rightfully chastised Jordan for being a controlling, manipulative parasite. Now he had sunk to his level. Although he hadn't directly stated it, there was certainly subtext to his body language. If he didn't follow his instructions he risked being viewed as an enemy himself. That meant he could get whatever was coming Clement's way. Somehow the lad was able to hold his own in a fight. Victor hadn't thrown a proper punch in his life. How could he stand up for himself?

"Can't you just keep away from him?" He begged the deranged male tearfully. "Just don't talk to him. I don't think he's going to do anything to you."

"Are you mad?!" He scowled at the boy with venom. "He's going to attack me again! Did you see what he did to me just now?"

Truthfully he hadn't seen it. He had, however, watched as the youth limped over to him. But what had he done to provoke him? Last night he had gone after Jordan. That morning he had forced his enemy into a brawl. He had no doubt that there was another side to this story. For the first time the young man caught a glimpse of Bryan's soul. There was something there he didn't enjoy viewing. It was as if dark veins were spreading towards his centre. These were corrupting his entire being. Whatever was happening, he didn't want to be infected with it himself. There was no better proof for the harm the camp does than this fellow. Even a dullard could see that he was teetering on the brink of utter insanity. His eyes pecked the boy's soul, breaking his heart. Rather than hate him for his violence he felt himself reaching out. Sympathy was what he deserved. This poor lad was a victim of the institution. They had taken an innocent prepubescent and turned him into a raging monster. If he was going to recover he needed love. Perhaps good care could reverse the decay of his very being. To comfort himself he pictured his mother's face. If she was here she would know what to do. There had to be something that would help the boy. Yet how was he supposed to heal the damage if his friend wouldn't let him in? Gently he reached out to touch his friend. His earlier thoughts had been correct. Hatred would only make things worse. He wasn't a bad kid; he just needed time to recover from the trauma he had experienced. Sadly he knew this wasn't going to happen during the month. Danger lurked behind every corner on the premises. A guard would beat someone for looking at them the wrong way. How was this fellow going to progress if the abuse was going to get worse? How would they react to an insane camper getting up to all sorts of strange activities? Once again the fear reared its ugly head. When he placed his hand on his shoulder he didn't know if the boy was going to bite into it.

"I think you should calm down," he begged him with all his heart. "Count to ten and breathe deeply."

"What are you talking about?" Bryan asked him directly with a bemused frown.

"You're not well. I think you're losing your mind. Just try to relax. Clement hadn't done anything really bad. You'll be alright tomorrow. Let go of the anger," his soft voice seemed to stir something within his chum's brain.

"You're right," he told him as he regained a little lucidity. "I won't attack him today. But this isn't the end of it. He's over there now thinking he's won. He's got another think coming!"

Victor smiled weakly when he heard that statement. Maybe by simply providing positive human contact he could make a world of difference. A simple touch from a friendly face had soothed his fragmented psyche. Still, there was a great deal more than needed to be done. While Clement wasn't in any immediate danger, the hostilities hadn't come to an end. Perhaps if he behaved as cordially as possible he could return him to a normal state. What else could he do? If he got the adults involved they would punish him. A spanking would only make things worse. It wouldn't heal the cracks running the length of his being. Before he knew it a guard announced lunch was over. This made the boy smile with glee. He could return to the safety of Mr Evan's friendly gaze. Victor struggled to understand how anyone could be happy to toil. His work was the hardest of the three on offer. He would do anything to avoid returning to the hot, dirty environment. Honestly he would rather take his chances against a worker than stroll willingly back into his prison. Fortunately he knew that taking on an employee was suicide. Strangely the best way to avoid being beaten was to throw himself into his work. As long as he kept busy the cruel supervisor didn't have a reason to interfere with him. Grumbles broke out amongst the campers as they began to vacate the dining hall. Remarkably there were no serious complaints. First of all they didn't dare voice them in the presence of the employees. Secondly, the salad they had consumed had filled their stomachs nicely. A healthy nutritious meal had given them enough energy to keep going through the afternoon. Secretly there was a reason for making sure the children loaded up on vitamins. Such things would drive their healing rates up a notch. Wounded children heal far better on vegetables than they do on gruel.

"See you later," Victor grinned at his damaged friend before heading towards the door.

Chapter six

Bryan took immense pleasure in his work. Once he started he tuned out all distractions. Occasionally he looked up, the pleasant smile of the manager providing great comfort. After a little while he wondered why he had confronted Clement. It was as if he had lost his mind. Why had he challenged him? What had he hoped to gain from a fight? His aching body pulsated with his heartbeat. Constantly it asked him why he had been so stupid. Fortunately he allowed the whole world to wash past him. Sewing was so enjoyable he felt he could lose himself in it. This didn't escape the notice of the adults. By the time he got into a routine they kept glancing at him. Their horrid scowls slipped slightly as the whispered to themselves. It was unusual for someone to show such promise so early on. Of course, those who shone began to glow early, but in their first year their potentially was normally still growing. This boy had the capacity to turn the activity into a career. So what if he would be questioned based on his choice? People would tell him that women tend to become seamstresses. Yet if he could make money from it he should seize the opportunity with both hands. After all, the best tailors in the realm were men. These people went home to their wives after a hard day's work in their businesses. Those who scoffed were jealous about the nice lives they lived. Bryan noticed that their gazes were falling on him more and more. In the time it took for some to produce one bag he had started his fourth. His hands were everywhere at once as he worked his fingers to the bone. Mr Evans sauntered over, his polite smiles greeting those who looked up at him. He had no doubt that the raw talent of the lad was extraordinary. Nonetheless, he found himself wishing to prove that the camper was as good as he appeared. Perhaps he was simply rushing the bags. Maybe they would be nowhere near the quality demanded by the management. Thus it was no surprise that he picked up one of the bags in his basket.

"This is amazing," he told the boy as he noticed the stitching. "If you keep this up you'll have no problems."

There was a tone of awe in his voice. Potentially this boy would break the record for productivity. Those around him turned to watch as he congratulated the male for his efforts. Receiving compliments from this man was better than all the gold in a bank vault. Such a cordial person was surely the epitome of geniality. Almost blushing from the praise, he watched as the man emptied his basket of the completed products. With a hand he signalled for one of his underlings to bring over more fabric. Seeing him grin from ear to ear inflated the boy's ego. It only confirmed what he had known all along. Surely this was proof he was better than everyone else. Having never done anything like this before, he had dove into it. Now the fruits of his labour were ready for picking. Some of those in the room began to inspect their own work. Was he going to check everyone? It came as a shock when he walked back to the middle of the room. Armed with the resources to make many more bags, he got cracking straight away. So great was his pride that the supervisor showed genuine happiness. There was no need for him to maintain his affable mask. For half an hour he ran on a true smile. Sadly no-one could tell the difference. He had maintained his persona for so long that it was as easy as breathing. Only he knew that the lad had filled his tank, allowing him to rest his psychological armament for a while. For that he was grateful to the lad. It was also nice to see that his tactics were working exceptionally well. By getting into the mind of this child he had turned him into a wonderful worker. If his productivity remained this high until he turned eighteen he would recommend him for a real job. Of course, he was too important to waste as hired muscles. Presumably he would be set to work in one of their other factories. Dotted around the realm were premises that constituted true workplaces. These legitimate businesses were crying out for people with such potential. He would definitely be appreciated there.

"I know it is," Bryan whispered after the man had walked away, agreeing with his assessment of his bags.

Clement was certainly enjoying what he was doing. However, he didn't have the benefit of a supervisor who had made a career out of hiding his psychopathic tendencies. Adam kept looking across, assessing how he was getting on. There really was no need for him to worry. He was just as skilled as Bryan was. Their manager stood menacingly as the front of the room. His glare was enough to keep everyone in line. They knew that if they failed to do their best they would be punishment. As if for emphasis a few of the lesser employees practised swinging their batons. It was as if they were trying to split thin air. Merely catching a glimpse of them made the lad feel sick. How was anyone supposed to try their hardest in such an abrasive setting? They might as well have kept them under armed guard. What difference would it make if they carried rifles rather than nightsticks? At least with the former they might expire quickly. Being beaten to death with a blunt weapon was a horrific fate. Picturing it almost made the juvenile wince. If they wanted the children to give the work their all they would be better off ditching the abusive behaviour. However, he couldn't deny that what they were doing worked. Obviously the money they received for the products was sufficient to support their continued existence. How else would they be able to pay people to work there? Not even the sadistic guards would be able to attend if they weren't offered salaries they could live on. It was strange to think that people were actually buying what they were producing. Maybe if he went into the right store he would see the frames they were decorating.

"Remember, we want original products. Don't follow the exact same pattern for every one you make," his booming voice startled him as it filled the room.

Despite the terror he experienced at the sight of the guards, he was still able to work very well. Last night he had found that giving the tasks his full attention made time fly past. Thus it was not surprisingly that he tuned the world out to focus on his labour. Very quickly all that existed was him and his desk. The rest of the room might not have existed. As far as he was concerned he was floating with his station in a white void. His brother's glances became fewer as he noticed he was managing the activities. His frames were truly beautiful when they were placed alongside his table. All sorts of colours were reflected off the glitter that coated every surface. He would buy one if he saw them in the shops. It was no wonder that there was a demand for such things. Someone could boast to their friends about how artistic their children are. It didn't matter to them that the product had been bought in a store. Why would it when it allowed people to score points over their friends? Their supervisor performed an inspection of the room once everyone had completed their first design. Clement didn't notice as he was besotted by the one he was working on. He didn't even look up when he reached his table. The man had no power over him when he was in this state. To feel fear one must devote thoughts to the cause of those feelings. The abusive fellow had long since been forgotten by the child. Adam was grateful to him that he passed his brother's table without showing a flicker of hatred on his face. That was usually the first warning that someone needed to buck up their ideas. If he wasn't satisfied with their improvement he would resort to physical means of manipulating their attitude. While he didn't show any anger when looking at the work of others, Clement was the only one who got a second glance. Was there a hint of less hostility in his eyes? Adam barely dared to assess him in his own mind. It was as if the mere memory of him had power in his psyche. Sadly it escaped his attention that this was true only insofar as he allowed it.

"Good," he uttered with a slightly hushed tone.

Walking further on, his older brother's work was passed without comment. That was more than enough for him to continue. This man appeared to deal almost entirely in negatives. His sibling had been lucky in receiving a single word of praise. For him to say anything at all must have truly impressed him. That always struck Adam as peculiar; spite flowed from him as if he was a tap, but only true amazement could bring out the slightest flicker of pleasantness. Looking over at his table, it wasn't hard to see why he had been granted such an honour. Most of the children were on their second frame. The older boys had started their third. However, Clement had managed to almost complete his fourth. None of them looked rushed in any way. If anything they surpassed the standards for sale. There was no doubt that what he had made would earn a high sum in a store. People would flock to the shops to obtain these wonderful ornaments. His beautiful designs would surely entice someone to buy them. Ironically the slavery of the children was the only thing keeping the camps running. If everyone refused to work the institute would go out of business in a few years. Either that or they would all come to an end. The same reason they returned year after year also compelled them to work until their fingers bled. Putting these nightmarish thoughts out of his head, he returned his gaze to his own work. He was just about to finish his frame when he heard screaming from the back of them room. Immediately their heads craned to get a better view. What was happening now? What minor transgression would earn someone pain? Clement was the only one who didn't stop working. Why would he want to see such a horrid sight? He had witnessed enough violence to last him a lifetimes. Willingly watching an adult assault a child was right at the bottom of his list of things to do.

"Look at that!" Adam heard him cry out as he dragged the boy from his seat.

"I'm sorry, Sir," he fumbled an apology as he stared at the spilt glitter on the floor.

"You'd better be!" He screamed in the boy's face at the top of his voice. "You've got ten seconds to clean that up or I'm going to rip your head off!"

Clement briefly looked up at the other workers when he heard this. Their faces were covered in gruesome smiles. They were obviously salivating in anticipation of the violence that would transpire. Spilling some glitter was not the end of the world. The first time he had decorated a frame he had spilt some. However, he had used it in the design. He hadn't swept it onto the floor in the hope that nobody would notice it. Yet he couldn't blame the fellow for what he had done. From the sounds of things he was the same age as him. His mind had probably frozen in terror. Was it really his fault that he had made a mistake? His brother continued to watch as the boy threw himself onto his knees. With as much speed as he could muster he desperately gathered the glitter with his hands. All the while the adult was counting down slowly, as if marking the time before a firing squad would end his life. By the time he had reached ten there were only a few sparkling fragments on the floor. It was obvious that the boy was praying for mercy. He had done what he had been told. The mound of glitter was now lying on his desk. Never again would he make such a mistake. No part of him could comprehend why he had swept it onto the floor. That was obviously asking for trouble. In a place like this he could count on the guards to be as petty as humanly possible. It wasn't as if their behaviour hadn't crossed the line of insanity already. How could they not make a fuss over something as trivial as spilt glitter? He risked glancing up at the man, awaiting instruction. Had he done enough to earn a suspension of his torment? For another five seconds he made contact with the aggressor. Constantly he hoped he would not be assaulted too badly. Watching a child being thrown across the room was terrifying even to watch. Perhaps the man would literally do what he had promised. Did he have the strength to decapitate him with his bare hands? Maybe not, but he could certainly break the neck of a ten year old. Eventually the worker gave him a malicious smile.

"Sit down and get back to work!" He bellowed so loudly the lad turned as white as snow.

"Lucky," Adam thought to himself as the man turned to walk back to the front of the building.

Clement barely noticed the ordeal. He heard everything that had happened, but he didn't let it register on his system. Running on autopilot seemed to repair something deep within him. The flayed edges of his soul were slowly stitched back together. Forgetting about the abuse he had suffered was a magical experience. In the recesses of his own mind he could rest in a silent crevice. To call such a state peaceful would be a huge understatement. Suddenly the work became a form of meditation. If he could keep up this condition throughout the month he might leave in a better condition than when he arrived. A memory of his brother entered his mind briefly. The disappointment on his face when he thought he was going to have to intervene was a knife in his heart. No longer was he his friend, someone he could share anything with. In a moment he had become a terrible burden. But he had shown the lad that he was capable of defending himself. Bryan had learnt that the hard way. What good would it do to dwell on such a thing? Previously he had thought that the only way they would get through the month is together. Now he was wondering if he even needed his sibling. Obviously he could hold his own in a fight. As he was good at his job he didn't need help from anyone. What exactly was Adam supposed to do for him? Furthermore, the look of embarrassment on his face had hurt him badly. He was his brother, not something a dog had left on the carpet. At that moment he found it hard to even enjoy his company. An urge to get away from him entered his system. Before long his blood had turned to acid. Even thinking about him was enough to make his head swim. As best he could he forced himself to focus on his work. Although it worked, the rage he felt wasn't extinguished. Instead it merely lay dormant, waiting for an opportunity to awaken. When it did so its roar might just shake the world.

Dinner came much sooner than Bryan would have expected it to. He found himself moaning when Mr Evans declared their shift was officially at an end. While he laboured he demonstrated his superiority to the world. Without saying a word he elevated himself above the others. At first his peers were amazed by his skill. However, as he repeatedly received compliments from the manager they began to grow jealous. The man had conditioned them to value his praise more than anything. Now one person was getting more of it than anyone else they were starting to see red. It wasn't fair that he was so good compared to them. It didn't matter that their work was more than passable. All they cared about was wishing this fellow nothing but pain. After all, pride was relative. Where was the thrill in earning a million pounds if everyone around you earned a billion? How can you enjoy your success when others have so much more than you? Adults would have been pleased that they simply weren't being beaten. However, these children had not matured nearly enough to follow these thought patterns. As far as they were concerned they wanted to be the centre of attention. If anyone else took on that position they would think the same of them. Only when an individual seemed to shine did that person think things had turned out correctly. It came as no surprise to him that the looks they offered were slightly hostile. Excellence breeds jealousy; he was good enough to make everyone hate him. This only served to increase his ego. How could anyone remain on the ground when their heads float in the clouds? If he was a helium balloon he would be large enough to raise whole cities. Their envy reinforced his belief that he was superior to them. Even though he wasn't very high on the pecking order, he was by far the best worker. There was a tangible swagger as he walked from the room. This bounce continued as he flaunted himself on the journey to the dining hall. It was as if a podium had risen from the bare soil, elevating him for the whole realm to see. Impressing Mr Evans would have been enough for him. Now he knew he was better than everyone else. In his fantasies he proclaimed himself king. Shouldn't the best in society rule? Where was the logic in not following an elitist pathway? To him it was madness that he hadn't been given far more responsibilities as soon as he showed his true worth. But there would be time for that later on. Everything would unfold nicely as long as he worked to further improve himself.

"Victor," he spoke loudly when he saw his friend.

Immediately the boy turned to face him. For a moment he was a bit worried about his state of mind. It was no secret that the workers were very cruel people. Had he emerged from the shack even more damaged than before he went in? It didn't seem that way when he walked over to him. If anything he looked better than he had done last night. The lines of decay in his soul had vanished without a trace. Reassured he wasn't in any danger, the boy allowed his friend to stroll alongside him. There was certainly something different about him. He didn't seem to care that he might find a razorblade in his food. Neither did he worry when they passed a harsh-faced guard. The fact he could have beaten them to a bloody pulp didn't bother the lad one bit. Victory was curious as to his chum's transformation. As they sat down he asked him about it. What was the secret that allowed him to regain his sanity? Regaining lucidity was one thing; this lad was grinning as much as the human face would allow. If he could he would cross the oceans with the ends of his lips. Something must have happened for this to have occurred. Maybe if the juvenile heard it he could apply it to his own life. He wouldn't mind being that happy in the darkest month of his life. It was the December of their days despite the weather outside. The summer sun had baked the mud dry, but in their hearts they were frozen solid. Seemingly the only way to avoid a nervous breakdown was to switch off the emotional parts of their beings. To act without truly feeling was horrid, even if it was necessary. Evidently Bryan had found a second option. From the looks of things it obviously worked.

"I couldn't believe the look on his face when he saw how many bags I had stitched together," he was speaking so quickly Victor struggled to understand him. "The other kids couldn't believe it either. Some of them frowned at me. It's such a shame some people can't control their jealousy."

His associate didn't know what to make of these statements. Certainly it was nice to see a recovery in his mental health. However, he wasn't speaking very nicely of his peers. Merely explaining he had done would have sufficed. There was no need to comment on the self control of his fellow campers. Even so, the glee oozed from every pore in the boy's body. That was the best thing he had seen in a long time. How someone could recover so quickly over so little he didn't know. Compliments were nice, but he didn't understand why they were so effective. What was it about this fellow that made his flattery so valuable? Naturally at the age of ten he wasn't old enough to understand true emotional manipulation. Even if he saw the man he wouldn't tell that his whole being was an act. How could a child see through such a thing? Adults were constantly falling for his tricks. He rarely met someone who even suspected something was amiss. Thus this lad had no chance of getting to the bottom of the matter. Regardless of his ignorance, he could at least be cheerful about his friend's transformation. Such a change was not to be questioned. After all, it was generally best not to look a gift horse in the mouth. That was something his father said frequently at home. Sadly it wasn't the best advice to give someone. The expense of his newfound joy came at a terrible price. His cheap ecstasy stemmed from allowing the man to infiltrate his soul. Whatever he was given this was far too hefty a fee. It didn't matter if the manager gave him a thousand realms to rule over. What good did it do someone to gain the entire universe at the cost of their essence? If he knew the truth about the supervisor he would know exactly what the cracks he saw were. They hadn't been erased. Those horrid black signs of rot had merely been bleached. His stranglehold over the children in his care was as strong as ever.

"I'm glad you're feeling better," he told the kid, genuinely pleased at the turnaround.

"Me too," he swiftly replied. "I'm not saying I'm not angry with Clement, but I think I can live with him."

At first this statement puzzled the boy slightly. Had he recovered at all? Why would he say such a thing if he had regained a positive spirit? Within seconds his anxiety had passed. It was normal for him to harbour resentment towards his peer. Twice they had fought within a very short space of time. The score was currently one-all. From his perspective it was a case of breaking the tie. That said, he was happy that he was no longer planning to hurt him. Just thinking about attacking him with weapons was enough to make him wince. It wasn't a nice thing to consider at all. The fact Bryan had got over this stage in his being was a great relief to the youth. With a warm smile he began to tell his friend about a detective story he had read online. It hadn't been published properly; it was a piece of fan fiction someone had written. Even so, it was an amazing read. Someone had obviously put a lot of effort into it. Alongside him the lad did his best to listen. However, there was something off about him. Deep down in his mind was a magnet pulling him into his own thoughts. Clearly this was a boy who would rather be dwelling on something else. If he knew him at all he could tell what it was. Obviously these comments from the adult had gone straight to his head. Perhaps this aspect of him was the only thing he didn't like. Why did he have to have such a high opinion of himself? It wasn't that he didn't want him to have confidence. Everyone needs to respect themselves to do anything. Still, he took it one step further. Imagining yourself as equal to others is perfectly fine. Holding yourself miles above everyone else was not. Victor couldn't bring himself to say anything about it. He spoke about the story he had read, knowing that Bryan was mentally condescending to him. In his own head he began to wonder how he saw his chum. Was he equal to him, or was he so far below him he was a speck beneath his feet? Trying to get inside his head was difficult. He could peer inside, but the door would quickly slam shut in his face.

"I can't wait for work tomorrow," he told the fellow as he bubbled with excitement.

"Why? Who would want to have to do it?" Victor immediately responded, not able to believe what he had heard.

"I'm going to impress him again. You'll see," he told the other boy while gazing up at the ceiling. "When I leave at the end of the month I'm going to be his favourite."

"You do realise he's one of the adults? He could beat you for no reason!"

It was Bryan's turn to be bemused. Did this lad know anything about Mr Evans? In shock he turned to made eye contact with him. One of the raging fires of bliss in his heart had gone out. How could anyone be so wrong about a man? He knew for a fact that his manager would never lay a finger on a camper. If he thought that he should try talking to him for five minutes. He would soon discover the truth of the matter. Mr Evans was the best person in the camp. Quite why he would lower himself into working in such a horrid place was nothing short of a mystery. Perhaps he thought he could change it. Maybe he believed the best way to stop the abuse was to lead by example. His group was incredibly productive. Even the slowest children could crank out six or seven frames in an hour. A wave of pride filled his heart when he realised how he compared to them. In the last half an hour before dinner he had decorated eleven. Once he got into a routine it was as easy as riding a bike. Running on autopilot did more than just blot out the world around him. It made his whole mind focus on one task. The result was that he was just as good as the older boys. In a split second he remembered his original train of thought. There had to be a way for the two of them to meet. Getting them together would show the lad that the adult was a good person. As soon as they had a chance to talk there would be no doubt in Victor's mind. Of course, he couldn't quite follow the logic in tarring the staff with the same brush. It was true that most of them were fatuous bullies. That would be putting it very politely. Yet that didn't mean that all of them were bad. Mr Evans certainly wasn't a psychopath. If anything he was the best man he had ever met. Who was that nice in the outside world? He was surely someone to be cherished. Anyone who had him working with them was blessed indeed. Victor could tell that he was besotted with the fellow. It could be that he was wrong; perhaps the man was as nice as the boy made out. Regardless of which way he looked at it, a few things remained that bothered him. They danced around his mind as if they were wasps out to sting him to death.

"If he's so nice, why hasn't be reported this place? He should have brought the police here a long time ago."

"I didn't think of that," Bryan eventually responded.

He certainly agreed that it was a conundrum. This was a valid point he couldn't explain away with ease. Despite this problem, his theory of improvement still appeared to hold validity. If he thought he could change things it was best for him to stay in the company. Somehow this didn't stop the deep itch within his body. There had to be something more to it than that. Summoning assistance would end the torment altogether. His eyes narrowed as he deliberated on the matter. Obviously there was a very good reason why he hadn't informed the authorities. Ironically the same could be said of the campers themselves. The other ten year olds could be excused based on their lack of experience. What excuse did the others have for not sorting this mess out? One call to the police could end their torture. They could ensure those responsible for the abuse were jailed. So why hadn't they striven to shut the institute down? Why hadn't anyone uttered a word of their experiences to their parents? Furthermore, why did people come back in the first place? Even if they didn't call the police they could save themselves. Simply spending the summer at home would solve all their problems. Nothing about this made sense. His head started to swim as he chewed it over. Was he the only one who wasn't completely brain dead? There was no way he was coming back next year. His parents had paid for him to be assaulted. Where was the sense in handing over cash for that? If someone actually wanted to hurt themselves they could do that in their own home. Bryan simply couldn't make head or tail of the situation. Was this how stupid everyone else was? Did they honestly not know that there was nothing stopping them from ending the madness themselves? Logically there were answers for all these questions. Victor could have told him that if he had bothered to consult him. Just because he was in the dark didn't make the entire population fools.

"Are you really sure he's nice?" His friend asked him, emphasising the third word.

"Yes," Bryan fired back, although less convinced this time.

"As long as you're sure," Victor softly stated, not wanting to start an argument with him.

"I mean, yes!" He was startled when Bryan reaffirmed his answer.

What in Inika was he doing questioning it in the first place? Nothing he had seen could possibly make him doubt the nature of the man. If there was a reason his suspicions should be raised he would pull them up himself. Yet there was nothing. Not once scrap of evidence existed to prove he was anything other than a cordial young man. At this point the juvenile began to wonder if Victor was slightly jealous. They hadn't really spoken about his supervisor much. Bryan didn't need to be told he was a cruel man. Could it be that he was merely trying to steal the concept of the fellow from him. Astronauts could probably see that he took pleasure from having him as a supervisor. It was certainly possible that the lad was trying to spoil something he enjoyed. This didn't exactly sit right with him either. During their lunch he had tried to get him to think clearly when he spoke of attacking Clement. When he realised he was feeling better he had been thrilled. So why would he be trying to steal enjoyment from him? This was something that didn't make sense to him either. Was this sinister motive even his true intention? Naturally he was going to be wary of adults. He is the same, knowing what most of them are like in the camp. Why couldn't he understand that Mr Evans was genuinely a decent human being? That had to be the answer; he wasn't the type of person who would intentionally cause someone harm. When he had been ready to kill Clement he had been horrified. Even the thought of a fist fight had been enough to turn his stomach. He just couldn't hurt someone, regardless of whether or not he knew them personally. So how could he be out to hurt his one friend in this nightmare? Feeling as if he could safely discount foul play, he wondered how he could get the two of them together. That was the only way he could put the doubt to rest once and for all.

"You'll see for yourself when you meet him," Bryan told Victor with a pleasant, if slightly smug, smile.

"I'm sure I will," he replied after a slight pause, praying that the encounter would end well for everyone concerned.

After a dinner of sausages and mashed potatoes the children were promptly sent to bed. As per usual they had thirty minutes to get themselves ready. Bryan barely noticed when Victor announced his attention to leave. He was desperate to see the girl again. Other than his friend she was the only person he felt he had a connection with. In terms of mental health she would barricade him against trauma. Surely he could weather any storm by thinking of those two. What else did he need to survive the rest of the month? Although it didn't seem as horrid as it had done the previous evening, the four weeks still stretched before them into infinity. How anyone retained their sanity at all was nothing short of a miracle. Frankly he was curious as to how he had avoided a nervous breakdown himself. In these conditions the chances of survival seemed infinitesimal. Yet everyone appeared to have made it through the first two days in one piece. Some of the lads were walking round on the edge of lucidity. These zombies always seemed poised to walk straight into brick walls. Others had been rendered as timid as mice. Their eyes constantly darted round as they massaged their badly bruised faces. Victor felt he should thank God he hadn't been assaulted yet. However, he didn't want to jinx his fate. There was still plenty of time for him to earn the ire of a guard. One wrong glance could send them into a mad rage. It had dawned on him that day that they weren't bad children. None of their transgressions deserved more than a smack on the backside. The problem lay with the workers running the establishment. They had infinite amounts of hatred within them. All they needed was an excuse to vent some on people incapable of defending themselves.

Bryan promptly left the dining hall. His friend was risking a great deal to speak to the girl. If he was going to put his safety in jeopardy it was only fair he did his best to keep his safe. Maybe if he remained just out of sight he could act as a lookout. In less than two minutes he had brushed his teeth. His peers were still giving him frosty looks as he went about his business. This only served to raise his ego. They were simply jealous of how well he was doing in the work detail. Presumably it wouldn't be long before the management officially recognised how good he was. Mr Evans had all but stated it several times that afternoon. Yet there was nothing to be gained in dwelling on that now. What he needed was a sharp eye. If a guard caught Victor by the fence he would be in trouble. The fact he is trying to interact with a female would surely spell doom for him. They would unleash the fury of God as they spanked him into the middle of next week. While he was content, he never allowed himself to forget how dangerous the place was. It would swallow you whole if you didn't have your wits about you. Thus the only expedient he could think of was to make sure his friend had a warning if a guard came his way. Quickly he reached the dormitory closest to the fence. Victor was up against the fence as his crush walked up to him. Exactly why he would risk so much for her he didn't know. She wasn't ugly, but she wasn't pretty enough for him to generate peril for himself. With a large smile on his face he stood just out of sight. He didn't want his friend to think he was spying on him. Someone of his intellect was fully aware that actions can be misinterpreted. He had been under the delusion that Jordan was his friend for years. For a little while he studied the soil beneath his feet. Why wasn't it covered in grass? Could it be that this place was so horrid it killed the vegetation? Having witnessed the horrors it had to offer he didn't struggle to imagine it. Emotions were very powerful forces. It wasn't unforeseeable that so much terror in one place would leave it stripped of turf. Maybe the workers deliberately treated it with herbicides. Grass would be nice for them to have. Anything that gave the children pleasure had to be destroyed.

"I'm so glad you could make it," he spoke tenderly as the girl walked up to him.

"Me too," she replied, her tone not a thousandth as loving as Victor's.

"How was your day?" He asked her with genuine enthusiasm.

"Alright I guess," she shrugged blankly, her voice one of chronic boredom.

"I was thinking about you today while I was working," he replied, rubbing her fingers through the chain link fence. "I hate it here, don't you?"

Another absent minded shrug followed. Bryan listened intently as the conversation progressed. This girl didn't seem to have an opinion on anything. Her head was about as full as an upturned colander. Bryan risked a look in her direction. If he was Victor he wouldn't bother with her at all. She was not the sort of person who deserved to have others put themselves in danger for. What would the two of them talk about if they met in the outside world? The way things were going he knew almost nothing about her. They might as well have been waiting at a bus stop in the rain. The lad followed an employee as he walked from the dining hall to an office block. With great suspicion he wondered what the fellow would do. Overhead the sun was still beating down strongly. In half an hour the traces of a glorious sunset would shimmer through the trees. He couldn't help but imagine himself fighting the fellow. If he thought it would help Victor he would certainly take him on. His best bet would be to attack from behind. Arming himself with something heavy was essential. One strike to the head could be enough to rid the world of him. His thoughts quickly began to digress into increasingly violent territory. After a few minutes he realised why he was there. Turning back to the couple, they were still struggling to find some common ground. It was almost pitiful to see the lad drag up the most obscure topics to try to please her. Even so, he had no choice. Almost nothing earned more than a shrug from the half-witted female.

"In school we have quite nice teachers. On Fridays they let us watch films afterschool," he began, the girl staring blankly back at him.

Suddenly the boy caught sight of an adult in the corner of his eye. His heart missed a beat as he realised the employee was heading straight for them. Taking a step forwards, he clapped to catch Victor's attention. Immediately the boy turned, Bryan entering into his vista. At first he was suspicious of his presence. Had he been there the whole time? This shock subsided when he saw the look on the juvenile's face. There was no time for verbal communication. A few seconds could make a world of difference in the outcome. Yet Victor knew everything he needed to. Such a fearful gaze could only mean one thing; there was danger around. Quickly saying goodbye to his girlfriend, he darted off round the back of a dormitory. Bryan, on the other hand, didn't bother moving. It was not against the rules of the camp to loiter in their free time. Nobody had told him that would be a problem. Even so, he didn't want to risk being targeted for something petty. A fleeting look over his shoulder revealed that the female hadn't moved. The idiot was still standing there, catching flies in her cavernous mouth. Why hadn't she gone? What was wrong with her? Did she have two brain cells to rub together? If she had she would have departed in an instant. Unfortunately not everyone can be as intelligent and wise as Bryan. He knew more than anyone that he had to make allowances for the flaws of other people, even if they did infuriate him. The employee marched menacingly up to him. Had he dreamt of joining the army as a child? He certainly had the stride needed for drill. There was great power radiating from him as he walked up to the boy. His baton hung loosely at his side, threatening him without the need for a single word. This climate of fear was something he would not forget in a hurry. It would remain with him for years to come. After all, it's not every day you step into the modern day equivalent of a concentration camp. The look on his face was rather smug as he contemplated Bryan. Nervously the fellow tried to work out what the adult wanted. Could it be the fact he was not running around that had aroused his suspicions? Or was it his proximity to the fence that had turned his head? Either way, he couldn't tell what his punishment would be. Who could say what would happen to him? If these people were simply violent they wouldn't be as scary as they are now. Their erratic applications of rage were what pushed people over the edge. They were bombs ready to go off, the screens of their timers having run wildly out of control. Nobody could tell if they would go off instantly or thousands of years in the future. However, Bryan feared this explosive would get him sooner rather than later.

"I heard you did good work today," he told the youth, amazing him with his topic of conversation. "Keep that up and you might just find yourself in a worker's uniform one day." Pride seemed to saturate his voice as he considered his own attire. "I take it you're trying to spy on the girls through the fence," he declared with a sense of uncertainty, hoping that was the reason.

"Yes, Sir," he lied, bowing his head with feigned shame.

"Give it a few years," the adult told him with a strange smile on his face. "That's when girls will become really interesting to you."

The pudgy male laughed loudly for around ten seconds. The lad didn't know how he should respond. He managed to choke out a giggle. If he hadn't he might have been beaten for insulting his sense of humour. Firmly the man gesticulated for him to return to his dormitory. Having cleaned his teeth he could go straight to sleep if he wanted. Naturally Victor wouldn't be there. It was a shame they weren't in the same work groups. Still, they would have a chance to talk over breakfast. He walked towards the shack with a grin stretching from ear to ear. Because of him his friend had evaded a nasty beating. He had also received a genuine compliment from one of the workers. In the vault of his heart that was a valuable substance. Seemingly all the others had taken from them was abuse. With his head in the sky he walked back to his dormitory. Although he was pleased it had gone well, he wasn't as happy as he should have been. There was absolutely nothing special about that girl. Either she didn't care about Victor one bit or she was incredibly stupid. He couldn't blame her for longing for someone to talk to. If the ugliest person in the world wanted to chat through the fence he would gladly oblige. Most of the other children in his group didn't care for him. The older boys treated him with an odd type of respect. Secretly they knew his productivity would earn him a job within the establishment. For that they were deeply sorry. Most people only lost their teenage years to the place. Evidently he might have his adult life stolen from him as well. Yet anyone younger than about thirteen already had resentment festering within him. How could he earn praise from him? What was it about him that enabled him to make so many bags? There really was no secret to it. He merely zoned out and let his subconscious mind get on with it. Frankly the rest was more valuable than the praise. While on autopilot he had a chance to heal the trauma that occurred when he was fully alert. That was something worth an awful lot to him. If it hadn't been for this bizarre meditation he would have beaten Clement to death.

"Have a nice sleep," the guard shouted over to him as he walked through the dormitory door.

That was something he certainly intended on doing. His body ached from the fight with his enemy earlier on. Even so, he was more than capable of working the next day. Once morning came his wounds will have healed. The throbbing from the blows he had taken would be but a distant memory. Even after a day spent labouring he was much better than before. His limp had completely disappeared. When he walked he no longer felt as if he would topple forwards. The flesh in his chest had long since stopped threatening to erupt from him. Such a thought had made him worried at first. Could something like that be possible? Quickly he realised how foolish he was being. He was supposed to be above the other kids. Why had he imagined himself in a playground urban legend? Of course his organs wouldn't fly from him. What was he going to do, swallow a grenade? Naturally he wished he did have a grenade. The guards would be digging holes for their fallen comrades. Picturing himself tearing the adults apart was pleasant after everything that had happened. Lying down in his usual spot, he placed his hands beneath his head. Tomorrow was bound to be a good day. If the previous two were anything to go by he would have a fantastic time. Now he needed to make sure he was well rested for the long day ahead of him. Closing his eyes, he had no idea that the other campers were staring daggers at him. If he had been more perceptive he would have felt the incredibly tense atmosphere in the shack. It wasn't yet at the point of erupting into violence. Still, he wasn't well liked amongst them. Fortunately the older boys seemed to maintain some semblance of order. Their presence ensured the other ten year olds couldn't launch any sort of attack. They would be on the kids before they could draw breath. This lad had attracted the attention of the management. That made him of note on the grand scheme of things. Attacking such a person would unleash greater fury in the workers than they had ever seen before.

"I will sleep well," he told himself as he began to drift off into a gentle slumber.

"Lights out in five minutes," a worker told them, appearing at the door.

Bryan barely noticed his statement. It didn't matter that it was shouted across the room. By this point he was already teetering on the edge of unconsciousness. His earlier thoughts filled his mind. Mr Evans was so nice he could barely wait to enter into his presence once more. When he was in there he felt safer than he did at home. What could possibly happen to him with that gentleman around? He would ensure nobody abused the children. It was upon thinking this that sleep swallowed him whole. The others were sitting around, desperately trying to extend their day. If they fell asleep they would soon be out in the factories again. With all the strength they could muster they began to fight their increasingly heavy eyelids. A few of the boys were crying, having been beaten just a few hours previously. Their sobs soon died out as the sandman took them too. Within ten minutes there wasn't a single person left awake. It is amazing how tired people get when they are in terrible conditions. Their energy had been zapped by fear for their safety. A shift adults would struggle with depleted their batteries as if they had run a marathon. In the other dormitories it was the same. A surprisingly pleasant silence gripped the rooms, the juveniles escaping their prison in their dreams. Bryan was perhaps the only person in the camp itching to get back to work. Thus it was no surprise he found himself dreaming of Mr Evans. In his reverie he found the fellow living with his family. They were gathered together in the living room, the television set on in the background. Sitting next to him on the couch was his pleasant manager. He placed his hand gently on the boy's shoulder. At that moment he had never felt such peace before in his life. It didn't matter that it was only a dream. Not once in the past ten years had he felt so loved. Compared to his parents he was a shining example of a decent person. This man would never anger, never argue and always provide the support he needed. As he slept it was as if he had never been trapped in the premises at all.

    Clement wasn't as lucky as Bryan. He didn't have a pleasant vision to heal his mental wounds. What he got was far more disturbing than family TV time. As soon as he fell asleep he found himself back in his school. He walked down the main corridor as he had done a thousand times before. Yet there was something different about it. The children were sitting rather awkwardly at their desks. When he studied their faces he found they were all staring at him. Their terrified eyes were so wide open they looked like golf balls. What was going on? Why were they so afraid? It was when he looked closer that he saw what the problem was. Every child was chained to the desk. Strong metal links connected them to their workstations. When he saw this he recoiled in terror. Suddenly a hand gripped his shoulder. When he turned he found himself face to face with the cruel supervisor of his work group. Still, there was something different about him. Staring at the man, he found he was much taller than he normally was. Judging by the size of him he had to be at least three metres. His hand was the size of a dinner plate as he began to squeeze the boy's shoulder. In pain he cried out at the top of his voice. With all the strength he could muster he began to kick the entity in the legs. Sadly his blows were too weak to have any sort of effect. Against Clement they might be effective. Even when taking on Graham they were strong enough to bring him to his knees. Yet this goliath was not just an ordinary human being. His legs were the same size as tree trunks. His arms looked as if they could rip through steel girders. Desperately he tried to beat the sadist back. Every ounce of power in his body was directed towards escaping the clutch of the fiend. With regret there was nothing he could do. None of his blows even made the ghoul flinch. He merely stared at the boy with a psychopathic grin. In terror he tried to summon help. There had to be someone around to hear him. The children were chained up, but the teacher was there, idly looking out of the window. If he could only attract his attention he might be alright. The member of staff would call the police once he saw what was going on. As hard as he could he punched the man while he called for help.

    "What's wrong with you?!" He screamed louder than he thought was humanly possible. "Can't you see I need help?! He's going to kill me!"

    The last statement finally made the man look over. When he did the boy started to relax. There was no way this freak could get away with restraining him. Even so, he wished the man would intervene sooner rather than later. The pain from where he was being held was unbearable. Looking at his shoulder was certainly a mistake. He cried out in horror when he realised what had happened. The man's talons had penetrated his flesh. Within his body his fingers were performing a hunt and search rescue mission. Blood poured from the wound as he studied it in disbelief. One final bellow managed to properly attract the gaze of the teacher. As he turned round he received yet another shock. This man was actually his brother. Naturally the body was completely different. This fellow looked as if he was in his thirties. He was almost twice as tall as the thirteen year old. Regardless of his size, this was definitely his sibling. His face was identical to the boy he had grown up with. There could be doubt about it. This person was the same boy he had spent all day playing with when he was in the nursery. All the times they had played hide and seek came back to him. School holidays were spent with each other, exploring worlds of their own creation. So why wasn't he helping him? He didn't even appear surprised that the giant was about to tear off a chunk of his flesh. Dozens of times he pleaded for help as blood cascaded from his wound. Around his feet a pool of the eerie red liquid was collecting. If it carried on much longer they would soon be swimming in it. The children seemed more interested in it that he did. Their faces were masks of sympathy as they sat in their uncomfortable plastic chairs. The only person who could help him was Adam. Yet the boy hadn't moved an inch. He simple watched with cold indifference as the creature rammed him into the blood. As he studied it he seemed to get bigger. Now the awful fellow looked set to burst through the ceiling. One of his enormous hands wrapped itself around the boy's arm. This was surely it for him. There was no way he could get away from his attacker.

"Adam, help!" He screamed with as much force as his vocal cords would allow.

"He's not bothered," the man told his victim with a spiteful tone. "Nobody cares about you; you're on your own!"

With that he leant forwards. His mouth opened impossibly wide as the boy struggled to get away. Unfortunately he could barely move at all. It was as if the beast had cast some sort of spell over him. His muscles were useless as the gaping cavern swooped down to devour him. The putrid air exhaled over him was nothing compared to the terror of being devoured. He had thought the camp was bad. All the things he had seen there had torn his heart to shreds. None of it compared to the emotions spiralling around his soul now. Even if Adam did come to his senses it was too late. By this point he was already inside the demon's mouth. As he began to bite him in half he screamed at the top of his voice. Suddenly the nightmare world in his mind began to dissolve. Sitting up, he continued screaming as he realised the events were not real. He was, of course, back in the living hell he had stumbled into. All around him the other campers began to groan. What was wrong with him? Couldn't they even sleep in peace? Still, none of them were angry with him. Kids are bound to have nightmares when they are trapped in a place of this sort. This didn't mean that they were happy about him balling. His cries echoed in the dormitory even thought his vocalisations had ceased. His uniform was soaked as his nocturnal sweat saturated the fabric. Had there been any cheese in their dinner? It would certainly explain the torment his mind had put him through. In his head he could still see the dark creature about to tear him in half. Its teeth were literally the size of tombstones as they had closed in on him. Never before had he suffered such a horrible event. Compared to his current situation it was a thousand times more terrifying. The guards could kill him, but they could never have his soul. Who could say what the giant worker would do if it had a chance to digest him. Perhaps he would be forced to live on as creature of hate. Wherever he went people would recoil in terror at the sight of the monster he had become. Fortunately that form of existence is not on the table. Still, he checked his limbs anyway to make sure he still had all four of them.

"Clement," his brother said with a tone of concern. "Was that you? Are you alright?"

"Keep it down," a boy groaned tiredly from the other side of the room.

"I'm fine," he replied, his throat hoarse from screaming. "Go back to sleep."

His brother didn't say anything after that. Why should he? There was no need for anything else. Even if teenager had offered to come over to sleep next to him he wouldn't have accepted. That vision, although horrific, had taught him a great deal about his sibling. Previously he had viewed the lad as his knight in shining armour. The first time Graham had attacked him his brother had been there. Obviously he considered himself partially responsible for the pair of them ending up in the camp. That had been translated into a need to defend him at every opportunity. But had it? He would have been on Bryan instantly if Rory hadn't mocked him. To save face with his friend he had let his brother be subjected to a vicious attack. Luckily he managed to claw back a victory without outside assistance. Those who saw it had been shocked. A small boy wasn't the person you would expect to turn into a prize-fighter. Nonetheless, Bryan had learnt valuable lessons about his victim. It was also no secret that Adam was fallible. Against one of the older boys he would be dispatched fairly quickly. Faced with a seventeen year old rugby player he would be almost powerless. If he was lucky he might just allow his brother to run. However, it would be no effort for the older male to break Adam's arm. Clement was also aware of how useless he was against guards. If he was being spanked for a minor transgression it would be madness for his sibling to intervene. That would increase his punishment, while getting the boy send to the coal shed for the night. Jordan had been locked in there for over twelve hours just for punishing a guard. That was after a fairly savage beating. If Adam tried to fight an employee he might not leave the camp alive. Maybe the guards would devise a punishment infinitely worse than a night in a crude cell.

"Yes, I'm alright," he thought to himself as he stared at where the ceiling would be in the pitch black room. "No thanks to you, though."

For the first time he found himself loathing his brother. Of course, he had been scared of him once before. The first night they had spent in the camp he had threatened him into using a communal toothbrush. Yet what he had done that day seemed unforgivable. There was a chance Bryan could have caused serious damage. If he had knocked him to the floor he might have hit his head. The only reason he hadn't rallied to his defence was the fear that dwelt within him. What would Rory have said if he had charged into battle once more? That was why he had left Clement to his fate. If a guard had been spanking him he would have understood his neutrality. However, this was a ten year old boy with a serious psychological disturbance. His only sibling had left him to sort out the situation himself. As far as he was concerned he was no longer friends with his brother. In the past he had argued with him over trivial matters. Yet within a few hours they were back playing together again. This time he had lost all interest in Adam. To him he was utterly alone in the camp. They were as distant as Jordan was from his victim. Those two would probably never even speak to each other in the future. Sadly Clement feared the same would be true for his brother. Turning over onto his side, tears formed in his eyes as he considered what he had lost. Losing his liberty was almost irrelevant compared to the situation with Adam. He could stay here year-round as long as he could overcome the hostility towards his relative. Did he even have a family anymore? A few choked sobs echoed through the building as he tried to return to slumber. After the nightmare sleeping had lost most of its appeal. Even so, it had provided an insight into the situation around him before. Hopefully he would reconcile with him if he slipped into another reverie. Certainly he couldn't drift any further from his only family member present.

"How could you do it?" He mentally asked his brother, praying that the pain he felt would evaporate by the time morning came.

Chapter seven

Bryan awoke feeling unbelievably refreshed. When the lights came on in the morning he gently awoke from his slumber. With a bit of luck his hopes could manifest in reality. Twice he had found enjoyment in his work. There was no reason why this wouldn't the case the third time round. He could barely wait as the door to the dormitory was unchained. Before he knew it would be back in the healing presence of Mr Evans. Why weren't people in the outside world as nice as him? If they tried to emulate his personality they would do well. Everyone else had known had lost their temper with him at one point or another. This man was certainly of a higher calibre than him. He might just be the best man he had ever met. How could he doubt this when merely being around him made everything seem alright? This didn't just include the so-called holiday at the camp. When he saw the man's smile his fears were washed away like sandcastles at high tide. There was no need to worry about such things as schoolwork. Wasn't he bright enough to do well? It had never been a problem for him in the past. He also didn't need to worry about finding a girlfriend. At the age of ten there was no need for such things. Plenty of time existed to find someone when he was older. For the time being he could just focus on being young. He would certainly miss it when he was an old man. In less than a minute the chain had been removed from the door. Even more light flooded in as the guard entered his vista. The usual notice of thirty minutes to breakfast was bellowed for the benefit of the children. Bryan began to wonder why he bothered to repeat it every morning. Wasn't everyone aware of the schedule by now? Were they suddenly going to call them five minutes earlier? Once people had done their teeth and used the toilet they tend to gravitate towards the dining hall anyway.

"Teeth," he thought to himself as the campers began to groan.

Only he seemed to enjoy getting up in the morning. The others didn't mind working for Mr Evans, but they wouldn't complain if they could have another hour in bed. A ginger haired lad was wiping sleep from his eyes as Bryan stood up. Seemingly once again he would be the first person in the queue. Slowly he sauntered from the building. The soil was slightly damp as he walked towards the washing area. Evidently there had been a slightly shower the previous evening. As he looked to his side he noticed the fog between the trees in the forest. A pleasant smell danced across his nostrils as he continued his journey. When he arrived at his destination he found it unattended. It was as if the older boys in charge of the stations had vanished into thin air. Picturing the day he would have brought a warm smile to his face. Jogging behind him was the fellow tasked with attending to their oral hygiene. He looked a little surprised when he saw Bryan standing there. Breakfast was still half an hour away. Most wouldn't be up for another ten minutes. He knew there was something different about this camper. His productivity was above that of the others. With more effort he could outshine the older boys. What was amazing was that he was only ten. At his age the management was only looking for items they could sell. As they matured they slowly increased in speed. This fellow had simply dived into the role. With no experience whatsoever he was able to shine brighter than anyone else. It was strange to think that by the time he came of age he might be responsible for half the group's output single-handedly.

"Good morning," he told the boy pleasantly. "You're a bit early, aren't you?"

"Am I?" He wondered, tilting his head to the side as he thought. "You don't mind, do you?"

"No, not at all," the fellow replied with a smile on his face.

Gently he squeezed a little paste onto the shared brush. So far he had not been struck down with illness through using it. By now his fear of contamination was almost gone. Even so, he had a little trouble gripping it at first. This would surely ebb away with time. Very few things didn't benefit from the healing power of the ticking clock. As he brushed his teeth he turned to face his dormitory. Two other older boys rushed from their cabins to attend to the pumps. Bryan still couldn't believe how quaint the whole setup was. He couldn't look at the area without picturing Victorian paupers filling buckets with muddy ooze. It was a step backwards in time that tickled something within the lad. The sun was still rising overhead. There was about an hour left before it would be of any great strength. Damp patches in the soil would be excised by its warm touch. Before they knew it the ground would be backed hard once more. Before he knew it he was rinsing his mouth out. Feeling rather refreshed, he strolled towards the dining hall. Frankly he had no idea if it would even be open yet. The teenager hadn't been wrong when he told him he was early. From the looks of things the shack was still chained shut. What was he going to do until he could sit down? He didn't fancy imprisoning himself in the dormitory once more. The smell in there was truly awful. The other boys had been sweaty all night in the stuffy environment. After three days they were all in desperate need of a shower. That was one thing he was clueless about. How were they supposed to wash? Nobody had told them they could attend to this need. As far as he was aware he hadn't even seen a faucet. Only the taps beside him had been set out for them to use. Maybe they simply hadn't been afforded this luxury. It didn't matter to the institute if they were clean or not. Why should they waste money so they could literally pour water down the drain? Even so, the boy longed to feel hot water flowing over his skin. At home his mother forced him into the bath once a week. If he had the opportunity he would throw himself into the bathroom. Neither hell nor high water would stand between him and the tub.

"Are we allowed to wash here?" He asked the fellow, eager for an answer that favoured him.

"Rarely," the man said, pretending to sniff the boy playfully. "I know what you mean. Us teenagers have to shower or we aren't fun to be around. Every two weeks is the rule," he replied with a nice tone.

"Thanks," he told him, walking away to let the next boy brush his teeth.

That conversation had been a pleasant experience. It was a miracle that they managed to maintain their sense of humour in such a place. Whatever the intentions of the guards were, it was a prison. He could go as far as to say it was a concentration camp. Not even prisoners are forced to work if they chose not to. How was it fair that murderers got to sit around while innocent children are forced to work? Such a concept seemed unfathomable to him. Luckily he found a distraction before he could let it get him down. A guard was standing outside the dining hall, unchaining the door. Immediately he began to salivate in anticipation of what lay ahead. A meal would fill the hole in his stomach. Without him noticing it had been carved out. He was sure he would enjoy every second of repairing the damage. As he walked towards it he remembered what had happened the previous evening. The narrow escape he had with the employee made him wince. Naturally he had come within an inch of a savage beating. It would have made the incident with Clement look trivial. Yet he had put himself in that position for a reason. If he hadn't maintained a vigil it would have been Victor in trouble. Surely the lad wouldn't forget the assistance he had provided to him. What he had done had been an amazing show of friendship. Now the youth couldn't doubt that Bryan was a faithful associate. Secretly he was hoping for more than just gratitude. Putting yourself in peril for someone else earned you a special place in their heart. This was the sort of thing that would bond them for life. Before he knew it he had reached the room. However, this time there wasn't an enticing odour. What was going on? Normally he could smell the food before he had even entered the shack. So why couldn't he this time? His mind concluded that it was still early. They had only just opened it for the campers. The cooks had to have time to put food on to cook. Probably they merely hadn't got that far ahead yet.

"Hello," he heard someone shouting from behind.

"Victor!" Bryan shouted, turning to smile at his chum.

"How are you? I'm so hungry I could eat a horse."

"Fine thanks," the juvenile responded sweetly. "I'm hungry too."

"I just wanted to say thank you for what you did last night," Victor blurted out, doing his best to keep his voice down. "You really helped me. If you hadn't seen him coming I'd be history."

There was no need for him to thank the lad. The look on his face told him exactly what he was thinking. This was what true friends do. He had no doubt that Jordan wouldn't have done it for him. By standing guard he had proved he was above that sullen bully. What he lacked, his former victim possessed in droves. One of his motives was to fulfil his own desire for greatness. Who could say he wasn't infinitely better than Jordan? Certainly he was above those in his work group. They were barely able to take steps while he was running marathons. There was pride to be taken in that. Last night he had broadcast the fact he was better than the monster that had abused him for a long time. Victor smiled back when Bryan offered him a grin. Despite knowing each other for only two days, there was certainly a deep attachment growing there. If something happened to the young man he didn't know what he would do. However, he wasn't keen on the girl he was jeopardising his safety for. The fact she wasn't that pretty was irrelevant. What bothered him was the lack of interest she showed in him. From the way she acted it was clear she was treating him as a curiosity. She studied him with the same disinterest as a person glancing at a crow. There was nothing there in terms of emotion. Couldn't he see this? It would break his heart to have to point this out to him. How would he do it without terminating the friendship he valued so highly? Still, he couldn't remain silent over the issue. If he truly cared about Victor he would be as brutal as he had to be. A caring word, regardless of how devastating it was, was the best thing for him. Yet when he opened his mouth he found himself speechless. Two parts of his mind fought against each other valiantly. One part ached to be honest with his first true friend. The other couldn't bring himself to destroy the only good thing the lad had. If he didn't have the girl to dream about, reality would become a lot harder. His time on autopilot told him that. There was only one way to escape the camp; that was to flee into your own head.

"Shall we sit down?" He found himself saying.

A nod from his friend caused them to enter the dining hall. Still there was no reassuring odour of food. Bryan began to worry over the issue. Every time they had a meal there was a delightful smell. It told them that decent grub was coming their way. What did it mean if this was conspicuously absent? There wasn't even a faint trace of last night's dinner hanging in the air. At the back of his mind he feared the worst. Could it be that the management had given them satisfying courses as some sort of trick? By now the children had learnt not to fear about their diets. Nobody could complain about what was being offered. It would be incredibly cruel to suddenly change things. He pictured the staff bringing in grass clippings with sadistic smiles on their faces. In seconds he began to feel deflated. Other than work, meal times were the only part of the day he looked forwards to. When he was eating he got to share kind words with Victor over the generous portions. Evidently that had been taken away from them. Still, he didn't let his fear get his friend down. What sort of person would dump their negative emotional load on a person they respected? He wasn't Jordan; he was a decent person. It seemed to him that the good time he had been having had come to an end. For three days he had actually enjoyed his time at the camp. It was the worst place he had ever been to, but he had etched out a comfortable existence. To him that confirmed that happiness was within the reach of every person. They simply have to clutch it with both hands. Victor noticed that his friend wasn't as cheerful as he had been earlier. This upset him slightly; he didn't want him to slide back into the dark place he had occupied yesterday morning.

"Are you sure you're okay?" He asked the boy, eager to get to the cause of the problem.

"Fine," Bryan's tired response echoed through the empty room. "I just wish I could go home."

"So do I," the boy quickly stated, his mind drifting away slightly.

"I did have a nice dream last night," Bryan told him in an attempt to raise his waning mood. "Mr Evans was living with me at home. It was amazing; I'd never felt so happy."

Straight away Victor's attention was consumed by the boy. Was he being serious? Had this actually happened? The thought of living with one of the guards was almost enough to make him lose control of his bowels. This had to be some sort of joke. If this was real there was something definitely wrong. Had he forgotten how he had been beaten by the guards? Did the memories of the abuse he had witnessed evade his recollection? He would do anything not to have a member of staff go anywhere near his family. Yet here this fellow was, pining for the adult who had some sick hold over him. His eyes narrowed as he considered what had been said. If this was true his friend had utterly lost his mind. Strangely he found himself consumed by conflicting emotions. Part of him wished he had a supervisor that was so pleasant. Obviously Bryan had been lucky in being assigned to work under him. Another section of his being was disgusted by the thought of his associate picturing a guard in such a way. The people who worked here were cruel all the way down to their cores. There couldn't be an ounce of goodness in any of them. He would rather take his chances with a pack of rabid wolves than spend a minute in a secluded place with them. He didn't care if they pretended to be nice. It had to be manipulation designed to work in the employees' favour. What other reason could there be? If this fellow was so nice, why was he working here? Why hadn't he reported it to the police? This was the question that had bothered him earlier. It didn't make sense for someone so pleasant to play a role in such a twisted operation. On the other hand, he knew better than to trust his own judgement. He had to admit that he was envious of the boy. How did he manage to have such a good time when every day was a struggle for him? As best he could he tried to put these thoughts out of his head. They would do him no good whatsoever on the grand scheme of things. He couldn't, however, get the sweet smile out of his head. Bryan had worn it while reminiscing about the man. Frankly it made him want to vomit. Something terrible was happening in his work building. That was obvious to him, despite his misgivings. He didn't like the fear it generated one bit.

"I think you should be careful around him," Victor dared raise his voice loud enough for the boy to hear him. "I don't think he's as good as you think he is."

"This again?" Bryan asked him, a slight hint of frustration in his tone.

"I'm just wondering why he's working here if he's so nice. If he's actually a good person why hadn't he reported this place? Why does he work here in the first place?" The apprehension in his statements didn't escape his friend's notice.

Of course, Bryan was pleased that his pal was showing an interest on such a deep level. There could be no mistaking the emotion he was investing in him. That was exactly what the juvenile wanted. With Jordan there hadn't been anything truly there. By the end he hadn't even pretended to take an interest in his victim. Victor was infinitely closer to him then anyone else had ever been. With the exception of family members, he was right at the top of the list of preferred people. Even so, he found himself growing exhausted of having this conversation. He couldn't answer the questions that were put to him. Yet he also was clueless as to why the campers came back here year after year. Very little of the place seemed to make sense when viewed closely. Neither of them had any idea that by the time they left they would know the answer to that question. Only then would they understand the secret that made even the older boys go quiet. It was something they would immediately wish they didn't know. For the rest of their lives they would search for ways to mask the fear the thought of it inspired within them. Ironically Bryan would be better off listening to his friend. Mr Evans was the master deceiver in the realm. He could convince people that the most ludicrous things were real. Bryan, despite having his eyes opened to Jordan's deception, couldn't see past the adult's mask. There was a perfectly good reason for this. The former bully was merely an errant school child with no discernible talent; the latter was a fully fledged psychopath. Mr Evans wasn't even his real name. It was something he went by in case the police ever did investigate the institute. Any statements given against him by the kids would send the police off in the wrong direction. In terms of misinformation he had fooled even the senior management. Now there was something that made him laugh when he was feeling down.

"I hope there's food coming," the boy voiced his concern, eager to change the subject.
"What makes you think there isn't?" Victor asked him swiftly.
"Can you smell anything?"

It was true; there was no wonderful aroma hitting their nostrils. At once the boy began to think the worst. Naturally this awful place would do whatever is in its power to hurt them. That included letting them starve for a few days. Suddenly the lad began to panic. What would they do if they weren't going to be fed? After a single night he was hungry. What sort of state would he be in if he didn't get anything until the following morning? By the end of it his stomach would be digesting itself. People would be eating the dirt outside. Yet somehow he wasn't as grieved as he would be. Why would they open the building at all if they weren't getting something? It would be far better to let them go straight to work. That was, of course, if they had more in mind than simply depriving them. The guards went out of their way to be as sadistic as possible. Sabotaging their food would carry far more emotional weight than simply denying them their meals. For all they knew there would be laxatives in the offerings. Not only would they have to work, they would have to do it in soiled clothing. Perhaps they wouldn't even let them change afterwards. Now there was a cruel act if there ever was one. Bryan hadn't considered that the meals might be vandalised. All he wanted was to get back to Mr Evans. Talking to Victor was an enjoyable experience. It was nice to know that someone his own age enjoyed his company. However, the juvenile didn't excite him in the same way the supervisor seemed to. With all his heart he yearned for the man's approval. In his own way he wanted his friend's acceptance as well. Even so, the adult's praise carried a lot more weight than that of the ten year old. Still, this didn't mean he couldn't enjoy Victor's company while he was able to. Chillingly it dawned on him that his chum might not be alive tomorrow. Who knew what torment the day had in store for him? Spanking could be taken too far. If he somehow enraged a guard he could be struck in the head with a baton. Picturing his friend as an inert corpse made him want to vomit. What would he do if the boy was taken from him? It didn't matter that he wouldn't have to suffer through the rest of the month. Selfishly he wanted the lad by his side. No part of him wanted to have to brave the nightmare on his own.

"Look who it is," Bryan told Victor as Clement walked through the door.
"You're in my group, aren't you?" Another boy told the ten year old before he had a chance to take a seat.

Slowly the fellow turned to view the other camper. The last thing he wanted was another fight. Had someone convinced this person to attack him? Graham could easily have bullied a younger kid into doing his dirty work for him. His mother always told him that bullies are cowards at heart. The morbidly obese teenager was certainly no exception. As far as he was concerned, the jury was out on Bryan. There could be doubt that he was spineless. Standing up to the boy who had manipulated him for years had taken guts. The only conclusion he could draw was the lad's sanity was slipping.

Was it any wonder given what was happening around them? To his surprise he found the youngster smiling pleasantly at him. What exactly was going on here? There was no hostility in his eyes at all as he offered a small wave. Clement subconsciously returned it out of politeness. His statement had been correct; this fellow's face was very familiar. Of course, the two of them had never spoken properly before. Until last night he had always been in his brother's shadow. That chapter in his life had come to an end. No longer was he the defenceless child in need of protection. Twice he had vanquished his foes with his bare hands. As far as Adam was concerned he could take care of himself. There was no reason for the older boy to stand guard, unknowingly scaring off potential friends. Without his sibling by his side he was far more approachable. Evidently this ten year old thought so. The boy's ginger hair danced beautifully under the influence of the gentle breeze. It was as if his head was on fire. Clement offered a pleasant smile of his own. At this stage he had no idea what his intentions were. Potentially he was out to cause him serious harm. Even if he was it wouldn't be the end of the world. He had shown the entire universe he wasn't going to be pushed around. If he could take on a fourteen year old, this lad would be a pushover.

"Yes, I think so," he replied as nonchalantly as he could.

"Sweet, I thought I recognised you." The youngster told him with a genuinely affable tone that caught Clement off guard.

"Mind if I eat with you?" He asked the boy. "I'm trying to meet as many people as I can."

There was no need for the boy to say no. As he studied his new associate he realised he was at least half a foot taller than him. A slight twinge of jealously rose up in his stomach as he considered his observation. Why was everyone bigger than him? Would he be forced to go through the rest of his life as a runt? That was what his brother told him when they argued at home. His mother was very quick to reassure him that he would grow. She stroked his hair and told him that people developed at different rates. Until recently he had always believed her. However, a few months ago he had realised that she was just guessing. She couldn't possibly foresee his future stature. For all she knew he could remain the same height for the rest of his life. Even so, he appreciated being comforted in such a way. Hopefully he would make it back home to see his parents again. With one hand he gestured for the lad to sit down on the bench. As soon as he did so he swung his leg over it himself. Within a few seconds the pair of them was sitting as if they were old friends. It was a bit silly for them to have dived in so quickly. He didn't even know his peer's name. Clement didn't care about this; he was just glad that someone besides his brother was taking an interest in him. When he thought about Adam he couldn't help but feel anger rising up from the depths of his soul. He had treated him as if he was an embarrassment. That, as far as he was concerned, had ended their relationship. He didn't care if he never saw the boy again. Why should he? If he was so embarrassing why would the teenager want to be around him anyway? Deep down he knew these thoughts were incorrect. Rory had infected his sibling's mind. For an adolescent there was great value in maintaining social ranking. If the obnoxious lad hadn't been there Adam wouldn't have minded stepping in. Currently he classed all this as irrelevant. For the time being he was happy to focus on the fellow who had gone out of his way to speak to him. The least he could do is make an effort to be attentive.

"My name's Clement, what's yours?"

"Leonard," the youth responded with an invigorating enthusiasm.

"That's nice, my uncle was called that."

"Thanks. I like yours too."

There was something delightful about the boy. In every word he radiated energy. If this boy was a machine he would be a nuclear reactor. Honestly it was refreshing to see someone with such fervour about them. If all the passion erupted from him the camp would be reduced to a smoking crater in the forest. Feeling as if he was talking to the embodiment of youth, he strove to continue the conversation. Clement was good at what he did. Decorating frames was incredibly easy for him. While the guards would rather kill him than admit it, he thought they were impressed by his productivity. It would certainly explain the less than hostile glances they frequently gave him. Just as he was about to speak his colleague began talking. Again he spoke with a tone that made the boy feel as if everything was going to be alright. At that moment he decided he was not going to let him go. Such a person was worth their weight in gold. Happiness in this place was not to be turned down so readily. For all he knew this could be the last meal he would ever have. Maybe he would be dead before he could take a single mouthful. You could never tell what sort of mood the lesser workers were in. Seemingly they would wear the same scowls if they won the lottery. Potentially one of them with pure murderous rage in their hearts would knock him from the land of the living. Perhaps a crack would open in the floor, hands dragging his soul to hell for all eternity. Before he could conjure them into existence he pushed the images from his mind. There was no point in tempting fate. Surely as long as he remained positive he would be fine.

"Do you know those two haurraks over there?" Leonard asked him, attracting the attention of Bryan and Victor.

"Is that some sort of insult?!" The trouble maker fired back, looking as if he would totally lose control of himself.

"Sorry, my aunty uses that word. It means kids," he shouted over to them in an attempt to ease the tension. "They're a pair, aren't they? Do you know them?"

"Unfortunately," Clement grumbled, not wanting them to start a fight. "The one you spoke to attacked me twice already for no reason."

Leonard's smile appeared to flee from his countenance for a brief moment. Less than a second later it was back, his beautiful blue eyes having refilled with joy. Clement replied with a joyful grin of his own. This fellow was wonderful. How could anyone remain so jovial in a concentration camp? There was obviously a great enigma behind those serene eyes. If the lad could discover his secret he would be the happiest child ever to have being imprisoned here. A quick look over his shoulder made Bryan turn away. Evidently the beating he had given him yesterday was still fresh in his memory. For that reason Clement doubted there would be a fight. Although the conflict hadn't been laid to rest, there shouldn't be any scraps between them. However, he knew that the lad enjoyed his feelings of superiority over others. Inevitably he would seek a third brawl to try to settle the score. If he wanted on he only had to ask. Anything that broke up the monotony of the camp had to be beneficial. Amazingly he wondered if combat would even be on the cards with Leonard present. Just now he had managed to diffuse the situation. How could anyone remain angry when his raw zeal for life registered in their psyche? His parents must be fantastic to have raised such an upbeat child. What would he be like as an adult? He would have all the friends he would ever need. Someone of his calibre couldn't possibly be friendless. People would flock to him to bask in his glee. Certainly Clement was doing just that. Genuine affection for the fellow began to form within him. Perhaps the seeds of true friendship would germinate into thick bushes. Hopefully they would be able to weather being slashed and burnt by the forces the camp would unleash upon them.

"I don't like him much," he whispered to Adam's brother, hoping the subject of his comment wouldn't hear. "He doesn't seem as nice as you."

"Thanks," he responded quickly, the compliment forcing the ends of his lips upwards.

"I don't like the adults, either," he dared add, hoping none of them were in earshot.

"Neither do I," Clement replied with a slight chuckle. "I don't think anyone does."

"I can't believe my parents paid to send me here. Can you believe it?"

"No," the other boy declared, wishing his parents had spent the money on clothes instead. "I came here with my brother."

"The older boy you sit next to when we're working?"

"Yes, that's him."

"He seems nice, too."

Clement nodded in response. He couldn't believe how friendly the boy was. It was as if the camp was throwing him a scrap from its table. Sadly he couldn't help but worry that something was going to mess it up. The institute had a way of ruining things when they took a good turn. Yet he tried his best to remain cheerful. It wasn't hard considering he was sitting next to a candle of optimism. How did he manage to be so positive about everything? Didn't he realise his life may well be in danger? For the time being he was happy to enjoy the boy's company while it lasted. If things didn't work out at least he had met someone nice. It was difficult to see how they wouldn't remain on cordial terms. Such a person would try his hardest to befriend everyone. This sort of person usually does well in life. After all, nobody wants to be around someone as frosty as an Arctic glacier. Out of the corner of his eye he spotted Adam entering the room. When he saw him he felt a deep longing in his heart. More than anything he wanted to be friends again with his older brother. It was only his petty rage that was preventing them from being intertwined again. Immediately he corrected his thoughts. He couldn't go through life in his sibling's shadow. If he ever wanted to be an individual he had to break free from Adam's grip. That was why he didn't call him over to sit with him. Instead he returned his gaze to his new friend. Truly it was an act of God that he could meet such a nice person. Now Adam didn't have worry about Clement embarrassing him in front of his friends. He never had to bother with the lad again if he didn't want to.

Adam saw the child sitting with one of his peers. At first he was a little afraid. Who was this person? Was he trying to hurt him? These worries evaporated as soon as he caught a glimpse of Clement's face. There was a smile stretching from one ear to the other. Such a sight filled his heart with joy. His brother had evidently found another fellow to play with. He couldn't say he wasn't relieved to have a break from his sibling. It wasn't that he didn't enjoy his company; at home they were inseparable at times. Yet it was nice to have a chance to socialise without him tagging along constantly. Now he had found someone of his own age he would surely make other friends. Before he knew it he would have a whole posse around him. They would be his own entourage, fighting Bryan whenever he reared his ugly head. Picturing this made him chuckle slightly. If anyone was going to act in such a manner, it would be Clement. He had no doubt that in his own little world he was a superhero. For the first time since they arrived he had no reason to worry about the ten year old. Finally he had a chance to be himself. Without looking at him he found a place to sit down. A look at the door revealed a group of older boys about to walk in. By now the room was filling up nicely. This didn't bother the two new associates. Clement couldn't believe how nice his new friend's hair was. It took an awful lot of strength for him not to run his hand through it. You don't have to have a degree to know that it wasn't a good idea. Although someone so nice probably wouldn't mind, he didn't want to risk the fragile bond. So far things were going swimmingly. He didn't want to do anything that could ruin things between them. Thus he resigned himself to imaging the act. Even this felt amazing. In his mind he felt as if he was stroking fire, his hand somehow resistant to the heat. A brief pause fell over the conversation. Before a few seconds could pass by the boy rushed to fill the space.

"Do you have any brothers or sisters?" His voice betrayed his genuine interest in his acquaintance.

"No, I'm an only child. It gets lonely sometimes, but I have friends to play with."

Clement listened intently to his response. Having an older brother he couldn't empathise fully with the predicament. Still, he had been alone often enough to know it wasn't pleasant. Perhaps there was a reason his parents hadn't wanted another child. Maybe he had brought them so much happiness they felt as if their family was complete. Now there was a thought that warmed his heart. As he felt it he offered another wide smile. His friend returned it with an even bigger one. Already he knew that something good had come from his time at this awful place. By the time he left he had to get the boy's address. Perhaps they could write to each other while waiting for the next summer. Realising what he had just thought almost made him faint. Could he really look forwards to returning to this awful camp? To him it was a sure sign that he was loosing his mind. What other explanation could there be? Anticipating the second month here would drive a normal person insane with fear. So why had he just acknowledged he would look forwards to it? As far as he was concerned, madness had already consumed him. It was just a matter of time before he was placed in a padded cell. Who could even guarantee that Leonard was even real? Perhaps he was a figment of his lunatic imagination? Maybe he had spent all this time rocking back and forth in the corner. After all, what were the chances he would be this lucky? A genuinely nice human being had come to this camp, then had been assigned to his work group. To top it all off, he wanted to befriend the lad. Things like this don't happen to him. For the first time in a while his outlook on life began to change. If this person could enjoy his company, maybe his lack of friends wasn't due to him being an obnoxious person. Perhaps it was simply of result of no common ground. This fellow was so nice that that problem wouldn't stop him. He would keep going until he found something they both enjoyed.

"I'm really glad we met," he told his friend honestly.

"Me too," Leonard responded with yet another beam. "I just wish we had met somewhere better. I hate it in here. Every time I'm around a guard I almost have a panic attack," he told Clement, his countenance falling.

Seeing him in pain was an awful experience. Someone so bubbly didn't deserve to be in this prison. Perhaps that was the catch in their meeting. He would meet the ideal chum, only to lose him to abuse. By the time he left there might be nothing left. The once brilliant personality could be hallowed out entirely. Considering this left Clement feeling despondent as well. Why was it that the institute had this power over them? Surely they could only control the children if they let them. As long as they distanced themselves from the torment it couldn't bother them. Sadly this was easier said than done. How do you switch off reality? The last time he looked there wasn't a button on the side of his head. Only when he was working did he allow himself to become a creature of his own subconscious. In this state peace abounded, healing the mental scars the nightmare had inflicted upon him. Mentally he was screaming for the boy to recover from his trauma. He wasn't going to lose his friend. Life was only as cruel as a person let it be. To get anywhere in the world you have to fight with everything you have. Obstinacy is the only way anything in history has been done. All of humanities achievements seem to have stemmed from the shedding of sweat and blood. There and then he resolved that he would do everything within his power to held Leonard. He would be in his grave before he let him become a ghost of his former self. Desperately he thought of something comforting to say. If he was in this state Adam would know exactly what to tell him. In a few minutes his flagging morale would be back where it needed to be. Alas, he was not his sibling. The only things that entered his head were platitudes. Even so, they would have to do. Surely he would appreciate the boy's effort, even if he wasn't particularly helped by what he was saying.

"Time is going by so quickly," Clement stated, agreeing entirely with what he was saying. "It's already been three days. In no time at all we'll be back at home."

"You think so?" His chum responded, his eyes betraying his concurrence with the declaration.

"Yes, of course we will. I don't think you've been bashed, have you?"

Leonard considered this for a moment. It was true; he hadn't yet felt the pain of a beating. Yet he didn't dare say this for fear of tempting fate. As a compromise he shook his head. Hopefully the universe wouldn't misunderstand it as a request. Ironically the guards didn't seem to pay him much attention. Despite his wonderful personality he had a tendency to fade into the background. He doubted if their manager would be able to pick him out of a line up. The only time they came into contact was when he glanced at his decorated frames. Although he had received a stern word on their practise run, he had learnt from it. The next time round he merely attracted a neutral look. That had been enough to reassure him that he had improved. Usually if the man had to give advice twice he followed the second serving with a nasty knock. The fact he hadn't earned such a punishment hadn't escaped his attention. He didn't know why he was so surprised. When he was working he gave the task everything he had. An order from the guards was followed to the best of his ability. There was no reason why he should be chastised physically. In this respect he was quite similar to Clement. Neither of them put one toe out of line. For that they had earned the best treatment of all; cold indifference. However, in Clement's case he was being actively monitored by the supervisor. He certainly had talent for what he was doing. For that reason they considered it prudent to keep an eye on him. If he could keep up his performance he might be offered a job at the end of his teenage years. If he knew this he wouldn't work anywhere near as hard as he had been doing. The thought of working for the institute would make him retch. In all honesty he would sooner die than be forced to strike children for money.

"That's something to focus on," he urged Leonard with a friendly pat on the arm.

"Yes, you're right," he replied quickly, a trace of a smile returning to his face. "I think breakfast's on the way."

Their heads turned as the kitchen staff brought out large bowls. Each of them carried a portion in each hand, their faces harder than usual. By this point the dining hall was packed with hungry campers. They could barely control their desire to gobble down the offerings. After a long sleep there was nothing better than stuffing their faces. To get through the morning shift they would need all the energy they could get. How could they face the hell they were in if they were hypoglycaemic? Bryan was in two minds over the presentation of the food. There was still no smell inviting him to gorge himself. The bowls in the hands of the workers were not steaming as they usually were. Normally the heat of the grub begged the boys to dig in with their plastic cutlery. Today there was no sign of the wonderful warmth that compelled him to devour the meal. Yet the boys who had received their portions didn't look disappointed. Another guard placed spoons alongside them. As soon as they released the tools the lads grabbed them eagerly. Bryan watched as they shovelled their breakfast down their throats. If the food had been sabotaged they show no signs of knowing. It was difficult to see where he was. The angle made the contents of the dishes invisible. However, as more bowls were put down, he realised what it was. This morning they had been given cereal swimming with milk. Finally he understood that his previous thoughts were misgivings. All the energy he had devoted to fretting had been wasted. Those kilojoules might have come in handy in future fights. They could be the difference between knocking an opponent over and merely causing him to stagger. If there was an uprising against the adults that energy could have allowed him to scrape a victory in a brawl. Sadly it was gone forever. An older boy would have known that these thoughts bordered on the deranged. Even so, the thought of a rebellion no longer caused adrenaline to surge through his system. Exactly why this was the case he knew all too well. He simply couldn't do that to Mr Evans. How could he risk the safety of the one man who treated him as a human being? For the first time he dared admit to himself that he truly enjoyed his time at the camp. He came here under the pretence that he would have a world of fun. Ironically, that was exactly what it was providing. He owned the place all the gold in the realm for helping him to realise he was under parasitic attack. If he had never come here he would still be under Jordan's spell.

"Full fat, I think," someone stated as they slurped a spoonful of milk.

Merely hearing that was enough to generate a chorus of stomach rumbles. Some of the guards looked at the food hungrily. Only when the children had cleared the hall could they tuck in to their own breakfasts. It was reassuring for the boys to see them viewing the food in such a way. If any of them doubted that it had been tampered with they could put their fears to rest. Why would the management allow them to interfere with the meals? Anything that negatively affected productivity was unacceptable in their eyes. Even in the eyes of Bryan it seemed strange. Surely all forms of cruelty would hamper the efficiency of the workforce. Naturally they didn't see it that way. Some abuse was necessary to bring out the best efforts of the campers. Above that threshold, however, things took a turn for the worse. Sometimes they could see the frustration in the eyes of the staff. When they were disciplining the children they longed to be able to cross that line. Yet even they knew the bosses would have their guts for garters. Only higher employees could kill a child and emerge with their careers intact. Lesser individuals would be reprimanded severely for their actions, even if though they would avoid legal trouble. Bryan wondered what would happen if one lad killed another. Without weapons at hand it would be very difficult to do so. Still, he couldn't help but consider the consequences an older boy would face if he beat a younger prisoner to death. Presumably the management would authorise the public execution of that fellow. He would be made an example of to discourage further violence against their peers.

"Thank you," Victor told a guard as a bowl was placed in front of him.

"Thanks," Bryan stated when he received his own helping.

Both boys made these statements with different intentions. In the former case he was simply trying to treat the workers with respect. He knew they were looking for reasons to satisfy their bloodlust. Discourtesy could not be used against him in such a way. The second fellow genuinely expressed gratitude to the adult. They were colleagues of Mr Evans. Surely that created some sort of fraternal bond between him and the wardens. In both cases their declarations went without response. Perhaps some part of the staff wanted to respond positively. After all, they were the only lads with enough manners to say such things. However, this urge was buried beneath miles of bile. Any love of children they once had had long since been driven from them. Who knew what abuse the employees had suffered in the journey to becoming part of the camp? Not for the first time Bryan found himself sympathising with them. It went against everything the other children felt, but he was a slave to the feeling. Logically he knew better than to let Victor know this. Already he thought he was mad for enjoying the company of Mr Evans. How would he react if he told him he was warming to the adults? Perhaps the lad would decide he no longer wanted to be friends with him. For a ten year old the thought of losing his only associate caused great concern. If anything came between them he would be totally alone. Sadly his lack of foresight had allowed him to make enemies during the past three days. The whole of his work group seemed to envy him, giving him scowls whenever they set eyes on his face. Not even the older boys were fully immune to this. They had to work to get as good as they were. Subconsciously this translated into a resentment of him. Perhaps most worrying of all was the mess he had made with Clement. Obviously the juvenile was a complete lunatic. Without Victor there to help in his defence he could be trampled into the dirt. Such an unstable person was erratic to say the least. Clearly that meant there was a serious risk to their safety. Together they were stronger as a unit. They would need to stick together if they wanted to defend themselves properly.

"I can't wait to get back to work," Bryan declared after chewing a mouthful of cereal. "Today should be a good day."

"Yes," Victor responded, not quite sure what to make of his comment. "We wouldn't want you to miss Mr Evans, would we?"

There was no sarcasm in his voice, but Bryan could tell something was amiss. Frankly he was tired to having the same argument over and over again. Victor felt the same way about the matter. He didn't want anything to come between them. That was why he had learnt there was no point in debating the issue. There were questions Bryan couldn't answer about him, but they had no power to convince him that the supervisor wasn't the man they thought he was. They chatted over trivial items for the rest of breakfast. Neither of them could find the strength to try to convert the other to their way of thinking. Despite a good night's sleep they both felt tired. Perhaps it was their night-time escapades that zapped their energy. Victor was very grateful for Bryan's help in evading the patrolling guard. If he hadn't maintained his vigil his contact with the female prisoner would have been detected. That wouldn't have ended well for anyone concerned. This way they could continue meeting in secret. Of course, the lad planned on speaking to her that evening. His close encounter hadn't dampened his passion for her. Bryan was curious as to why he continued to risk himself. Naturally he didn't risk offence by questioning him on it. However, it seemed that she treated him as a curiosity. She didn't even seem to care for him as a friend. There was no reason for him to spend energy on her. He would be better off developing his skills in the factories. At least way he would reduce the chances of receiving a beating.

"That was a close shave last night, wasn't it?!" Bryan whispered enthusiastically to him.

"I know, I can't believe we got away with it," Victor replied softly, his voice laced with excitement.

"What exactly is it that you like about her?" He asked, genuinely interested to hear his response.

"She's so beautiful," he told him as he began to daydream. "She's nice, too. You don't find that in a lot of people."

"She's alright, I suppose," Bryan managed to bite his tongue to avoid insulting her directly.

"More than alright," Victor quickly corrected him. "I could see us living together when we're older."

When he heard that he almost dropped his spoon. How could anyone be so deluded? She had no interest in him whatsoever. Unfortunately desperation does this to people. She was one of the few good things he had in the place. That meant she had value in his heart. He would fight to the death for this female if he had to. It didn't matter that their conversations were one sided. Victor couldn't see that she sighed miserably when he attracted her attention. He might put himself in danger for her, but she wouldn't bat an eyelid for him. It was heartbreaking to see him devoting so much time to her. She had entered his soul and stolen a piece of his being. From the looks of things she was either too stupid to realise or didn't care that he was infatuated with her. This female, who he dreamt about for hours at a time, was about as interested in him as the guards themselves. If he didn't seek her out she would forget him in a day. Sadly Bryan couldn't begin to raise the issue with him. How would he react if he stripped away this pleasant notion? For his emotional strength he leant on the female camper. Without her he would crumble internally. His only friend would be left a hopeless wreck. It dawned on him that lies can have more value than the truth. Being honest with Victor would have the same effect as a stick of dynamite strapped to his heart. That was, logically, if he could bear to believe what the boy was saying. Most likely he would storm off in a huff. His mind didn't want to accept the truth of the matter. In contrast to honesty, reinforcing the lie would heal him. While he kept up the pretence he could lift himself up from the depths of despair.

"I hope everything goes well for the pair of you," he wished them well, even though he knew it was doomed. "Just make sure she feels the same way about you before you do anything silly."

"Who are you, my father?" Victor playfully responded, narrowing his eyes.

"I don't want to see you getting hurt. Even if she likes you too the guards will beat you just for talking to her."

"Do you think I don't know that?!" He raised his voice, surprised that the boy had made such a statement.

"Of course you do. I don't want to see either of you getting hurt."

There was no doubt in his mind that Bryan was being honest. Every time he spoke to her he was taking a great risk with his safety. It was only a matter of time before his communications are discovered. When the affair was exposed he would have to face a hefty punishment. Such a transgression would not be dismissed for any reason. He would be spanked so hard he wouldn't sit properly for weeks. The guards would beat him further just for the fun of spilling his blood. The images in his head shocked him. In a moment of clarity he realised just how much he had matured in the past few days. Before coming here he would never have conjured such disturbing thoughts. Now they were as much a part of him as his left arm. Sighing, he nodded in agreement with what his friend had said. Why couldn't things be simpler? If they had met at school they might have had a chance of getting together. Instead he had to almost risk his life just to catch a glimpse of her pretty face. As he considered her further he heard a commotion from outside. Suddenly the air was alive with screams. Immediately the room fell silent. What was happening now? Just as they were getting used to the camp, something happens to upset everything. The boys' hearts raced as they listened to a child screaming an apology. There were tears in Victor's eyes as a worker bellowed obscenities as a response.

"What's going on?" Clement asked Leonard, not brave enough to raise his voice higher than a whisper.

"I don't know," his chum replied, wondering why he thought he would know anything.

"I don't like this," someone declared at the other end of the room.

"Quiet," the boy next to him hissed, not wanting him to draw attention to their group.

"Please, I wasn't trying to escape!" They just about deciphered the wheezes of the lad.

"Then why were you digging by the fence?!" A male employee queried, scarcely believing the cheek of the camper.

Suddenly the whole workforce knew what was happening. Someone had been caught trying to get out underneath the fence. Exactly why they had tried it he didn't know. As long as you worked you could evade punishment. Trying to leave was the most serious act they could commit. Perhaps he was as good as dead in the eyes of the management. Peradventure they would kill him to send an example to the others. The thought of being forced to watch him die almost brought Clement's breakfast back up. Fortunately he managed to control himself. However, the sound of dry retching didn't earn him favourable glances. Who wanted to hear that just after they had eaten? Regardless of the noises he was making, nothing could drown out the sound of the boy's crying. All the group could think about was the escape attempt. Suddenly every mind in the room became focused on it. Obviously the guards knew fleeing wasn't impossible. If it was there would be no need to chastise those caught trying. The sound of screaming grew closer as the boys made out more of the conversation. Horrible swear words filled the air as the guard dragged the boy to the dining hall. Clement didn't know the escapee. From what he could out the voice wasn't familiar at all. Leonard thought he recognised it, however. When he searched his memory he saw a ten year old with pitch black hair. Then again, he wasn't certain of it at all. Perhaps he was simply clutching at straws.

"This brat was caught trying to escape!" The guard shouted as he appeared in the doorway.

"I'm sorry!" He pleaded pitifully with the worker, struggling against the hand that held his shoulder.

Leonard was both surprised and saddened to see that his memory was correct. On the bus journey down he had sat next to this fellow. Although he had been quiet he had been pleasant enough for them to become associates. Sadly they could only interact at mealtimes. They hadn't been placed in the same work groups. He was a rather handsome looking lad. His hair was as black as newly mixed bitumen. The Roman nose was a little too large for his face, but he would grow into it. That was, of course, if he wasn't killed for his transgression. Why did the adults have to treat children in such a way? Just thinking about it made the ginger juvenile feel sick. Once again the smile ran from his face. This didn't evade his friend's notice. For the second time Clement wondered if he had lost his friend. There would be time to worry about that later on. For the time being he was fixated on the sight in front of him. As hard as he could the child was tugging himself away from the employee. With his other hand he did his best to break the man's grip on him. Unfortunately there was no way he could get out. Not even Adam would be able to dislodge a single mighty finger. Deep down his victim knew he was trapped. A moment of madness may cost him his life. His screams grew increasingly hysterical as he anticipated the worst. All he wanted was to run away. Maybe if he hid for a while the mess would blow over. That wasn't an option in this place. If he did find a secluded spot he would be found. They would turn the camp upside down to find him. When they did he would be in even more trouble than he was now. Every word that came out of his mouth begged for mercy. In desperation he made all sorts of oaths. He even offered to work through the night in exchange for his safety. Naturally the guards weren't going to comply with his requests. It was important they drove the notion of getting away out of their wards' heads. If a trace of it remained it would contaminate their whole psyche. Before the guards knew it there would be missing children in the woods.

"Are you going to tell them how you tried to escape?" His captor teased him with an eerily calm tone.

"I tried-" he started, but couldn't find the strength to finish.

"You tried to do what?" The man asked him, his voice taking on a familiar harsh edge.

His victim couldn't answer. He couldn't even look the other boys in the eyes. All he wanted was for this to be over. How could anything be alright after this? They would surely kill him for desiring freedom. One of his hands wiped the tears from his eyes. By now they were stinging, the crowd in front of him a blur. Clement could see that the dam within him was breaking. Piece by piece the wall was crumbling to dust. It would only be a little while before the reservoir flooded the valley. When that happened he would never be the same again. Trauma had a way of changing people. A flicker of innocence his parents admired would blink out forever. Part of his soul would be ripped from him to satisfy the bloodlust of the guards. His silence infuriated the worker. How dare this boy not speak when he was asked a question? What sort of ape would try to escape in the first place? Perhaps it wasn't surprising that he couldn't talk. If he tried to dig under the fence he obviously wasn't as intelligent as the family dog. With a raised voice he repeated his question. Even the lad could sense that he was making things worse for himself. If he thought it would help he would get down on his knees. With his hands together he would pour his soul out, imploring him for mercy. Logically this would not be enough to save him. As an unjust being, this worker was incapable of forgiving. He would remember this for many years to come. Just to be cruel to the male he would torment him with it every time they met.

"Answer me!" He shouted so loudly the young man flinched.

"I tried to dig my way under the fence!" He bellowed at the top of his voice. "Are you happy now?!" The victim added, turning to face his abuser. "Do you like hurting me?!"

Gasps filled the room as they comprehended what he had just said. By challenging the man he had written his own death warrant. Instead of digging his way to freedom he would have been better of digging his own grave. At least that way he wouldn't be thrown out for the wolves. The anger that left the boy's body shocked the whole crowd. Did such a small person really generate such fury? It took a few seconds for the worker to understand what had just happened. Clearly he hadn't expected such an outburst either. Yet before the children could draw breath the atmosphere began to boil. Rage evaporated from every pore in the older male's body. Clement didn't need a degree to know this could only end badly for the youth. With a clenched fist he punched the young man straight in the teeth. Goblets of saliva flew through the air as the target fell backwards. The grimace on the adult's face could melt steel. Few adults would be able to take him on in such a wrathful state. In the blink of an eye the man kicked the child in the stomach. A scream emanated from within the wounded cub. Another kick followed before the cry could echo off the walls. A third cracked something within the boy's body. Picking the writhing mass from the floor, he punched him in the stomach again. Upon letting go he watched as his victim flew through the air. Two metres away he came down heavily, screaming in agony. Words could not describe how much pain he was in. Every nerve in his body was on fire after the ordeal. Regrettably his punishment hadn't ended there.

"Kyle," the adult smirked as he walked over to the failed escapee. "My apologies for that, I'm normally not so lenient on kids that try to get away."

This statement relaxed the boys slightly. Did he mean it was over? Had he served his punishment for his actions? Kyle certainly didn't think this was the case. One of his eyes was shut; the other was half open. Despite his limited vision he knew there was something wrong with the worker's body language. After what he had been through he didn't trust the guards as far as he could throw them. If the gaoler wanted to talk to him he could do so from a safe distance. His chest heaved as he struggled to inhale. What had happened inside him? He felt as if something had broken within his abdomen. Picturing it made him want to vomit. There was no way he was going to get medical treatment out here. If something was seriously wrong he was as good as dead. Just enough strength persisted for him to drag himself along with one arm. Even that was an enormous struggle. At most he managed to pull himself a few inches towards the bench. That was the only plan he had. Perhaps if he took refuge beneath the furniture he could somehow evade further torment. Yet the man continued to insist that nothing further was coming. Even so, the sadistic look on his face told him he was lying. Indeed, after thirty seconds the man sighed deeply. Clement couldn't take his eyes away as the adult silently advanced towards the kid. Across the room Bryan was secretly siding with the guard. Who would want to escape from here? It was awful, but it was survivable is a person was prepared to work in the factories. As far as he was concerned the male was getting everything he had coming. Although he knew he was right, he didn't dare say this out loud. They were bound to disagree with him, just as they did with everything else.

"So I'll beat you some more!" The guard joked, advancing menacingly at the poor kid.

Immediately his writhing became more frantic. If he could only get under the table he might be able to shield himself. Obviously this wouldn't work. The adult would simply pluck him from where he had been lying. Still, his terrified mind clung to the idea that he could find shelter there. Thus he moved as fast as he could towards his sanctuary. Unfortunately there was no way he could get there in time. His injuries were agonising already. Never before had he experienced such pain. Frankly he wouldn't mind curling up in a ball and dying. At least that way there would be no more discomfort. He wouldn't have to worry about the workers again. His mind would simply lose itself as he slipped into the afterlife. Like a shark the man descended upon him. The prey didn't even have time to wince as he was lifted from the floor. In desperation he lashed out as hard as he could. He knew this was no longer a matter of evading a beating. This man had no idea what he was doing. New recruits didn't know how far they could take abuse at first. They had to learn from observing their colleagues. If he had worked there for longer he would know he had already done his job. The other boys prayed silently as he slammed his small fists into the man's torso. If they were causing him any pain he wasn't showing it. A smile grew on his face as the blows rained down on him. His flesh was much stronger than that of his victim. It would take a lot more than he had to bruise him. With one hand he threw the boy into the wall. Every mouth hung open as he slammed head-first into the masonry. A sickening crunch filled the air as he fell to the floor.

"He's killed him!" Someone shouted from behind him.

"He's not breathing!" Another lad shouted.

For a moment there was a horrific look on the man's face. Picturing the boy as a corpse had filled his heart with psychopathic joy. When the other campers saw it they wanted to run for their lives. This was surely a madman. At any moment he could turn on them. If they had the strength they would head for the door. It didn't matter what they guards did to stop them. No part of them wanted to be near the fellow. Why had he done that? Naturally they didn't believe he was dead. How could they? These boys were just children. How could they truly comprehend what it meant to be dead? None of them had truly started living. Clement couldn't take his eyes off the crumbled body. From where he was sitting he couldn't tell if he was breathing. Certainly there was no tell-tale movement of his chest. If he was still alive he had been knocked out cold. Leonard was stunned by what had just happened. Why had he been sent to this place? Tears flowed down his cheeks as he implored the boy to move. That was all he wanted. One little twitch would remind the world that there was life in him yet. Honestly he wouldn't mind if he swore directly at the ginger boy. As long as he was speaking he was still alive. He would live on to see their time at the camp end. His abuser merely stared at his body. For thirty seconds nothing was said. What could anyone say to make this alright? A pool of blood was collecting underneath the boy's head. Was that a good sign? Surely if he was bleeding his heart hadn't stopped. Clement knew it wasn't actively flowing. If anything it was dripping from his wound as water flows across concrete. Unbelievably the man shouted an insult at him. Was he so cold that he would treat the wounded in this way? Wasn't it enough that he had caused him such a great injury? When his taunt didn't inspire a response he ordered him to stand. Again he received not even a speck of a response. The lad didn't even groan. If he was conscious he would have made every effort to stand. Through fear of further pain he wouldn't have dared defy a worker.

"I'm not playing around with you!" His shriek threatened to rupture the eardrums of everyone in the room. "Get on your feet now!"

Another ten seconds passed without him moving. The skin of those watching rapidly grew pale. An alien would think he had descended upon a planet of albinos. Their colour change was ironic in a way. The snow-coloured skin matched the frostiness in their hearts. Nobody could bring themselves to say what they were thinking. This boy was stone dead. One of the adults had killed him in cold blood. There and then Clement decided he was going to get out of the camp. Whatever happened, he would make sure the man was punished for what he had done. Why couldn't he have left him after the first beating? There had been no need to go back for a second helping. Only his bloodlust had driven him back into the thick of things. If he had simply left him he wouldn't have made himself a murderer. No longer was the male happy that he had injured his ward. With frantic jerks of his body he bent down to inspect his handiwork. What was going through his mind? Did he feel anything for the fact he had murdered a child? Or was it a case of fearing for his position? He must have known that slaughtering the workforce was frowned upon. The terror in his head must have been palpable. What would he do if he lost his job? He didn't know anything other than the camp. All through his teenage years he had been coming here. The adults had been his carers here, just as his parents were at home. That made his abusers his family in a twisted sort of way.

"What have you done?!" Someone managed to whisper.

"Come on; turn over onto your stomach. I know you're pretending. If you drop the act now I'll give you a bowl of cereal." He screamed into the boy's ear so loudly he probably heard him in heaven.

For ten of the longest seconds in history they waited. Was he going to respond? His attacker didn't care about the food. He could have another ten bowls if he wanted. All he needed was some conformation that his victim was still alive. Immediately after finishing his statement he began to grow impatient. What was it going to take to wake him up? Suddenly a hole appeared in his mind. From it poured all sorts of thoughts. Part of him that had lain dormant was roused by what he was doing. How could he have accepted the position? Fearing what would happen if he refused it was no excuse. For years he had dreamt of being free of this place. For some reason he thought it would be a good idea to spent his adult life here too. Why? What lunacy had compelled him to take the job? Now he had ruined his whole life. His sadistic programming was smashed by the sight of the dead child in front of him. There was no going back now. He would have to hand himself in to the police. It was only fair he took whatever sentence they handed down to him. Frankly he considered execution too lenient. What worse crime was there than child murder? A life that had barely started had been so tragically cut short. More than anything he wanted to sacrifice himself so his victim could live. What good would it do him to keep hold of his worthless life? He was sure the juvenile could make far greater use of it than he had done. It dawned on him that he hadn't even checked for a pulse. A glimmer of hope appeared in his heart. Maybe the boy had simply been knocked unconscious. There was nothing to say he wasn't perfectly alright. Once they had treated his head wound he might be up and about in a few hours. There was always hope that things would turn out for the best. Perhaps he hadn't murdered a child in cold blood. He had every reason to believe that the lad would go on living for another sixty years.

"What have you done?" One of the female guards asked him tiredly.

"Do you know how much trouble you're in?" The man next to her asked him.

Their manners disturbed Clement greatly. These were not the attitudes of someone hurt by the tragedy. They were the voices of people who were worried for their colleague. Leonard so no concern in their eyes for the boy's safety. Why should he care? The others could easily pick up the slack in the sweatshop. However, their peer was in danger of having his career come to a messy end. What would the management say when they found out he had killed an inmate? By rights the children should have gone off to start their morning shift. Every second they wasted here was losing the company money. The first thing they had to do was get the kids back to work. On the verge of hysteria the man fumbled around for any sign of life. Turning his victim onto his stomach was a mistake. The sight of the huge gash in his head was overwhelming. Staggering backwards, he couldn't take his eyes off the crescent of bone visible through the split in his skin. Before he knew what was happening he was doubling over. Vomit poured from his mouth as his grief gripped him. What had he done? Not too long ago he had been a child in this camp. He had been abused badly by the guards. This cycle of abuse would continue to infinity because of people like him. Turning to look at his colleagues, he wondered how they could stand to work for the institute. He couldn't believe he had fallen for their brainwashing. It was as if he had been possessed by a fallen angel. Now the light of God had shone on him, freeing his mind from the poisonous influence. His look surprised his peers. It wasn't someone who was about to beg for a second chance. He might as well have told them he was going to blow the whistle on their operation.

"He's dead," the woman told him, fearing what the man would do. "There's no reason why you have to go the same way."

"Have you seen what you've become?!" He screamed bitterly at the frosty female. "Look at what I've done. Can't you see this whole camp is wrong?!"

"What's happening?" Victor asked Bryan with a whisper.

"I don't know. I think he's lost the plot," his friend responded with a concerned tone.

"Everyone here needs to get to work," the woman urged the children to head for the shacks.

"Norman," the other male approached the murderer. "You know we can take care of him," he stated calmly, glancing towards Kyle's remains. "Just let us help you."

"No, Harry, I killed him. I have to turn myself in."

There was genuine remorse in the man's voice. Tears were streaming down his cheeks as he began to sob. Even the stupidest in the crowd could see that this was a penitent fellow. Bryan could tell that there was something different about his eyes. Prior to the incident with Kyle he had been totally consumed by his brainwashing. He had been a firm believer in everything the management had dumped on him. Now he had woken from their spell. Once again he was a normal human being, repulsed by what was happening around him. Bryan didn't enjoy seeing the change one bit. Surely he was a man who was out to cause trouble. He would never say it, but he knew that what was happening was right. History could tell him that since human beings appeared children have been working. People changing their attitudes didn't negate the role of juveniles in society. In his mind he begged the two adults to do something. They had to stop this failed employee before he brought the whole system crashing down on their heads. Slowly they began to walk towards him. Evidently they had received his orders. All they needed to do was show him that he had the potential to be a good worker. As soon as he took a swig of their morality he would drink the whole glass. Did this man seriously want to go to prison? He was looking at a sentence of thirty years. Why should he lose three decades for an event that didn't last three minutes? It was inconceivable for him to choose such heavy punishments over the power they offered him. Evidently the trauma of what he had done had driven him insane. No person of sound mind would vacate the position he had been offered. After all, a fish doesn't throw itself onto a river bank for no reason. Why would it when it meant leaving behind everything it needed? If he refused to let them help him he would blow the secrets of the company. In a few days the children would all be liberated. Every single member of staff would end up in jail for their part in it. If he wouldn't accept their assistance they would have to stop him from reporting the facilities.

"Norman, we're giving you one last chance. Help us help you. Just come with us to the staff room. At least here what we have to say. If you still want to go to the police after that we won't stop you," the woman told him, picturing how she would take him down.

"She's right," Harry added, realising that she had one hand on her baton. "We won't stop you from leaving as long as you wait a few days. Why not hear what we have to say?"

Bryan could tell they were getting ready for a fight. He would not enjoy the consequences of standing up to him. If he didn't accept their terms they would do things the hard way. He couldn't deny that he was enjoying what was happening. The man was a fool; he had been given a perfect ultimatum. If he submitted himself to them they wouldn't spill a drop of his blood. Failure to do so would leave him just as dead as Kyle. None of them other children could believe what was happening. More than ever they wanted to go home. Just seeing the dead eyes of their peer was too much. Sobs rose from the crowd as they realised they were in hell. Would they be allowed to leave now they knew he had been murdered? They were witnesses in a homicide case. Surely when the truth was revealed they would be forced to testify. For that reason they were in a great deal of danger. Even they knew that dead bodies can't talk. That would make slaughtering the workforce an ideal option. His eyes fell across the room to Clement. Why hadn't he died instead? It wasn't as if the world would be worse off for losing him. Logically he was the sort of lunatic who would dream of escaping. So why hadn't he tried it? Why hadn't be been caught and had his head slammed into a wall? It didn't occur to him as odd that he was having these thoughts. The camp had altered his thinking massively since he arrived. Of course, he knew he was superior from a very young age. All around him was power, exerted by those who had it against children who didn't. For someone who considered themselves better than others it was quite an attractive concept. He didn't know it, but it could be him walking around with a baton one day. Without people of his nature it would difficult for the facilities to continue operating. Normally they took years to get someone ready to accept the camp. If Bryan had the chance he would volunteer willingly. Such people were highly prized by the administration. He was someone they wanted to keep a close watch on. Mr Evans had already highlighted him to the overall manager. Although he didn't know it, he had taken the first steps on a dangerous path.

"I don't want to hear what you have to say!" Norman spat his reply so loudly he made the children jump. "You're all sick, twisted monsters. I wish I'd never come here. Then he might still be alive."

"This is a perfectly normal response," Harry told him through gritted teeth. "You're bound to feel shocked the first time you take a life. You didn't exactly enjoy the first spanking you gave, did you?"

Bryan felt a sense of pride when he heard those words. These people deserved credit for what they were doing. The advice given here may one day help him if he was offered a position. For the first time he evaluated how he would feel about that. Three days ago he would have told them exactly where they could stick their job. However, all that had happened since he had arrived. Jordan had been revealed to be a parasite of the highest order. When he realised this he had never felt so angry or so powerless in his life. Now he had been offered a glimpse of true power. Weren't most people a little like Jordan? Don't most people take the easiest possible route if they can? That was all he needed to justify the abuse in his own head. Surely the guards were helping these people by attempting to quash their weaknesses. The only people who were against personal improvement were those who didn't want to let go of their easy lives. Frankly he would dig a grave for such individuals if he had the chance. Jordan was a foul creature that didn't even deserve to be called a human being. Why was locking him up in a coal shed overnight a bad idea? Naturally he didn't say these things out loud. He didn't even dare tell Victor about them. He would think that the boy was some sort of deranged criminal. Nothing could be further from the truth, of course. However, in this day and age an unpopular view automatically made you a fascist. This was true whether or not the common belief had any validity at all.

"I can't believe you killed him!" He heard Clement shouting.

Immediately all eyes were upon the lad. He had risen to his feet to shout it. Adam prayed that nothing bad would happen to him. These people were just looking for an excuse to beat someone. Directly confronting the worker was bound to lead to bloodshed. Was his sibling completely insane? Wasn't watching a camper being beaten to death enough of a warning? What would it take for him to learn to keep his head down? Once again the youth was the victim of Bryan's dark thoughts. Honestly he had no idea how someone could be so wrong about the situation. The worker was the hero in all of this. He had taken a stand against the children, demonstrating the superiority of the guards. If he was an adult he would make an example of Clement. Obviously one death wasn't enough to keep everyone in line. What better sacrifice than someone who would never be fully under the spell of the employees? He had the feeling that nothing they would do to him would be enough to instil discipline. Thus the only suitable course of action would be to end his life. If there was trouble in the facility, it would inevitably start with him. He listened as the juvenile screamed obscenities at the murderer. Hearing them drove the bile to Bryan's throat. He wished there was a knife in his hand. Clement would be on the floor with a slit throat. Maybe that would be enough to silence him. The two workers fired dirty looks at the ten year old. Evidently they agreed with him about the boy's conduct. Still, they weren't in a position to punish him. They weren't even ready to send the kids back to the work groups. If they tried to use force against the children they would be attacked. The killer would be on them in seconds. Worryingly Norman had noticed the female reaching for her baton. If they attacked he would do his best to fend them off. Only then did he stand a chance of getting out of here. What the police decided to do to him was irrelevant. No part of him cared if he died at the hands of his former colleagues. As long as he released the children he will have done his job. Once they dispersed into the forest the management would never be able to round them all up again.

"You're a murderer!" Clement howled at the top of his voice, his eyes saturated with revulsion.

"I said that's enough!" Harry bellowed in response, although he had lost some of his authority.

"You're all sick!" Adam's brother stated with the taste of vomit in his throat.

"He's right!" Leonard declared as he stood up.

"Sit down!" The female shrieked with a tone of impatience.

This was going horribly wrong for the two guards. How were they going to take him down now? He would help the children if they were silenced with force. Likewise, the children would assist him in a brawl. How could today have gone so wrong? A perfectly normal meal had ended in disaster. One camper was stone dead at the hands of a traitor. Now the kids were on the verge of joining him in a revolution. Presently it appeared that they would have to call reinforcements. Without other staff members around, they were doomed. Who could tell what would happen if they were attacked? If all the prisoners banded together they wouldn't last long on their own. Two adults were nothing against dozens of children. Before they could escape they would be on the floor. Boys who have held grudges for years would pour their aggression out onto them. In a short while their blood would be flowing across the rough concrete. All hope would be lost as their lives were slowly extinguished. What would happen after that? Armed with batons, the children would run riot. Reinforcements would be brought in, but the traitor could have opened the gates by then. In hours news of the camp could reach the outside world. If they survived they would spend the rest of their lives in hiding. Wherever they went they would be terrified of being identified. People wouldn't understand what they had been doing. They would hear about beatings and presume they were evil. Hadn't the members of the public been spanked as children? Had it done them any harm? They wouldn't ask themselves these questions. All they would do is point the finger in blind ignorance.

"Don't sit down!" Norman ordered the boys. "Why should you listen to her? What power does she have over you?!"

"I have the power to kill you like he did Kyle!" She informed them as she drew her baton.

"She's right. Do you think we haven't got enough weapons here to massacre the lot of you?" Harry warned the children sternly. "What about the guns we have? Do you think there aren't enough bullets to turn you into pepper pots?"

This seemed to steal some of the fight from the lads. Still, they were not defeated yet. All they were waiting for was a spark. One burst of energy was all it would take to ignite their gunpowder tempers. Even the workers knew that when it came all hell would break lose. The female trembled a bit when a group of older boys gripped their bowls. It didn't matter if the adults dodged their crude missiles. From history class they remembered the story of Draco. He was a lawmaker, apparently killed when the crowd he was speaking to threw cloaks into the auditorium. The legend states that he was suffocated by the sheer weight of the things piling up on top of him. Whether or not it was true she didn't know. One thing she was certain of was that small actions can have massive consequences. One thrown bowl could bring down their whole organisation. She knew this had to be dealt with quickly. But how could she summon reinforcements without arousing suspicion. Unless she left the building she couldn't contact anyone. However, she could sense that there might be some hope for them. Most of the faces in the crowd were stony towards them. Their countenances revealed just how much resentment they had stored up from their treatment. Naturally they didn't have the wisdom to realise that the abuse was for their own good. How else are they supposed to iron out the weaknesses that plagued them? Those aged around sixteen and below bore these dirty looks. They stared at the guards with nothing but contempt in their heads. Still, she knew that there were some supporters in the crowd. The oldest boys, seventeen and upwards, would come to their defence. If the children attacked them they would throw themselves into the brawl. These lads had been shown what it meant to be part of the institute. More than anything they wanted places in it. Saving the lives of two wardens would make them stand out when their cases are reviewed. Even some of the younger campers looked as if they would attack the errant kids. Some as young as ten had witnessed the power that was radiated constantly by the adults. Who could resist such an attribute? They would do anything to help advance them relative to their peers. For that reason they would rally behind the guards. Even so, they were in the majority. Perhaps twenty of the group would assist them if it came to a brutal battle. That number was simply too low for them to defeat an uprising. Whatever they were going to do, they would need help from the other staff members.

"For goodness sake," Bryan muttered as he rose to his feet.

"Sit down, kid," Harry warned him. "I know you're one of the good ones. We don't want anything to happen to you. Nothing with happen to Norman, either, as long as he does what we say."

"You don't get it!" The renegade soldier screamed as his former friend. "I have taken a life! Nothing will ever make this right!"

"You know you won't get in trouble with the police," the female replied tiredly. "We'll take care of that. All you have to do is apologise to the manager. He'll go easy on you."

This snapped something within the mind of the killer. Was this woman playing a joke on him? Did she seriously consider murder a minor transgression? Just because he wouldn't get in trouble doesn't make it right. By that logic she could justify genocide providing the bodies are never found. The children had never seen such a disgusted look in their lives. Bryan didn't pay one bit of attention to it. Although the heavy door to the kitchen was closed, he knew there were still people in there. Anyone could see that this was about to get ugly. Without reinforcements the adults wouldn't stand a chance. As soon as the man began to fight them the youths would get involved. Through sheer numbers they would be swamped. Their lives would end as showers of blows pummelled them into submission. Logically summoning assistance was the best expedient available to him. After all, it wasn't as if he could pull an army out of thin air. Without worrying about the consequences he began to walk towards the door. Kyle hadn't moved under his own power since he had hit the wall. His blood had also stopped flowing. Not one trickle had left the wound in over two minutes. Surely he had gone; his transgression had signed his death warrant. Of course, it was terrible that he had perished for his crime. Still, that didn't change the fact he shouldn't have tried to escape in the first place. An executioner is not bound to feel any sort of guilt over his profession. If people didn't want to be killed by the state they shouldn't commit murder. He was glad he couldn't see his face fully from where he was. His somewhat floppy neck had pushed his face to one side. One of his eyes, however, was on show. Immediately after seeing it the boy stopped. It was as sudden as turning off a light switch. Straight away he knew he would never be able to get the sight out of his head again. Although it was blankly staring at nothing, it was an embodiment of fear that could cleave a soul in half. For a moment he doubted whether or not he was fighting for the right side. Norman had done this before his mind had slipped. His actions stemmed from his participation in the activities of the camp. A boy around the same age as him had died at the hands of a warden. Even so, Mr Evans had done his job very well. The hole in his thoughts disappeared as soon as it had formed. Norman surely couldn't be the one to blame. He was simply reacting to the misconduct of his victim. If he hadn't committed the worst act possible he wouldn't have suffered disciplinary action. Frankly he got off lightly. While they are here they are supposed to respect the authority of the adults. Kyle was incapable of doing that. For his discourtesy he had paid the ultimate price. Before he lost his mind he hurried past the corpse. No good would come from dwelling on the unpleasantness for too long.

"What are you doing, boy?!" Harry asked him fearfully, not wanting to risk a talented slave.

"You'll see," he told the man, earning a glare from the rogue guard.

Clement didn't know what to make of this. What could he possibly be doing? He would be better off keeping as quiet as possible. This situation was more volatile than any oil pumped from the ground. Exactly what he intended was unknown to his peers. Could he be siding with the man? Was he about to stand next to him? If so, Clement would never fight him again. Why would he when he was actively staging a revolution? These boys were waiting for someone to take a swing at the adults. As soon as they did that there would be no stopping them. Some of them had been here seven times in their lives. That sort of hatred could consume a person. They would fight until only one side was left breathing. Either they would die in battle or slaughter every enemy that dared get in their way. Leonard smiled when he saw the man walking towards Norman. In a few hours they could be on their way home. If the fellow would open the door for them they could escape into the outside world. Evidently it had taken someone as mad as Bryan to take the first step. All eyes were on him as he walked towards the fighter. There was a smile on his face as he saw the ten year old approaching. This was it; the first of the boys had come to his side. With glee in his heart he waited for the male to reach him. When he did so he would be welcomed with open arms. For choosing freedom he would have a place in the history books. Maybe one day people would be taught how he bravely sided with the rebel cause. Yet there was something wrong with him. As he came closer he could tell that he wasn't looking at him. How could he have made this mistake? The child was looking past him. In disbelief he watched as his ward walked straight past him. What was he planning? Everyone watched as he stopped in front of the kitchen door. Immediately the two guards realised what he was doing. How could they not have seen it before? In there were four adults responsible for the catering. Who was on the rota for breakfast that day? Frankly in all the excitement they had completely forgotten. The female also knew that this could backfire on them. Naturally the staff would support them if it came to a fight. Even so, in there were enough weapons to fight a war. Lethal knives would help them maintain order in their hands. Unfortunately they were just as deadly regardless of who was yielding them. If they were shunted aside by the children, these weapons would definitely be used against the staff. Once they possessed these blades there would only be one course of action left available for them. They would have to break out the firearms kept in storage. Batons lose their effectiveness surprisingly quickly when the opposing side is also armed.

"What are you doing?" Norman asked him, not willing to play around with him.

"I can't let you spoilt things here," the lad replied, his voice so serious there was no question of him joking.

"Don't you want to get out of here?!" He shouted, stupefied as to his behaviour.

"I will get out of here," he answered without any hesitation at all, "just as soon as the month is over."

As hard as he could he banged on the kitchen door. The female smiled when she realised what he was doing. Now there was a kid who could go a long way here. If it was up to her he would get a medal for what he was doing. Obviously he would make a very guard when the time came. That was, of course, if the older children didn't kill him. The looks on their faces were unmistakable. They knew that the rogue employee was their best shot of going home. If he summoned the kitchen staff there was no chance they would be able to leave. One of the boys closest to him stood up. He couldn't believe what he was seeing. Bryan was shouting at the top of his voice for them to open it. Harry couldn't take his eyes off their young helper. Without him they might have been facing a rebellion. Now there was a light at the end of the tunnel. It came in the form of a ten year old who knew what was right. There was no way he would let a trouble maker ruin this for him. Finally they understood why Mr Evans had such a high productivity level. His children were completely infatuated with the concept of such a kind man. Evidently he utilised some sort of psychological programming they couldn't understand. He didn't even care that she was the same person who had struck him in the arm on the first day. All he wanted was to preserve things as they are. The adults relaxed slightly as they watched the door open. A man in his thirties gave him a curious look. What did this boy want? If he was after more food he would be punished. The portions they gave were bigger than they needed to be as it was. To make sure he would never ask again he would feed the lad until he was sick. Maybe then he would learn not to be so greedy.

"He's not misbehaving," the woman quickly informed the man of the situation. "This fellow," she announced, pointing towards Norman, "has turned against us. We need to take him down."

"Thanks, kid," he told the juvenile before disappearing back into the room.

"Do you know what you have done?!" Norman shouted at him, charging towards the boy. "You spoilt your one chance of sleeping in your own bed tonight. I hope you're happy. You don't even know they've brainwashed you. I didn't know until a few minutes ago!"

"I know exactly what I've done," Bryan turned to face him with an unpleasantly smug smile. "I have stopped you from bringing down this place. Can't you see it's good? Children are meant to work. My father left school at eleven. He went straight into a mine."

"You stupid boy!" He declared angrily as he reached the youth.

"Get away from him!" The female warned him with an extended baton.

"If you touch him you're dead!" Harry added, his expression fierce enough to melt steel.

Bryan flinched as his attacker pulled his arm back for a strike. At the end of it was the heavy metal baton all guards carry. What would be left of him once the man had finished. He knew he would be a hero amongst the staff for his actions. He could sense the pride emanating from them. Frankly he didn't care what happened to him. During the time he spent in the camp he had been shown a picture of a great society. Although his peers lived in terror, they conveniently forgot that if they did nothing wrong they would not be punished. Evidently he was the only one smart enough to understand that. So what if the man killed him? He would forever know that he had found the closes thing to paradise that existed in the mortal coil. Maybe if he lived on as a ghost he could inhabit the camp for all time. That would certainly be a worthwhile eternity. Never before had he seen such anger in a man's eyes. This emotion was far stronger than the usual resentment the fighters had for the campers. It was as if his soul had turned to acid. For some reason he had lost his mind. Upon killing Kyle his sanity had snapped. Why else would someone condemn what was happening in the premises? He just wished he didn't have to die at the hands of this man. Luckily for him he never even felt the breeze of a blow across the face. Before he knew what was happening the kitchen worker had shunted Norman aside. One of the children screamed when he saw the knife the cook was holding. It had to be at least twenty centimetres long. If that was used on him he wouldn't stand a chance. His entrails would be hanging from a slit in his abdomen.

"Get off me!" Norman shrieked as the man pinned him to the floor.

"Help me!" He screamed as the man slowly began to jerk his way to freedom.

A second male charged from the kitchen. This one looked as if he was in his mid-twenties. There was certainly more muscle on him than the first employee. In less than a second he crossed the distance to the pair. One massive yank tore the baton from his grip. Bryan knew this was a good move. Without his weapon he had no chance of bringing about the revolution he had threatened to start. When he looked into the sea of faces he could feel their souls cleaving. Some of them were so white they wouldn't be noticed if they lay naked on a glacier. It was a shame they were doing this to themselves. If he had been older he would have taken Norman on himself. Alas, his young age prevented him from taking such action. However, his wisdom had compelled him to seek assistance from the other staff. Harry winked at him reassuringly as two more workers poured from the kitchen. By this point there was a unit on each of his limbs. Still he fought desperately for freedom. Naturally the boy had no reason why. As far as he was concerned the man would be punished for what he done, then allowed to return to work. Unfortunately this was not what the management would have in store for him. Although he didn't know it, he had condemned this man to a horrible fate. Ironically the child would benefit greatly from this tragic turn of events. Still, he was potentially in a great deal of danger. His actions had smashed the dreams of his peers. Perhaps the only chance they had of bringing down the institute had gone. While they fantasised about tearing him apart, Norman would pray that they would take his life quickly. Fear of torture was worse than the apprehension dying generating within him. Kyle, the true victim in all of this, would soon cool as if he was a cup of tea left out for too long. However, Bryan would come out of this smelling like roses. Neither of the adults would ever forget how he had risked himself to save them. Mr Evans would certainly hear of this. When he did so there would be more feigned love heading his way than ever.

"Do something!" Norman's muffled voice begged the inmates. "If you don't help me you're going to be stuck here for the rest of the month!"

Sadly the kids were glued to their seats. What could they do? The figurehead of their rebellion had proved himself to be utterly powerless. Without any sort of struggle he had been restrained. If a trained soldier couldn't fight his way out of here, what chance did they stand? At the end of the day they were not revolutionaries ready to destroy everything that crossed their paths. Even the sixteen year olds were frightened children who wanted to wake up in their bedrooms. Peradventure if they wished for this hard enough the room would manifest itself around them. There was an enormous grin on the face of the ten year old. It didn't matter that the other kids were poised to rip his head from his body. If there were knives in their hands they would perform a vivisection for his betrayal. The jealousy his peers felt previously was nothing compared to what was running through their heads now. They knew Norman was correct. If they didn't take action their hopes of freedom would come to nothing. On the other hand, the sight of the knives stopped them dead in their tracks. Merely seeing the lights reflect off the grey metal made their hearts race. Batons would do little more than sting in the grand scheme of things. Blades offered a one way ticket to the grave. If they were unarmed there would be no question of stepping in. However, the presence of the makeshift cutlasses took this option completely out of the equation. Feeling like cowards, they hung their heads in shame. Harry bellowed at them to head back to the work buildings. The start of the shift had been delayed long enough. Hopefully they would still be able to make some money that morning.

"Not you, though, kid," he told Bryan the moment he had taken a step forwards.

"Stay were you are," the female spoke to him with a sweet tone.

"No!" Norman whined, realising what their desertion meant for him. "Attack the guards or you've killed me!"

Upon hearing this a few of them stopped. Something stirred within their hearts for a minute. A trickle of adrenaline momentarily resurrected their dreams of going home. With regret it wasn't enough to make them forget about the danger they would be in. How could they defend themselves against knives? Shamefully they continued marching towards the door. It didn't matter to them that they knew he was speaking the truth. Goodness knows what his colleagues would do to him for betraying them. More than one was crying as they passed through the door. Why were they here? What awful thing had they done to deserve a place in this nightmare? Bryan watched as they shuffled hopelessly through the doorway. The last one to do so paused for a moment. From the looks of him he was around fourteen years of age. A quick look over his shoulder refreshed the carnage in his mind. Seeing Kyle was enough to make him retch. Worse than that was the look in Norman's eyes. By now the anger had been lost to the ether or his soul. All that remained was an insane fear for himself. The fact he had taken a life no longer played on his mind. How could it when his own existence could be about to be snuffed out? The atmosphere was choking as it absorbed so many emotions. Mostly these were negative, enough to make a person's eyes water. Hate directed towards the guards hung in the air. It had been oozed by the majority of people in the room. Yet this was strangely not as horrible as the positive ones. These essences were echoes of what could have been. Desperate hope for escape attacked those present. It ate away at them as if it was acid. A bitter happiness was also present. This had been generated by the prospect of seeing two sadistic guards getting their comeuppance. By lunchtime none of these things would be present. The horrid air would have cleared by then. However, none of the children would forget what they had done. Norman's commands would have led them to victory. Instead of heading back to work they would be doing battle with the remaining hostile adults. For all time they would have to live with their spineless natures. When they matured a bit they might realise the deeper implications of what they had just done. The death of Kyle would not be enough for the camp to come under scrutiny. By the time the management had dealt with it no-one would even link it to the establishment. Worse than that was the second life that would be lost. Norman was just as much a victim in all of this as the boy he had killed. As he was no longer loyal to the camp he would have to be dealt with. None of this mattered to Bryan as he milled around as instructed.

"You're going to pay for this!" Norman shouted to the smug lad as more guards entered through the front doorway.

"What do you mean?" He replied nonchalantly, genuinely wondering what the traitor was talking about.

"When they get a chance your friends are going to slaughter you. You ruined their one chance of getting out of this place. They're stuck here because of you. They wouldn't forget it."

This struck a nerve deep within the boy. He hadn't thought about his peers when he had walked towards the door. He couldn't deny that the man was right. There was no way Victor was ever going to talk to him again. His smile vanished when he realised he was alone once again. It was worse than before; now he was a pariah. Who would want to be friends with him given what he had done? He knew that this was the price good people pay for doing what is right. Summoning help had been the only correct cause of action available to him. Now he was going to be universally reviled for it. Still, this was the best outcome for it. Not being a fool, he knew exactly how much danger he was in. People would kill for a chance to leave this place. He had blocked their chance of tasting freedom prematurely. Because of him they would probably have to come back here every summer until they turned eighteen. Naturally they were going to produce enough bile to fill the oceans. In their eyes his actions were unforgiveable. Surely they would attack him directly for what he had done. Tears formed in his eyes as he contemplated this. How could he have been so stupid? For the first time he came to regret helping the two guards. Yet, he didn't repent of having considered doing so righteous. Once again his mind considered the role of children in society. Until recently it was natural for them to do so. Attitudes changing didn't alter the truth of the situation. This place should exist; Bryan supported it wholeheartedly. Unlike others he wasn't a hypocrite. He wouldn't defend it as long as he didn't have to go there. He was standing in the middle of a dining hall in such a place. If anyone slandered the establishment he would be on them in a second. Nobody had any argument against this facility. Only logical fallacies would provide the vapours of an argument, just as it was with atheist fascists.

"Don't worry about him," Harry told the frightened juvenile as he strolled towards him.

"He can't hurt you, he's being handcuffed," the female added, gesticulating towards a pair of steel rings one of the new arrivals had brought with him.

"It's not him I'm worried about," Bryan told them with scarlet eyes. "What will the other kids do to me? They're going to hate me!"

"I wouldn't care about them," the female told him, tenderly touching his arm. "You obviously think this is a nice place. Am I wrong?" Her face seemed to harden slightly when she asked her question.

"No, I do enjoy the camp. I know that you only punish those who deserve it."

When he spoke those words, the faces of the guards lit up. Here was a boy who had fully embraced what they were out to create. If he was like this after only a few days, what would he be like after eight months here? The upper management could be shunted aside by the rising star of the payroll. There was no doubt about it; he was going to go far. Still, if they wanted him to get anywhere they would have to protect him. Children could be malicious about the most trivial things. Something as large as preventing an escape would fill their hearts with bloodlust. The fact he had helped the guards had sealed the deal for them. He had indirectly renounced any kinsmanship with the other boys. If they caught him on his own they would beat him to death. The blood of their new recruit would saturate the parched earth outside. That could not be allowed to happen. Having told the others he was not one of them, they would welcome him into the fold. He was as much a member of their family as Norman used to be. Together they watched as the raving man was dragged from the dining hall. He did everything in his power to try to get away. First of all he vowed to kill those who had imprisoned him. Secondly he begged for another chance. Finally there was nothing left but to hurl abuse at the boy. Bryan knew better than to listen to him. Would he listen to a supporter of genocide if they shouted loudly enough? To do so would be a sure sign of a weak mind. He was proud of his ability to take such insults without breaking. Harry ran his hand through Bryan's hair playfully. With a giggle he made eye contact with the worker. It truly was nice to feel positive human comfort. Hopefully Mr Evans would hear about his fortitude. Norman could easily have caved his skull in to stop him summoning help. A hug from that fellow would be heavenly.

"That's nice to hear," the female encouraged him. "I'm sure our colleagues would enjoy meeting you. I am going to take you to see someone now if you don't mind." Her voice was pleasant, albeit firm as she spoke.

"Okay," Bryan replied simply.

She gave him a cheerful grin before leading him towards the door. Kyle had not been attended to yet. Presumably someone would clear the mess up before lunch. Nobody would enjoy eating next to a corpse. You would have to be a lunatic to even have an appetite when one is in the room. Even so, the other boys couldn't understand that the camp was right. Who could be more insane than them? Deliberating on the issue further, he allowed himself to be escorted by the pair. Harry was behind him, just in case he decided to make a break for it. Luckily he knew it was only a formality. Both adults had long since put away their batons. There was no need for them to be out around the lad. He was truly one of the best young men to walk through the gates. If he hadn't come there was no telling what sort of mess they would be in now. Maybe the children would have escaped into the forest. Once they dispersed there would be no way of recovering them all. At least one would find his way back to civilisation. One word of what was happening would bring the wrath of God down upon their heads. Together they walked towards the offices that sat behind the work buildings. These were usually the last places a camper would want to go. However, after everything he had done, this lad would be welcome. Surely the overall manager of the camp would want to hear about his actions. Perhaps there would even be a little reward in it for him. Logically what he had done was worthy of such special treatment. If he hadn't taken action there would have been a disaster. For that reason he would be cherished by the staff members. Someone as special as Bryan deserved to be welcome into their family with open arms. He wasn't of the same stem as the other troublemakers. Here was a boy with enough intelligence to understand how the world works.

"He's going to find you very interesting," they encouraged him along the way. "We can't thank you enough for stopping the riot."

"I was just doing my duty," he replied with a greater sense of belonging than he had ever felt in his life. "You don't have to thank me."

***

Nobody said a word as they marched towards the work buildings. Why wasn't there a bottomless pit they could leap head first into? The whole camp would gladly queue up for it. Escape was there for the taking. If they had reached for it nothing could have stopped them. Granted, it would have been a struggle, but so was anything worth doing. All the achievements of humanity were forged from the grace of God and hard work. If they hadn't been so lazy they would have had the former in abundance. Getting down and praying for help would have sealed the deal for them. For all they knew the walls would have come tumbling down around them. Clement didn't know what to do as he made his way through the doorway. One thing he did know was that Bryan was going to die. He was going to make sure the lad paid dearly for what he had done. If he had any sense he wouldn't have taken a step towards that door. They would have admired him if he had taken on the guards. Instead he helped the adults by summoning reinforcements. Why had he done that? As far as the boy could fathom, he was either deranged or malicious. Deep down he was aware both were probably. To side with the guards a person would have to be insane. To stop his peers from fleeing the camp, he had to be malicious. They wouldn't have left him behind if they found a path to freedom. He would be as welcome to use it as anyone else. It didn't matter that the pair of them had come to blows in the past. No child deserved to be imprisoned in this place. The prospect of escaping now seemed further away than ever. Why hadn't he thrown his bowl at Harry's head? That was exactly what the juveniles would need to start rioting. Rather than be a man he had covered. His actions always betrayed his age, regardless of how smart he was. What was intelligence if he lacked a spine to manifest his thoughts in reality? Now they were going to have to trundle back to the sweatshops. He had no doubt that the workers would increase their aggression to discourage further violence. If he was in their shoes he would do exactly that. How else were they going to extract vengeance from the lads?

"That kid is in trouble," he heard a boy in front of him declare angrily.

"I'll kick his head in if I ever catch him!" His friend spoke so coldly it made the hairs on the back of his neck stand up.

"Join the queue!" A third fellow piped up.

"This Bryan kid is horrible," Leonard whispered to him. "One of the worst haurraks I've ever come across."

For a moment Clement was utterly lost. His memories had been covered with a frost shed by his very soul. Only after deep searching did he find what he was looking for. When they had spoken earlier he had used that word. Apparently it meant children. Even if it didn't, he was happy to repeat it in his head. It helped distract him from the shame of his cowardice. Naturally he had no way of knowing that everyone else felt the same. All the kids had regrets; it wasn't just him who should have done something. Where were the muscular fifteen year olds pumped full of testosterone? Leonard would tell him not to worry if he could see into the boy's soul. The atmosphere of the crowd was horrific. They had just watched a ten year old being beaten to death. How were they ever supposed to get over that? Adam's brother would have expected far more people to be crying than they were. In his heart he knew why he could only hear a few choked sobs. Extreme distress had a way of chilling the heart. His peers were living in emotional vacuums. Days could pass before the events registered on their systems. Even then their minds would dissociate themselves from it. What other defence mechanism was available to them? They were children, not psychologists. What had transpired that morning would be imprinted on their memories for all time. Not able to bring himself to say goodbye to Leonard, the two parted in silence. Both of them were far too deep in their own heads to truly comprehend their separation. It was as if a neurological court had declared them emancipated from their spirits. Only time would tell if their psyches would ever thaw. Perhaps they would remain in their frigid states for all time. In a way that was worse than having to deal with the torment head-on.

One thing he did know was that he was going to get out of this place. He didn't care if he died trying. Kyle had been killed for making his escape. That didn't deter the lad in the slightest. Although he had left the land of the living, the murdered child was free. No guard would cause him anymore pain. The poor conditions would not cause him even the slightest bit of distress again. Wherever his spirit was, he surely knew that he had beaten the system. Clement was determined to make a bid for freedom. As long as the blood flowed in his veins he would not give up planning. Everything he did would be for the good of this end. No force in the world would keep him from breaking out of this death camp. In his mind he pictured himself in the forest, being chased by guards. He knew they had guns. If they caught him they could shoot him dead where he stood. That was perfectly fine by him. As long as his success inspired others to choose freedom he didn't mind. After all, they couldn't imprison a corpse. Either he would end up in an urn on his parent's mantelpiece or feed the worms in the soil. Another image entered his mind. This one concerned the traitor in their ranks. His transgression would not go unpunished. Hopefully the guards would stab him in the back when he wasn't looking. That was a bittersweet ending, however. Before he came to this place he would never dream of taking a life. If there was one person he would like to kill it was the smug prat that had alerted the kitchen staff. His heart raced as he pictured himself strangling the life from the boy. Was this something that could happen or something that was going to happen? Frankly he had no idea. Did it matter? Such a person wasn't going to last long when there was so much hatred in the air. He hadn't let in a goal that cost a football team the match. That was forgivable in eyes of humanity. What the lads wouldn't overlook was the fact he had forced them to spend many more months in this nightmare. Although the camp had given him a frosty welcome, his peers would give him a cold goodbye. The others were welcome to do that if they liked. Hopefully he would be back with the police before his spilt blood had dried. The adults were far from victorious yet.

***

    Writing the story kept the old man in the office far later than he had ever been before. The cleaners came shortly after everyone else went home. With a single glance he told the woman not to enter his office. He didn't know what they thought about his continued presence. Frankly he didn't care. The only thing that mattered was putting word after word down on the paper. When he finally got to Kyle's murder he looked at his watch. His eyes bulged when he realised how much time had passed. Even the security guards would be finishing their rounds. As quickly as he could he concluded the first part of his testimony. It was odd to think that this would be the last normal day that particular camp ever had. From now on things would become far more bloodthirsty. Reaching this point was a bittersweet milestone. He was proud of how much he had churned out so far. His original thought had been correct. With every word he felt he was breaking free of his misery. Yet this confirmed the events had actually taken place. No longer could he lie to himself, pretending the fiasco was a dream. His trauma was reduced slightly, but now set in stone. With a sigh he placed his briefcase on the table. In a few seconds the papers disappeared from his desk. He wished the horrendous events could be hidden from view so easily. It would be a glorious moment when the story was finished. Closure is truly a gift from god.

    One thing he feared most of all was the dark turn the story would now take. There was no escaping the fact the camp had been irreparably damaged by Kyle's death. In all honesty he was clueless as to how the death of one camper could stir up the masses. If he had the chance he would happily go back in time to save his life. Of course, he didn't care about the boy himself. He was about as important as an ant crushed by a grazing cow. Yet his demise would bring unbelievable torment to those he truly cared about. To spare them all the heartbreak he would happily give his own life to bring back the urchin. In a way his passing brought the whole institute to its knees. It would remain there for some time, but there is light even in the darkest times. When it got back on its feet it would double in size. Its skin would be totally impervious to any attack. Only God himself could knock it back even a few inches. But there was still a long way to go before he reached this point. To see the majesty of the camo they would first have to see it at its weakest. It would be an understatement to say producing the account would destroy him. All he knew was that at the end he would be fully healed. He had to cling to this mantra, even as the corpses piled up around him.